TRAITOR!

Calabar tried drawing his sword, but the belt had shifted, and he c_____ _____ _____ _____ d, he drew his knife, la_____  _____sed.

De Gama came _____ _____ _____abar was ready. De G_____ _____ with his left boot, catc_____ _____lling him over. Now, t_____ _____ own knife ready and thrust it toward Calabar's stomach. Calabar twisted but felt the blade tear his wet shirt. He struck de Gama's chin, sending the man reeling back just enough to allow Calabar to roll the other way.

Calabar lurched up onto his feet. As de Gama came at him, Calabar raised his pistol and pushed it into the captain's throat. De Gama halted abruptly.

"It's over, de Gama," Calabar said. "You are beaten."

De Gama's bloody, puffy lip quivered as sweat rolled down his face. He grimaced as if a shot of pain had pierced his eye, but his voice was clear and unwavering.

"Traitor!"

Calabar wavered at the word. He held the gun firm against de Gama's throat, but the joy of victory was gone.

Looking into de Gama's eyes, a man he had fought alongside and whose life he had saved, Calabar said, "I am no traitor." His voice was quieter than he had wanted.

De Gama nodded. "You are. Come, traitor," he said, slowly turning to offer Calabar his back. "Shoot me as I flee. Helpless. Show the world what you are."

THE RING OF FIRE SERIES

1632 by Eric Flint • *1633* with David Weber • *1634: The Baltic War* with David Weber • *1634: The Galileo Affair* with Andrew Dennis • *1634: The Bavarian Crisis* with Virginia DeMarce • *1634: The Ram Rebellion* with Virginia DeMarce et al. • *1635: The Cannon Law* with Andrew Dennis • *1635: The Dreeson Incident* with Virginia DeMarce • *1635: The Eastern Front* • *1635: The Papal Stakes* with Charles E. Gannon • *1636: The Saxon Uprising* • *1636: The Kremlin Games* with Gorg Huff & Paula Goodlett • *1636: The Devil's Opera* with David Carrico • *1636: Commander Cantrell in the West Indies* with Charles E. Gannon • *1636: The Viennese Waltz* with Gorg Huff & Paula Goodlett • *1636: The Cardinal Virtues* with Walter H. Hunt • *1635: A Parcel of Rogues* with Andrew Dennis • *1636: The Ottoman Onslaught* • *1636: Mission to the Mughals* with Griffin Barber • *1636: The Vatican Sanction* with Charles E. Gannon • *1637: The Volga Rules* with Gorg Huff & Paula Goodlett • *1637: The Polish Maelstrom* • *1636: The China Venture* with Iver P. Cooper • *1636: The Atlantic Encounter* with Walter H. Hunt • *1637: No Peace Beyond the Line* with Charles E. Gannon • *1637: The Peacock Throne* with Griffin Barber • *1637: The Coast of Chaos*, ed. with Bjorn Hasseler

1635: The Tangled Web by Virginia DeMarce • *1635: The Wars for the Rhine* by Anette Pedersen • *1636: Seas of Fortune* by Iver P. Cooper • *1636: The Chronicles of Doctor Gribbleflotz* by Kerryn Offord & Rick Boatright • *1636: Flight of the Nightingale* by David Carrico • *1637: Dr. Gribbleflotz and the Soul of Stoner* by Kerryn Offord & Rick Boatright

Time Spike with Marilyn Kosmatka • *The Alexander Inheritance* with Gorg Huff & Paula Goodlett • *The Macedonian Hazard* with Gorg Huff & Paula Goodlett

EDITED BY ERIC FLINT, ET AL.
Grantville Gazette I–IX • *Ring of Fire I–IV*

To purchase any of these titles in e-book form, please go to www.baen.com.

1636
CALABAR'S WAR

CHARLES E. GANNON
ROBERT E. WATERS

1636: CALABAR'S WAR

This is a work of fiction. All the characters and events portrayed in this book are fictional, and any resemblance to real people or incidents is purely coincidental.

A Baen Books Original

Baen Publishing Enterprises
P.O. Box 1403
Riverdale, NY 10471
www.baen.com

ISBN: 978-1-9821-2605-6

Cover art by Tom Kidd
Maps by Michael Knopp

First printing, April 2021
First mass market printing, April 2022

Distributed by Simon & Schuster
1230 Avenue of the Americas
New York, NY 10020

Library of Congress Control Number: 2020058603

Pages by Joy Freeman (www.pagesbyjoy.com)
Printed in the United States of America
10 9 8 7 6 5 4 3 2 1

For my son, Jason Michael Waters.

—Robert E. Waters

To my editors and collaborators:
Jacqueline Lichtenberg, Anji Valenza, John Carr,
Steve White, Toni Weisskopf, and Eric Flint.

Their kindness, generosity, and wisdom has been,
and remains, indispensable. If a reader enjoys
my writing, it's because I listened to them. If
a reader finds little of value in my prose, it's
because I didn't listen to them carefully enough.

—Charles E. Gannon

Special Thanks:

To Dr. Robert Finegold, for his invaluable assistance with historical data pertaining to the Jewish communities and personalities in the New World.

Contents

The Caribbean
as of Jan. 1636

Atlantic Ocean

Bermuda

Anegada Passage

Anguilla
St Maarten
St. Barthelemy
Saba
St. Eustatia
St. Christopher
Nevis
Montserrat

Vieques
St. Croix

The Bahamas

Tortuga
Luperón

Havana

Cuba

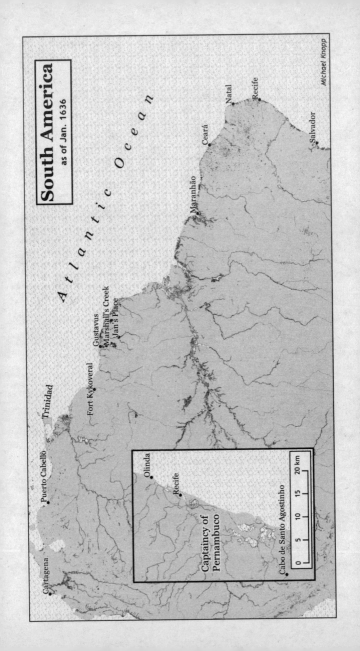

South America
as of Jan. 1636

Atlantic Ocean

Michael Knopp

Cartagena

Puerto Cabello

Trinidad

Fort Kykoveral

Gustavus
Marshall's Creek
Jan's Place

Maranhão

Ceará

Natal

Recife

Salvador

Olinda

Recife

Captaincy of Pernambuco

Cabo de Santo Agostinho

0   5   10   15   20 km

1636
CALABAR'S WAR

Prologue

Ed Piazza didn't look up from the day's security reports since he already knew, from the casual cadence of the footsteps, who was approaching his office. "Hiya, Mike. Have a seat."

Mike Stearns stopped in front of Ed's desk. "Shouldn't we be meeting in your new office, Mr. President?"

Ed heard the grin in Stearns' voice. "I suppose we should. There's more room than in this one. We can move there, if you like."

"I'm okay either way. Question is: why haven't *you* moved in there, yet? It's been two weeks since you became President. You need the space. And the imposing desk."

Ed sighed, leaned back, looked up to see the crooked grin that was one of Mike Stearns' habitual expressions. Particularly when he was trying to lay on the homespun charm. Which hardly made any sense, since Mike's educational credentials made him anything but a yokel. But

1

somehow, he got away with the "just folks" demeanor when he needed to. "What's up, Mike? You're being excessively congenial for having just traveled down from Magdeburg."

Mike's grin widened. "It's that obvious?"

"It surely is. Did you pick up Nasi on the way?"

Mike nodded. "Yeah. He was up to his elbows in reports." The grin returned. "Like you."

"Which means you can see for yourself why I haven't moved into your old office. I haven't had the time." Ed glanced balefully at the stack of folders in his "in" box. "You were a great President, Mike, but not a very tidy one. Lotta loose ends."

Mike glanced at the ceiling innocently. "Now see, that was just me deciding to leave you plenty of room for creative evolution of my policies."

Ed stood. "Nah. You just move too fast for bureaucrats to keep up." Which, all things being equal, wasn't an entirely bad trait. "Let's go to your—my—office."

Stearns smiled. "Good. The chairs are nicer."

"Just remember: the chair behind the desk is mine now. You flop down on the other side."

"Fine by me. I sit at the pleasure of the President of the State of Thuringia."

Piazza managed not to roll his eyes as he led the way out of the office.

Francisco Nasi was already there. The Jewish commercial-magnate-turned-intelligencer was still handling covert matters for Mike even though he was technically retained by Ed and the State of Thuringia. And given Mike's new role as the Prime Minister of the United States of Europe, Nasi now had what were effectively two full-time jobs. Or would, as soon as Ed began availing himself of the young spymaster's capabilities. Which looked pretty imminent.

Ed sat down in the big chair behind the even bigger desk and thought, *I've got to move in here. If for no other reason that this chair will not irritate my hemorrhoids into open rebellion. Literally.* "So, what's hit the fan?"

Nasi frowned. "I beg your pardon?"

Mike's lopsided grin came back. "I'll translate later." Nasi was still learning the slang that American English had bequeathed to the hybrid dialect Amideutsch. He was particularly out of step with the more profane additions.

Mike had turned toward Ed. "We've finally got news about Dutch survivors from the Battle of Dunkirk."

Ed nodded, sighed in relief. The fleet under Tromp had been betrayed by its strange allies, the English and French, who had attacked from their position at the rear of the fleet as it sailed into action against the Spanish. Caught between that known rock and the traitorous hard place behind them, only a few ships were reported as having escaped. Ed, like others, feared that the final report would reveal that the tally of surviving Dutch hulls would be effectively zero. "What's the source of the information? Is it reliable?"

"Two sources," Francisco Nasi corrected mildly. "Dutch fishing boats operating out of the Frisians who were coming back from the waters off the Channel Islands, and two small Irish ships carrying 'assorted cargoes.'"

Ed smiled at the latter. "So, smugglers. But how, or more pertinently why, are we getting information from the Irish?"

Mike shrugged. "Anything to stick their thumb in England's eye. Also, it seems that old Mike McCarthy has been trying to initiate some sort of correspondence with members of the exiled Irish nobility."

Piazza leaned back. "You mean Mike McCarthy *Senior*? Damn, I didn't even know that he knew how to write." Which was a lie, of course, but the old Fenian radical had never struck Ed as the type who would devote himself to "opening a correspondence" with anyone. "So some of the Dutch ships *did* make it out?"

"Yep. Pretty big ones, too. Thirty-two guns or more."

"And just how did they manage to give their far more numerous enemies the slip?"

"By crowding sail and heading due west," Nasi answered. "And running dark all night long."

Piazza frowned. "I'll assume for a second that the Dutch reputation for sailing by sextant and compass alone is mostly accurate, rather than exaggeration. Even so, how did they keep their ships together while running dark in the Channel?"

Nasi nodded. "In addition to having many of the world's best living captains and navigators, it seems that the Dutch vessels kept only their stern light on, but covered. Except for a single, simultaneous fifteen-second reveal every ten minutes."

"That's a neat trick. Timed it with hourglasses, I assume."

"Or pendulum clocks. Their design was the first technology the Dutch carried away from the high school library." Nasi waved a hand in its direction. "It was reported that Admiral Tromp bought one earlier this year for his fifty-four-gun *Amelia*. If his flagship survived, and she remained in the lead, the timing of the light reveals could have been maintained with admirable precision."

Mike leaned back with a satisfied smile. "Unless someone was looking in exactly the right place at exactly the right time, the Dutch would've been safe by the middle of the first night. Best guess puts them off Dungeness Point during the night after the battle."

"Who spotted them there? English?"

Nasi shook his head. "No. It is an estimate."

"Based on what?"

"Back-calculated from where the first of the Frisian fishermen spotted them just before sunset the following day: drawing abreast of the Isle of Wight, albeit well offshore. To get there by that time, Tromp's ships would have had to pass Dungeness Point the preceding midnight, given the winds."

"How many ships were spotted?"

Mike frowned. "The fishermen weren't sure, but not enough. Less than ten. Perhaps as few as half a dozen. Which matches the after-action estimates we've intercepted from Spanish couriers."

"Any sign that the League of Ostend fleet is still looking for them?"

Mike's grim laugh was closer to a grunt. "Firstly, no: too many weeks have passed. Secondly: 'League of Ostend,' my butt. League of thieves, more like. The smoke hadn't settled when the English beat for home and the French 'withdrew to their own waters.' Only the Spanish might still be on the lookout for Dutch stragglers. But if they are, they aren't devoting a lot of ships to the effort.

"Besides, since most of the grandees at the Escorial

are still convinced that radio transmissions are whispers from the Devil, news of the battle is following well behind Tromp's fleeing ships, not spreading out in front of them."

Ed looked from Mike to Nasi and back to Mike. "Okay, so what am I missing? You two wouldn't be here if all you had to report was good news."

Mike sent a sideways, and broadly histrionic, smile at Nasi. "I told you Ed was bright."

"With respect, Michael, I already knew that. Quite well." He kept his eyes on Piazza. "The complication is that, if, as we suspect, Admiral Tromp or a successor is withdrawing to a port in the New World, it would be profoundly advantageous if the Spanish were slow to become watchful for his possible appearance."

Piazza nodded. "You want the Spanish to conclude that any surviving Dutch hulls scattered and then foundered." Nasi nodded. "And how do we do that? Or, probably more pertinently, why do you need *me* to do that?"

Mike leaned forward. "Because, Ed, it would be doubly risky for me to try to mount the necessary disinformation campaign using the assets and imprimatur of the United States of Europe. Firstly, the USE is a pretty ragged patchwork quilt, right now. It's amazing it holds together at all. It will be easier with every passing month, but"—Mike tilt-waggled his palm-down hand—"the infrastructure is still, to put it mildly, in disarray. Everybody with any authority is used to being a chief, not an Indian. And what isn't compromised by dueling egos is undermined by the lack of clear delineation between the newly minted USE administrative units and the old national ones alongside which they have to exist for the foreseeable future."

Ed stared at his folded hands. "So essentially, you're telling me that right now, a USE-initiated intelligence operation would turn into a Keystone Cops scenario."

Nasi may have tilted his head. "If I understand your expression, that is one concern, yes, Mr. President. But we must also be mindful that where there are disgruntled officials, there are also opportunities for enemy subornation."

Ed nodded. "So you're worried that a secret operation would be anything but. And that Philip would probably get wind of it and deduce that if we were trying to get him to believe that none of the Dutch ships survived, it surely meant that some of them had. And might reemerge as a significant force in being, somewhere down the line."

"Correct."

Mike had leaned well back in his chair, watching almost sleepily. Ed suppressed a smile. *Getting me used to working with Nasi directly, eh, Mike? And that look on your face tells me that you know that I know that's you're intent. And it's not a half bad plan, either. Gustav may not yet be familiar with the term "plausible deniability," but he'll become intimately acquainted with it soon enough. And he'll probably keep glancing toward Grantville—meaning* me—*to handle that kind of operation for a while, yet.* "So, Mr. Nasi, I presume you have a plan for duping the Spanish into believing that the Dutch ships were all lost at sea?"

"I do. We will ensure that they intercept one of our couriers who will be carrying a modified version of the report we received from the Dutch and Irish boats."

"Modified how?"

"That our sources reported only three surviving ships, not six, and that all were listing or low in the water when they began to flee. Furthermore, they will be reported as individual sightings, not together as a flotilla. A following report will be invented for each, indicating that, late the next day, our sources encountered wreckage consistent with such ships. The Irish will report the foundering of either one or two ships off the far Channel Islands, near Les Casquets, West of St. Anne. The Frisians will report passing considerable debris fifteen miles south of the Isle of Wight."

Ed shrugged. "Plausible, but how do we make sure the Spanish believe it? Particularly when I'm not about to let you compromise one of our couriers."

"Of course not. That is why the information will be entrusted to an inherently *unreliable* courier."

Ed felt his left eyebrow rise rapidly. "And who would *that* be? From what I hear, our people have been pretty successful screening out individuals who would be security risks."

"Quite true. But Mr. President, bear this in mind: the same skills which allow a counterintelligence chief to screen out potential risks also gives them the ability to detect couriers that would be intrinsically untrustworthy."

Ed smiled. "Let me guess: you're planning on having Gretchen Richter run this."

"Of course. She has shown admirable native ability in being able to distinguish reliable persons from those who are not, or who are in fact attempting to infiltrate either the Committees of Correspondence or our legation in Amsterdam. Secondly, she has the right...sensibilities for this particular task."

"You mean recruiting someone who she knows is either an enemy agent or some unreliable loudmouth."

"The latter, yes. The former is not operationally sound."

Ed Piazza crossed his arms. "Really? I would think that if we let one of their own get access to one of our diplomatic pouches, they'd have complete confidence in the information."

Nasi took a moment collecting his thoughts—or probably, Ed revised, the wording whereby he would gently and tactfully educate his dunderheaded superior in the actual best practice of espionage. "President Piazza, you are correct that the Spanish would have complete confidence in their own operative. But that is not the same as having complete confidence in the veracity of the information he brings them."

Now Ed saw it. "Sure. Because getting their hands on the intel so easily would seem just a little too convenient."

Nasi nodded, allowed one hand to drift in the direction of distant Amsterdam. "This is particularly true in the case of Gretchen Richter, Mr. President. Her record at rebuffing or eliminating security risks is essentially unblemished. For her to suddenly 'miss' detecting one of their confidential agents would cause them to wonder if that outcome is, in fact, too good to be true. They will wonder if their agent's success at gaining her apparent trust was because that was Richter's actual intent. And so, the Spanish spymasters would likely deduce that whatever intelligence they had intercepted was not merely inaccurate, but carefully crafted to ensure that they came to completely incorrect conclusions."

Ed shrugged. "Okay, so Gretchen is going to have to recruit a pigeon."

This time it was Nasi who frowned in uncertainty. "A what?"

"Pigeon. American slang—*dated* American slang—for a person who is recruited to be an unsuspecting part of a confidence racket."

Nasi nodded quickly. "Yes. A pigeon."

"I'm guessing he'll be the kind of courier that likes to impress the ladies with big talk, or has a big taste for liquor?"

Nasi nodded again. "Preferably both."

Piazza frowned. "Except that's not our modus operandi either, Francisco. Gretchen hasn't yet recruited any couriers with those failings. Besides, with access to the radio, we use damn few live couriers, anyway."

Nasi nodded approvingly. "An excellent point, Mr. President. I agree; both her, and our own, modi operandi must remain unaltered if we are determined not to alert the Spanish to our disinformation operation.

"Accordingly, Ms. Richter shall initially retain this unreliable courier for nonsecure messages. He will be a mere convenience for maintaining mundane coordination with her various subordinates in and around Amsterdam. But, with the onset of late fall, the weather will soon enough provide us with a perfectly plausible cover story."

Ed Piazza smiled, shook his head in appreciation. "Sure, because we're moving into that time of the year when the storm fronts start coming in waves, sometimes back to back. And at some point, when that weather has degraded our radio reception to nothing, we occasionally have to resort to live couriers, entrusting them with some lower level confidential reports. And that's precisely when Gretchen gives the doctored data to Mr. Unreliable, and pays him handsomely up front. That way, he has enough pocket money to indulge the vices that will compromise him and his 'secure' pouch."

Nasi's smile matched Ed's own—and maybe had hints of relief that the President of Thuringia was actually going to be easy to work with and was a quick study. "Fortunately, when the weather is at its worst and ruining radio reception, it will also be making the roads nearly impassable. If the pouch's delivery is defined as nonurgent, the courier will not need much—if any—encouragement to wait for the weather to improve slightly. During which time his vices will have ample opportunity to undermine whatever weak conscientiousness he brings to his employment."

Mike's smile was more expansive than the two of theirs put together—probably because he had just successfully midwifed the birth of a beautiful professional relationship between his two friends. "And I can tell you without a doubt that Gretchen knows just the right inn at which to put up Mr. Unreliable to wait out the weather: the kind of place where the clientele will be sure to see and work a mark like him and turn him over to the Spanish. And of course, she'll put a tail on him to make sure it goes down just that way." Mike's smile faded a bit. "What's wrong, Ed?"

"It's a good plan . . . but it could take a while for all those elements to come together. For instance, how soon can Gretchen actually find and hire Mr. Unreliable?"

"Seriously, Ed? The typical problem is making sure you *don't* hire one of them. And I don't foresee a sudden drought of unscrupulous would-be intelligencers in Amsterdam.

"Besides, we've got plenty of time. Whatever Dutch get to the New World are sure to lay low. Meanwhile, the mere fact that Spain will now be pretty relaxed about getting the word to the New World will send a message of its own to the viceroys there: that it's presumed that the Dutch were wiped out to a man. Which is to say, they've got no reason for worry.

"And when the Dutch hopefully teach them otherwise in Brazil or the Caribbean? Well, unless Philip has lifted the ban on the devil-magic of radios, it's going to be even more months before word bounces back across the Atlantic and shows Madrid that they fell for our misinformation."

Ed shrugged. "Fine. So what do you need from me?"

Mike stretched expansively, smiled at the ceiling. Nasi leaned forward, a leather portfolio secured with three buckles in his hand. "If we could start by sending these messages and documents..."

November, 1633
Recife, Brazil

The silhouette of the forested coast was dark against the night sky. Darker than any place Admiral Maarten Harpertszoon Tromp had ever seen. Darker than any port, city, or wilderness he'd known in Europe, Africa, or even here in the New World.

But as he stood upon the prow of his still-wounded

flagship *Amelia*, watching faint specks of light emerge, flicker, and mark the length of the port town of Recife, he couldn't help but feel profoundly lucky. And, incongruously, sorrowful.

Two months ago, he had almost been killed upon the cold, fall waters near Dunkirk. Now he was here, alive and breathing hot, exotic air while contemplating how the fortunes of war had changed. Not a stranger to the vicissitudes of fate—what sailor was?—today he found himself reflecting upon whether his fortunes had actually changed for the better. Tromp remembered the faces of those who'd gone down with his fleet and shook his head as the imagined ghost of Dame Fate rose up behind them; *there's no way to call this "good fortune."*

The *tap-tap-tap* of Cornelis Jol's wooden leg shook him from his reverie. "She's a marvelous port," Jol said, breathing deep and coming to an abrupt stop alongside the admiral, "a jewel in the Dutch crown here in this Garden of Eden. She'll get your fleet up and running in no time."

Tromp nodded. "I pray that is so. But I did not come all the way from Europe just for a refit, Jol. I have a greater purpose."

Jol sighed. Just as when the old privateer had met them earlier today, Tromp could smell rum on his breath. This time, he longed for a draught himself. He'd rather it were gin, of course, but there was none left after the perilous crossing. Still, if a lack of gin was the greatest accommodation Maarten Tromp had to make to life in the New World, then he did indeed lead a charmed existence.

Jol leaned on the railing and tapped out a rhythm

with his leg. "So you've a greater purpose, eh? What do you propose?"

Tromp turned back toward Jol. "The world has changed, my friend. The arrival of the Americans through their Ring of Fire; the French and British in an alliance; Europe in turmoil: it is too soon to know how it will all play out. But one thing is certain: we Dutch must change our strategy here if we hope to keep the West India Company from meeting the same fate as my fleet. Our settlements are spread too widely, and our available forces are overextended trying to protect them all. We must consolidate."

"It may be a mistake," Jol murmured, "ceding too much territory to the Portuguese just to reduce our vulnerabilities."

"It would be a worse mistake to depend upon luck, Jol."

"As if you should speak ill of luck! If your good luck hadn't kept the Spanish from intercepting your fleet, we'd be having this conversation at the bottom of the sea."

Tromp pushed down his earlier ruminations upon luck, forced himself to chuckle. "You have the consummate wit of an admiral. Perhaps I should make you one."

"Only if you're a fool."

"I've been called worse." Tromp turned, made his voice loud and authoritative as he gave the orders that set in motion the delicate one-sided dance of docking at night. Although it was long habit, he was conscious and careful not to allow the slightest hint of impatience or threat to slip into his tone. An effective leader always behaved as if he *presumed* that his orders would be obeyed, quickly and attentively.

And he could not afford any failures now. During the crossing, his flotilla had picked up four more stragglers, and all ten hulls were damaged, most of them heavily. He did not want further disruption or injury to his men and ships by sloppy handling in the dark, even though Jol had sent his ship back to Recife to surreptitiously prepare the port to receive Tromp's ships. Even so, docking at night could be a risky business, and in this case, it was not strictly necessary. But it was worth it if it bought Tromp a few extra days before the Portuguese became aware of his presence.

Jol's hands turned restlessly on the fo'c'sle's forward rail. "So, you're thinking of consolidating our holdings. What, specifically, do you have in mind?"

Tromp shook his head. "I can't say right now. I have an idea, but I must think on it some more. I don't want to make a rash decision, because it will necessarily be a bold one."

He watched *Amelia*'s deckhands—the middle watch larger than usual in order to dock her at night—and suppressed a relieved sigh. Those men—and boys, in some cases—were preparing the mooring lines and fenders with the graceful speed of seasoned sailors, so familiar with their tasks that performing them was now second nature.

If only he had advisors whose knowledge of the New World was as ingrained, as natural. Not the Company men who'd carved out a place on the wild coast of the Pernambuco. They knew the region from having subdued it; they had not grown up in it. And that was exactly what Tromp needed if he was going to make the right choices, take the wisest steps to maintain a

Dutch presence in the New World despite the terrible reduction of the fleet upon which it depended.

"I need someone I can trust," Tromp said suddenly, almost harshly.

Jol started, then laid his hand almost cautiously on Tromp's shoulder. "You can trust *me*, Maarten."

Tromp smiled, tried to show he hadn't meant his abrupt proclamation as a denigration of his old friend. "That is a comfort indeed, and I thank you. But I need someone who knows these lands from having grown up in them, my friend, someone who understands the people of this country, and who can help keep the Portugese, particularly Matias de Albuquerque and his brutes, guessing while we plan. I need someone who, from birth, has lived and breathed *Brazil*."

Jol nodded, patted his shoulder, and lurched to the rail just beside the centerline, from where he stared out over the bowsprit. Tromp could hear Jol breathe deeply, as if trying to pull all the nighttime mists of the Pernambuco into his barrel-shaped chest.

"Well," Jol said eventually, "if it's personal reliability and knowledge of Brazil you need, you are once again in luck." In answer to Tromp's quick glance, he nodded and exhaled. "I know just the man."

Part One

March–May 1634

*"...the hour has come for you to wake from sleep.
For salvation is nearer to us now
than when we first believed."*
—Romans 13:11

Chapter 1

Outside Pontal, Brazil

The guns in Fort Nazare fell silent, and although their deafening salute to the invading Dutch had sent a few to a briny grave, enough ships had gotten through to threaten the Portuguese town of Pontal. Now, the Dutch fleet lay at anchor at Cape Agostinho as soldiers, under Captain Sigismond von Schoppe, spilled out onto the shore and marshaled up into ranks five deep. Musket troops mostly, flintlock pistols, a few wheellocks, and even a few pike.

Pike seemed silly in such close quarters, under the blasting heat and glaring sun of the Brazilian coastline. But Domingos Fernandes Calabar, who stood beside a much-delighted von Schoppe, knew old habits were hard to break. The fair-skinned Dutch had done well for themselves along the Brazilian coast since they had arrived in force a few years ago, but no amount of pike would take this fishing town. It would take skill, speed, guile, and a clear understanding of the forest that lay further inland. Calabar knew this. He wondered if his friend did as well.

"I can always tell when you are troubled, Domingos," von Schoppe said, looking through his spyglass to monitor the first wave of men he had sent forward. Muskets sounded in the distance.

The battle for Pontal was on.

"How so?" Calabar asked.

Von Schoppe chuckled. "You become...quiet."

"*Eu nao estou*—" he paused, realizing that he had lapsed back into Portuguese. He sighed. *Old habits, indeed.* "I am not troubled, Captain," he said again, this time in Dutch, "just concerned."

"Speak your mind."

Calabar cleared his throat. "Fort Nazare's guns have stopped, yes?"

Von Schoppe nodded.

"To me, this means that its commander has decided to abandon the position and lead his men out to defend Pontal. He will bring them through the jungle to strengthen its rear defenses."

Von Schoppe scoffed. "That is no concern to us. De Gama has but a handful of men. No more than a hundred."

"Much less than that, I'd suppose," said Calabar. "But he does not need that many men, Captain. No matter the number, they are all Portuguese veterans. They understand defensive warfare. All de Gama needs is to get into Pontal and hold us off long enough for Albuquerque and that son of a bitch Bagnuoli to bring reinforcements. If he does that, we will not be in a position to defend against them, no matter who controls the town."

Von Schoppe lowered his spyglass and shook his head. "I've got nothing but fishermen in front of me, and you are asking me to split my force."

"Just give me two hundred men." Calabar motioned to the left. "One hundred. Luiz and I will work them around behind Pontal and lay in wait for de Gama."

Von Schoppe eyed Calabar carefully. The German-born commander's weathered face was worn, dirty. If the situation weren't so dire, Calabar might have smiled. Life in Brazil had not been easy for the Dutch. It had not been easy for any of the European countries which had tried to stake out their claims upon the lush potential of Brazil. The Dutch, the Spanish, the Portuguese, even the French and English had all made attempts at controlling portions of it. And now the Dutch and Portuguese were in a death struggle for the very heart of Brazil, the captaincy of Pernambuco. The Dutch held the coastline; the Portuguese, much of the mainland. Where one would gain advantage, the other would fall back, and vice-versa. On and on it went, and it seemed to Calabar that the ceaseless struggle had written itself directly on to von Schoppe's face. The man looked twenty years older than he was. So did Calabar for that matter. But what was bad for the body was sometimes good for the soul. Calabar had promised himself that he would never regret the decisions that he had made in this long struggle.

Von Schoppe leaned in close. "Are you so sure that de Gama will do what you say?"

Calabar nodded. "Yes, I am. I know him, Captain. I . . . served with him."

Von Schoppe stared for a long moment, then smiled.

"You're lucky that I like you so much, Domingos. You're lucky I'm so fond of your wife."

From any other man, that might have been seen as a threat, but not from von Schoppe. He was a good family friend. He had even been present at the recent baptisms of Calabar's two oldest children.

"We are both lucky in that regard, Captain."

Von Schoppe chuckled and waved him off. "Take your hundred. Whomever you wish."

"Thank you, sir."

Calabar turned and walked to the soldiers gathering on the shore.

Most of them were Dutch, but not as many as he would have expected. Among them were Tabajara tribesmen and a smattering of Caetés. Some of the tribes of Brazil had aligned themselves with the Dutch, having been repeatedly and thoroughly ravished by the Portuguese. But alliances were easily bought and sold in Brazil: whoever made the most appealing promises won the most support.

Many of the soldiers Calabar wanted for his ambush *were* the tribesmen. They were far more skilled in subterfuge and guerilla warfare, but they were carrying pikes, which he did not need. So he would have to mix his force; some natives, some Dutch. And how would that go, he wondered, as he walked among the ranks, lightly tapping the shoulders of the men he wanted. *Will they follow me in battle?* He gave them their orders, and they fell out of their ranks and waited near the tree line.

He was about to shout out Luiz's name when his young adjutant-in-training appeared at his side.

Luiz Goncalves had very dark skin. The seventeen-year-old was believed to be the product of a Portuguese *bandeirante* and an African slave. But he had grown up an orphan among the Jesuits and knew many of the native languages far better than Calabar ever would. He knew the lay of the land pretty well also.

"O Calabar, sir," Luiz said in his surprisingly deep voice. He made to salute as the Dutch did, but Calabar waved him off.

"Not necessary, Luiz," Calabar said. "Tell me: what have you discovered?"

Luiz pointed toward the tree line where the soldiers awaited them. "The way through there is typical, sir. A dirt road that ends near the river. And then it's footpaths from there on. Very narrow going. A migration of ants will cause us trouble in one place, and there are howlers everywhere."

Indeed, Calabar could hear those loud monkeys from where he stood. He nodded. "A hundred men aren't many, in truth, and being spread out so much, we will not be able to bring fire to bear as nicely as I had hoped."

"Did he give you *all* the men you wanted?" Luiz asked.

Calabar shrugged. "Enough, but now we have to put them to good use." He looked up into the bright sky. He wiped his brow. Humid, hot, and sticky. Not much of a breeze off the sea. A scent of rain in the air. That would not help their shooting. "Let's begin," he said, turning Luiz around and urging him forward. "I want you to stay with the Tabajara, yes? You convey my plan to them. Understand?"

Luiz nodded. "Yes, sir, I will do so. But...what is your plan, sir?"

"To be where we are not expected, and to attack

when they are not watchful, Luiz." Calabar smiled and slapped the boy on the shoulder. "In short, to defeat them. As usual."

"I suspect," Luiz said, frowning slightly, "that the men will want details."

Calabar could not keep from smiling. "Yes. They are trying, that way."

Calabar huddled quietly behind broad leaves and thick vines, his wheellock pistol loaded and ready in his hand. Twenty soldiers waited nearby for his signal. Their muskets were leveled toward the path that led roughly two miles northeast into the small, uneven streets at the rear of Pontal. Von Schoppe's frontal assault was going well, but from this distance, Calabar could not tell if the town had been taken yet. Probably not. Von Schoppe was showing enormous patience, giving Calabar time to spring his trap. Finally in position, and enduring a clinging humidity and clouds of biting flies, he waited for Pedro Correia de Gama to come.

Calabar had set himself up in the vanguard of the ambush, instructing the rest of the men to spread out so as to be able to bear along several routes that their enemies might use. Invisible only a few yards within the jungle, they were gathered in clumps of about a dozen. It was logical to assume that de Gama would use the widest of the pathways to facilitate the speed and ease with which he could insert a force into Pontal, but Calabar knew that the Portuguese captain was too smart for that. If his ploy was expected, then he would likely stick to a smaller trail, accepting a slight decrease in speed for the near-certainty of dodging an ambush. And de Gama would certainly know the next best route to take; he had been in the country for over ten years, and knew the lay of the land. Hardly surprising: the Portuguese had first arrived in Brazil almost one hundred and ten years earlier, more than a century before the Dutch began attempting to wrest it away from them.

How ironic, Calabar thought, that one could easily consider the Dutch to be "foreign invaders," as if the Portuguese were the native peoples of Brazil. Certainly some considered them that. Calabar had pondered the contending arguments a good deal over the past couple of years, but right now, waiting behind damp foliage, trying desperately to keep his powder dry, he was not merely unsure of the answer; he was unsure that it mattered. He had never known a Brazil without the Portuguese. He had also never known a Brazil without slavery and the bigotry it spawned. He shook his head to drive away the questions, smacked a fly from his neck, and reaffixed his broad-brimmed hat against the first droplets of rain.

Rain was a blessing and a curse when attempting an ambush in the jungle. Rain would help keep the howler monkeys from giving away their position to the Portuguese. But it would also hamper gunfire. Perhaps, Calabar had reasoned, the pikes weren't wholly ridiculous weapons after all, but they were too long, a weapon for the vast fields of Europe where the role of neatly formed blocks of soldiers was to repel cavalry charges, push the enemy from the field, or into places where gunfire could do its worst. That was not the warfare for Brazil. Here, small units, cover, and surprise worked best. It had taken a long time for the Dutch—primarily a seafaring power—to understand that. Calabar was doing what he could to help. And now here he was, leading Dutch boys into battle, some of them almost young enough to have been sons of his.

So, taking the helpful advice of Luiz, he had instructed all the pikemen to saw their pikes in half and then wield them like spears. Von Schoppe would not like having his weapons ruined, but Calabar was willing to risk the wrath of his friend. Such anger would not last long anyway, assuming they won.

A young Dutch soldier stumbled through the underbrush and came up at his side. "Calabar," he said in a labored whisper. "They are coming."

Indeed they were. The whinny of a horse and the slosh of its hooves through the mud confirmed it. Calabar drew his pistol from beneath his coat and listened. Soon, he could hear the rumble of steel-banded wheels coming up one of the smaller paths. More horses trotting closer, and then the shuffle of men's legs. He craned his neck to see above the dripping leaves.

Through the hazy air, he spotted a mass of twenty or twenty-five men, moving in a defensive ring around a cannon being pulled by a single horse. It was a smaller piece than what would have graced the walls of Fort Nazare, but large enough to have three men behind it, pushing against its wheels as the horse pulled. An old Spanish saker probably, a gun brought in to provide close-range firepower if the walls of the fort had been breached. The rest of the Portuguese guard carried muskets.

"When I give the signal," Calabar said, mouthing

the words more than speaking them, "we rise up together and shoot together. Understand?"

Everyone nodded.

"Then we rush the gun and take it before they can respond. *Wait* for my signal."

They waited. Calabar rose to his knees, pistol aimed, hand in the air.

The cannon train hastened forward. Now, he could see the small caisson being pulled from behind, more of a handcart than anything, hastily assembled to make the short journey to Pontal. He waited until the rumble of the cannon's wheels were clear, until he could clearly see faces of the Portuguese soldiers in front; their eyes were shifting back and forth beneath tarnished morion helms, searching nervously for trouble. *They will get plenty soon enough*, Calabar said to himself, as he raised his hand higher, ready to signal.

A shot rang out on his left before he dropped his hand.

A young Dutch boy fell back from the recoil of his own musket. Perhaps he had gotten scared, or the trigger was slick with water or sweat. Whatever the reason, the premature round nicked the cannon barrel, and the Portuguese guards turned and fired into the underbrush.

In a moment, everyone was firing. Calabar hit the ground and covered his head. *Goddamn!* He spit the curse into the soil. The Jesuit priest who had baptized him as a child would have beaten him black for such blasphemy, but he didn't care. The ambush was ruined.

Calabar rose up, aimed and fired at the closest Portuguese soldier. Despite the rain, the pistol barked, and the bullet tore through the man's shoulder, knocking

him back against the horse's flank as it was riddled
with shots. The horse smashed through its twisted
tackle, taking the man down with it and stopping the
procession in its tracks. While the other Portuguese
soldiers desperately reloaded their muskets, Calabar
gave the second, final signal.

"Now!"

Men sprang from their hiding places, rushing the
piece, some yelling and holding their muskets like
spears, others trying to take aim as they skipped
forward. The Portuguese held firm, huddling around
the saker and trying to fend off the attackers. Calabar
raised his pistol and drove it straight and hard against
the jaw of a young man guarding the cannon. Bits
of chipped tooth, blood, and spit flew from the boy's
mouth as another Portuguese stepped into the gap.
Calabar took a swing as the new defender raised his
pistol. As Calabar's own pistol batted it away a split
second before it went off, he pulled his sword and
slashed out with it. The hasty cut parted the man's
gruff cheek with a gush of crimson as he jumped aside
and was lost in the writhing mass of men.

An unseen object found Calabar's ribs and drove
the wind from his chest. He fell back a pace, steadied
himself, and slashed again, this time at another Portuguese soldier who was trying to spike the gun. The
blade found the man's fingers, tore two from his hand,
left him screaming, and the iron spike in the mud.

Then it was over. Those Portuguese lucky enough
to have survived were fleeing back from whence they
came. A couple of Dutch soldiers tried to follow them.

Calabar called after them. "Stop! We do not chase
stragglers. Let them go!" The boys seemed upset at

that. Calabar did not know if their annoyance was due to their blood being up or from the fact that it was *he* who was ordering them to stop. But that did not matter right now.

"Who's the *rotzak* that fired before my signal?" he asked, helping a soldier up.

"Jansen, sir," one called, pointing to a dead Dutch boy lying face down at the side of the path.

Jansen's was not the only corpse. Calabar counted another six dead, mixed among the Portuguese. *Na morte nos todos somos o mesmo*, he thought as he holstered his pistol and sheathed his sword. *In death, we are all the same.*

"The next one of you who disobeys my order, I'll—"

Echoes of musket fire and shouting men interrupted his speech. He recognized a voice in the chaos.

Luiz!

Calabar abandoned the gun, his men following him through the thick wood. The rain had tapered off, but the howlers were back, announcing their approach. But they could no longer allow that to delay them: the battle was on, and Luiz was in trouble.

Calabar ran for nearly a quarter mile, the stink of wet, decayed leaves and the fresh scent of musket fire in his nose. The distant but constant sound of battle from Pontal rumbled in his ears. Calabar could feel his heart pounding against his ribcage as his legs began to weaken. But he mustered the strength to keep going, jumping a fallen tree and blowing through a patch of thorny vines. They broke free of the brush in a clearing near the back of the town, and all Calabar could see was a mass of men fighting: intermittent discharges of pistols, broken pikes clashing, swords striking, blood spilling.

At the center of the carnage, Luiz and de Gama were locked in combat, swords flashing, faces taut and sweaty. The boy tried to repel the Portuguese captain's relentless attack, but was faring poorly. His shirt was torn, his arms cut.

As Calabar raced across the clearing, a drift of musket smoke obscured the two momentarily. He charged harder, straining to see—and knocked over a Portuguese soldier as he cleared the dispersing cloud. He avoided another, almost stumbling but keeping his feet until, howling, he threw himself into de Gama's back. His hat flew off as the full impact of his weight thudded into Luiz's attacker.

The Portuguese captain grunted as the blow sent him reeling, his sword knocked from his hand. Calabar righted himself quickly and tried to find Luiz in the spreading smoke, but the young man wasn't nearby. In that moment, de Gama regained his feet and was on him quickly, punching his jaw and pushing him back. Calabar tried drawing his sword, but the belt had shifted, and he could not find the hilt. Instead, he drew his knife, lashed out at de Gama, but missed.

De Gama came at him again, but this time, Calabar was ready, catching the captain's wrist and turning it. De Gama screamed and struck out with his left boot, catching Calabar in the thigh and rolling him over. Now, the Portuguese captain had his own knife ready and thrust it toward Calabar's stomach. Calabar twisted just in time but felt the blade tear his wet shirt. He balled his fist and struck de Gama's chin, sending the man reeling back just enough to allow Calabar to roll the other way, coming up short against the body of a dead soldier.

Calabar pulled his pistol, and then remembered it was not loaded. He cursed and tossed it away, then found another, primed and ready, in the hand of the dead man alongside him. He thanked God quickly, pulled the pistol free, and lurched up onto his knees. As de Gama came at him, Calabar raised the pistol and pushed it into the captain's throat.

De Gama halted abruptly, the knife in his hand suspended in mid-thrust.

"It's over, de Gama," Calabar said. "You are beaten."

De Gama's bloody, puffy lip quivered as sweat rolled down his face. He screwed his dark eyes up and flicked a tongue between uneven teeth. He grimaced as if a shot of pain had pierced his eye, but his voice was clear and unwavering.

"*Traitor!*"

Calabar wavered at the word. He held the gun firm against de Gama's throat, but the joy of victory was gone. Only that word now hung in his mind, that simple yet damning word. He had heard it before, more than once, but somehow, at this particular moment, it held new meaning, had extra power that it had never had before. Looking into de Gama's eyes, a man he had fought alongside and whose life he had saved, Calabar said, "I am no traitor." His voice was quieter than he had wanted.

De Gama nodded. "You are. Come, traitor," he said, slowly turning to offer Calabar his back. "Shoot me as I flee. Helpless. Show the world what you are."

It was the right thing to do. Here in the jungles of Brazil, the tactically sound thing to do was to pull the trigger. This was a tough, dirty war, and if he let de Gama go, he was likely to face the man on some later battlefield, his old comrade fully willing and ready to put a bullet in Calabar's chest. His mind told him to pull the trigger, and yet the words kept echoing in his ears: *Show the world what you are . . . traitor.*

"Calabar!"

Calabar turned toward the new, vaguely familiar voice. Pedro Álvares was standing amid the scattered bodies of both sides, wet and dirty, a spent musket in his hand. He lowered the weapon and waved peaceably. "Please, don't kill him."

Calabar knew Álvares mostly through reputation. He had served in the past as a liaison for both Duarte de Albuquerque and his brother Matias when, three years ago, they had sent an offer to the Dutch that could have meant peace, or at least a truce. The offer, of course, had not been accepted. But here on the outskirts of Pontal, Álvares was a long way from Matias and his inland stronghold, Bom Jesus.

"Serving swine now, eh, Pedro?" Calabar said, pushing the barrel of his pistol deeper into the nape of de Gama's neck.

"I serve Duarte, Matias, and my king," Álvares said. "As you once did."

"Shoot, you mameluco dog!" de Gama blurted, and began walking away.

Pedro fell silent, and Calabar stared deeply into his eyes. Yes, shooting de Gama would be best. *But . . .*

He lowered the pistol. "Go," he muttered quickly, "before I change my mind."

His former comrade turned, and the anger on his face was gone, replaced with surprise. Calabar let the pistol fall from his hand as he watched Álvares lead the wounded de Gama away. They disappeared into the tree line. De Gama looked back again, but

Calabar did not meet his gaze. Instead, he turned to greet Luiz who approached holding a cut on his arm.

"Why did you let them go?" Luiz asked.

Calabar ripped a piece of fabric from his shirt and wrapped it around the young man's wound. He tied it tightly in place. *I'm no mameluco dog. I'm no traitor,* he thought, but he said, "It doesn't matter now. Listen."

They listened. Through the humid air, they could hear Dutch soldiers cheering.

Pontal was theirs.

In the cool shade of a tree, Calabar watched von Schoppe approach. His friend carried a bucket and a ladle. Calabar smiled weakly. No Portuguese captain had ever condescended to bring him water.

Von Schoppe laid the bucket down and scooped out a ladle full. The water spilled over the sides, and Calabar nodded and took it gently with his hands. He drank deeply, then said, "Congratulations, Captain."

"I should be thanking you, Domingos," von Schoppe said, dropping the ladle back into the bucket. "You were right again. And now we have time to reinforce before Matias arrives."

"Do you think he will?"

Von Schoppe nodded. "He's a dog with a bone, a most persistent creature. He'll come. It'll do no good, but he'll come." After ladling out a drink for himself, he stood. "Rest up, and then come find me. I need you to reconnoiter up toward the fort. De Gama is still out there, and—"

"Captain," Calabar said, standing slowly. "I wonder if I could beg your leave and return to Recife with Admiral Lichthart."

Von Schoppe wrinkled his brow. "Are you injured?"

"No, Captain. I'm just... Well, it has been several weeks since I've seen my wife, my children."

Concern spread across von Schoppe's face. "How is Carlos?"

Calabar shook his head. "I don't know. I haven't heard anything of late. I take that as a good sign, but I need to see my children. I will leave Luiz here with you. His wound looks worse than it really is. He's capable. He can assist in anything you require."

"He's a good scout, yes, but he's not as good a soldier as you. Few men are, even though you've been at it for less than half a year." When Calabar's only response was a one-shouldered shrug, von Schoppe sighed. "Very well. When ready, report to the admiral. He'll be leaving under cover of night...if he can find a way past the cape in one piece."

Chapter 2

Fort Nazare, Brazil

Pedro Álvares watched Dutch sailors prepare to disembark. He watched them through a small window from the safety of Fort Nazare, as de Gama fumed behind him. There were no guns firing at the ships. What purpose would it serve now but to waste ammunition? Von Schoppe and the Dutch had taken Pontal, and no amount of gunfire from a small fort would make any difference.

"I have sent word to Matias," de Gama said, fiddling with papers at his desk in an obvious attempt to mask his rage.

"You do not trust me?" Álvares turned from the window.

De Gama paused, set his harsh gaze on Álvares' face. "I'm a soldier, Pedro, not a politician. My men and my current military position matter most, and time is precious. If *you* cared about time, you would already be in the saddle, riding hard up the coast."

Álvares nodded but could not help letting a smirk

cross his lips. "Do not worry, de Gama. The fate of your men and of Pontal will be articulated to Bom Jesus. I shall ride by dusk, and I will give them a full assessment of the situation. Something your courier cannot do."

De Gama grew quiet, then said slowly, deliberately, "Do you think Matias will send us men?"

"I'm sure he will." *But he would be foolish to do so.* Álvares did not bother to speak his true thoughts. De Gama was a decent field commander, but he was prone to angry outbursts. Telling him the truth of the tenuous strategic situation in which the Portuguese found themselves in Brazil would be foolhardy, and serve no purpose other than to force de Gama's hand. If de Gama believed that no reinforcements were forthcoming, he might very well abandon the fort again and try to retake Pontal on his own.

And next time, Captain, I will not save you from Calabar.

De Gama rose from his desk and stood beside Álvares. He peered out the window toward the Dutch ships, said, "He should send enough men to kill that mameluco dog, at least."

Álvares winced. Those words stung him more than he thought they would. "He stayed his hand, Pedro. He let you live."

De Gama nodded. "That he did, and I wonder why."

Álvares acted as if he were insulted. "I begged him not to shoot, if you recall."

"And why should he care what you, Matias' man, would say? That should have made him pull the trigger straight away."

"But he *didn't*. So perhaps he isn't such a traitor after all, yes?"

De Gama cleared his throat and spit through the window, as if he were trying to strike the mast on Lichthart's flagship. He wiped his mouth, and said, "He's a traitor. Any man who fights beside me one day, and who then pledges his allegiance to the enemy the next, is a traitor. And as I stand here breathing, I pledge to God that if Matias doesn't put Calabar into the ground someday... I *will*."

Álvares opened his mouth to continue arguing the point, but closed it promptly. Any further discussion on the matter would draw too much suspicion to himself, and de Gama was not a man he wanted as an enemy. Besides, the more important matter before them now was why the Dutch had suddenly taken an interest in Pontal. What strategic significance did a small fishing village hold for the mighty West India Company? And why send so many to take it, when a force half its size would have sufficed, even taking into account the reinforcements of de Gama and his men from Fort Nazare? All of this had something to do with Admiral Tromp and his arrival in Recife. There was a connection, and Pedro Álvares had his suspicions. But he was not about to share them with de Gama. But with Matias?

No, not yet. Or maybe never...

De Gama returned to his desk and fiddled with more papers. "Be ready to ride by dusk. Tell Matias of our situation, and implore him to send more men. I want Pontal back under my command in a fortnight."

Álvares nodded, but turned back to the window. One week, two weeks, a month. How long it took to recapture Pontal no longer mattered. The inexplicable Dutch assault implied that something far more important than the fate of a small Portuguese coastal town was at stake, and Álvares would make sure he learned of it before it was too late.

He picked up the spyglass that sat nearby on the window sill and trained it at the Dutch flagship. On the deck stood a dark-skinned man, disheveled, his shoulders limp, speaking to Admiral Lichthart. Even though he had no way of knowing what they were saying, he knew the context of their conversation.

"Take him home, Admiral," Álvares whispered so that de Gama could not hear, "and let Calabar see his family again ... before everything changes."

Hours later, with Calabar's assistance, three Dutch ships navigated quietly past Fort Nazare in darkness and proceeded up the coast to Recife. Calabar stood on the deck of Vice Admiral Lichthart's flagship for the duration of the journey, despite calls from the admiral to go below and rest. He needed it, no doubt, but the trip was short and besides, he couldn't sleep. Try as he might, he could not erase de Gama's words from his mind, nor the face of his wife and children.

At the break of first light, the rocky reef of Recife came into view, and Calabar found the strength to smile. It was a beautiful sight, almost as lovely as Porto Calvo, his place of birth, but far more important, more so than nearly any other point along the Brazilian coast.

The ships slipped into the harbor through the narrow passage between the reefs, and Calabar marveled at the number of tiny forts lining the approach. Just four years ago, the entirety of the area had been under Portuguese control. Now, it was in Dutch hands: precariously so, in the long term, but firm enough right now. The forts were an impressive indication of their resolve to ensure that the strategic hub of those possessions, Recife, would stay that way. Calabar put his hand over his eyes to shield them from the sudden brightness of the rising sun.

The buildings of Recife caught that light, standing out from the green and blue that surrounded them. The walled town sat like a fist at the tip of a long island that snaked into the harbor from roughly six miles up the coast near Olinda. Three rivers, the Afogadas, the Capiberibe, and the Beberibe spilled their brackish water into that harbor, its broad waters a natural barrier that separated—and protected—Recife from the mainland visible just beyond. A long bridge connected Recife to the much larger island of Antonio Vaz, which was also protected by forts. It had to be, for the Portuguese were still close, in numbers large enough to be a constant threat.

The three ships moved their way up and through the anchorage of Admiral Tromp's fleet, which had arrived four months prior. Combined with the ships that had already been in port, Calabar had not seen so much naval power in Recife since the days when the Portuguese held the harbor. But apparently that massing of force had not been entirely a matter of choice, as many of the Dutch ships had limped in with splintered masts, breached hulls, and fire damage nearly beyond repair. The fortunes of nations were apparently changing almost as rapidly as the tides themselves, or so it was whispered in the streets of Recife. A strange group of people had arrived in Europe, seemingly from nowhere, announced by a bright flash of fire. Their ideas and influence had begun changing the balance of power that prevailed there, and perhaps in the wider world beyond. At the very least, these so-called Americans had, directly or indirectly, triggered a chain of events that prompted Spain to send a fleet to engage the Dutch in a place called Ostend.

That was all Calabar knew. When he tried to learn more, he was told "just do your duty." So that was exactly what he had done. But Tromp's ships were still impressive, even as damaged as they were. Repairs were being made, though slowly, and as Admiral Lichthart's ship came to rest alongside a sturdy pier that jutted out from Recife's dockyard, Calabar wondered how long it would take for the Dutch fleet to be back at full strength. Not much longer, hopefully.

He hoped too that, by some miracle, Celia and their children would be waiting for him. But alas, the pier held only Dutch sailors who helped moor the ship firmly into place with strong hemp lines. Calabar gathered himself and carefully made his way down a rope ladder. He hopped off, turned and nearly ran into Cornelis Jol.

"My apologies, *Houtebeen*, I mean, Admiral," Calabar said, bowing politely. "I did not see you there."

Calabar immediately regretted using the Dutch word for Jol's wooden leg, which was affixed tightly above his missing calf and knee. The Portuguese called him *Pé de Pau*, but the last man who used that term in Jol's presence lost an eye. Calabar winced and reflexively covered his face as if he were about to sneeze. Jol laughed heartily, his fresh but graying whiskers twinkling in the morning light. The man's breath carried its customary scent of rum and half-stale bread. Calabar held his breath until Jol stopped laughing.

"'Admiral'?" Peg Leg Jol said, ignoring the Dutch nickname. He screwed up his pinched face as if he had eaten a lemon. "My superiors may call me that if they wish, but you know better, my friend."

Calabar smiled. Indeed, Jol was more of a pirate, a privateer, than he was an admiral. But the rank was genuine, bestowed upon him for great deeds performed in the service of the West India Company. He was much revered among the Dutch colonists in Recife, despite the wooden stump that forced him to lurch through the streets like some terribly grizzled monster.

"I did not expect you to be here," Calabar said.

"Nor did we necessarily expect you to return so quickly from Pontal," Peg Leg replied, "but we hoped you might. And how did we fare in that engagement?"

Calabar told him.

"Very good. Now, come," he said, taking Calabar by the shoulders and slowly turning around. "Let's be off. There is much to discuss."

"Sir," Calabar said, resisting being pulled up the pier, "I returned so that I might see my family."

"And you will, you will, I promise. I will take you there myself. But now, we have much to do. Your presence is required."

"By whom?"

"Admiral Tromp."

Calabar stopped and kept his expression firm as he looked straight into Peg Leg's amiable face. "Sir, if he plans on giving me another assignment so quickly, I must humbly—"

"Heavens, no! He wants to speak to you about a far more serious matter."

Calabar paused. "What matter?"

Peg Leg grabbed Calabar's arm and pulled him over to a pile of crates. He looked about, ensuring no one was near. He spoke low, his friendly eyes now turning dark and serious.

"The Dutch are leaving Recife."

Maarten Tromp was young, not much older than Calabar, but he commanded great respect in the Dutch navy. He had only recently been promoted to admiral, but was held in high regard by the local Company representatives, despite the fact that he had come into port with a crippled fleet.

He was waiting for Jol and Calabar in the kitchen of the governor's home, helping himself to some boiled cabbage, sweetened pawpaw juice, and bits of dried *pirarucu* fish. Calabar didn't realize how hungry he was until he smelled the fine breakfast.

"Please, sit," Tromp said. "Have whatever you wish."

Calabar was messy, smelly, and was not prepared for dining, but he accepted Tromp's offer and took a seat. Peg Leg stood behind him.

"Pontal went well?" Tromp asked.

Calabar nodded. "Yes, sir. We took the town."

"I have not received the official report from Admiral Lichthart, but that is good to hear." Then his expression turned serious. "It may very well be the last town we ever take in Brazil."

Calabar accepted a piece of bread and helped himself to a jug of juice. He swallowed the bread in one gulp. "I don't understand, sir."

Tromp stopped eating, shot a glance at Peg Leg who nodded approval. "You saw what was left of my fleet when I arrived?"

"Yes, sir."

"Then you have seen the damage that we are still repairing," Tromp said, finishing his meal and patting the sides of his mouth. He placed his napkin on his plate, pushed away from the table, and stood up. "It is time for us, for the Dutch, to leave Recife."

Tromp walked across the room and gazed out the window. Had they been in the dining room, he would have enjoyed a wide panoramic view of the harbor. Here, he looked out over a humble but tidy herb garden. "Europe is changing, Domingos. Europe has *already* changed in many ways and, in consequence, we can no longer maintain our position here. We must leave before the Portuguese, and the Spanish for that matter, learn of our weakened position."

"They have not yet heard of the destruction of your fleet at Dunkirk?"

"No. It is not unusual that news from the Old World is delayed by half a year or more."

Jol nodded. "Particularly down here."

Calabar nodded back. "So. Where are we going?"

Tromp turned and looked straight into Calabar's eyes. "I cannot tell you that right now, Domingos." He crossed the room again and sat back down. "I've called you here because I need your help. You are respected and admired among the colonists," Tromp began. "You hold special status among the *mestizos* and mamelucos in particular, although many of them are of Portuguese descent. I suspect you are one of the reasons they have supported our position here in Brazil, so far. And if our departure is to occur smoothly and on time, we will need their continued support. Or, at least, their silence."

"I understand, sir. And you cannot tell me where we are going?"

"No, not today. But I want you to attend a meeting on my ship, four days hence." He leaned in close. "Assuming that I can *count* on your aid?"

Calabar had completed a few assignments for Tromp since the admiral's arrival, but they did not know each other that well. They were certainly not close, not like he was with Peg Leg and von Schoppe. But Calabar and the young admiral had gotten along well whenever they met, and Tromp had never given him any reason to be concerned with his service or loyalty to the Company, or to the Dutch in general. Thus, there could only be one reason why Tromp was being so persistent in securing a clear, unambiguous declaration of support.

To serve them, I had to become a traitor. A mameluco dog. And now they wonder: will I turn again?

"Admiral Tromp," Calabar said, pushing away from the table and standing. "I serve the Dutch and have given my oath to them. I will not break that oath. I will help you in any way that I can. In fact, I would ask that I and my family be allowed to leave Brazil as well when the time comes."

Tromp smiled at that request, and Peg Leg slapped Calabar's shoulder. "That's good news, my friend. You are most welcome to come along."

"You are indeed, Domingos," Tromp said, his quiet voice and somber nod a strangely reassuring contrast to Peg Leg's good humor. "But I do want to warn you: the type of service that you have provided us here in Brazil will likely stop in the new colony. At least for a while. In addition, there are already Dutch colonists there who own the choice land, and the Dutch relocating from Recife will have claim to most of the rest of it. You might not have the opportunity to own land, Domingos, and thus I cannot guarantee what kind of life you and your family will find there."

Calabar had owned property once before, under the Portuguese. Not that long ago, in fact. It had been a small cane plantation that would have been dwarfed to invisibility if set beside the vast *fazendas* of the wealthiest Portuguese *fidalgos*. But oh, how he missed it sometimes. It had started as a small *trapiche* mill, one powered by horse and cattle, and with three wooden rollers used to extract the juices. Over time, the Portuguese had honored him with a larger *Engenho* plantation that allowed the cane to be ground and processed by water power instead of livestock, thus making the process more efficient and lucrative.

To this day, if he closed his eyes and surrendered to the memories, he could almost smell the cane juice boiling in the cauldrons as the impurities were cooked out. The molasses was then placed into clay sugar-loaf molds and sent to Europe. Europe craved sugar, and Calabar had been part of that trade for the Portuguese. Once upon a time.

He shook the recollections from his mind. "I serve the Dutch now, Admiral. I will serve them here and wherever it is we are going."

Tromp nodded and stood again. He offered his hand. "Very well. Then I will impress upon you the importance of keeping this conversation quiet, until noon, four days from now, when you arrive on my ship. All will be discussed and revealed then. Is that clear?"

"Yes, sir." As Calabar made to depart with Jol, Tromp gave him the remaining food and pawpaw juice. After accepting it graciously, Calabar stepped out of the governor's house, feeling both elation and fear.

Chapter 3

Recife, Brazil

Tromp stared at the door that had closed behind Calabar's exhaustion-sloped shoulders. "He is not a talkative fellow."

"Surely you'd already noticed that." Jol slipped a piece of bread out of the woven reed basket at the center of the heavy, much scored, tabletop.

Tromp shrugged. "Yes, but Calabar has always been part of a group, before. Meetings, always with senior commanders present. Under more private circumstance, I had thought"—*well, hoped*—"that he might become more expressive."

Jol smiled around the remains of the bread in his mouth; he never looked more like a sea dog than when he was eating. "I told you he was a man of action and few words."

"So you did."

Houtebeen glanced at the basket again. "And is he not the man I claimed him to be? Ideal for your—our—needs? And a most agreeable fellow, besides?"

Tromp nodded. "He is all that. And he has adapted admirably to his role as not merely a leader of scouts, but a commander of soldiers."

Jol pocketed another piece of bread. "Maarten, even when you agree with me, when you end on that tone I know there's a 'however' waiting just behind it."

Tromp's smile was slight but genuine. "It is annoying that you know me so well."

"I'd better. You're not exactly an open book yourself. So tell me: what is it that bothers you about Calabar? Do you still doubt his loyalty?"

Tromp shook his head. "No. But I am uncertain if he is sufficiently...prudent."

"Oh, that. So you've heard that he can be a bit of a hothead?" Jol shrugged. "Occasionally, yes. But that's not a cause for worry, Maarten. That's a trait for which you should be grateful."

Tromp felt the frown growing on his face before he could suppress it. "You are saying that we *want* a hothead leading our troops?"

Jol sighed, shook his head, grabbed another piece of bread without the faintest hint of subterfuge or shame. "Maarten Tromp, you are a fine commander of ships. Probably the best I've ever seen. Except when I'm looking in a mirror, that is." They both smiled. "But as chaotic as a battle at sea can become, it always requires a measure of reserve, of restraint. There are too many details, both of devices and tactics, that a good officer must always bear in mind.

"But that is not the way of commanding men on land, Admiral—of which I have done much more than your lofty self." Jol's grin became positively piratical. "That, my friend, is a dirty, nasty business, and one that often rewards split-second decisiveness which looks like impetuosity to those who have not struggled at close quarters." He stole another piece of bread.

"So you are saying that Calabar is *not* hotheaded?"

Jol grinned. "Only when he should be."

Tromp refused to return the smile. "That is not an answer. That is an evasion."

Jol's smile disappeared. "In truth, Maarten, it is not. Particularly not here in the New World. Given the ranges at which we usually fight, a high temperament is a weapon unto itself. What Calabar lacks in training and physical size he makes up for in courage, passion, decisiveness, ferocity. He would not be a very successful soldier in Europe, you know. Imagine him there, carrying a musket in a formation that marches to and fro, the front line of muskets firing at the enemy and vice versa, like ships pouring broadsides into each other.

"But when the day is decided by a final charge, when those tidy ranks become gangs of desperate savages murdering each other with pistols and swords, then Calabar would be your man. There, as here, in the chaos of personal combat, his temperament is no longer a handicap. That is what makes him a dangerous opponent and an inspiring leader, because that is precisely the nature of the wars we wage in the New World. Here there are no set-piece battles, only sudden, brutal skirmishes."

Jol dusted crumbs from his hands, set them on his knees. "People born in these lands, they are different because they see the world differently. Back in Europe, we grow up surrounded by roads, and tall buildings, and complex tools and skills of every kind. Even for those of us who happily leave all that behind"—Jol leaned back with a broad grin—"it is nevertheless the lens through which we always see the world: a place dominated by the handiwork of humans."

His grin diminished, became more reflective. "Not so here. Look at this place, this Recife we've built. Here, this grand town is not the rule, but the oddity. It is the untamed continent that crowds up against our small streets which shapes the people of Brazil."

He frowned. "Europeans call them 'savages.' I say they are simply more direct. In Europe, we put layers between who we are and what we may do. Feelings, instincts, reflexes; we filter and alter them like a dog pulling back on its own leash. And so we congratulate ourselves on being 'civilized.' This place and its people are more truly human, more honest."

"You are saying there is no treachery among the peoples of the New World?" Tromp tried to keep his voice from veering toward incredulity.

"Now, Maarten, you know I am not so foolish as to claim that. But this much is true: whatever normal measure of deceit already existed here has grown a hundredfold in response to our own, nourished by the manure of the 'civilized' duplicity that lurks behind our laws and religions and dainty manners."

"I think," Tromp murmured, "that I now understand your choice of a career much better than I have before."

Jol nodded. "That is why I spend so little time back home. I would rather be around men like Calabar. He, like many other people of the New World, may occasionally seem rash, but they are fundamentally honest—except when they are lied to. Then . . . well, why *should* they keep promises to us when we prove ourselves faithless?"

Tromp raised an eyebrow. "And is that what happened with Calabar and the Portuguese?"

Jol nodded. "They not only lied to him, but made promises in the name of a God that he respects more truly and fervently than they. You wanted a man you could trust, both in terms of his knowledge and his character. Calabar is that man."

Tromp frowned. "I do not question his basic honesty, and certainly not his effectiveness. But it is imperative that his actions do not become an—an embarrassment to our nation or William of Orange."

"As if similar concerns ever give the Spanish a moment's pause."

Tromp thumped his knuckles against the table. "Are we to hold ourselves to no better standard than theirs? Jol, when we arrived and I said there are many changes coming, and that they will be bold, I was utterly serious. I was somewhat uncertain then, but since that first night, I have watched, have read, have thought carefully. And so what began as a sympathetic impulse has become a reasoned, ethical resolve: that here in the New World, we must not merely prevail on the battlefield, but in the eyes of God."

Cornelis Jol stopped chewing the latest piece of bread. "Maarten . . . Admiral, are you contemplating—?"

Tromp did not let him finish. *One difficult debate at a time.* "It is not enough that Calabar can win battles. He must also understand the need for restraint. And on this matter—his ability to think clearly in the heat of combat, to separate his thought and responsibilities from his passions and his impulses—I have no report. His men speak highly of him, yes. And yes, he betrayed his Portuguese masters to join us. From what I can tell today, he also has good manners when visiting a superior's house. But none of that tells me what manner of man we are trusting with our future. For that is exactly what we are doing." Tromp sat, locked eyes with Jol, arms crossed as he waited for the other to reply.

Houtebeen sighed and settled into a chair opposite Maarten's. "Do you not feel there is a certain irony in ascertaining the better points of a man's character by asking the opinion of a pirate?"

"Privateer," Tromp corrected.

Jol waved away the distinction. "There are none among Calabar's superiors or soldiers who speak ill of him. Indeed, he is said to be sensitive to the needs of his men and genuinely dedicated to his religion."

"By which you mean—?"

"By which I mean he does not simply pay lip service to his faith—not the way so many of the Spaniards and Portuguese do, sinning like devils because every Sunday they can step into a confessional and settle their conscience and their account with God. And so, start all over again as soon as they exit.

"Calabar is not often described as being a warm man, but his men know him to be just, and his devotion to his family is unswerving. And, as you must already realize, he is most discreet."

Tromp nodded. Not quite the insights he had hoped for, but they were promising. And besides, that was the most he was going to be able to ascertain. "Very well. Then trust him we shall."

Jol scratched his slightly furry ear. "Given all the

missions he's been sent on, I thought you already *did* trust him."

Tromp shrugged. "Managing a battle is a short-lived and straightforward matter compared to what lies before us."

"You mean abandoning Recife? Yes, that will be quite a—"

Tromp shook his head. "Leaving this place is only the beginning of the challenges that we will need to address. And endure."

Jol squinted at his friend and commander for several long moments. "Maarten, what you said earlier, about prevailing in the eyes of God: are you proposing—"

"The end of slavery."

Jol pulled back as if Tromp's words were a fist aimed at his face. "Maarten, you know I share that sentiment, but—"

"It is not simply a 'sentiment.' Nor can there be any 'buts' about this matter. Piety, morality, and prudence all argue against manumission, and our break from Recife gives us an opportunity to break with this 'institution.'"

"Yes, it might," Jol allowed. "But you must expect trouble." The pirate sucked at the uneven collection of yellowed teeth that remained in his gums; it made a sound of anxious misgiving. "If you do this, you are putting your hand in the landowners' pockets. And the only reason they braved the perils of the New World was to fill those pockets with gold."

"And so they may, but without owning other human beings to do so. Human beings who must have freedom and fair recompense for their labor."

"'Must have'? History's great empires were built

on—depended upon—the backs and labor of slaves. It has ever been thus, from before the time of Moses."

"You make my point for me, Jol. The Pharaohs were ultimately made weaker as they increasingly *depended* upon slaves. Exodus shows the inevitable outcome. The same holds true for Rome; Spartacus' revolt was inevitable. And if slaves themselves do not rebel, they are ready friends to the foes of those who keep them in chains. We cannot afford that risk to our colony's safety any more than we can afford the risk to our individual souls."

"Maarten, I know how personal this matter is to you. Twice a slave, first in Salé and then Tunis: surely that has left its mark upon—"

Tromp waved aside Jol's explanation for his fervor. "No, Jol. That was not truly slavery. It was labeled so probably to quicken the grief and loosen the purse strings of relatives they hoped would pay my ransom."

Jol's smile was rueful. "Yes . . . and a pity you were not the son of a wealthy man."

"Perhaps . . . or perhaps those years of bondage shaped me for the better. How would I have felt about slavery without those experiences, as mild as they were?"

"Mild? Maarten, to be deprived of one's freedom is not—"

"Is not synonymous with the horror that is true slavery." Maarten scoffed. "When held by the Dutch Bey of Salé, I was more a pampered pet than anything else. Later, while a prisoner of the Bey of Tunis, he honored me above his own captains, and ultimately set me free."

"Because you were, on both occasions, both unbowed and ten times the sailor of the best in their service. They *admired* you, Maarten."

"Which is quite beside the point. In European terms, I was not truly a slave, merely a prisoner on open parole. I was not abased, I was not deemed subhuman." Tromp jabbed an index finger toward the cane fields surrounding Recife. "That—that out there—is true slavery. Our practice of it may be less harsh than that of the Spanish or Portuguese, but the fact remains that those people, those children of God, are property. Their owners may treat them like animals, and work them even harder. In the face of that, I cannot say that what I experienced among the Barbary pirates was slavery."

Jol grunted. "You will get no argument from me that it is evil for one human to own another. But still, I ask that you tread lightly on this matter. At least for a time. If the Spanish and Portuguese have slaves and we have none, then it will be *their* plantations that run more efficiently, produce more goods. If that occurs, the backbone of our colonies—the cane growers—will lose their profits, and you will lose their support. Which will destroy us more certainly than all Spain's ships and men. So, sadly, the West India Company must keep slaves, too, if only for a while."

Tromp shook his head, even though he heard and could not debate the bitter, pragmatic truth of Jol's warning. "I will not be"—he gritted his teeth—"rash. But the time is coming when we must—*must*—eradicate slavery."

"Agreed. Our safety—and perhaps our souls as well—depend upon it."

Tromp shook his head less violently this time. "It goes beyond that, Cornelis." Jol seemed to wince at the use of his given name. "For a century, the winds of social change have been rising. The up-time histories provide a perverse hindsight which confirms that trend. But now, whether they want to or not, the up-timers—and their ideas—are now whipping those winds into a hurricane. And slavery and autocrats will be the first to feel the full fury of that tempest. Accordingly, it is both wise and just to set our sails to catch those winds, to not merely accept the change but be a part of it."

Jol grinned. "Well, then you can surely place all your trust in Calabar, Maarten. He has been treated as half-human all his life and hates slavery with a passion."

Tromp shook his head. "No, Jol. That is precisely where you are wrong, and why I am worried. I know Calabar hates slavery. And it is that very passion which could get him—and us—into trouble."

Jol was frowning again. "How so?"

"You said it yourself: whether or not we wish it, we must tread slowly in addressing the issue of slavery. But will he, Calabar, be *able* to tread slowly? Will his passions let him?"

Two of Houtebeen's unprepossessing teeth came down softly on his lower lip. "I wish I could say, Maarten."

Who nodded gravely. "So do I, old friend. So do I."

Chapter 4

Recife, Brazil

Calabar's home lay near the western wall of Recife, a small one-level *apartamento* that still contained many of the furnishings from when the Portuguese controlled the town. His wife Celia and children Lua, Martim, and Carlos, greeted him warmly. Celia hugged her husband and kissed him repeatedly on the mouth and face. Lua and Carlos giggled at the lively affection, and Calabar was more than half embarrassed.

Not a man who showed his gentler emotions freely in any situation, he tried pulling away to get in a word, but ultimately failed. He was drawn into the living room and his martial accoutrements—pistol, knife, sword, and powder horn—were removed by the children. They tried playing with them, but Calabar put a stop to that quickly. So, they pretended that they were soldiers, saluting and marching in the service of the Dutch, just as they imagined their father did. Even Lua, who most often refused to play soldier games with her brothers, allowed Martim and Carlos to chase her about the room, making popping noises while pulling the trigger on her make-believe gun. Calabar watched his children play for most of the afternoon, laughed and danced with them, and felt more relaxed than he had in weeks.

That evening, they praised God and dined on tender capybara meat, dried iguana, boiled radishes, and the remains of the bread and juice given to him by Tromp. They talked about the weather, Celia's cooking, the sewing repairs that Lua had finished on her doll, a picture of a bird that Martim had sketched in writer's ink. Calabar practiced Dutch with the children, and he was much pleased with their improvement. Lua especially, who showed great skills with languages just like Luiz. Her intonation and inflection were near perfect now, and Martim's was improving. But Carlos grew weaker and weaker as the day wore on, and by supper, he could only take a few bites of meat and radish. Celia put him to bed early while Calabar read passages from the Bible to Lua and Martim until they too were nodding off. One after the other, he carried them to their own beds.

The house now was quiet, and Calabar followed his wife into their bedroom, where he slipped off his clothing and sat in a tub that Celia had filled with warm, clean water. He dozed, but when Celia began scrubbing his right arm with lye and a rough-bristled brush, he awoke, startled.

"I want Carlos baptized by September," Celia said. "Father Araujo will do it gladly."

Calabar frowned. "Baptized by the Jesuits? We are under Dutch protection now, Celia. Perhaps he should be baptized by them, in their own church. What do the doctors say?"

She shook her head. "He was strong today because he wants to impress his father. But he is weak, Domingos," she said, her voice quavering. "He is weak and getting weaker. He has a blood affliction, and there is nothing they can do about it. Maybe he will outgrow it, but I want him baptized before... before..."

She could not finish her sentence, and Calabar did not press the matter. They were silent for a moment, then he leaned forward to let her scrub his back. He wanted to stay silent while she did her work, but de Gama's foul accusations came back like an echo that had somehow lodged in his ears.

"I was called a traitor yesterday, Celia," he said, letting water rush down the sides of his face. "Pedro Correia de Gama, a man I served with, looked me straight in the eye, and called me a traitor."

"That is a lie."

Calabar shook his head. "No, he's right. I *am* a traitor. I stood before Matias de Albuquerque, his brother Duarte, and swore an oath to them both, and to the king. They repaid my loyalty with land and sugar mills. And I turned on them. I've burned their plantations, killed their soldiers, stolen their property. I've done all that. My father was Portuguese, my mother Tupi. To them, I am now just another mameluco dog."

Celia dropped the brush in the water and cupped Calabar's face in her warm, wet hands. "You are a child of Brazil, Domingos. You are a child of God. You did what you thought was best. And it hardly matters now anyway. We are, as you say, living under Dutch protection. No harm will come to us here."

Calabar took her hands away from his face. "No, Celia. Things have changed."

He told her about his meeting with Admiral Tromp, about the imminent departure of the Dutch, despite Tromp's explicit order not to speak of it to anyone. Celia was his wife; he had to tell her. She asked questions he could not yet answer. She grew frustrated, stood up and paced back and forth. He climbed out of the tub, wrapped himself in a fresh bed sheet, and followed her. "If we are truly under the protection of the Dutch," he continued, "then we must go all the way with them. We must go with them to this new colony. For when they leave, the Portuguese will seize Recife and everything in it. There will be no safe place for us then."

Celia shook her head. "No, we cannot go. Carlos is too weak. He won't survive the trip."

"We must risk it."

"No!" she yelped, louder than she wanted, and looked toward their door, fearing her children would be there. She went to it and closed it all the way. "I will not risk putting his life in danger."

"If we stay, it surely *will* be in danger."

"Then you must beg their forgiveness," she said, coming to him and putting her hand on his chest. "Go to Bom Jesus and throw yourself on Matias' mercy. Plead for your life, for your children's lives."

"Bah!" He said, pushing her away and turning toward the tub. "That is silly. They will shoot me on sight."

"Then I will go. They will not dare shoot a woman."

"You will not involve yourself in these matters, Celia," he said rounding on her and giving her a stern look. "I am your husband. You will do as I say."

A deep, bitter silence filled the room. In the distance, Calabar could hear laughter, some music, the bark of a dog. All the sounds of a town contented and free, at the moment at least, from danger and war. *How wonderful it would be*, he thought, *if it could always be that way*.

He heard her come toward him, careful steps, and felt her tender hand on his shoulder. "Yes, Domingos, you are my husband, and I have sworn to obey and to serve you." She was speaking Portuguese now. "But I am also the mother of your children, and I have made many sacrifices for you. I have raised our children almost entirely on my own, while you were off fighting this admiral's battle or that general's war. I have cried myself to sleep at night wondering if you will ever walk through that door again, and I have given strength to the three *filhos* who sleep in the beds that you have provided. They deserve a mother *and* a father. You may yell at the top of your lungs, you may strike me if you wish. But I will not, God forgive me, put our son's life at risk for the Dutch, now that they are leaving. They are abandoning us, and so we must do what we have to do to survive. Do not allow them to break up our family. Promise me, Domingos, that you will go to Bom Jesus and *try* to speak to de Albuquerque. Please . . . that is all I ask."

Calabar had to admit that Carlos seemed too weak to move. And having no idea where the new colony was located, he could not, in good conscience, risk Carlos' life with a potentially long and difficult journey. Was Celia right? Were the Dutch really worth the uncertainties and probable risks? They traded slaves just like the Portuguese and the Spanish, albeit not in the same vast numbers. Not yet, anyway. There were more than a few bigots among them, and they were even more brutal in some ways than the other European powers in Brazil when it came to trade and commerce. But try as he might to diminish their standing in his mind, he could not deny one important fact.

No Dutchman had ever called him a mameluco dog.

He softened, let the sheet fall, and hugged his wife close, feeling her warm body against his. *Oh, Celia. May God strike me dead if I ever strike you.*

"I promise to try to make it right, my love. I promise to try."

Bom Jesus

The official name of the fort and surrounding village was Arraial do Bom Jesus, or Real do Bom Jesus, depending upon whom you talked to. The Village of Good Jesus...the Royal Good Jesus. But to those who lived in it, served and protected its walls, it was simply Bom Jesus, though some of its soldiers often referred to it in passing as *o forte*. It was the strongest Portuguese fortification in the Captaincy of Pernambuco, and Matias de Albuquerque was in charge.

"Your counsel for discretion is noted, Pedro," Matias said, finishing a chunk of meat and washing it down with a gulp of red wine. "But I have already sent men to retake Pontal. I do not expect them to be long in recapturing it." Matias chuckled, cleared his throat. "It'll be like Bahia. The Dutch occupation will be short-lived. So I may need you there again soon. Do not get comfortable here, old friend."

Pedro Álvares nodded. "Yes, my lord. I serve wherever you deem necessary. I only express caution because

Admiral Tromp's fleet remains at anchor in the harbor, just a short distance from here. I'm sure that your men will retake Pontal in time, but with respect, it will not be like Bahia. If Admiral Tromp decides to move even a portion of his fleet to support von Schoppe, there will be no combined Portuguese and Spanish armada to block and hopefully, by God's grace, destroy him."

At least not in the short term, Álvares knew, and perhaps not even in the long. The so-called Ring of Fire and the "up-timers" who had come through it, were changing the face of Europe, politically, spiritually, and socially. Reports were sketchy indeed, but the New World colonies could no longer afford to believe that such changes would not find their way across the vast, blue Atlantic. To Álvares, the presence of Tromp's fleet was a probable harbinger of that trend. Clearly, judging by his cavalier attitude, Matias was either too stubborn—or too stupid—to perceive it.

Pedro tried a new tack. "With Tromp's fleet in harbor at Recife, I'm also concerned that the Dutch will try to attack us in a more strategically important place."

Matias looked up from his meal, furrowed his brow. "Like where? Olinda?"

For a time, Olinda had been under Dutch control. The small, strategically important town north of Recife occupied a soft spot in Matias' heart, for that was where he had been born over fifty years ago. He always looked toward it with fierce, protective eyes.

"No, my lord. Here . . . *o forte.*"

Matias rolled with laughter. The man had a guttural, undisciplined cackle that was difficult to appreciate. He spent most of his time handling military matters in a deadly serious manner, and the Dutch had given him few opportunities to laugh. But on this occasion he laughed, and Álvares winced.

"Nonsense," Matias said. "The Dutch have tried many times to breach us here, and they have failed each time. Bom Jesus is stronger now than it has ever been. The redoubts are well defended. Sending men to Pontal has not changed that."

"Yes, my lord. You are correct. But I fear that if they do choose to attack again, they will have the guidance of Calabar, and that will improve their tactical planning."

Matias' mirth disappeared from his thin face. Álvares watched as anger seemed to collect in the man's cheeks, making them swell and redden. He squeezed his fork as if he were going to plunge it into Álvares' eye. "I want that traitor brought to me, in chains. Do you understand, Pedro? I order it. I want that son of a bitch captured and brought to me. I will hang his head and bowels from the battlements."

Something about Matias' deep, dark expression told Álvares that he was serious this time. He had given that order before, and then had promptly forgotten it when other, more important matters of state emerged. But this time, Matias' gaze remained fixed on Álvares' face.

"Yes, my lord," Álvares said, letting the lie linger in the air. "I will see to it."

Matias nodded, dabbed fatty juice from his mouth, and called for a servant. An African boy scampered into the room, groomed and nicely dressed in white linen, his dark face expressionless but gentle. He did not seem afraid of his position and place, Álvares observed, but more resigned, listless, as if it were all a bad dream. Had he been born in Pernambuco?

It was hard to know. Slave ships arrived in Brazil on a regular basis, in Bahia primarily, and in Rio de Janeiro, as often as they used to arrive in Recife before the Dutch. Álvares watched as the boy cleaned up Matias' scraps, plate, silverware, and wine glass, then as quickly as he had arrived, disappeared.

Matias rose from his chair. "So, what do your spies tell you of the admiral?"

Álvares cleared his throat. "Not as much as we would like, my lord. Whatever battle Tromp fought in Europe, his fleet was badly damaged. Some hulls are still lashed to the largest pier: spars broken, fire damage, and still requiring occasional pumping. They are all being repaired and refitted, but it will take time to get them seaworthy again."

Matias grunted and shook his head. "I'm amazed he made it all the way across the Atlantic."

"Maarten Tromp is a skilled seaman," Álvares said. "The best they have, in my humble opinion."

"Then you don't think he and his fleet will remain here for long?"

Álvares shook his head. "I do not know, my lord."

"I find it hard to believe that the Dutch would simply let their best admiral tuck tail and run all the way here, and leave it at that. Based on all reports I've heard, they need skilled military men in Europe now more than ever. Wouldn't you agree?"

No. "Yes, my lord. That would be my assessment as well."

"Very good." Matias turned and headed to his study. He stopped and said, "Keep eyes on Recife. I want daily reports of all activity. In the meantime, I'll pass the reports to de Oliveira, in Bahia."

"Our former governor-general?"

"Who else? He will want to keep the Spanish informed. We may have an opportunity here, my friend, an opportunity to destroy Tromp in port as he licks his wounds." He chuckled, then raised his hand and pointed a sharp finger right between Álvares' eyes. "And bring me Calabar. I want him found. And if not him, then his family. Let's see how quickly a snake rises from the grass if his lovely wife's head is twisting in the wind."

"Yes, sir."

Álvares clenched his teeth as he watched Matias leave the room. It was one thing to demand the capture of Calabar; he had, after all, betrayed de Albuquerque's trust. His reasons for doing so may have been noble, or it may have been an act of necessity, but he had still broken his oath. But to go after the man's innocent wife, and his children . . . that was beyond reason. And it was well beyond the Christian faith that Matias supposedly professed.

Álvares shook his head. "No," he whispered. "Not as long as I have something to say about it, my lord. You will never lay hands on Celia. Never."

Chapter 5

Recife, Brazil

Calabar woke with the dawn, making sure that he had the time to bathe before arriving on Admiral Tromp's flagship at the appointed time. He had considered dressing for war, wearing his sword and pistol, but thought it proper to shrug off those military symbols and wear his finest, instead: a slashed gold-and-brown doublet with paned sleeves, pressed breeches, a fresh pair of boots, and a new black broad-brimmed hat. They had been given to him by the wife of a Dutch merchant for his dedicated service to Recife, but he had never worn them until now. He'd had little enough opportunity.

Besides, dressing for war on this particular day might prompt speculation of a fearsome announcement, especially given the nature of the people who came aboard even as he did. They were merchants and planters mostly, who were accustomed to seeing Dutch soldiers, but might be either alarmed by the presence of an armed mameluco or, worse yet, might begin to wonder more critically at what his presence and dress portended. Calabar knew little more than they did about what would be revealed, but he knew enough not to risk becoming the cause of unnecessary excitement or concern on a day when the Dutch would surely be agitated enough by the coming announcement. Plus, wearing street clothes, as Celia called them, kept her from asking too many questions on his way out.

They assembled on the deck of the ship, twenty in total. Calabar knew most of them.

Admirals Tromp and Jol had been joined by Admiral Joost Bankert and his son Adriaen, who was beginning to show signs of becoming at least as great a seaman as his father. Calabar was disappointed that von Schoppe was not in attendance, but it was understandable; he was currently holding off a counterattack by Portuguese troops at Pontal. All reports indicated that the defense was going well, but von Schoppe obviously could not pull himself out of the fight to attend.

There were several other high-ranking Dutch officers, namely Major Schutte and Krzysztof Arciszewski, a Polish nobleman and engineer who had fled his homeland ahead of a murder accusation. Like Calabar, he was a bit of a duck out of water, an outsider among these Dutchmen, but one who had made a name and a place for himself on the Brazilian coast. Calabar had served under him once, and considered him a fine officer.

The government officials included Matthijs van Ceulen and Johann Gijsselingh, Councilmen Jehan de Bruyne, Philips Serooskereken, and Servatius Carpentier. Their presence was not merely predictable but essential . . . and yet, Calabar eyed them carefully. He had never heard anything negative about any of these men, and had no other logical reason to be distrustful, but on the other hand, he had never met a government official who did not have a hidden agenda or two. He moved to the other side of the deck, hoping that the distance would keep any of their bureaucratic nonsense—or possible double-dealing—from rubbing off on him.

Among the handful of merchants were a few clergy from the Dutch Reformed Church. Calabar made a mental note to talk to them after the meeting about his son's baptism. Celia continued to insist that Carlos be baptized by the Jesuits, like their other children had been, but Calabar could not see how that was possible given their current situation. It was true that the Jesuits did not have any legal or political affiliation with the Portuguese; indeed, they were often at odds with them over the *bandeirantes* whom the plantation owners hired to rove inland and impress whole native tribes into slavery. However, getting Carlos to the church near Olinda, or getting a priest into Recife, would prove difficult, even if the Jesuits were willing.

The attendee who impressed Calabar the most was Moses Cohen Henriques Eanes, a Sephardic pirate who had served the Dutch well in their capture of the Spanish treasure fleet at the Bay of Matanzas some years back. Moses now worked primarily in concert with the Dutch in the Caribbean, but his ties with the small Jewish community in Olinda were well known. A physically vital man with an expressive face, Moses was a person that Calabar had one day hoped to meet, but not here, not today. Because his presence at this meeting was a sign of how likely it was that Tromp's plan for relocating the colony would in fact take place, and soon.

Confronted with Celia's strong and understandable desire to remain in Recife had led Calabar to hope, perhaps beyond hope, that when he arrived, Tromp would call it all off, declare all was well with the world, and pop open a keg of rum to celebrate the good tidings. Such was not the case. Moses' presence meant only one thing: the Dutch were serious enough about leaving Recife that they had called him in for counsel and possibly direct assistance.

Admiral Tromp emerged from the door leading back toward the captain's cabin, strolled into the gathering, cleared his throat, and put up his hand to still the conversation. When it stopped, he said, "I want to thank you all for coming. I was hoping that this meeting could be held in the stern cabin, but given the heat of the day that is already upon us, I think here in the open breeze will be more comfortable. We have much to discuss."

Calabar pulled at his collar to let a breath of ocean-scented air soothe his hot neck. It was going to be a warm day indeed.

Tromp continued. "Some of you already know what this meeting is about. Some of you have no idea. Let me bring us to the point quickly. The Dutch fleet, due to the treachery of the French and British, was nearly destroyed as we sailed, as allies, against a new Spanish Armada with designs on invading the republic. Such an act of treachery has put us in an extremely dangerous position in Europe. And with the political disruptions stemming from the arrival of these so-called Americans who claim to be from the future, our efforts to predict what might occur next becomes so problematic that it is essentially pointless to include such considerations as we address our changed situation here in the New World. So, our only reasonable course of action is to proceed from what we know, rather than conjecture."

He pointed to his fleet in the harbor. "In our retreat from Dunkirk, I only managed to withdraw with six hulls. We came across four more afterwards that were in serviceable shape. Losing all but ten ships of our European fleet was not merely a devastating blow to our nation, but has completely changed the long-term prospects for our continuing occupation of Brazil. Bluntly, the Netherlands can no longer support or supply reinforcements for our position here."

Calabar saw the trepidation and fear on the faces of those around him.

Tromp sighed deeply. "Therefore, by the end of May, we will be abandoning Recife and moving to Saint Eustatius in the Leeward Islands of the Lesser Antilles. Its colony, Oranjestad, will be our new base of operations here in the New World."

A collective gasp went up among those who were just hearing this for the first time, primarily the merchants and the clergy. Calabar eyed them carefully, keeping his mouth shut, waiting and watching. He was happy to see that the officers were taking the news better than the civilians, but then they would. A soldier is mobile, going where he is needed. The others had families and roots and businesses and religious interests that would, inevitably, be disrupted significantly by such a move. Calabar thought about Carlos, and then Celia's exhortation...

Promise me, Domingos, that you will go to Bom Jesus and try . . .

A merchant's voice rose above the clamor. "With respect, Admiral Tromp, if our position is as tenuous as you say, then what was the purpose of attacking Pontal? Which, by the way, men are still fighting and dying to hold."

It was a valid point, Calabar had to admit, although he felt he already knew why.

"The Portuguese and their Spanish masters are well aware of our defeat at Dunkirk," Tromp countered, "but they do not know yet that Recife has been cut off. Pontal is a feint, in strength, but one absolutely necessary to keep them believing that we are maintaining a strong presence here . . . at least until we put our plans for withdrawal into motion. If we do not, Matias de Albuquerque will learn of our situation, and it will embolden him. He will strike hard from land, the Spanish will surround the harbor, and we will lose everything. We cannot afford that; the Company will not tolerate that. And thus, our only course of action is to leave in secret. And soon."

"By God's graces, Admiral, how do you propose to leave?" A clergyman asked, folding his arms with a look of indignation.

"By ship, of course," said Jol, moving forward to give Tromp support. "Do you think we would force you to carry your crosses and bibles up the coast like a porter?"

Tromp put up his hand to kill the argument before it started. "Father, Admiral Jol is right. The colony will leave by ship. We have now roughly forty-eight hulls in harbor, including my ten, Jol's and Bankert's warships, yachts and *paraguas*, sloops, fluyts, and several fishing boats. We will leave in strength, and we must be at sea by late May or early June so that you all"—he pointed to the merchants and farmers—"are settled in time to plant a new crop. We cannot wait much longer anyway, for if our departure slips into July or August, we run the risk of hurricanes. Our ships must be in a safe anchorage by the end of June. At the very latest."

"The Spanish are all over the Antilles, Admiral," said a merchant. "What keeps them from attacking us as we go?"

"Nothing," Tromp admitted, "but they are not typically active in numbers that would concern us. Their fleet in Saint Maarten's, which is the closest colony to Eustatius, is small and not in a position to cause us trouble. Their other, far more sizable fleets, remain close to their home ports in Havana and Santo Domingo, tasked with protecting general commerce and the safety of La Flota. If we are in place by June, we will be safe on St. Eustatia."

The merchant scoffed. "I see no difference between there and here."

"Oh, there is a big difference," said Arciszewski. His Dutch was reasonably good, but he stumbled over his words every once in a while. "In Eustatia, we fear only the Spanish by sea. The island is ours total. But here, we fear both the Spanish by sea, the Portuguese by land. It is a far more difficult place to hold."

"But a much more fertile, and financially advantageous, one as well," another merchant pointed out. "And that is why the Company chose it, why we have sacrificed so much to keep it, despite all of the losses we have suffered. Are we going to abandon Recife so quickly, so readily?"

"You do not understand what has happened in Europe, my friend," Councilman Jehan de Bruyne said. "The Republic *cannot* protect us here. It is the only way we may remain in the New World. We must shift the location of our resources in order to protect them better. If we don't, we *do* run the risk of total annihilation."

One of the farmers stepped forward. "The sugarcane that we process each year in Brazil is almost enough to sustain Recife by itself."

"Only if the sugar continues to flow to Europe," said Tromp, his voice rising in agitation. "Our ports there are closed to us, blockaded. And once word of our incapacitation reaches the Spanish, they will encircle this grand harbor and stop all commerce. And no amount of sugar waiting unshipped on our wharves will feed the bellies of your starving children. And there is no incentive for the Portuguese or the Spanish to just let us walk out, once they know that *they* are in a position of strength. Why not surround us and destroy us and be done with it—with the Company—forever? No. The matter is decided. We must leave Recife by end of May . . . with or without you."

All fell silent as that last stinging point brought an end to the argument. Calabar looked carefully around as the reality of the situation begin to sink in. There was a helplessness, a near terror, on their faces.

"Admiral Tromp," said Major Schutte, "a practical matter: how do you propose to keep the Portuguese from learning the truth? There are several living here in Recife still, as well as on Antonio Vaz where our position is quite tenuous. I'm certain that many of them are still sympathetic to their king."

Tromp pointed to Calabar. "That is why I have asked Domingos and Moses to attend." He nodded at them. "You two will be in charge of planning our exodus, especially from the island and from Olinda. The Jewish residents in Olinda will be quite helpful in the new colony; they have skills we lack, and commercial contacts with other communities in the Caribbean."

Another merchant pointedly avoided looking at Calabar or Moses. "And why must we rely upon... outsiders to overseeing our relocation?"

Tromp nodded slowly. "Moses has long experience navigating the waters from here to our new home undetected. That and his excellent logistical expertise makes him an invaluable organizer and guide. Domingos understands the Portuguese better than any of us. Plus, he has ties with the native tribes. We will need their help as well to make this work."

"Why? Are we taking every Tupi we can push into a hull?" a merchant asked.

There were a few derisive snickers from the merchants and farmers from that remark. Calabar kept quiet, although judging from the expression on Tromp's face, he knew they would not like the Admiral's answer.

"No," Tromp said. "But the Tupi will have to cooperate with us nonetheless if we are to get our people out of here safely. And if they won't help us actively, then you, Domingos, will have to ensure that they at least stay out of the way, and refrain from alerting the Spanish or causing trouble themselves."

So, Calabar was to connive with the Dutch to use the native populations to beat a hasty, but safe, retreat . . . and then abandon them once again to the depredations of the Portuguese. He managed not to roll his eyes. Perhaps Celia was right that the Dutch were no better than anyone else; once again, their self-interests took precedence over any darker-skinned folk who happened to be inconvenient to their plans.

But as Calabar fumed, he could not deny what he saw in Tromp's eyes: hurt and bitter regret. The admiral hated what he had just said, had just ordered, but even he could not do anything to change it. The situation was thus, and he answered to a higher authority as well.

"With all due respect, Domingos," one of the merchants said, this one turning fully to look Calabar straight in the face. "Why should we trust you? You were, after all, in service to the Portuguese. How can we put our lives into your hands?"

"I have every faith in Domingos Fernandes Calabar, sir," Tromp said. "I . . . I trust him with *my* life. He has the respect and admiration of all the officers here. He has earned that respect with deeds. His service to the Company has been invaluable."

But Tromp's protestations earned only a moment of respectful silence before almost half of the gathering began muttering oblique objections, then voicing related accusations and concerns. The conversation fragmented quickly, different groups veering off into different topics that bore upon their own self interests. The merchants wanted to know how their goods would be packed and transferred safely. The clergy fretted over what kind of congregation they could expect to find in the new colony. The farmers argued over the kinds of crops that would fare well in a more northerly, island climate. The officers debated how best to load and move the colony and the special burdens it would place upon ensuring sufficient supplies and logistics.

Tromp and Jol moved from discussion to discussion, urging the groups to remain calm while also trying to maintain some control on where each conversation was leading. Their success was limited, at best. Even when Moses sidled up to Calabar, suggesting that they meet later to begin formulating a plan of exodus, Calabar could not fully focus. Instead, he could not take his attention away from the sad spectacle unfolding before him.

All of these important, fair-skinned men, crisping in the sun, trying to figure out how to protect their interests and unable to remain focused on finding the best strategy to facilitate their departure. Instead, they kept stepping all over themselves with one petty argument after another. And here Calabar stood, a piece of dark clay among white pillars: a half-Portuguese, half-Tupi beast. Just a *mameluco dog*, even to them, even though they didn't say it aloud...

Mother of God, am I the only *one who sees the way forward?*

Calabar closed his eyes. "Attack Bom Jesus!"

He blurted out the words before he knew what he was saying. He said it again, and this time, the conversation stopped. The men all turned to him in silence.

"What did you say, friend?" Admiral Jol asked, his peg leg clicking against the sturdy deck.

"Attack Bom Jesus. Attack the Portuguese at their strength."

A farmer huffed. "We have tried that before, Calabar. It did not work."

"That's because I was not involved in that effort."
He couldn't believe how bold he was being, but who
among them would try to talk him down? If these
people hoped to escape successfully, they would listen
to him now. "Since then, I've helped you defeat them,
but simple ambushes in the forest do not threaten
the strategic balance. Pontal was the right move, but
too far away. We can attack a dozen Pontals, and it
will do no good.

"The key is Bom Jesus, Matias' stronghold. It
remains the center of Portuguese power here in
Pernambuco. If it falls, or if we can threaten it
enough to force the Portuguese to pull back their
military assets from Antonio Vaz, Olinda, and some
of their other forts, you will have the breathing room
to move your people out of harm's way. Keep the
Portuguese occupied with a real battle, and you will
give yourself a chance."

It took a few moments for his words to sink in, but
once they did, the midship deck was soon noisy with
renewed conversation. This time, however, everyone
was speaking about the quality of his plan. Suddenly,
he was the center of their attention, their petty squab-
bling silenced and replaced with focused consideration.
They pelted him with questions, and Calabar tried
answering as best he could, but he hadn't given the
attack much thought himself. And perhaps he had
spoken out of turn, put himself into a situation that
he was ill-equipped to handle. The largest force he
had ever led into battle was two hundred fifty, and
that had been for the Portuguese.

But now here he was, proposing a major assault
against them. And how would he coordinate such an

attack? He had to think of something. They were all counting on him now.

Celia's words came back to him. *Promise me, Domingos, that you will go to Bom Jesus and try…*

I promise, Celia. I will go to Bom Jesus, and I will not just try…I will kill Matias de Albuquerque myself.

Chapter 6

Near the Capiberibe River, Brazil

Calabar was no stranger to *o forte*. He had been inside its daunting walls many times, and could not have cared less about its many impressive names and nicknames, so long as at the end of the day, it lay in ashes. Or, at least, had suffered enough damage to force the Portuguese to pull back or capitulate on other fronts. Its main fortification, and Matias de Albuquerque's headquarters, was a heavily built and much-reinforced house at its center, once owned by a settler named Antonio do Abreu. Calabar had met the man and knew that he had had no hesitation in giving up his home for the protection of Portuguese interests. There were a lot of Albuquerque sympathizers on the mainland of Brazil; most of them were Portuguese themselves, which made Calabar's mission all the more difficult. Even with the cover of night, it would be hard to move against Matias' position when one had to deal with a population where even the smallest among them, children capable of listening to and understanding directions, could deliver a message to the walls of Bom Jesus and warn it of Calabar's approach.

And so what was he to do? Apprehend every child, every family, from here to the fort? It was an almost impossible task, but Calabar had agreed to his central role in carrying out this attack. He had been the one who had recommended it in the first place. He could not back down now.

It was a relatively simple plan that Major Schutte had devised, with Krzysztof Arciszewski's and Calabar's assistance. All available Dutch soldiers and all tribesmen that could be convinced to attack the Portuguese were gathered and divided into three columns, each of which was assigned a different line of approach to Bom Jesus. But they would be attacking at different times, so as to take full advantage of changes in the Portuguese defensive positions. Several small forts and redoubts guarded the way there, so it was nearly impossible not to encounter resistance, sometimes in force, as the Dutch columns moved inland. The only way to approach without encountering the enemy was to ship a force several miles to the south along the coast, disembark, and then swing up behind the fort and attack from the protection of the jungle. But that would take far more time, and very likely the column would be strung out and exhausted if and when it reached the walls.

So, no: time was not on their side for that kind of operation. The Dutch attack had to go in frontally, but carefully, taking full advantage of Calabar's knowledge of the terrain and his understanding of the Portuguese defenses and their probable responses.

So it was Calabar's job to attack first, in darkness, to surprise and shake the resolve of the Portuguese before Schutte's and Arciszewski's assault commenced at first light of day. Consequently, Calabar's was the riskiest part of the plan, one that could go awry easily. Although Calabar and Luiz knew the countryside well, at night there was always the potential for losing soldiers who should have turned left instead of right, who kept moving forward instead of stopping at a rally point before reaching the objective. The column could easily stretch out to meander over a mile or so of the difficult terrain, and with a thousand men at his command, it was all too likely. And that kind of vulnerability was a significant risk, if they were detected while still approaching.

To be entrusted with a force that size was more than he, a mameluco turncoat, could have asked for. He had even been offered cannon, two in fact, but had refused. He was not going to be slowed down by hefty guns that could get mired in the Capiberibe's mud. Besides, it would have been difficult, to carry enough shot for those cannon to make a difference. So let the others have their heavy guns. Calabar would do what he always did and better than anyone else on the Dutch side: prevail with speed and subterfuge. Cannon fire bothered his ears, anyway.

"We will face at least two redoubts before we reach Bom Jesus' walls," Calabar said to Luiz who knelt at his side as they took a small break near the bank of the Capiberibe. "We must strike them hard and fast, causing a lot of noise and disruption."

"Noise, sir?" Luiz asked.

Calabar nodded. "Once we engage, there will be

no way to conceal our attack. Nor would we want to. Once the fight is on, it is essential that we cause as much trouble—and noise—as possible to make them think a massive force is at their flank. If all goes according to plan, they will pull soldiers out of Bom Jesus to meet our threat. We don't need them to send that many, but enough that we may be sure to have redirected their attention, and for long enough for Schutte to begin his assault with an advantage."

"And do you think things *will* go according to plan?"

Calabar smiled at Luiz, though the young man probably could not see it in the intermittent moonlight that shone through the high, scudding clouds. Luiz was a smart lad indeed, with an appreciable measure of natural wit and skepticism. That pleased Calabar. "Nothing ever does go *completely* the way one plans, Luiz, but we can always hope." He placed his hand on the boy's shoulder. "And now I need you to position your force just as we discussed—and no more debate about it being an unusual order. You take your hundred musketeer tribesmen and swing around the fort until you reach the Paranamerim. Then lie in wait for me there."

"Yes, sir, but it's just a dry stream bed now. Maybe enough water to cover the ankles. Do you really think it will provide the cover, and so, the surprise, that you imagine?"

"We will find that out soon enough. You have your orders now. Take the men and wait there. Remember: muskets primed and ready, trained to the south. Understood?" Calabar looked into the sky at the gathering clouds. They seemed lower, closer. "And let us pray that the rain holds off this time."

The last time a large attack had been planned against Bom Jesus was a couple years ago when Dutch commander Stein-Callenfels had sent six hundred men against it. That attack failed, due in large part to heavy rain which had made musket fire near impossible. Subsequent smaller attacks had been made, but nothing had worked. Calabar had been part of Bom Jesus' defense during that initial attack. Now here he was, planning to attack it himself, and this time praying to God to hold off the rain.

How things have changed. How I have changed.

"Go, now!"

Luiz scrambled into the darkness. Calabar watched until he could not see the boy anymore. He sighed. *Is this too big a task for him?* Calabar wondered. Perhaps it would have been better to put a Dutch sergeant in charge, one of his other commanders from the regular ranks. Calabar shook his head. No, a Dutch officer would have had difficulty finding the stream in the dark. Luiz knew exactly where it was and would understand instinctively what to do once he got there. The best move would have been to put himself in charge of that task, but that was impossible. He needed to lead the main attack against the redoubts that lay ahead, before the walls of Bom Jesus, just a half mile up the river.

Calabar rubbed sweat from his rough face, stood, and motioned quietly for his men to follow. They fell in behind him as he picked his way through the darkness along the bank of the Capiberibe.

By God's grace, he thought as he led his men along the riverside noiselessly. *Let the battle begin.*

❖   ❖   ❖

Calabar waited long enough to give Luiz time to get into place. Then he rose up into the darkness at the edge of the tree line along the river and roared proudly, "Fire!"

Primed and ready, the musket line fired. A massive wave of smoke and a deafening roar reached across the small field where the redoubt lay. A few small lanterns twinkled in the darkness, giving away the fortification's position. Calabar could see little else, but he heard the collective snap of planks and low-velocity shots hitting the packed dirt and the chest-high stone walls. Following that were cries of shock and surprise from the redoubt's occupants. Calabar figured that there weren't many behind those make-shift walls, but whoever was there now knew that they were under attack.

His musket men reloaded quickly while spearmen began crawling across the field, their faces mere inches from the wet, cool ground. It was near impossible to see them, as Calabar had wanted. Their dark skin, coupled with their knowledge of silent movement, would get them up to the redoubt almost before its occupants would detect them.

"Fire!"

They fired again, and this time, he heard a Portuguese defender's roiling screams die away into the night as the second volley found its intended targets. Finally, shots began to answer from the redoubt, bullets whizzing over the heads of the Caetés tribesmen as they crawled forward. One of them lurched up on his knees; his spear dropped and his left arm jerked uncontrollably as small shot hit his chest, shoulder, and face. *Damn it all!* Calabar cursed to himself. He blurted out a command in the Caetés language, hoping it was the right phrase for "keep low."

The third volley was almost ready. "Forward," Calabar shouted. The musketeers stepped out from the protection of the trees, took ten paces forward, knelt, and waited.

"Fire!"

The third volley exploded outward, and now Calabar could see and hear frantic voices inside Bom Jesus, far behind the redoubt. The light coming from there was more distinct, cressets burning along the backlit walls, little silhouettes of men scurrying here and there. Calabar's heart skipped a beat; *perhaps Schutte should press his attack now*, he thought as he rose and walked slowly through the field alongside his musketmen. A young Dutch boy standing next to him crumbled after a shot from the redoubt. Calabar flinched, but quickly regained his composure. It would not do to appear weak or uncertain to the men around him. That, at least, he had learned while under the command of the Portuguese. A commander—a good one, at least—had to be more stalwart and brave than even the most experienced line soldier.

"Hold!" he yelled. His soldiers took a knee and waited.

A final smattering of muskets fired from along the redoubt, downing a few more boys in the ranks but then falling silent. Calabar girded his courage, stood, and shouted for the general attack.

The Caetés tribesmen came out of the tall grass, howling like mad bush dogs, and struck the redoubt walls. Clashing swords and spears, wheellock fire, and screams erupted as both sides struggled hand to hand. Bodies pitched everywhere, fingers scraping at throats, eyes, and mouths. Spears broken off in shoulders, knives piercing legs and chests. It was difficult for Calabar to see it all, to know clearly who had the advantage, but he called out to his men to move again. This time, cannons began to fire from Bom Jesus.

A round struck nearby, blowing a hole in Calabar's line, tearing his men away and into the darkness behind. He pulled his sword from its scabbard, shouted and jogged forward. His men followed.

If they got to the redoubt in good order, then they could man its walls, and protect themselves from the fire coming from the fort. That was the plan anyway. His recollection of these redoubts was that they held well against cannon fire, although not forever. But he didn't need forever. All he needed was to pull assets away from other parts of Bom Jesus long enough for Schutte and Arciszewski to attack. *Hurry up*, he voiced silently to Schutte, as errant musket fire from Bom Jesus pelted the ground around him.

The light of morning was coming, but not fast enough for Calabar's taste.

He reached the edge of the redoubt, climbed over the first wall, and fell to the ground on the other side. His ankle gave a little and he winced. A body fell on him in the next instant—two, in fact, struggling to tear at each other's throats. He worked his sword out from beneath them, turned the blade inward, cut the neck of the Portuguese soldier, then pushed him away. The tribesman, confused, scared, disoriented from lack of light, tried plunging his spear through Calabar's gut. Calabar swung his sword, deflected the spear and put his fist across the tribesman's face. "Not me; them!" he shouted and pushed free.

More cannon fire from Bom Jesus forced him to crouch behind the wall, but Portuguese resistance in the redoubt was gone. The Caetés had prevailed and were now finishing the attack, going through the wounded Portuguese and stabbing them in the chest. It was one of the brutal necessities of war in Brazil.

Calabar stopped and took a deep breath. Somehow he was both shaken and pleased. The attack had gone as planned, so well, in fact, that the redoubt's defenders had not even gotten their small falconet loaded and fired. The entire gun crew had been slain where they stood. Calabar pushed a dead crewman out of the way and leaned against the cold barrel.

"The next redoubt will not be so easy to take," he said to Sergeant Bosch who stood nearby waiting for orders. "We'll be heading into a field of fire."

"Let us swing around and take it from the west," Sergeant Bosch said.

Calabar shook his head. "We cannot make such a bold move against its flank, lest we give Luiz's position away. No, we have to move against it frontally, take it, and force Bom Jesus to send help. We must follow the plan."

"Do you think Luiz is in place?"

Calabar shrugged. "I don't know, but he knows his duty."

He instructed Bosch to stay and defend the position with four hundred men, turn the falconet against Bom Jesus, and keep it firing. There was not as much ammunition for the cannon as Calabar would have expected, but if they expended all that was available, that would give him some cover as he and his remaining five hundred moved toward the fort. He glanced around; well, less than five hundred now. They had not suffered as many casualties as he had feared, but there would be gaps in the line.

As Bosch got the falconet firing at Bom Jesus, Calabar lined his men up behind the redoubt, the Caetés leading in a skirmish formation that, he hoped, would create some semblance of order amidst the chaos. Cannon fire from Bom Jesus scarred the ground, leaving thick gashes in the soil agitating the tribesmen as parts of the redoubt's wall were struck as well. Under the barrage, they were having difficulties maintaining discipline. They knew that they would no longer be able to move in secret, or stealthily through the tall grass, any longer.

But ironically, that too was part of Calabar's plan, the part he had not shared with them. Their purpose now was to draw the musket fire from the second redoubt while the larger body of men moved up to mass for a more focused attack.

Calabar shook his head. This was not the kind of fight he liked or wanted. But it was necessary in order to take these outer fortifications. The second redoubt had to be overwhelmed with superior numbers and forcefully enough to send an unmistakable message and sense of urgency to Matias. *However*, Calabar thought as he took his place behind the Caetés line, *if these tribesmen break and rout, I will not stop them. They've done more than enough already.*

"At the quick step!" he said, brandishing his sword and moving forward through the haze of smoke and faint sunlight.

The Caeté skirmishers moved quickly forward, the lower half of their bodies disappearing in the grass. Calabar let them move about fifty yards ahead, then marshaled his own men forward, their firearms freshly reloaded and half-cocked. Through the murky darkness, musket fire from the second redoubt began to bark and blaze, and tribesmen began to fall. But none of the enemy's sporadic fire made it through their thin line to the far larger mass of men behind them.

Calabar smiled, yelled orders to wheel. His men complied.

The Caetés hit the second redoubt. Calabar could hear the crack of clubs and then the screams of the Portuguese as they fell beneath spear thrusts. The tribesmen were not merely fighting savagely but enthusiastically. Calabar had promised the Caetés that they could loot the bodies afterwards, peeling off any jewelry and clothing that they could carry.

The noise diminished and—slowly at first, but then in a rush—the tribesmen fell back, pouring through the advancing Dutch lines, holding bloody spears, swords, waving a few torn Portuguese shirts. They had not been able to take the redoubt—as Calabar had expected—but they had weakened it, penetrated its defenses, and hopefully killed a few officers. Now they would likely keep running until they reached the Capiberibe.

Calabar could hear the men he had left defending the first redoubt pour fire upon Bom Jesus, along with a slow but relentless hammering of falconet rounds. This had the effect of compelling Matias' guns to return fire, thus taking pressure off Calabar and his men as they moved forward. He barked another order, and his troops wheeled again, this time toward the second redoubt, making themselves vulnerable to enfilade fire, but he did not intend on leaving them in this formation for long. Still in good order, his troops stopped, the first lines of each block kneeling, the second lines coming up closely behind. The third lines held their guns over the shoulders of the men in front of them. Calabar waited two desperate minutes to see them all in place. He raised his sword, waved it furiously in the smoky air, then brought it down with a scream.

Hundreds of muskets roared, a sound so deafening that Calabar could not even hear himself think, but he already knew what his next order would be.

The echo of the musketry fell away. The outcries of surprise and pain subsided among the Portuguese defenders as they returned fire from the redoubt. Before their resistance could stiffen, Calabar once again raised his sword, and shouted in Portuguese, "*Ataque!*" He let the word linger on his tongue, willed it to echo over that battlefield, so that anyone on the other side, any soldier, any officer who could hear the order, would know that it was he, Domingos Fernandes Calabar, who had given it. *Let them know that I am come*, he thought as he kept himself beside his men in the charge, *and that I will bring these walls down*.

Across the field they ran, through the darkness, howling like the Caetés had, but this time in Dutch and in far greater numbers. Perhaps too many, Calabar thought, as they sprinted forward. All the surviving Portuguese had to do was point down and pour fire into his men as they approached. But the fire was still sporadic and his men were in a headlong charge, sure of their target. They could already see the outline of the redoubt through the growing morning light that was brightening the sky over the tree line and over the low, angular silhouette of Bom Jesus.

A bullet nicked Calabar's shoulder, cutting through his coat, and knocking him off course. But it was just a graze. He collected himself quickly, pulled his wheellock, and kept pace.

A cannon fired from the second redoubt, but it sounded like only a half load. Ineffective, the ball went uselessly over the heads of the sprinting Dutch. Calabar smiled, raised the volume and pitch of his exhortations even further, and kept running.

The mass of Dutch soldiers hit the sloped outer face of the redoubt. The weight of the first line cracked the fragile planks that held the wall's rock, mortar and dirt in place. That first line began scrambling over it and into a point-blank repulse by Portuguese swords and muskets. The men behind them stopped and tried to reload their muskets and fire instead of following.

The assault broke down into a mass of bodies twisting and contorting for advantage, utilizing every open space for killing. Men shouted in Portuguese, in Dutch, calling each other such terrible names, names that, in any other time and place, would have caused Calabar to feel a sudden, collective shame for their profanity before the omnipresent Holy Trinity.

But surely God was not looking down on them now. Surely he was looking away, for how could he allow such carnage, such terrible murder to persist beneath his gaze? And for what? To simply force the Portuguese to recoil long enough to allow a few Dutch ships to escape in the night? Were such transient, paltry ambitions worth all the blood?

Yes. For my family, a thousand times...yes.

Calabar pushed his pistol into the throat of a Portuguese captain and pulled the trigger. The man crumpled dead against splintered planks that were already slick with gore. Before a second had elapsed, Calabar caught a sword swipe against his spent pistol, feeling something break on it but hadn't the time to look. He smacked the desperate soldier across the jaw with the smoking barrel, leaving a powder smear that paralleled the man's lacerated flesh.

Someone kicked Calabar in his side; he fell into the dirt. Not even stopping to look, he hooked his right arm through the legs of his assailant, brought the man down, and squeezed his throat until the thrashing stopped.

When he looked up again, men all around him were punching, kicking, screaming, dying. He was not in any immediate danger, down there in the muck, shielded by dead bodies, but he saw no safe way to extricate himself. The instant he raised his head, a sword or pistol or boot would surely smash his skull. But he was the commander. He had to move. He had to marshal his men forward to finish their duty.

He sucked in a gut-filling breath, gathered his strength in his thighs, and pushed up, knocking one of his own soldiers aside, but gaining his feet. His spent pistol was still in his hand, and he used it like a club, driving its handle into this face, that face, breaking cheek bones, making widows with each hacking blow. His soldiers did the same, some able to turn their muskets upon and fire at those Portuguese who tried retreating through a gap in the back wall of the redoubt. An errant Caeté spear found its way into

Calabar's hand, and he pushed it into the stomach of a boy crying at his feet. He turned the blade, yanked it upward, and ended the screams, seeing for a brief moment his own son's face in the dying boy's eyes. Calabar blinked away the image and continued fighting.

Then it was over. There were no more Portuguese in front of or around him, just his own men and the dead piled within and along the grimy redoubt walls. A scattering of musket and cannon fire echoed across the field, but even that died away in the cool morning breeze. Calabar dropped his broken pistol and leaned exhausted against the stone and dirt wall. His heart beat so fast he felt like he might pass out, but he kept his feet, wiped his sword clean on his sleeve, and sheathed it carefully. He closed his eyes and tried to relax.

"What are your orders, sir?" a Dutch soldier asked. He was a footman, no rank, helmet gone, hair mussed and caked with mud and sweat.

Calabar eyed the boy carefully, smiled, and said, "Now, we wait."

They did not have to wait long for Matias to do what he was supposed to do. It was a risk, indeed, but a necessary one given the circumstances. To let both redoubts fall, and so quickly, could not stand. Calabar smiled as Portuguese soldiers streamed out the back gate of Bom Jesus.

He counted through the haze and smoke. Company strength perhaps, maybe two. They lined up smartly, following directions being barked at them by a captain that Calabar did not recognize. Their faces were eager, their motions brisk. Calabar looked around: all his men were worn out, many with wounds. And was ammunition running low? Behind these earthen walls, they could hold off an assault reasonably well, but not forever, and in the end, Matias had more men. *But I don't need to hold them off forever,* he thought, grabbing a discarded musket and checking its load twice with careful hands. *And Luiz will do his duty. He must.*

The Portuguese lines moved forward, tightly packed, muskets ready. From the back wall of the redoubt, Calabar allowed his men to fire at will, picking off a soldier here and there, reloading and firing again. Men went down, but were quickly replaced by the following reserves. Slowly, slowly, the Portuguese lines moved forward, silhouetted against the rising sun. Calabar looked beyond them, toward the Paranamerim, prayed to God, reloaded his own musket, fired, and prayed again.

The Portuguese soldiers halted, redressed their lines. The first row fell to a knee, raised their muskets and waited. The second and third rows fell into place. A simple call from their commander, and over one hundred muskets fired together with such a violent rush of smoke and lead that certainly those sleeping in Recife would have heard it, startled from their warm beds.

The walls around Calabar's men exploded in showers of wood, stone, and dirt. Domingos couched behind the wall, shielding his head from chips of stone and splintered plank. Men around him moaned, grumbled, yelled—sometimes wordlessly—just to keep their courage up. He patted a young boy on the back, told him to keep strong, reload and get ready. And in time, the echo of the Portuguese gunfire subsided.

Calabar poked his head up and dared a sustained

look. The Portuguese lines were advancing again, reloading awkwardly as they came. Scattered Dutch fire from the redoubt began anew, and a makeshift crew had even managed to load the cannon and fire it. But Calabar knew that it was a fruitless effort. In time, the lines would be so near that all the Portuguese had to do was simply scale the back wall and fire down upon their heads, and the redoubt would become a Dutch grave.

Now or never...

"Doe den tap toe!"

A Dutch trumpeter nearby sounded the call, meant for Luiz...and, perhaps, to confuse the Portuguese if any were listening and trying to interpret the signals. If the circumstances weren't so dire, Calabar might chuckle at the notion of using such a silly string of notes in a battle, but it was the only Dutch call he knew, and he had taught it to his young assistant. Calabar screamed at the trumpeter to sound it again and again, until the boy's face was as red as the dawn from blowing. Then Calabar heard the Portuguese commander give the order to dress ranks and ready to fire a second volley. Then there was silence for a long, dangerous moment.

From the protective line of foliage along the edge of the Paranamerim came the sound of musket fire, scattered at first, then more pronounced and steady. Calabar looked up again and saw the Portuguese line, which had moved into their firing position, suddenly stumble to their left. And now the cannon at the first redoubt fired, followed by a strong volley of musket fire, pushing the Portuguese back toward the creek. Luiz's men, hiding in that creek, fired once more.

The Portuguese broke.

Calabar kept himself from roaring with joy. It had worked. Matias' men had walked right into a lethal enfilade position, taking fire from three sides. Calabar ordered his men to add their own waves of lead to the growing torrent, his scratchy voice barely able to articulate the complicated Dutch words. But they understood what he meant. The only order that mattered now was to fire.

Although ... maybe not. Through the smoke, Calabar began to see another opportunity. The enemy soldiers were falling back, leaving behind many dead but even more wounded as they reached the back gate and the protection of its walls. It was folly to allow them to find safety. Why not kill them all now? After all, that was the ultimate objective. But if he waited too long—

"Up!" Calabar said, forcing the words through a hoarse throat and dry lips. "Prepare to charge!"

A captain beside him frowned. "Sir, Major Schutte made it clear. Our orders were to take the redoubts and then hold them against counterattack. We should not come out from behind these walls—"

"Major Schutte is not in charge here, soldier. I am. No more Portuguese are to reach that gate alive. I said up, and ready the men."

The order went down the line. The men climbed out of the protection of the redoubt and waited. Calabar climbed out, stood with them, smiling and nodding, then shouted, *"Ataque!"*

They charged like the Caetés, muskets forward like spears. Some of the men had real spears, opting instead to cast their muskets aside and attack unhindered by heavy barrels. Calabar fired as, screaming, he ran headlong into the rear of the fleeing Portuguese, knocking over an enemy soldier and smashing the head of another with the turned butt of his musket. And right behind came his men: savage, wide-eyed, sensing victory and yet fearing defeat if they did not seize it.

The Portuguese fought as best as they could, scattering backward. Some reached the gate, but more fell to swords and spear strikes. Calabar worked through the mass of men, cutting and counting as he went. *That's for my son...my daughter...my wife.* Before him, the joints of mortar holding together Bom Jesus' thick walls were visible. He was close, so close. *And now all I have to do is get inside and find Matias, as I promised Celia. And then—*

A sharp blast. A blow to his upper body. A stagger and a losing struggle to stay on his feet.

Calabar fell to his knees, looked down and saw a ragged wound in his shoulder, blood pouring out and covering his sweat-browned shirt. He looked up and saw the fuzz-bearded face of the almost petite Portuguese soldier who had fired the round, standing proudly and looking at a mameluco dog kneeling just feet from the gate. Someone came up and drove a spear through the boy's liver. Calabar blinked and fell over.

He felt the warmth of the sun. His face began to sweat. A tear rolled down his cheek, not out of fear or pain, but failure. *I have failed you, Celia,* Calabar thought as he tried rolling onto his back. *I have failed us all.*

Hands grabbed him and pulled him through the wet grass. From a distance, he could hear cannon fire. Major Schutte's cannons. Calabar smiled, closed his eyes, and let the darkness come.

Chapter 7

Recife, Brazil

Calabar heard Celia's voice. It seemed both distant and muffled. She was speaking with someone, another voice that he recognized but could not quite place.

He opened his eyes. The world was blurry, with blurry shapes standing before him. His head hurt, his face. He tried moving but pain in his shoulder stabbed through his chest and made his stomach ache. Hands were on him immediately. Male hands.

"Steady, Domingos. Praise God, you are alive, but you are in no condition to move."

Calabar blinked several times, shook his head, and the world came into focus. He was home, in his own bed, the windows open to catch a light breeze off Recife's harbor. Before him stood Admiral Tromp, Admiral Jol, and Celia. He raised his hand to take hers. She smiled politely, for the sake of their guests he supposed, but refused his hand and stepped away.

"Admiral Tromp," Calabar said, clearing his dry throat. He dropped his hand. "I apologize for my ... condition. I'm sorry that I cannot rise—"

Tromp waved him off. "As I say, you are lucky to be alive. Do not concern yourself with formalities at this time."

"How long has it been?" Calabar asked.

"Six days," Jol said, stepping forward with a woody tap of his leg. "Six days you have been drifting in and out, almost conscious one moment, on the edge of a coma the next. Thankfully, you have an excellent wife with a tender hand. And luckily, the ball made a clean exit, no clipping the bone or any arteries. You lost a lot of blood, but you may thank Luiz for pulling you to safety before you bled dry."

"Did we prevail?"

"We did," Admiral Tromp said, nodding, "but barely. Your attempted assault against Bom Jesus nearly cost us the advantage. Luckily—and God forgive me for saying it—you were struck early. Your captains realized the blunder and pulled back in time to bolster our position in the redoubts. Had you remained on the field and continued to press that attack, your whole column might have been smashed, giving the Portuguese an avenue for reinforcements." Tromp cleared his throat. "You made a foolish move, Domingos."

"I saw an opportunity and took it," Calabar said.

"You got angry," Tromp said, "and you sought revenge. Understandable. Not a day goes by that I do not *seek* revenge in my heart against the Portuguese, or the French, or the English, for that matter. But we do not have the time or resources to settle personal grudges. We must maintain self-discipline, particularly if we are to expect it from those under our command. Do you understand?"

Calabar sank back into his pillow. "Yes, sir, and I apologize. I take full responsibility for my actions. If you wish, I will resign my services—"

"Quiet with that foolish talk," Jol said, working his jaw muscles, a stern gaze in his eyes. "We are not here to relieve you from our service. We are here to discuss the next move." He paused, then nodded toward Celia. "That is, if your lovely wife will give us a moment alone?"

Celia stood a step back from the bedside, a bowl of cauliflower soup in her hand. Calabar eyed her carefully, his heart pounding. She looked back at him, her jaw muscles tightening with each breath. She put the bowl down on a table beside the bed, laid the spoon beside it, and curtsied. "Of course, my lords. This is my *husband's* house."

She left the room and closed the door quietly behind her. Calabar swallowed hard and felt the hair on his neck rise. Celia was in a foul mood. *God help me...*

He turned his attention back to Admiral Tromp. "What is our current situation, Admiral?"

"Bom Jesus is surrounded. It is, in effect, under siege. The situation is becoming desperate for Matias. The Portuguese do not know what to do. But we cannot press the attack either; we, too, lack sufficient resources. But a decisive victory wasn't the purpose of this affair, as you well know. We merely want them to relent enough to give us enough room to slip away. Matias has agreed to negotiate terms, and of course, the Company has agreed as well."

"Have negotiations begun?" Calabar asked.

Tromp shook his head. "There is no one in Bom Jesus that we trust. On principle, Matias has refused to chair the discussions. We will give him that small face-saving gesture. And obviously, if their commander does not sit at the table, then, particularly as the victor, I shall not either. Which is fortunate, since I do not have the time." He placed his hand on Jol's shoulder. "Cornelis has agreed to negotiate for our side, along with Major Schutte."

"And for the Portuguese?"

"We have agreed to the representative they have proposed: Pedro Álvares."

The name was fresh in Calabar's mind, having just seen the man outside Pontal. It was a good choice.

Calabar nodded. "Very well. The matter is done then."

"Not quite," said Jol. "Álvares is currently with de Gama in Fort Nazare. As part of *our* good faith gesture, we have agreed to discuss the withdrawal of our troops from Pontal," he chuckled. "As if we weren't going to do that anyway. When you are able, we want you to return to Pontal, coordinate the withdrawal with Captain von Schoppe, and bring Álvares back."

"Forgive me, Admiral, but . . . why me?"

Jol eyed Tromp carefully. "Because Álvares has asked for you personally."

Calabar's heart sank slowly under the weight of vague misgiving. *Me? What could this mean?* He hadn't a clue. They had met briefly on the battlefield. Álvares' plea for de Gama's life had, indeed, stayed Calabar's hand. *But why does he want* me?

"Have you had dealings with Álvares recently?" Tromp asked.

What should I say? "No, sir. I haven't seen him in a long time."

"Well, he has asked for you. And we will oblige. I want you to get as much rest as you can in the next few days and eat well." Tromp eyed the hot soup at the bedside. "Start with this bowl here. Also, once Álvares has been returned and negotiations have begun, we will need you and Luiz to begin preparing the local population, and the various tribes, for the move. There is still much confusion and uncertainty in Recife. Some colonists are aware of our plans; some are not. So far, we have been successful at keeping our preparations relatively quiet, and Moses has already begun organizing the departure, but there are still many people to make ready. We'll need your skills to both move Dutch families currently on the mainland into Recife, and Portuguese families who have been living under our protection into custody. That's the only way to prevent some of them from becoming spies for Matias." Tromp sighed, removed his hat, and scratched his dry scalp. "I fear that no amount of care will stopper all the holes, but we will do our best. The fleet will be ready soon, and so too must everyone else. Are you with us?"

Calabar shot a glance toward his bedroom door. It stood ajar, but there were no signs of feet shadowed at the bottom; no one was listening in. He nodded. "Yes, sir. You have my service."

"Good," Jol said, "then I will be back in a few days to continue this discussion."

Jol turned to leave, but Admiral Tromp stopped him. "There is one more matter," he said, moving closer to Calabar's bed, "that I wish to discuss with you, Domingos. It is not an issue that we can resolve today; it is not even an issue that we can discuss in *detail* today, but as we prepare to relocate, we must also prepare to bring a terrible institution to an end."

"What institution is that, sir?" Calabar asked.

Tromp looked at Jol as if he were seeking guidance—or, at least, in Calabar's mind—agreement. Jol seemed to sigh, but nodded. Tromp turned back to Calabar, and said, "Slavery."

The word hit Calabar's consciousness like a rock going through a glass window, sending his thoughts reeling in many directions, hurtling toward many startling possibilities. *End slavery?* Slavery sickened him, indeed, but the notion of ending it, once and for all, everywhere, had never crossed his mind. *Is it even* possible?

"I apologize for dropping this on you now," Tromp said, "but it has been ... much on my mind over the months that I've been here. And having seen the practice of it by the Portuguese, I am determined that it needs to go. So you see, Calabar, your continued service is not just so that we Dutchmen can escape Brazil safely. It's about changing the future of life in the New World. For everyone."

Tromp wrung his hands as if he had just finished a meal. "Now, get some rest, eat well, and Jol will return in a few days to discuss the next move in our exodus."

They bid him farewell and stepped out of the room. As they made their goodbyes to his wife, Calabar sat up slowly and pulled himself toward the bowl of soup. He leaned over, grabbed it and the spoon, and dug in heartily. He was quite sure it was the best soup he had ever tasted.

Celia entered by throwing the door open. She pretended to ignore him while she placed a few linens in a footlocker. Calabar did not intrude upon her moment of anger. He was finally about to say something, when she said, "The soup is poisoned."

He hesitated, letting the spoon waver over the warm broth. Then he huffed. "Do not play games with me, Celia. I'm in no mood."

"Nor am I," she said, slamming the top of the footlocker down. "You lied to me, Calabar. You lied to our children."

"No, I didn't. I went to Bom Jesus as I promised. Matias just didn't like what I had to say."

"That is not how we discussed it, and you know that."

Calabar set the bowl down. "I am doing the best I can for us, Celia. For the children."

"And your best is to nearly get killed?"

"Yes," he said. "I think our lives with the Dutch are worth it."

"So you say, but I'm not so sure."

He held his hands up as if he were worshipping God. "Look around you. All of this is courtesy of the Dutch. They are the reason we live like this."

"What did Jol say just now?" Celia asked. "He said, 'We are not here to relieve you from our service.' *Our* service, Domingos." She blew out a great, indignant breath. "Tromp talks about establishing a colony that has no slaves, but he treats you no better than one."

So, she was listening.

"Enough, Celia! I don't know Tromp as well as I should, perhaps, but I promise you, he is sincere. These men are working for the benefit of us all."

"So you have decided, yes? We are going with them?"

Calabar said nothing. He swallowed hard, let the sudden pounding of his heart settle. He pinched his eyes shut, dreading this moment. "No, we are not going. *I* am going."

Celia stood there, stunned, her lips parted. Her angry eyes gave away her true feelings. "You are abandoning us?"

"No, you can't think of it like that. Yes, I am going to Saint Eustatius by myself; that is where the fleet is headed. But you are right: Carlos is too weak to travel...at least right now. I will get us established there, and then I will come back for you."

Celia shook her head violently. "The Portuguese will sweep into Recife when you and the Dutch are gone. They will take all the mamelucos and jail them...or worse, sell them into slavery."

"That will not happen to you, Celia, I swear it. It has already been arranged. Luiz will be staying behind. He will deliver you in safety to the Jesuits. They will protect you."

"Luiz?" Celia threw up her hands. "He is too young, too inexperienced!"

"He is a man now, and a competent one. I trust him completely. He has saved my life more than once. And he will save yours. Trust him, like I do."

Celia did not answer, nor could she look at him. His wife turned and moved to the window. She stood there for a long while, staring out at the harbor, across the short roofs of Recife, out toward the mass of Dutch ships, their tight clustering almost suggesting an anxious impatience to depart. Three times he wanted to say something, but fell short. What could he possibly say to change her mind, to get her to trust in his plan? In him?

Finally, Celia turned to him. "Domingos...Tromp is fooling you. Don't you see it? He is trying to keep your spirits up so that you will continue to help them leave Recife. The Dutch aren't going to end slavery. They rely on it just like the Portuguese and Spanish."

"I trust him, Celia," Calabar answered, trying to keep anger from his voice. "I absolutely trust Peg Leg Jol. They would not stand in my own home, stare me in the eyes, and lie to me. We shall not discuss it any further."

Celia turned back toward the window, her face streaked with tears. "So it is done, then," she said without looking at him. "You are the head of this household, and you have made your decision. I pray that it is a good one. I pray that these Dutch, in whom you place so much trust, keep handing you swords instead of driving them into your back. And I pray that Carlos survives another night." That brought more tears to her eye. She blinked them away. "But remember this, my love, that just a few short months ago, Recife was the crown jewel of the Dutch settlements in Brazil. One to stand forever, they said.

"Now look at it, on the verge of collapse. Things change, Calabar. People change; nations change. You know this all too well. Trust your Dutch friends, if you must, but put your faith in God, and always, *always*, put your love for your children first. Whatever you decide to do, Calabar, make your choices for them."

She came to him and he laid his head on her stomach. He pressed into her, wrapping his arms around her waist, letting her rock him like a child. She kissed his sweat-matted hair, rubbed his back. Then she pulled away, walked out silently, and closed the door behind her.

Am I making the right choice? Calabar did not

know the answer to that. *Perhaps I will never know.* But to be asked to help end slavery, to put an end to the terror and brutality and disgrace once and for all? How could he turn his back on men who had declared such an intent to his face?

To the sound of Celia's muffled sobbing, he lay back down, pulled the sheet over his legs, closed his eyes, slept, and dreamed of a better day.

Tromp walked, hands behind his back, making sure he did not outpace Jol, whose weary *tap-ta-tap-ta-tap* was growing slower all the time.

"Cornelis—"

"Don't say it. And don't call me 'Cornelis.' Yes, you asked if he was a hothead. And I told you he was."

"You said he was a hothead *at the right times.* I'm not so sure his impulsive charge at Bom Jesus was one of those 'right times.'"

"Maarten, please; when your irony becomes patronizing, it becomes unbearable. You were right, yes? This is what you wished to hear?"

"No, old friend. What I want to hear—to know—is this: will it happen again, do you think?"

Jol was quiet a long time.

Tap-ta-tap-ta-tap.

"Well?"

"I'm thinking," Jol growled. "And I think better when I've had a drink."

"Just one?"

A sigh that ended in a chortle. "You know me too well, old friend."

"Don't I, though? Come: let's find you a chair and a bottle."

Chapter 8

Pontal, Brazil

Calabar waited on the deck of Captain von Schoppe's flagship, watching as a small boat came alongside and off-loaded its precious human cargo. He greeted Pedro Álvares with a nod and offered his hand: his right hand, since the wound healing in his left shoulder was still sore, the muscles weak. Álvares accepted the lift, and Calabar could immediately feel the man's strength. Álvares was older than Calabar. By how much he did not know. Five, six years perhaps.

Once aboard, Álvares nodded curtly and saluted. "It is good to see you again, Calabar."

Really? That surprised him, for why would a Portuguese sympathizer be happy to see a mameluco dog? He ignored the kind greeting. "Pedro Álvares, I have been instructed by Admiral Tromp to personally deliver you to Bom Jesus, so that you may participate in our negotiations with the Portuguese. Matias de Albuquerque has agreed that you shall be his spokesman, and that—"

Álvares waved him off. "I am aware of my duty, Calabar." He hesitated, then said, "Is there some place that we can speak privately?" He looked at Captain von Schoppe who stood nearby.

Von Schoppe hesitated, then nodded. "You may use my cabin."

Calabar led the way. They entered the small, humid compartment. He closed the door behind them, and Álvares took the liberty of sitting in one of the two chairs near a small, three-legged round table. He motioned for Calabar to do the same, as if it were his cabin. "Please, sit down."

Calabar did so reluctantly, pushing his own chair against the wall. He wanted as much room as possible between himself and Álvares in case the man tried something.

Álvares began. "You've been wounded. Is it serious?"

Calabar shook his head. "Not so much. I will live."

"That is good to hear. The world would lose a fine person if you were to die."

"I'm . . . honored, Pedro, that you hold me in such high regard. I did not realize."

"Your exploits, or shall I say, service, to both the Portuguese and the Dutch are well known to everyone. Everyone that counts, at least."

"My service to the Dutch is unwavering, good sir. If your intention here is to soften my resolve with platitudes, I promise you will not succeed. As for my past service to the Portuguese, the less that God is reminded of such folly, the better. Now, enough of this pleasant talk." Calabar leaned toward Álvares and stared him in the eye. "Admiral Tromp said that you had asked for me personally. Why?"

Álvares smiled. "You showed great courage, fortitude, and patient will when you let de Gama live."

Calabar huffed. "He deserved a bullet in the back, the filthy pig."

"Perhaps," Álvares agreed, "but you did not pull that trigger. You showed a side of your character that he assumed was not there. You impressed him. But more importantly, you impressed me."

"And why is impressing you important?"

Álvares leaned forward as well, his face now very close to Calabar's. He whispered. "Because you and I are probably the only men in this whole affair that can make it play out the way we want. The way it needs to play out."

Calabar screwed up his face. "What are you talking about? There is nothing here to play out. The Dutch are simply strengthening their position on the mainland so that we might live in peace."

Álvares smiled. "So you say. But don't you think it a little strange that shortly after Admiral Tromp limps into port, the Dutch throw so many of their assets into taking Pontal, laying siege to Bom Jesus—and then suddenly they stop to negotiate? And now they are willing to withdraw from Pontal, so soon after acquiring it with loss of life. Come, now, Domingos; you are one of the canniest commanders in Brazil. Something far more important is taking place here. What is it?"

Calabar tried not to sweat as he stared into Álvares' insistent eyes. He swallowed, shook his head, and said, "I don't know what you mean. It is as I told you; the Dutch are resolved to secure their position on the Pernambuco coast."

Álvares leaned back. "Very well. Loyalty has come to you at last." He stood up and went to a small porthole that looked out onto the low swells of the bay. He opened it fully to let a breeze rush in. "I did not ask for you to come here just to confirm what I already know. I, too, am a smart man, Domingos." He chuckled. "That, I suspect, is the product of my mother's influence."

The compartment was silent except for the faint creaks of the hull being caressed by the modest risers. Álvares took his seat again. His face grew stern, serious, but Calabar could see the man's hand shaking. "I asked you here for another reason. What do you remember of your mother?"

Calabar shrugged. "She was a saint. She raised me almost entirely on her own, with some help from the Jesuits. I was schooled by them."

"And what do you know of her life before you were born?"

"Not a great deal. She never spoke of it to me. I was too young to understand much of it anyway, and frankly, too young to care."

Álvares' face grew even more solemn and quiet. He became slightly pale, sweat beading on his forehead. "Well, I am here to tell you that your mother's name was not Angela Fernandes, as you remember her and from which you draw your own name. She was born Angela Álvares, and she was my mother as well."

Calabar leaned back in his chair. It felt like an anvil had fallen on his chest. He struggled to breathe. "You lie."

Álvares shook his head. "It's true, Domingos. We share the same blood, the same mother. I was not sure of it until recently. But I have spoken to the Jesuits about you, and they have confirmed it. It is true whether you wish to accept it or not.

"My father was a Portuguese soldier. He died in service to the king when I was very young. But his family did not approve of his union with our mother, and so they took me away when he died. I was raised Portuguese, and could not learn much about our mother. But what little I remember of her confirms what you have just said: she was a saint. And I imagine I saw a bit of her in you, in your eyes, when you faced de Gama on that field of battle. I would like to know more about her."

Calabar did not speak at first, still absorbing all he had just heard. On the surface of it, it seemed both too convenient and too fanciful to be true. But perhaps it was, nonetheless. Indeed, Calabar's mother did have a very different life before he was born; she had mentioned it, but had never given details. She seemed ashamed of it, as if she had fallen in some way, had been responsible for her diminished lot in life. Calabar had never known his own father, and when he brought it up, she would grow quiet and change the subject quickly.

Calabar stared at Álvares, his ostensible half brother. They did not look the same. Álvares had far, far lighter skin. How could they be related? But again, it was possible. Some Portuguese were very fair, even had blonde hair.

Calabar sat tall in his chair and shook his head. "None of this matters now, Álvares. What you say may or may not be true. Perhaps you are trying to confuse me to gain advantage in the negotiations. I cannot know the truth of your claim, so I cannot know your reason for advancing it at this time and place. But what I do know is that, right now, only the negotiations matter. If we survive this ordeal, then perhaps we will have another conversation about this. So: will you or will you not negotiate in good faith with the Dutch on behalf of the Portuguese?"

It was Álvares' turn to force himself to smile. "You must have gotten your stubbornness from your father... whoever he was. Very well: for now, I will put aside the discussion of our mother. But we will come back to it someday, Domingos, I am sure of it.

"Now, you too must understand one thing right now: I know what the Dutch are up to, and if you want me to negotiate in good faith so that your plan does not fall apart, then you must do something for *me.*"

Slowly, cautiously, Calabar nodded. "What do you want?"

Álvares told him.

Chapter 9

On the road to Olinda, Brazil

Under heavy guard, Calabar delivered Pedro Álvares to Bom Jesus as promised. He delivered him personally, at the front gate, and stood once more before Matias de Albuquerque. In his presence, Calabar felt a chill reach down his spine. On the one hand, he felt the urge to do what he had promised Celia: to negotiate a private peace between them. On the other, he longed to drive a knife into Matias' neck. It was a strange feeling and one that Calabar did not like: the uncertainty of emotion, the inability to have a clear sense of his relationship with this man whom he had stood beside many times, and had fought for. Now they stood face to face as enemies. What was Matias feeling? Calabar wondered. Anger? Embarrassment? Humiliation? Perhaps all three.

For his part, the protector of Bom Jesus did not give Calabar the satisfaction of looking him in the eye. He accepted Pedro Álvares from the Dutch guards, turned and walked back into the fort. The matter was concluded and any last consideration to implore upon Matias' Christian goodwill, as Celia desired, was gone. The door to Bom Jesus was shut, and so too had any possibilities of personal reconciliation with the Portuguese.

Three days later, the negotiations began, on the island of Antonio Vaz, in an old Capuchin monastery that now lay damaged and abandoned from when the Dutch had made their assault against Portuguese positions on the mainland years ago. Calabar did not like the site, feeling that it was too close to Recife, which stood just across the harbor. Dutch movements and activities could be too easily observed from the water's edge. A Portuguese spy, or several in fact, could have been placed in Álvares' entourage, which arrived each morning for the talks. These guards lounged around outside the building as the negotiations took place, and Calabar wondered who among them were there strictly to protect Álvares, and who had been given instructions by Matias to keep a sharp eye angled toward Recife.

Calabar shared his concerns with Major Schutte, who responded by making it perfectly clear to Álvares that it was paramount for the Portuguese to agree, immediately, to pull their military and mercantile assets away from the harbor, in order to give, ostensibly, a buffer zone of increased safety and comfort to the Dutch. Álvares agreed to this in exchange for the Portuguese prisoners that the Dutch had captured during their assault against Bom Jesus.

Four days later, the Portuguese forces had pulled back to a fort which lay a mile or so further inland and near the intersection of the Capiberibe and Afogadas rivers. But to make sure there were no Portuguese eyes trained toward the harbor, Calabar assigned picket duty to tribesmen, who, according to his instructions, remained scattered along the shore and as far up the coast as Olinda. They were to report any strange activities or persons they saw.

The next issue to negotiate was the removal of the Portuguese among Recife's population and their resettlement on the mainland. When the Dutch had captured Recife, several Portuguese families had remained in the fortified town. Why the Dutch had insisted that they stay in Recife after the capture, Calabar could not guess. But now their continued presence in the Dutch colony was untenable and dangerous. If they were allowed to freely move about, they would most certainly learn of the Dutch plan, and find ways to send that knowledge to Bom Jesus.

So far, Admiral Tromp had done a canny job confounding queries into his fleet's activities by stating publicly that the food, dry goods, stores of sugar, and livestock being placed upon his ships were for his inevitable return to Europe. That statement seemed to quell any suspicions that might have stirred among the Portuguese population. However, the matter of these families had to be resolved well before any removal of Dutch colonists could take place.

But Tromp did not want to simply hand these families over to Matias and thus lose a bargaining chip for any issues that still needed to be resolved. And thus it became Calabar's charge to remove these families and place them in protective custody in forts San Francisco and San Jorge, where they would remain until Matias agreed to any additional requirements.

Calabar hated the task. Not because there was fear that the families would be harmed in any way. No, he hated knocking down doors in the middle of the night, scaring children and pulling their mothers and fathers out into the street. But now that the Dutch were in a position of strength, their actions had to reflect that strength. Matias had to believe that the Dutch were serious, and that they intended to stay in Brazil for a long, long time.

As part of that deception, Admiral Tromp offered Álvares a five-year cessation of hostilities, and if Matias agreed to it, the Dutch would end their siege of Bom Jesus and pull all Dutch forces from the mainland, including Dutch farmers and plantation owners who clung to a few choice pieces of land. All that the Dutch required to sign this agreement was a removal of Portuguese soldiers from Olinda, for one month, so that the Dutch might extract the Sephardic Jewish families living there and move them into Recife. There were six Jewish families living in Olinda under Portuguese control, estimated at twenty-two souls in all, and rumors of their privations were both convincing and grim. The Portuguese had not allowed the Dutch to enter Olinda since they had recaptured it, so there was no way of determining if the reports were accurate or exaggerated.

Álvares carried the offer—five years of peace for the evacuation of six Jewish families—to Matias. The offer was rejected. Matias did not trust the Dutch when it came to Olinda. He believed that it was a ploy to get the Portuguese to pull back, thus allowing Dutch soldiers to come in and retake the town.

Mere days before the negotiations were set to

Álvares smiled. "You showed great courage, fortitude, and patient will when you let de Gama live."

Calabar huffed. "He deserved a bullet in the back, the filthy pig."

"Perhaps," Álvares agreed, "but you did not pull that trigger. You showed a side of your character that he assumed was not there. You impressed him. But more importantly, you impressed me."

"And why is impressing you important?"

Álvares leaned forward as well, his face now very close to Calabar's. He whispered. "Because you and I are probably the only men in this whole affair that can make it play out the way we want. The way it needs to play out."

Calabar screwed up his face. "What are you talking about? There is nothing here to play out. The Dutch are simply strengthening their position on the mainland so that we might live in peace."

Álvares smiled. "So you say. But don't you think it a little strange that shortly after Admiral Tromp limps into port, the Dutch throw so many of their assets into taking Pontal, laying siege to Bom Jesus—and then suddenly they stop to negotiate? And now they are willing to withdraw from Pontal, so soon after acquiring it with loss of life. Come, now, Domingos; you are one of the canniest commanders in Brazil. Something far more important is taking place here. What is it?"

Calabar tried not to sweat as he stared into Álvares' insistent eyes. He swallowed, shook his head, and said, "I don't know what you mean. It is as I told you; the Dutch are resolved to secure their position on the Pernambuco coast."

Álvares leaned back. "Very well. Loyalty has come to you at last." He stood up and went to a small porthole that looked out onto the low swells of the bay. He opened it fully to let a breeze rush in. "I did not ask for you to come here just to confirm what I already know. I, too, am a smart man, Domingos." He chuckled. "That, I suspect, is the product of my mother's influence."

The compartment was silent except for the faint creaks of the hull being caressed by the modest risers. Álvares took his seat again. His face grew stern, serious, but Calabar could see the man's hand shaking. "I asked you here for another reason. What do you remember of your mother?"

Calabar shrugged. "She was a saint. She raised me almost entirely on her own, with some help from the Jesuits. I was schooled by them."

"And what do you know of her life before you were born?"

"Not a great deal. She never spoke of it to me. I was too young to understand much of it anyway, and frankly, too young to care."

Álvares' face grew even more solemn and quiet. He became slightly pale, sweat beading on his forehead. "Well, I am here to tell you that your mother's name was not Angela Fernandes, as you remember her and from which you draw your own name. She was born Angela Álvares, and she was my mother as well."

Calabar leaned back in his chair. It felt like an anvil had fallen on his chest. He struggled to breathe. "You lie."

Álvares shook his head. "It's true, Domingos. We share the same blood, the same mother. I was not sure of it until recently. But I have spoken to the Jesuits about you, and they have confirmed it. It is true whether you wish to accept it or not.

"My father was a Portuguese soldier. He died in service to the king when I was very young. But his family did not approve of his union with our mother, and so they took me away when he died. I was raised Portuguese, and could not learn much about our mother. But what little I remember of her confirms what you have just said: she was a saint. And I imagine I saw a bit of her in you, in your eyes, when you faced de Gama on that field of battle. I would like to know more about her."

Calabar did not speak at first, still absorbing all he had just heard. On the surface of it, it seemed both too convenient and too fanciful to be true. But perhaps it was, nonetheless. Indeed, Calabar's mother did have a very different life before he was born; she had mentioned it, but had never given details. She seemed ashamed of it, as if she had fallen in some way, had been responsible for her diminished lot in life. Calabar had never known his own father, and when he brought it up, she would grow quiet and change the subject quickly.

Calabar stared at Álvares, his ostensible half brother. They did not look the same. Álvares had far, far lighter skin. How could they be related? But again, it was possible. Some Portuguese were very fair, even had blonde hair.

Calabar sat tall in his chair and shook his head. "None of this matters now, Álvares. What you say may or may not be true. Perhaps you are trying to confuse me to gain advantage in the negotiations. I cannot know the truth of your claim, so I cannot know your reason for advancing it at this time and place. But what I do know is that, right now, only the negotiations matter. If we survive this ordeal, then perhaps we will have another conversation about this. So: will you or will you not negotiate in good faith with the Dutch on behalf of the Portuguese?"

It was Álvares' turn to force himself to smile. "You must have gotten your stubbornness from your father... whoever he was. Very well: for now, I will put aside the discussion of our mother. But we will come back to it someday, Domingos, I am sure of it.

"Now, you too must understand one thing right now: I know what the Dutch are up to, and if you want me to negotiate in good faith so that your plan does not fall apart, then you must do something for *me*."

Slowly, cautiously, Calabar nodded. "What do you want?"

Álvares told him.

conclude, and with the matter of the Jewish families in Olinda still unsettled, Calabar found himself alongside Moses Cohen Henriques Eanes on horseback. They rode under a flag of truce to the Portuguese stronghold, as agreed to by Matias, in order to view the conditions of the Jewish families for themselves. Their escort—two mounted guards—followed close behind, muskets ready, eyes forward on the foliage of the narrow passage through which they were moving.

Moses had been livid since before the sun set. "That son of a cow," the pirate blurted, as he and Calabar sat their swaying mounts. "Matias is doing this to anger me personally. What other reason could there be?"

"Despite the fact that he was born there, I don't think this is actually personal, Moses," Calabar said, sitting firmly in the saddle, rubbing his thumb across the handle of his pistol and keeping the horse steady. "Matias is just being stubborn. Olinda has always been an important town and refuge for the Portuguese. He will relent in time. He's not in a position to refuse."

Moses shook his head. "He had better relent quickly. We don't *have* much time."

That fact weighed heavily on Calabar's mind. They had five days, maybe. Perhaps only four. Admiral Tromp wasn't sure. He had already sent a part of his fleet and Admiral Banckert's as well to Saint Eustatius in preparation for the arrival of the colonists. There were still enough war ships in the harbor to support the main exodus, but if something went wrong, if the negotiations fell apart, there might not be enough Dutch soldiers left to conduct a fighting withdrawal. Tromp had ordered some of the forces from their positions around Bom Jesus to fall back into Recife, and had put some of them on departing ships. Calabar was worried that that move might have been seen as weakness, thus emboldening Matias to remain stubborn over Olinda. And so here he was, with a Sephardic pirate, both charged with getting the colonists ready to leave in haste and in the dark of night, traveling instead to Olinda... and for what?

Mostly because Moses had insisted that they do so as a precaution. If Matias refused to pull his troops from Olinda, and time ran out, then those families would need to be removed using other means. And of course Moses had already formulated a plan incorporating those other means: a plan which necessitated seeing precisely where the families lived and having Calabar to help him do so.

Calabar spurred his horse forward. One of their guards held a lantern but it was still very dark, the moon hiding behind a bank of clouds that had threatened rain all day. He could feel the moisture in the air, the oppressive heat close around him. He uncorked his wineskin and took a drink.

A firearm roared nearby; a lead ball ripped the wineskin from his hand. Calabar's horse spooked, reared up, and threw him to the ground.

Calabar groaned as a sharp pain flared through his hip, and he rolled toward the bank on the opposite side of the path. More muskets fired, and one of their escorts fell dead, his horse following his tumble into the bushes after three shots in its flank.

Calabar cocked his pistol, aimed it into the darkness across the path, waited until he saw the flash of a gun barrel, then fired at it. A yelp followed and a limp body tumbled into view and slid down the embankment.

The guard that held the lantern had managed to survive the ambush, but his lantern was broken; its oil spread along the ground, burning slowly. The flames cast a flickering, irregular light along the embankment. Squinting, Calabar looked for reflections upon the faces of their ambushers, trying to divine their numbers. He'd only heard five shots before the present lull.

"Moses," Calabar whispered, reloading his pistol, not daring to raise his head out of the brush. "Where are you? Moses?"

"Here," a faint voice replied from behind a heap of dead horse flesh. "I'm here. My leg...I have been hit."

Damn! "Can you fire?"

A cough. "I think so. I'm not bleeding too badly."

Calabar nodded, though he knew Moses could not see it. "They're going to fire again soon. Load as fast as you can and keep firing. I'm going to try to work around them. You, there, come with me."

He motioned for the remaining guard to follow him, and they slowly picked their way under protection of bushes and darkness, back down the path, until they reached a fork in the road. Quietly, they took the other path, working up a rise until they were just behind the ambushers. Calabar winced every time he heard one of them fire, then felt relief when he heard Moses firing back. But that would not last for long. Their small party had not carried that much ammunition with them; they had been moving under flag of truce.

On hands and knees, Calabar slipped swiftly through the brush, ignoring the biting brambles and clinging vines. The Dutch guard had a more difficult time of it, getting stuck once, but otherwise keeping good pace alongside Calabar.

They cocked their pistols under muffling hands, rose up behind their assailants, and fired.

Two fell heavily, shot in the back. The other two, in mid-reload, tried turning to face the threat behind them. The Dutch guard swung his pistol and knocked one of the Portuguese men senseless, following the boy closely down the embankment to continue beating his face until he lay still and dead. The one facing Calabar began cocking his pistol even as he raised it, but Calabar was on him.

He knocked the gun from the boy's hand, grabbed him by the waist and bodily shoved him down the embankment. The boy sprawled out of the brush and fell hard on the path, tried scrambling away. Calabar followed, raised his pistol, and swung it across the back of the boy's head, who staggered, stunned. One more stroke and he went down, limp.

Fumbling in the darkness, Calabar fumbled after the boy's collar, grabbed it, then pulled the boy over to lay beside Moses. The Sephardic pirate was still, eyes closed, a solemn expression on his shadowed face. Calabar placed a hand on his chest. His heartbeat was faint, but there was still life.

"Fix him a tourniquet," Calabar said to the Dutch guard. "Quickly!"

He turned to the young Portuguese soldier, who was coming around slowly. Calabar slapped him, then harder a second time. Wanted to continue. Harder and harder.

He was angry, and rightfully so, damn it. To be attacked under flag of truce. He wanted to fire into the boy's chest, point-blank, and watch him die the instant after the ball tore through his heart. *If Moses does not survive, I swear . . .*

He sat back, prayed, appealing to God to calm his rage. He breathed deeply, several times, then said in Portuguese, "Tell me, who sent you?"

The boy did not respond at first. Calabar shouted the demand. "Matias," the boy said, jumping at the deep harshness of Calabar's voice.

"Why? We are under flag of truce. A truce he agreed to."

The boy coughed. "He wants you dead."

"Me? Why?"

The boy did not say at first. He coughed, laid his head to the side. Calabar screamed at him again. The boy flinched: "Because he said that you are a traitor."

Calabar waited in the ruin of the sugar mill. It was not his mill; that had been taken by the Portuguese, briefly held, and then abandoned and left to the elements. The machinery of the mill itself still showed signs of newness, of being capable of production, but Dutch cannon and fire had destroyed many of the outlying buildings. And now here he stood in one of those buildings, watching from darkness, as Pedro Álvares climbed off his horse and walked alone toward him.

Calabar cocked his pistol beneath the derelict table at which he sat. The sound echoed through the empty room. "Come no closer."

Álvares stopped just outside the door and put up his hands. "I'm unarmed."

"Unlike those men you sent against me last night."

"I had nothing to do with that."

Calabar slammed his fist onto the table. Dust rose, then settled to the dirt floor. "You represent Matias in the negotiations. You speak on his behalf. Do not condescend to tell me that you were not aware of his actions, that you did not know that he would be sending assassins against me."

"I confess," Álvares said, gaining the courage to continue walking through the entrance and toward the table. "Matias *did* order me to capture you, so that he might put you to death himself. But I never put that order into motion. I would never do that to you or your family. I swear it before God. Matias went behind my back and ordered last night's attack on his own. I only learned of the plan after it had been put in motion. There was nothing I could do then. I just wonder what my own fate holds, now."

"What do you mean?"

Álvares raised one eyebrow. "Domingos, you know perfectly well what I mean. If he is no longer sure that I will carry out an order to take you captive, but rather, takes it upon himself to make arrangements for your assassination, I must tread very carefully. Matias may have begun to consider me a liability rather than an asset."

Calabar shook his head angrily. "But it makes no sense that he would wish to kill me *now*. Why would he risk the negotiations, the safety of his own position, to kill just one man? I have no power."

Álvares uttered a single muted laugh. "You have more power than you know, Domingos. Matias blames you for everything. Before you switched sides, the Dutch were losing. Well, perhaps not losing, but they were certainly not gaining any new ground. You changed that. You taught them how to fight back. And now here the Dutch stand, encircling Bom Jesus, forcing Matias to give ground everywhere. The Portuguese are angry; they are hurt. Most importantly, they are embarrassed politically."

Álvares put his hands down and moved to the table. He took the rickety chair opposite Calabar. He cleared his throat. "You also embody something that they cannot abide, cannot allow to stand."

"And what is that?"

"The mere notion that a mameluco dog could hold such respect and authority with a European power. Think of it, Domingos. If a person of your background can be held in such high regard and respect, then how can they hold sway over 'lesser' races? How can they continue to maintain their slave trade? Their whole position here is in jeopardy if such a man as you is allowed to continue to breathe free."

Calabar considered letting Álvares in on what Tromp had told him about slavery. *Could Matias' agent—my alleged half brother—be trusted with such* dangerous *knowledge?* Álvares might indeed be against slavery, but was he against it enough?

Calabar shook his head. "I'm not that important."

Álvares leaned in close. "You are. The Bible speaks of a divine spark in all of us. I cannot speak for myself, but many have seen that spark in your eyes."

Calabar shrugged. "I suspect they are simply seeing the rage I struggle to contain when I find myself on a battlefield. Or enduring European arrogance."

"Maybe. But maybe that is part of your divine spark. The Old Testament is full of heroes whose greatest quality was neither wisdom nor temperance, but a fury to be free."

"I see. So what would be a rash action for others is the eruption of righteous anger for me?"

Álvares waved away the ironic quip. "Whether you wish to believe it or not, Domingos, you could become the Spartacus of Brazil. You are a clear threat to Portuguese rule, and Matias will not stop until you are dead."

"You are a mixed-blood yourself," Calabar said, "if we share the same mother as you claim. You hold tremendous sway with Matias, with the Portuguese. So tell me: why does he rely upon what goes on in your head, rather than just putting it on a pike?"

Álvares seemed to consider that question, then said, "It is one thing to be an advisor, Calabar. You served in that capacity, too, for Matias. So long as you were his servant, he controlled you: your position was no threat to his authority. But since then, you have commanded steadily increasing numbers of men for the Dutch, and your importance and influence continue to grow." He shrugged. "And I suppose it is helpful that he does not know of my parentage. My light skin shields me from suspicion, from questions that could lead to persecution."

Calabar leaned back, his mind a maelstrom of contending emotions, desires, and apprehensions. What was he going to do? What *could* he do?

I must do my duty, do what I have pledged to do.

He uncocked his pistol and stood. From his pocket, he pulled a small package, a white cloth wrapped in cord. He placed it on the table. Álvares stood as well.

"Thank you, Pedro," Calabar said. He pushed the package across the table until it lay in front of his half brother. "This is yours now."

Calabar nodded respectfully, turned, and walked out into the night.

Chapter 10

Recife, Brazil

Although restless, Calabar was resolved to conceal it from Luiz as they walked through Recife at dusk on the next day. While the light had lasted, he had helped Dutch families board ships in anticipation of their imminent departure. Most were willing to go and accepted his help gladly, even giving him small hugs and tiny presents of food for his service. Many of them assumed he was staying behind. *Why would such a fellow leave?* he imagined them wondering. A mix of native and European blood, they knew him best as the former owner of a Portuguese sugar plantation. Surely he could go back to that life once Recife was abandoned. He didn't bother to disabuse them of their unvoiced speculations.

Some of the families, merchants mostly, refused to leave. At one point, a sugar trader took a swing at Calabar and tried pulling a pistol. Luiz subdued the man and removed the firearm from his shaking hands, only to get a nasty scratch across the cheek from the trader's enraged wife. In the end, they, like the others, were left to their fate. Their hope of future profits was far more important to them than loyalty to their country or the potential threats to its continued stability or even sovereignty. Perhaps the Portuguese would be kind to them; perhaps they would not. Matias would certainly require they swear fealty to his king and take a heavy sum of any profits. And because of Calabar's fateful decision to switch sides years ago, Matias was unlikely to just let those who remained behind give their oath and be done with it. They could expect to be watched, hounded, perhaps even harassed for as long as they remained in Recife. Matias would not be forgiving of even the most innocent misunderstanding.

But there was nothing to be done about it now. Admiral Tromp refused to force anyone onto ships that was not willing to go freely. And anyway, there was no time left to argue.

Tromp's remaining ships were leaving tomorrow night with everything they could carry.

"How is Moses?" Luiz asked Calabar as they walked the last street toward his home.

"He's doing well. But he lost a great amount of blood, and he won't be able to walk for a while. They've already put him on Tromp's flagship."

"What about Olinda?"

What, indeed? With Moses incapacitated, Tromp had reluctantly abandoned the plan to remove the Jewish families there. Matias was just not going to give in, and there was no further time to discuss it. After the assassination attempt, the negotiations had been suspended, and Tromp had pulled the remaining soldiers away from Bom Jesus, positioning them instead along the coastline for final embarkation. As far as he was concerned, Olinda was lost. Just the prior night, the pirate had wailed his misery over the decision, but Tromp would not budge.

"I'll do it," Calabar had told Tromp before the day's work had begun; the matter had cost him most of his sleep. He had few doubts about what the Jewish population of Olinda could expect in the long run. When Tromp blinked in surprise, Calabar had merely nodded. "I'll get them out."

The admiral had appeared ready to argue the point, but a second look into Calabar's eyes apparently showed him that the mind behind them was already made up. Tromp had waved a permissive, albeit reluctant hand in response to Calabar's resolve, but made it clear that there would be no delay in the fleet's departure, whether Calabar succeeded or not. "I understand," Calabar had assured him.

The plan that he, Moses, and Luiz devised sounded simple enough. Two hours before the fleet departed, Calabar's men would slip into Olinda under cover of darkness, remove the Jewish families quietly, and place them on small boats that would meet the fleet out in the harbor.

This meant, of course, that there was no time to alert the families of their impending removal. This fact caused Calabar greater concern than any other aspect of their plan: it was one thing for a Jewish pirate to waltz into the town and declare that Jewish families should pack up and leave. For a mameluco to try and do the same . . . what would be their response? And there would be no time to take anything beyond what they could carry without encumbering themselves. It seemed to Calabar that the plan could easily evolve into seizing rather than removing people. And if so, then how much resistance would he meet?

Accordingly, Moses had personally handwritten six letters in Hebrew, one for each family that Calabar would hopefully convince—quietly—of the legitimacy of his plan to remove them. The letter explained everything, but that was still no guarantee that they would believe it.

With Calabar's hand resting on the breast pocket that held the thin pieces of paper, he and Luiz rounded the corner into his street, and discovered a small crowd of neighbors huddled around Celia. She sat sobbing on their front porch, a handkerchief against her face. One of the neighbors pointed to a patch of deep red paint smeared against the wall of their apartment.

Drawing ahead of Luiz, Calabar pushed hastily through the crowd and saw the mad scarlet scribble across his porch, front door, and newly broken window. The words had been hastily painted on, whole letters smeared and stretched beyond easy comprehension. Celia stood and threw herself into her husband's arms, laid her head on his shoulder. As he stroked her hair and let her tears wet his shirt, he mouthed the foul red words silently. He then said them out loud: "*No confe este cachoro traidor. Ele e portuges.*"

"Portuguese spies," Luiz said. "We must tell Admiral Tromp that Matias has eyes in town."

Calabar shook his head, read the phrase again, and then again. "No," he said. "Matias' eyes are not here."

"But that is Portuguese," Luiz said pointing at the red words.

"Poorly written Portuguese, as you can see," Calabar said. "*Very* poorly written. Even the word 'Portuguese' is misspelled. It should read '*Nao confie este cachorro traidoroso. Ele e portugues.*' . . . 'Do not trust this traitorous dog. He is Portuguese.' No. This was done by Dutch hands." He touched Celia's face gently. "Did you see who did this?"

She wiped away tears, shook her head. "No. We were out, making final preparations, getting some bread. When we came home, it had already been done."

"The window too?"

"Yes, a stone. Nothing on it. Just a big black stone. Thank God we were not here, Calabar, or it might have struck our children."

She began to cry again. Calabar held her tight and looked around at those gathered. He wondered, *Do any of them know who did this?* Their eyes, faces did not give anything away. They seemed almost embarrassed to be there. "Go away," he said, obliging their silent discomfort. "Leave my family alone, all of you. You should be finishing your preparations to depart, not standing out here in the street. Go and make ready, or Admiral Tromp will leave you behind!"

The crowd dispersed. Calabar turned and went inside, holding Celia close.

The children were there. Lua hugged his waist the minute they stepped through the door. Martim stood tall, silent, like a man, showing strength for his father. Carlos sat nearby, seemingly strong as well, but his eyes revealed the truth in the room. They were scared, all of them. Their home had been violated, the window smashed. Their father was leaving them soon, and now they faced physical danger. So many uncertainties, so many confused questions lay in their young minds. And their father would soon be too far away to help.

"We must tell Admiral Tromp at once," Luiz said. "Those who did this must be found and punished."

"Luiz, this is a ploy by those staying behind to discredit me. To make those in this community balk when I go to them and tell them it is time to leave. They are trying to turn Recife against me, here at the last minute. Although they are fools if they think that such bad grammar will trick me into thinking that the Portuguese are the ones who wrote it."

Calabar fell into a chair, removed his hat and wiped his dirty brow clean. He considered the situation. The Portuguese wanted him dead. The obstinate Dutch wanted him discredited—some might even want him dead, too. He stared at his children, watching Celia comfort them all, and in that moment, he realized that no matter where his family was, they would not be entirely safe. Not so long as Matias sought his death. And if Matias found him, they'd find Celia and the children too. He sighed. *Perhaps it would be best for everyone if I just died . . .*

He paused, considered his situation again, his plan for Olinda. Then he grit his teeth, stood, and turned to Luiz. "Tonight. I want you to get Celia and the children to the Jesuits, to Father Araujo, tonight. As per our plan."

"Tonight?" Luiz's face showed concern, confusion. "But I thought we were to wait until the ships departed, until after Olinda."

Calabar shook his head. "Tonight, Luiz. I will take care of Olinda myself. You stay here, help Celia and the children prepare, then leave within the hour. You *must* do this for me."

He turned to Celia. She had heard everything, but still her face, her accusing eyes, did not relent. Despite everything, she still did not want him to go, or for her and the children to be taken to the Jesuits. But she came to him anyway and hugged him one final time, letting the curves of her body join his, letting her warmth press deep into his chest.

He did not want to let go, but finally pushed her away, refusing to look her in the eye, fearing what might happen if he did, fearing that he would give in, stay with them, go to the Jesuits as well. But that would be death...for all of them.

One by one, he hugged and kissed his children, gave them little tickles around their necks, promised each with simple words that they would be together again, soon, and everything would be all right. God would see to it, he said. He knelt and together, they prayed. Then he stood, shook Luiz's hand once more, bid them all goodbye, and passed through the door.

He emerged in the humid darkness and was ambushed by the recollections it prompted. Creeping toward Bom Jesus, sneaking up on Matias' assassins, meeting Pedro Álvares: always in the same suffocating darkness. Would his life ever be different from what it had now become: always skulking in heat-thick shadows, dripping as he waited for—or led—men bent on death, destruction, or possibly betrayal? If there was a spark that some saw in his eye, he found it hard to believe it was put there by divinity.

Fixing his hat upon his head and pulling its brim low, he stalked toward the blackest alley that would take him to the outskirts of Recife.

Chapter 11

Olinda, Brazil

It was near midnight when Calabar and a handful of tribesmen slipped onto shore from four small boats that they had rowed up the harbor in full darkness. Crewmen from Moses' ship had accompanied them to man the boats and then guard them while Calabar and local allies waded through the fens south of Olinda, up a small bank, over a hillock, and then into the town proper. Luckily, the Jewish families were clustered on the marshy side of the town, near the wall which protected Olinda from sea bombardment and invasion. It would have been best if they could have rowed up the harbor and landed on the north side, but the shoreline there was too rocky, too treacherous underfoot. There were at least eight children that would have to be removed, along with their mothers, fathers, and grandparents. Would the boats hold them all? They had to. There was no alternative.

He and the tribesmen waded through the marsh without torches or lanterns. The darkness was essential if they were to infiltrate the town, but it would then pose a problem once they were within and had to face the families. How would these town dwellers react to dark-skinned natives suddenly emerging from the gloom, breaking down their doors and pulling their children from beds? Calabar tapped the letters in his pocket to ensure they were still there.

"I will personally deliver a letter to each family," he reiterated to the leader of the tribesmen who lay beside him in the tall grass of the hillock just outside town. He hoped his words were correct. *I wish Luiz were here*, he thought as he slowly repeated the words in his broken Tupi. "And they will, I hope, understand what we are doing. It will be difficult, but we must get them all out of the town and back to the boats. Do you understand?"

The tribe's leader nodded.

"You and your men must get them back. I will not be helping you. You must do this on your own. Do you understand?"

The leader nodded again. "I understand. And what will you be doing?"

Calabar ignored the question. "Let's go."

Together, they rose out of the grass and moved down the hill, following Calabar into Olinda. They stopped behind the first line of homes. Calabar peered around a corner. There were a few faint lights scattered around the town, but not enough to reveal them. He spotted a Portuguese soldier, then another, and another, walking the empty streets, muskets in their hands. He waited until the closest turned a corner and disappeared. He then motioned and led the tribesmen stealthily across the street and behind a line of shops, all lightless and empty. They waited again until another soldier passed out of view. They crossed another street, and finally they were behind the first Jewish home.

The house was dark, but the back door was easily pried open. Calabar closed his eyes, said a small prayer, then put his shoulder into the door. It fell open and the people in the house jumped up. A woman tried to scream. A tribesman was on her, his hand over her mouth, a knife at her throat. Calabar grabbed the lantern on the table. With one hand, he advanced the wick so that the almost invisible flame grew; with the other he pressed his index finger to his mouth. "Shhhh!"

He pulled a letter from his pocket and motioned the father to come and read by the lantern light. The man, terrified, did so, read it twice, looked up as if he could not believe the words there. Calabar nodded and then instructed him quietly to gather a few things and follow his men out. The man's wife and their two sons did as they were told. They slipped through the back door and toward the boats.

The next house and the next followed similar patterns. The fourth house, however, had an elderly matriarch who could not walk on her own, and the Portuguese had done nothing to help her condition, or that of her family. But Calabar kept his frustration in check, helped the woman to a stretcher that the family had constructed when they needed to move her, and directed two tribesmen to carry her back to the boats.

As they were slipping out the back door, the woman's granddaughter dropped her doll. She tried to turn back to get it, but Calabar blocked her path. She could not be allowed to delay the family's departure.

She had to go, *now*. Calabar did not like the movement of Portuguese troops in the streets. As careful and quiet as they had been, Olinda was beginning to rouse. More soldiers began to drift into the area, attracted and curious about the faint but uncommon noises and disruptions coming from there.

"No, sweet one," Calabar whispered to the little girl. "Go with mama!"

The girl pouted but allowed herself to be drawn away.

The next house was not so easy. The man had a pistol which he pulled from beneath a broken slat in the floor. He aimed it at Calabar, tried cocking the hammer. Calabar swung with his own pistol swiftly. Struck in the jaw, the man stretched his length upon the ground.

His wife screamed, running at Calabar with her small fists curled up and ready to strike, but a tribesman pulled her away. They dragged the man out behind her. There would be no reading a letter to them.

But the commotion brought the Portuguese soldiers directly to the house. A soldier began to beat on the door. Calabar motioned a tribesman over, then opened the door abruptly: the tribesman put a spear through his chest. The soldier fell forward, tried to scream, but a knife across his throat silenced him.

Another soldier appeared behind his dead companion, raised his gun and fired. The tribesman with the knife fell, a gaping wound in his own chest. Calabar shot the soldier, who fell limply before he could charge the door.

Secrecy was no longer important or possible. Olinda was coming alive, and one family still remained. "Go get them," he told the tribe's leader. "I'll hold off the Portuguese as long as I can."

When they were gone, Calabar reloaded his pistol, used the muzzle to push open an unlatched shutter, discovered another Portuguese soldier creeping toward the house. Calabar waited until he was within ten feet, then fired: the pistol ball tore through his shoulder, dropped him writhing to the ground. Other soldiers fired back a mere moment after Calabar fell to the floor, reloading and considering his options. It was not possible to hold them off forever, but he only had to slow them down long enough for that last family to be secured.

He scuttled to the back door, found an unlit lantern, smashed it against the floor: oil spread across the weak slats. From his pocket, he fished out pieces of flint. He struck them together once, twice, three times until a spark hit the oil. The faint blue flames raced across the floor, yellow flickers starting up where the wood was already starting to catch.

He went to the next house and did the same. As the flames leaped up, the tribe's leader brought the last family behind the smoky cover of the burning houses. Calabar slapped him on the shoulder. "Get them to the boats. Now!"

"Are you coming with us?"

"No. I will hold them off. Go, get the families out of here. Once they are on the boats, leave. Do not wait for me."

The leader seemed confused, tried to argue. Calabar shoved his pistol into the man's chest. "Go, or you die!"

The man, shocked and wide-eyed, nodded and led the family away. Calabar watched them leave, then turned his attention back to reloading and scanning the massing Portuguese soldiers.

Fortunately, the fire had brought out a confusing rush of civilians as well, who were trying to organize a bucket brigade to keep the fire from spreading to other homes and businesses. Calabar ducked as a lone musket discharged; the ball blasted a jet of dirt out of the mud brick wall of the house against which he was leaning. He finished reloading, then stepped out into the open to get a better look. Across the street he saw a Portuguese soldier frantically trying to reload his musket. Calabar raised his weapon, steadied it, squeezed the trigger and watched as the young man staggered and then fell.

That attracted the expected attention. From several different locations, musket fire answered his own. He reacted by falling with a scream, feigning a hit in the meat of his thigh. Gripping his leg in apparent agony, he crawled back into the first house they had entered. Once inside, he kept low and flattened himself against the wall. He waited, waited until a soldier burst through the front door.

Calabar threw himself against the man, yanking the musket out of his hands and forcing the length of the barrel against his throat. The man fell back, slamming Calabar into the chairs and table. A lantern fell, its oil burst against the wooden floor, setting it afire. But Calabar did not let go, despite the flames, despite the terrified strength of the soldier. He held the musket tight and pushed the barrel down into the soldier's throat, held it there until he heard a brittle crackling sound of a crushed windpipe; after a moment, the thrashing stopped and the man lay dead.

Despite the heat of the growing fire, Calabar turned the young man over and looked into his white face. He wasn't much more than a boy. "I'm sorry," he said to the body, turning the musket over in his hand and hefting the stock. "I know you were just following your orders, but it had to be done. Go with God."

Without remorse, without regret, Calabar slammed the butt of the musket into the boy's face, again and again, until there was nothing left to recognize. He tossed the bloody musket into the fire, and, as the flames grew higher and hotter, began to undress.

Pedro Álvares walked carefully through the charred wooden skeletons and cracked adobe rubble of the burned homes, noting the occasional remains of Portuguese soldiers. All told, four homes had been reduced to soot, cinders, and scorched brick: a grim reminder of what had transpired in the streets of Olinda the night before. Matias de Albuquerque followed Pedro, surrounded by his personal guard of five men. Álvares proceeded slowly, looking for survivors.

"God's grace," said Matias, his voice dry and raspy, "look at it. The bastard will hang for this, I swear."

"They are gone, sir," Álvares said, kneeling down. He pulled aside a superficially blackened board, tossed it aside, and found a small doll, its little cloth dress singed, its wooden face rough and split by the fire's heat. "All of the Jewish families are gone."

And so too the Dutch. Most of them, at least. They had apparently slipped away from Recife in the night, on board Tromp's fleet. Some Dutch had remained behind: mostly merchants, a few farmers, and those with more Portuguese blood than Dutch. But where were Calabar and his family? Matias had ordered a house-to-house search in Recife for the *traidor*. He would be found and executed for all of his crimes.

Álvares shook his head, stood, and looked toward the protective wall of the town. He could not see the harbor from where he stood, but somewhere out there, far up the coast, Maarten Tromp's fleet was headed north, probably toward the islands of the Caribbean. Maybe Curaçao, maybe one of the Antilles. Where exactly, he could not say. That was the only part of the plan that he had not been able to figure out, and Calabar would not tell him.

Perhaps the Spanish would get lucky and catch the Dutch before they arrived at their destination. Álvares smiled and shook his head again. No reason to imagine the impossible: it would take an act of God for a sufficient number of Spanish galleons to stumble into the Dutch, who they had no reason to expect to be fleeing Recife at all, let alone in such force. Besides, there were too many good captains and cunning seamen in the Dutch fleet, and no matter what had happened in Europe to bring Tromp to Brazil in the first place, one thing seemed certain: the Dutch always survived to fight another day.

Matias, who had insisted on inspecting Recife before Olinda, was pleased that the Dutch were gone. When they had walked across the long bridge connecting Recife to Antonio Vaz, Álvares could tell that the man was elated. The long-standing goal of Portugal's captains in the Pernambuco had been to free Brazil from the West India Company and now it had finally been accomplished.

But there was a haunted look just behind the seeming satisfaction in Matias' eyes, a furtive hint of humiliation, anger, and embarrassment that he would not, could not, admit. Not even to himself. Because even though Matias de Albuquerque could stand proudly in the main square of Recife and say that Brazil was once again fully under Portuguese control, one traitor—a man that he had once respected and admired in spite of his mixed blood—had apparently escaped.

Álvares turned that fact over and over in his mind as he continued walking through the ruin that had been the small Jewish quarter of Olinda. Had he told Matias of his suspicions of what the Dutch had been doing, the entire matter would have played out differently. The Dutch would likely have been surrounded in port and eventually destroyed. All it would have taken was just one word.

Álvares pondered the power, the decisiveness, and the risk of that one unspoken word as he picked his way forward, fiddling with a silver ring on his right hand. It was an unspoken word that could become a de facto death sentence, if his decision not to utter it ever became known to Matias. Logically, it made little sense: risking everything for one small, intangible reason. He flinched his fingers away from the ring. But his focus upon it, and the fateful reason for his silence remained: *I did it for Calabar. For your— our—family. And for all mixed-blood peoples here in Brazil. All us mamelucos, both secret and known.*

There was a commotion ahead. Several Olindans had come to a halt around the last pile of rubble, pointing at something buried beneath it. Álvares went there and began helping the men push away the soot-blackened beams and stones.

Underneath lay a body, dressed in Dutch clothing. A man, his face smashed in, apparently, from fallen stone. Beyond that his clothes were nearly burned off. What remained of them clung, tattered and black, on his roasted, husk-like corpse. Álvares gently picked a few remaining locks of wet, gory hair away from the dead man's forehead, but the face was too damaged to recognize.

Nearby, rumpled and flat, lay a hat. Álvares leaned over the corpse to grab it. He unfolded it in his hands. Black felt. Excellent quality and still wonderfully smooth, despite the heat of the fire.

Calabar's hat.

"Who is it?"

Álvares ignored Matias' question. In the tight, balled-up hand of the corpse lay a small scrap of paper. Álvares carefully, with subtle motion, pulled the note from the stiff fingers, opened it quietly and read it to himself. Two simple Portuguese words were scrawled in the center of the paper. Two hateful, derogatory words. Álvares could not help but smile. He looked to the wall again, toward the harbor.

O Calabar, you clever bastard!

"Is it him?"

Matias' question could not be ignored again. Álvares stood, turned, and offered up the hat. He nodded. "Yes, sir, it is him. Domingos Fernandes Calabar is dead."

Up the Wild Coast

On the deck of *Amelia*, Admiral Tromp stood beside Calabar who was dressed in a poorly fitting Portuguese uniform and wrapped in a quilt. He had developed a small cold, shivering despite the unrelenting humidity of the Wild Coast. Through the early morning haze, the coast itself could not be seen. But Brazil was still there, far beyond those brightening mists, and it would always be there for Calabar.

"Excellent work in Olinda," Tromp said.

Calabar sniffled. "Thank you, sir. All the families have been placed on ships. No losses, praise God."

Tromp nodded, glanced toward the mist-wreathed shore. "I hate to leave it behind. Brazil, I mean. I'm not sure that the Company will ever find a paradise as rich and plentiful ever again. As many of the colonists bitterly continue to point out. But imagine what would have happened had we tried to stay."

Calabar could not imagine it. All he could think about, all he could see, were the four faces he had left behind.

Tromp turned toward him, a small inquisitive smile on his face. "What did Álvares want for his silence?"

Calabar shrugged off the quilt and let it fall to the deck. He leaned against the portside railing. "A silver ring. It was my mother's. She had gotten it from his father."

"He knew you had it?"

"No, but he hoped, and when he mentioned it in von Schoppe's cabin, I knew immediately what he meant. *Minha mae* gave it to me when I was a boy. 'Keep this in remembrance of me,' she had said, 'and someday it will bring you good luck.' She was right."

"Do you think he'll keep silent? Keep the truth from Matias?"

Calabar nodded. "He will. He's family. As far as the Portuguese are concerned, I am dead."

They stared out across the water. Calabar thought

of Celia, of Martim, Lua and poor, sickly Carlos. What would happen to them now that he was dead? Would they live in peace? Would the Portuguese leave them alone? With his death, perhaps Matias' need for revenge would subside.

Calabar's family would mourn his passing; of that, he was certain. Indeed, his concern was whether Celia could carry on, could endure it. Calabar prayed to God that she would. Besides, she was tough, resilient, just like his mother had been. She would survive because she had to, if not for herself then for her children. And someday, soon, he would return.

"You said before that you wanted to speak to me about slavery," Calabar said. "Can we have that conversation now?"

Tromp perked up, nodded. "Yes. I don't have many details finalized yet. It's a complicated matter."

Calabar shook his head. "Not to me. Not to those in bondage. It's a simple matter. Men and women being held against their will, forced to endure privations and inhuman suffering and work, want their freedom. It is a simple matter."

"I understand that, Calabar." His voice lowered and he seemed to be speaking to himself, as well. "Trust me, I do. It sickens me. I cannot speak for all of my people, but I can assure you, it sickens a lot of them as well.

"Now, presuming that the Dutch are allied with the Americans in order to work together against our common enemy—Spain—the United States of Europe will begin to change as well. They have to. The Americans' original constitution does not allow slavery, and I imagine that it will be untenable for them to have a strong alliance with any power that is not similarly aligned. There were murmurings even before we sailed into ambush at Dunkirk that Gustav was willing to accommodate himself to that requirement, and the United States of Europe is a power which Amsterdam cannot be at odds with, not if it is to survive.

"All that said, many of our own people may not wish to see the institution end too quickly. Or at all. They argue—and they are not incorrect—that the Spanish have slaves. The Portuguese have slaves. Those slaves are the basis of their economic power, and the WIC cannot reject that same loathsome institution without weakening itself, without drastically, maybe fatally, undermining its ability to resist those powers in the New World. Still, slavery *must* end; not only is it a moral atrocity, but it will be as fatal to our ability to succeed here as will Spanish superiority. So the question is: how? How do we end slavery and ensure our own survival?"

Calabar was not certain whether Tromp was asking him to answer. He had an opinion about the matter, but he waited.

"Given enough time," Tromp continued, "slavery will end on its own. The technological advances that the Americans brought with them through the Ring of Fire will almost certainly render slavery obsolete, needless. So, if we were ethically and innovatively lazy, we could simply step aside and let the matter take care of itself. But how many hundreds, thousands, of native peoples, of Africans, will be captured, enslaved, and die while we wait?"

"What are you proposing, sir?" Calabar asked.

"I have yet to find the right balance between justice

and prudence, Domingos," Tromp sighed. "Our first priorities must be to get the fleet to Saint Eustatia, get the people settled, and the first crops in the ground. Then we'll have the time—and enough safe months ahead—to think on it. And my solutions will be much dependent upon whether the Americans come to the New World. If they do, their forces and knowledge will begin to change the balance of power on these two continents, I am sure of it. From there, I can finalize a plan and a timetable to put an end to this wicked institution once and for all. At least in the Caribbean."

"What about Brazil?"

Tromp nodded. "That's where you come in, Calabar. I know no man who understands Brazil better than you do. You are a representative of its culture, of all its people: half colonizer, half native. And insofar as you understand the Portuguese foe far better than anyone I know, I believe you are the best man to help make it free."

Calabar perked up as if his cold had suddenly disappeared. "When do we start?"

"Again, I must ask you to give me time," Tromp implored. "We need to get the fleet and our people secure. Then we can discuss it in full. Give me a few months at least, a year at most. Then we'll be in a position to help."

Calabar nodded. "And what do I do in the meantime?"

Tromp rubbed his chin. "There's no scouting or military work for you right now. Our conflict with the Spanish here in the Caribbean will be more of a maritime endeavor, in which our primary objective must be to remain undetected, at least initially. So...no disrespect to you, my friend, but you aren't a seaman."

Calabar nodded agreement. He could not argue that point. He wasn't totally incompetent at sea, but he wasn't at home there, either.

"I know I told you that cropland would be scarce on Eustatia," Tromp continued. "The population is going to increase quite a bit, and that's going to make things difficult for a while. But I am resolved to find you some land. Perhaps not the choicest, but enough to get a good sugar mill going, if that's what you want to do. You can build a new home for yourself, your family. Then we'll continue this discussion." He found and held Calabar's eyes: "I give you my word."

Calabar rubbed his own chin in thought. If Celia were here, she'd caution him not to just accept the admiral's promise as gospel. And perhaps he shouldn't. Still, there was something in Tromp's steady, serious gaze that gave Calabar hope. There was sincerity there, and it told him that the Dutch admiral truly believed what he was saying.

But things can change, as his wife had so eloquently told him one evening in Recife. Calabar knew that if Admiral Tromp ruled the world, the slaves would have already been set free. But he didn't. Spain was still the dominant power in Europe and the New World. On the other hand, if Tromp was right—if these mysterious Americans were coming and bringing their machine-sorcery with them—it seemed quite likely that things *would* change.

But, Celia would have countered with, "Who could truly say in advance what those changes would be?" Changes for the better, Tromp seemed to think. He might be wrong, of course. But so far, he had proven a shrewd judge of character and an excellent commander, one whose viewpoint was more pragmatic than visionary. So if Tromp actually felt certain that the arrival of the Americans in the New World would reinforce the Dutch and hasten the end of slavery, Calabar was inclined to believe the man. Or at least, not to doubt that he had arrived at that conclusion through careful, sober consideration of what information he had.

Calabar picked up the quilt and draped it back over his shoulders. "Sir," he said, "I accept your call to action. I also accept that, for now, you have little use for my services. So I will sail to Saint Eustatius with you and build a new home for myself and for my family. And one day I will return to these shores and help you end slavery if God deems it so. Celia called me a child of Brazil. Álvares said I could be its Spartacus." He shook his head. "It is hard to know if these statements are wise or mere wishful thinking. Perhaps I will be more like Moses, leading my people out of bondage, yet never enjoying the Promised Land myself."

He chuckled. "I'm just one man, and I can only do what I can do. But Brazil *is* my home. One day, I will free my family. And then . . . I will free Brazil from the Portuguese. Or I will die trying." Calabar stood tall, saluted Admiral Tromp after the fashion of his own sailors, turned, and headed into the depths of the Dutch ship.

Part Two

August–November 1635

*"Please listen and answer me,
for I am overwhelmed by my troubles."*
—Psalm 55:22

Chapter 12

Bom Jesus, Brazil

Life was good once again. Or, at least, Matias de Albuquerque could find no immediate fault in it. A mountain of paperwork, yes. Too many soldiers and local merchants and political interests who, officially or otherwise, drew from the swelling store of coins in his treasury, certainly. But Recife was again in the hands of the Portuguese. Trade goods were rolling through the port; sugar flowed like water to Europe to accommodate its insatiable appetite. And slaves—fresh, healthy Africans—arrived in Recife monthly to meet the growing demand from plantations up and down the Brazilian coast, and from the mines inland and further south. Spain was in an increasingly difficult situation against the combined power of the Dutch and the so-called United States of Europe whose forces had arrived in the Caribbean, but happily, Brazil was far away from that turmoil, and Matias cared not a whit about it. Brazil was thriving, and may the Lord keep it so.

If he thought about it for any length of time, he was quite glad that the Dutch had slipped away in the night. In retrospect, if he had known about their plans ahead of time, he might have let them go freely, just like the Dutch fleet had been allowed to escape Bahia some years ago during another conflict. But that was, after all, the perfect vision of hindsight. Just a year ago, the political will was, and would logically have always been, against allowing Tromp's fleet to go. The possibility of catching it unawares in port, and burning it to the last mast, had promised too great a victory to ignore.

But now, given the outcome for the Pernambuco, had he done the unthinkable and let them leave uncontested, why, the king might have called Matias back to Lisbon to rain praise and plaudits down upon him. He would have been declared a hero of the state, and perhaps bestowed large tracts of land, or more. Matias sighed. *Opportunities lost*, he thought as he finished the last swallow of wine before returning to his papers. But no regrets, for at least, in his little corner of paradise, things were wonderful, if not a little tedious. And who cared if Madrid was still angry with him for having failed to detect and disrupt Tromp's plans to leave Recife? He never cared for Spanish wine anyway.

A knock came at his door, followed by a meek voice. "My lord, you have a visitor."

"Who is it, Filipe?"

A boy pushed the door open and shuffled in a few paces. He was a small lad, dark-skinned, African descent. Matias had given him the name Filipe. He always liked that name. "My lord, a physician from Recife is here to see you. A Dutchman."

"A physician?" Matias raised his brow. "Why?"

Filipe shook his head. "I do not know, my lord. But he says that it is urgent. He has visited four times this week begging admittance. We have turned him away each time, but he is very persistent. Shall I turn him away again?"

Some of the Dutch had elected to stay in Recife when their countrymen departed. At first, Matias had wanted to round them up and lock them away, to make room for Portuguese professionals, who, in his mind, deserved to be enriched by the local commerce before all others. But Pedro Álvares had convinced him to stay his hand, urging restraint. "You have won, Matias," he had said. "Why aggravate the situation any further? Show compassion, and perhaps they will become dedicated Brazilians in the service of their Lord." Perhaps those hadn't been his exact words, but if not, it had still been some similarly annoying, albeit ultimately profitable, exhortation to show mercy.

"Check the Dutchman for weapons," Matias said, waving his hand at his servant, "then let him in under guard."

Filipe bowed quickly and left. He returned a few minutes later with a guard and a tall Dutchman, richly dressed, politely holding his felt hat.

"What is your name, sir?" Matias asked, setting his paperwork aside.

"Bram Erckens, my lord," the man said. "I am a physician with a small practice in Reci—"

"I am aware of that. What service do you offer to me, to the Portuguese crown, today?"

Erckens smiled. "I can serve you today with information. Information that I am certain you will want."

"What information?"

The Dutchman cleared his throat and said, "Three times now, a young man calling himself Raúl has visited me. Each time, he purchases a powder that I administer to patients for nausea and dizziness. The amount he purchases varies, but it is the same powder every time."

Matias waited, then shook his head. "Why does this concern me?"

"Because the man's name is not Raúl, I'm certain of that. I do not know his real name, but I'm equally certain that he assisted Domingos Fernandes Calabar during the Dutch exodus."

Matias stopped breathing. *Calabar.* He hadn't heard that traitor's name in almost a year. He was embarrassed to admit that, on his better days, he had forgotten the swine, now that he was dead. But this young man, this "Raúl": he had to be Luiz Goncalves.

"For whom is this man purchasing the medicine?" Matias asked.

Erckens shook his head. "I do not know, but this powder is not a mild remedy, my lord. It is strong. Whoever it is for, that person is very sick."

Matias rose from his chair. He gritted his teeth, his face reddening. "You are a physician, sir. You did not bother to ask this Raúl who he was purchasing it for?"

The man shrunk under Matias' angry gaze, then straightened and said, "Forgive me, my lord, but I did inquire upon his third visit, yes. He told me it was for his mother, suffering from a stomach affliction, but I found his manner unconvincing. I offered to see her—without consideration of a fee, in fact—but he declined and rushed out. So, although I do not know who he is purchasing it for, I still thought you might wish to know, since I supposed it was possible that he might be getting it for Calabar himself."

Matias slowly sat back down. He took a few deep breaths, forcing his anger away. He stared at the physician. The fact that this man would come to tell him of this matter was comforting, but how far could he be trusted? He was a Dutchman after all, and in the end, did he not hold some residual pride and loyalty for his own country? Clearly, he did not care about some useless mameluco dog, such as Calabar, but to betray the man that had helped his own countrymen escape . . . well, perhaps Pedro had been correct: show tolerance, kindness, and gain an informant.

"I thank you, sir, for the information." Matias offered a few coins across the desk. Erckens took them humbly. "If this young man returns, you will alert me immediately."

"Certainly, my lord."

Matias nodded. "Filipe will see you out now."

When they left, Matias flung his paperwork across the room. So, Luiz had not left with Tromp's fleet, as was largely suspected and as Matias had hoped. Did it matter? In the broader sense, no. If Luiz, the cast-off bastard of a bush-dwelling *bandeirante*, had just faded away, never to be seen again, his whereabouts would be meaningless. But he was here, in Recife, and actively buying medicines.

For whom? He certainly wasn't buying it for Calabar. That *traidor* was, praise God, dead. No; Luiz was using his alias as Raúl to buy it for Carlos, Calabar's son. It was no secret that Calabar's youngest was a sickly child, and rumors had suggested that his days remaining were few. But he was still alive and close, although still in hiding. And where Carlos was hiding, so too were Celia and the rest of the children.

"Filipe!"

The boy appeared instantly at his door. "Yes, my lord."

"Find Pedro Álvares, and bring him to me . . . now!"

Chapter 13

Overlooking Oranjestad Bay, St. Eustatia

Calabar wiped sweat from his dirty face as he climbed down the ladder. A Dutch boy who had come with them from Recife offered up a ladle of cool water.

"Care for a drink, sir?" he said politely. The smile on his face was as bright as the sun.

Calabar took the ladle happily and downed the water in one gulp. He took another, and another, then offered one to the boy, who shook his head. "No, thank you, sir. Will there be anything else for the day?"

Calabar looked up into the noon sky. There was much daylight left and still much to do, but the boy had been at it since dawn, and his father didn't like him spending all his time at Calabar's meager plantation, while his family's own much larger homestead lay waiting for attention.

Calabar patted the young lad on the shoulder and handed him a few copper *pennings*. "Go on, Diederik. And tell your father I said 'thank you.'"

The boy nodded, fixed his broad-brimmed hat, and was gone.

Calabar breathed deeply. He could smell the salt from Oranjestad Bay; he was that close, and thankful for that. He enjoyed waking up every morning and looking out over the water, breathing deeply and smelling the fresh air, and then watching the sun set every evening. Of course, he wanted a bigger plantation, but he was hardly in a position to complain.

He had thirty acres of land, given to him grudgingly by Diederik's father at the behest of Admiral Tromp. *For dedicated service to me and to the West India Company*, so said the good admiral, who had followed that up with a handsome sum of guilders as starting capital for food, supplies, and oxen to power an old *trapiche* mill that had seen better days. Such a wonderful gift was more than Calabar could have asked for after their dangerous flight from Brazil. He had accepted all of Tromp's gifts humbly, and his gratitude had not dimmed.

But it had been over a year since they had arrived on Saint Eustatia, and he hadn't spoken to or seen Admiral Tromp in months. In fact, he hadn't seen his friends Peg Leg Jol or Moses Cohen Henriques almost as long. The missions and objectives of the Dutch and their slightly larger fleet were focused elsewhere and did not include Calabar.

Of course, that was in keeping with what Tromp had envisioned in the immediate future, first in the governor's kitchen in Recife and then later at the start of their voyage from Recife. Indeed, how could Calabar's service to the Dutch undergo any dramatic change once they arrived on the island? How could

Calabar possibly establish a new sugar plantation if he was always running off on errands for Tromp and the WIC? But still, it had been a year, and things were not running or progressing either as swiftly or smoothly as Calabar had hoped.

He was building his house. Generous merchants from Oranjestad had given him building materials on loan: hardwood, some red brick, stone known as coral rag, and linseed oil-based paint. But they expected him to pay for it all within a year, and the money was nearly gone. He had a part-time foreman and five runaway slaves working his cane field, his *trapiche*, and a small personal garden of radishes, cabbage, and peppers.

It was both gratifying to think of all he had achieved, and yet difficult not to allow the associated frustrations to overwhelm him. Trying to focus on the former, Calabar walked down the dirt path to his cane field.

It was the hottest time of the day, and so he allowed his workers time off to rest, gather their strength, and come back in the evening to finish whatever they needed to do. His foreman didn't approve. Calabar didn't care. He had seen how African slaves were treated in the Pernambuco. He had seen them worked to death in the relentless Brazilian heat. The speed with which slaves weakened and died was staggering there, and yet, few seemed to care. There seemed to be an endless flow of fresh labor coming from across the Atlantic all the time, and for many landowners, it ultimately cost more to maintain field slaves over years than it did to work them hard until they died, thereby taking any thoughts of flight or rebellion with them into their shallow graves. In the Caribbean, the Spanish were no less dependent upon such cheap and expendable labor. Even the Dutch had them, though their numbers were smaller. *But I won't. Never!*

Calabar pulled his machete from his belt and cut a stalk. He squeezed it tightly, letting the juice drop onto his tongue. God, but he loved it. Every stalk, every acre. This was what he was born to do. This was the talent that God had granted him. His talent for waging war and for scouting was for the benefit of others: for the Portuguese, for the Dutch, for those who could not settle their problems without shedding blood. But his talent for growing cane and for managing a plantation was personal, was for him and for the benefit of his family.

His family: memories of faces suddenly seemed more real than the cane breaks around him. *Celia.* The thought of her made him weak. Lua. Martim. Carlos. Poor, sick little Carlos. Were they safe? Healthy? Happy? He stared out past the cane, back toward the southward rolling sea.

Upon arriving at St. Eustatia, he had immediately sent word back to Luiz in a letter only that young man could have interpreted, saying that all was well. Calabar had gotten a response from Luiz a few months afterwards, but nothing since: no answer to the many letters that had followed.

Ultimately, Calabar stopped writing altogether, fearing that his messages were being intercepted by Matias or his henchmen. There was no way to be sure of it, but he could not risk endangering Celia and the children even more: their lack of response might well mean that his letters were no longer being put in Luiz's hands, but those of Calabar's—and therefore, his family's—enemies. As far as he knew, his wife was still unaware that he was alive, and for now, that was for the best, though it was painful to keep the truth from her.

What he needed now was to get them all out, including Luiz, and soon. But how? How could he depart now? There was so much more to do, and so much which made it imperative that he succeed here, on this small bit of land. How could he leave his small farm without risking that it would fail in his absence?

"Calabar!"

His foreman, Willem Dircksens, approached from the tree line. He was a short, pudgy man, muscular and amiable. He served Diederik's family, had done so for nearly a decade, and had volunteered to work with Calabar when able, which was not as often as Calabar liked.

"How goes it?" Calabar asked as he accepted Willem's hand. "What did he say about the land?"

The pained expression on his foreman's face told Calabar everything he needed to know. Willem sighed, averted his eyes, and said, "I'm afraid to say that he's decided not to sell to you. He says he can get twice as much as you are offering for that land. Additionally, he pointed out that you haven't settled your payment with him for the coral stone."

"Lies on both accounts," Calabar spit, throwing down the hacked sugar cane. "He gave me a full year to settle on the stone—you heard him yourself—and he told me not a week ago that my price for those fields was reasonable. Now he is reneging on the deal? Those additional acres allow me to build better living quarters for my workers, Willem, and gives me access to more tillable, profitable land. It gives me *options*.

Options to plant more cane, to make more money, so that I *can* pay them all back. He's doing this because of who I am, isn't he? He's declining because of my skin. A white man comes along and suddenly the mameluco dog's money is no good? Son of a bitch!"

Willem put his hands up in peace. "Please, Calabar, I beg you. Show restraint. I'm on your side, you know that, but take caution in your tone. You are well-respected here, but some of these men, well, they have slaves in their fields with lighter skin than yours. It is hard for them to accept you as an equal. Things are changing, you know that, but it will take time. Be patient. He'll come around. When he can't sell that land for what he claims he can, he'll come back to you. I'm sure of it."

I don't have *time*, Calabar almost said aloud. *I need that land...now!*

Willem continued reluctantly. "I must also point out that you are running out of money, and our next yield will likely not bring in the revenue you need. Now, I know we have had this discussion before, but I implore you to reconsider: you need to stop paying the men their weekly stipend."

"I will not have slaves!"

Willem shook his head. "You do not have to be a cruel master. You may feed them and board them generously. You may treat them kindly. But you cannot afford to keep them as indentured servants. Doing so is forcing you to get by with a smaller labor force, but you must have *more* labor if you want to be competitive with other owners on this island. Your...economic viability is lessening by the week. Your competitors see this, Calabar, and they are just waiting until you default on your payments. And then, they will seize your property."

"Diederik's father would be the likely person to take it," Calabar said. "It was his to begin with."

Willem nodded. "Perhaps, but there are others out there, waiting. So I implore you, sir, please reconsider treating, and paying, your workers as if they were indentured servants. It is hurting your cause."

Calabar wanted to lay into the cane with his machete, to cut a deep swath through his field, to crush it under his boots, just to show the world that it was his land, his cane, and he could do whatever he wanted with it, and no hateful, deceitful white men were going to tell him otherwise.

But instead, he closed his eyes, took a deep breath, ran his hand through his thinning hair, and took a step back. *Still, I will* never *have slaves . . .* "You're right, Willem. I thank you for your concern. I will consider your advice." He gave his foreman a brief smile. "Will you kindly see to the men, determine if they need anything, and if you wish, you may put them back to work by three this afternoon."

Calabar said nothing else. He turned and walked back up the path to his house, half-built and surrounded by piles of stone and wood that he had yet to pay for.

He found the bucket of water and ladled out another drink. He drank slowly this time, savoring every drop. Then he dropped the ladle into the bucket.

Oh, Celia, what am I going to do?

A boy, running fast, came up the narrow cart track that joined his farm to the Oranjestad road. Calabar stepped aside to give him room to stop. The boy skidded to a halt and offered Calabar a note. "For you, sir."

"Who is it from?"

The boy shook his head, turned, and headed back down toward the road.

Calabar read the note once, twice. It wasn't from Celia or Luiz, sadly, but he had been expecting this reply for months.

Why had it taken so long?

St. Eustatia, Oranjestad Bay

The water was warm, as always, even at midnight, with gathering clouds and the threat of rain. Calabar gasped for air as he finished his swim. He reached out and touched the hull of the ship, thought about hitting it, as if that might alert those tucked away behind its treated planks.

He didn't need to, however, as the crew was expecting him. Lantern light caught his face as he crested the surface of the water, and the weighted end of a rope ladder was tossed down. He shook it straight against the hull and then climbed slowly, securing his feet and hands on each coarsely threaded rung until he was safely aboard.

He didn't recognize the men that pulled him to safety, but he recognized their captain.

"Moses," Calabar said, using his shirt to wipe the brine from his face and then wringing his sleeves dry. "It is good to see you upright and walking."

In the lamplight, Moses Cohen Henriques limped forward. With a big smile on his face, he wrapped his arms around Calabar despite the seawater. He squeezed generously. Calabar felt small in his arms, even though the man wasn't much bigger than he was. "It is good to see you *too*, my friend. It has been too long."

"I sent word to you months ago," Calabar said. "Where have you been?"

Moses pulled away. "I apologize for the delay, but I've been quite busy addressing the requests of our good Admiral Maarten Tromp. A most polite man, I must allow. Even so, I did not want to unnecessarily enter Oranjestad Bay lest Spanish eyes learn of our colony here."

"You could have at least sent a boat to shore for me. I'm not a good swimmer, even in daylight."

Moses laughed and tugged at Calabar's collar. "Ah, it's good for a man to go on a midnight swim once in a while. It strengthens the lungs, heightens the senses. Now come, to my cabin. Get dry and let's talk."

Calabar followed Moses across the deck. He looked around him, admiring the clean sails, the fine rigging, the pitch-scented planks. "This is a new vessel?"

"Yes, indeed. Not five years old, I would think. The largest patache I've ever seen. Courtesy of a Spanish rogue who now breathes salt at the bottom of the sea. I call her the *Sword of Solomon*. Do you like that?"

Calabar nodded, though he knew very little about King Solomon or what he meant to the Jews. The Jesuits who had educated him did speak often of events in the Old Testament, but Calabar had always concentrated his prayers and scripture readings elsewhere.

They entered the cabin, and Moses offered Calabar his best chair. "Don't refuse," Moses warned him, politely, "I would be insulted if you did."

Calabar took his seat, feeling an uncomfortable

squish as air and water pressed out the sides of his pantaloons. Luckily it was a hardwood seat. He crossed his legs and leaned back carefully, enjoying the comfort.

Moses poured healthy amounts of rum in two earthernware cups. He offered one up. "Fresh batch, courtesy of that same Spanish fellow."

Calabar waved him off. "No, thank you, my friend. I have to swim back to shore."

Moses laughed, tossed back one cup, then the other. Calabar watched as Moses let the warm, powerful liquid go down slowly and then took a seat. "How are you faring?" he asked.

"I'm surviving, though my life as a farmer is proving difficult. I'm being prevented from buying more land."

Moses curled his lip. "Why?"

"Because I'm a mameluco."

Moses leaned back in his chair and exhaled loudly. He removed his hat, rubbed his eyes. "I feared that that might happen. Admiral Tromp made his feelings clear about that kind of behavior, but he isn't around all the time."

"As is the case now. He's been gone for more than a month with most of the fleet, heading south. But you probably know that, already."

Moses nodded slowly. "I do."

"And so you also know that the up-time ships arrived three weeks after he departed and then headed south after him?"

Moses shrugged. "No, but I suspected as much. Before coming back to Statia, we spent almost two weeks scouting the waters around Curaçao, trying to find a way to make landfall. But the most savage 'Brethren of the Coast' are circling that island like sharks. We couldn't get close enough to go ashore in the northern shallows near Hato, the salt lake. Entering the harbor at Willemstad was impossible."

Calabar crossed his arms. "I am very familiar with impossible tasks. I am a mameluco asking for cooperation, or simply compassion, from the white landowners who hold my debts."

Moses sighed. "As I said at the outset, I feared this might happen. Old habits are hard to break, particularly bad ones that are expensive to put aside. Prejudice is everywhere, my friend. I know all too well. When the admiral returns, I will talk to him, see if he can speak to—"

"I don't want Tromp's assistance or anyone else's," Calabar said, more forcefully than he had intended. He lowered his voice. "Having *Admiral* Tromp force my neighbors to treat me better will only make them resent me more. I will fight and win my own battles, so long as the ground is fair and balanced. The Company has to change its policies. Until then..."

He trailed off. What was the point of finishing the thought? And why burden Moses with such talk? He was just one pirate—or maybe a privateer, now?— who held little sway with the Dutch when it came to financial and social matters.

"Let me tell you why I have come to you tonight," Moses said, leaning forward. "Admiral Tromp has completed a survey of Saint Eustatia, and he is concerned. The need to keep this colony a secret hampers our ability to resupply, lest the traffic be followed here and we be discovered. Once Dutch ships resume traveling to the Caribbean, such concerns will be moot, but for now, the colony needs more food, more supplies, more everything. I don't doubt your problems, but I wonder if part of your neighbors' intransigence is lack of basic resources. When food and equipment are scarce, men can become beasts."

"How will this ever change, Moses?" Calabar asked. "The Spanish are far more powerful here than we are, even with Tromp's fleet."

"You've seen the Americans', the up-timers', ships, haven't you?"

"The big ones that seemed to be on fire? Yes. From a distance."

Moses was smiling. "Oh, those ships weren't on fire, Calabar. They were using furnaces to boil water, to make steam that forces propellers to push them through the water. Like a well-digging screw boring into the earth."

Calabar smiled tightly. "I didn't actually think they were on fire, Moses."

"So: Tromp has told you about them?"

"A little," Calabar nodded. "Shortly after we arrived. Some of the colonists here arrived a few weeks after you reached Recife. They had news, or at least rumors, of the strange engines with which the up-timers propel their ships. Have you met or seen these Americans yourself?"

"No, but apparently they are not the devils or the angels that some would like them to be. They are people, like you and me, but those ships are not just large and powered by engines. They are far more powerful than anything the Spanish can float. Once they commit to battle, things will change, and Eustatia will be able to live openly in peace and, God willing, free."

That will be a wonderful day, Calabar thought. He admired Moses' enthusiasm and his oration. If things had turned out differently in life, the pirate might have been a good public speaker. Or a rabbi. He had a soft, but powerful voice, and his enunciation was superb. When he spoke, it was difficult not to listen.

"So," Calabar said, "why have you come to see *me*?"

Moses' expression grew even more serious. "I need you, Calabar. Tromp needs you. He has asked me to do what I do best: raid. All along the Spanish Main, supported by safe harbor in any Dutch port. Now that the up-time fleet is here and preparing to engage, I am to keep the Spanish occupied in the heart of their empire by raiding, pillaging, stealing: everything a good pirate can do."

Calabar shook his head, leaned forward in his chair. "You don't need me for those things. You and your crew are more than capable of doing all that on your own. I'm a farmer now, Moses. I have a plantation to build for my family. I have to finish that first, and then I have to get them out of Brazil."

"Domingos, not five minutes ago, you were telling me of all your troubles here. Do you not need money and food? Wouldn't more of both go a long way toward relieving your problems? And the action upon which I am embarked is just as important to your survival as that of the rest of Saint Eustatia."

"Still. I can't abandon my mill. My neighbors will steal it from me."

"No, they won't."

Moses stood and walked across the room. From a drawer in a small table near his bunk, he produced a folded letter, bearing the seal of the West India

Company. He handed it to Calabar. "The Company will take hold of your property while you are in service to Admiral Tromp. Your debts will remain frozen until your services to the Dutch Admiralty and to the Company are complete. Which, I personally promise, will not be long. You'll be back walking through your cane by year's end."

Year's end? Calabar did the math. Four months. So much time away. *Too much* time away. How could he possibly do it? "Who will take care of it while I'm gone?"

Moses shrugged. "Whoever you wish. Your foreman, those runaways you have under employment. Who do you trust?"

Calabar stood and went over to the small bank of windows at the stern of the ship. It was not, properly speaking, a "great cabin," but the view was wide enough to show him the whole of the dark bay. It had begun to rain. The waves had picked up. The ship rocked back and forth. *Who* do *I trust?* he wondered.

He trusted his foreman to run the plantation in a professional manner, that was certain, but could he trust Willem not to fall back on his racial biases and turn Calabar's workers into slaves? And what of the Company? They had guaranteed his rightful ownership of the land on paper, but would they have someone there watching his neighbors day after day? And what would they do if, by some chance, his primitive irrigation system broke? Would they even know when an acre or two was sun-scorched here, or a half acre was suspiciously overcome by vermin there? Who would have the authority and courage to act before his crop was reduced to what could be grown in the small rocky strip that ran along the bay? How could the Dutch authorities truly protect his interests if they weren't *there* to protect them?

Celia had once asked him if he trusted the Dutch. The memory of that question, and the persistent uncertainty behind his affirmative answer, now hung like the nighttime mists around Moses' ship, concealing whatever might lurk beneath the waves in the same way that Calabar's confident response had concealed his own reservations, then and now. Did he truly trust the Dutch? Was that where he had put his faith? Or had he committed to them solely because he trusted Tromp and Jol? Having never thought on his actions and resolution in so pitiless a fashion, he discovered he did not really know.

But he did trust Moses, and the eloquent pirate was correct: he needed money and food, and scores of other things. If he refused to help Tromp now, it was quite possible that no further personal assistance would be forthcoming from the admiral. And not because of spite or hard-heartedness; there were so many other hands constantly tugging at the good admiral's coattails. Calabar could not rule out the possibility that he might be forgotten like so much sand in the wind. If he refused to help now, his land might be taken, and furthermore, how could he ever hope to find a way to liberate his family from Brazil?

Calabar turned from the window and stared into his friend's big, hopeful eyes. "Very well, Moses. I give Admiral Tromp and the Company my services once again. When do we leave?"

Chapter 14

Antonio Vaz, Brazil

Pedro Álvares waited until Luiz reached the crumbled entryway of the ruined sugar mill. Then he seized him, grabbing the young man's worn collar and pushing him roughly against the dirty stone wall. "You fool!" he said, letting his anger get the better of him. He hissed the words like an asp spitting venom. "I told you never to go into Recife. Never! Why did you do it?"

Luiz was paralyzed by the ambush. He tried speaking. Pedro loosened his grip and waited. Finally, Luiz replied.

"I apologize, Pedro. I did not mean to cause trouble. But the boy I sent the first time got the wrong powder. It made Carlos very, very sick. I could not afford to have that happen again. I had to go and get it myself, to make sure it was the right medicine. I could not ask any of the Jesuits to do it, lest someone tell Matias that they are involved."

"Someone already told Matias," Pedro barked, but let go of Luiz's collar. "That traitorous physician who sold it to you. I should drive a spike through his head! He recognized you, Luiz. Now that arrogant half-wit Matias is asking questions and wants me to find the truth. He knows very little as of yet, but I just hope your blunder hasn't doomed Calabar's family."

Luiz straightened, fixed his collar, rubbed his neck, said, "I did as you instructed. I passed the powder to a courier, who gave it to another, and another, then to the drop-off point. The trail runs cold to the Jesuits, I promise you. No one knows that the powder is going there."

Not yet, Pedro thought, *but how long will that last?* "The deliveries must stop," he said. "We cannot afford to let Matias learn the truth."

"Sir, if they stop, Carlos will die."

The night air seemed to freeze in the burdensome truth of that statement. The powder was not a cure, but it helped with his symptoms. If the boy was vomiting less, he could eat more. He could keep his strength up. He could sleep better. And his poor mother would not have to watch him wither away in such agony. At least not so soon.

Pedro sighed deeply, lowered his head. His left temple throbbed. His eyes ached. He needed sleep himself. He cleared his throat. "Does Celia know that Calabar is alive?"

"I don't know. I have not spoken to her since I left them at the church. But she is a very smart, capable woman. I'm sure she wonders."

"She deserves to know, but neither of us can afford to visit the church now, and it is not something one should reveal in a note." He shook his head, trying to whisk away the growing headache. "Don't worry about the medicine, Luiz. It is my responsibility now. I will find a way to get the powder to our friends." He fished around in his pocket and pulled out several silver coins and a small rolled letter, tied up with a thin piece of twine. He handed them to Luiz. "I have one more request for you, and then you must disappear, must leave Brazil. Do you understand me?"

Luiz nodded slowly. "Yes, sir."

"Take these to a merchant in Olinda named Alvaro Cardoso. Ask him to give the letter to that French buccaneer with whom he trades Spanish trinkets. Tell him to deliver the letter to any Dutch captain who may know the name Calabar, so that they may deliver the letter to our friend of the same name. Go now! I don't ever want to see you again."

A tear rolled down Luiz's cheek. He nodded and disappeared into the night.

Pedro leaned against the wall and felt a pang of guilt work through his stomach. Those last words to Luiz had not come out right. He wasn't angry at the young man. Well, he was, but more importantly, he wanted Luiz safe and away from the long reach of Matias de Albuquerque. That's what he had meant, and he hoped Luiz would understand that in time. *I do hope I see you again, my friend. I do.*

There was a scratching outside the wall. Pedro dropped low, waiting to see if the sound persisted. He waited, waited, his headache gone, his heart beating rapidly. There was no further sound.

He stood and dared to look around the corner of the dilapidated wall. Tree limbs scraped the stone in the breeze. He breathed relief, fixed his dark hat, and made for his horse.

The headache was back, aggravated by the slow, sinking realization that everything was falling apart.

Off the northern coast of Nepoia Territory, Trinidad

It took time for Calabar to acquire his sea legs. He had been on ships before, of course, most recently with their journey from Recife to St. Eustatia. But that was different. He had developed a cold and was belowdecks more often than not.

But on this voyage, Moses insisted, and rightfully so, that Calabar serve his ship like a member of his crew. This brought him into contact with all the critical practices and parts of a ship: masts, sails, rigging, the cannons. Everything. Up and down the length of the hull, ever moving and ever aware of the incessant motion of the waves. For ten days, his complexion took on a decidedly pale—some said greenish—color. He and the portside railing developed a comfortable relationship, as Calabar hugged it tightly while vomiting day after day worth of meals into the waves. Another month had passed and, finally, he was getting the hang of it. All the while Moses had teased him roundly. "You are the worst pirate I've ever seen," he'd say, just as they would move into contact with an enemy ship. "You leave the seafaring to us, and we'll leave the killing to you."

They didn't leave the killing to him alone, however. In their dozen or so engagements with Spanish ships up and down The Main, eight crewmen had been killed in close combat. The *Sword of Solomon* had suffered

mast and hull damage. Moses himself had earned a
bloody slash across the face from a Spanish first mate,
who had been about to deliver the death blow, only to
be torn away by a pistol blast from Calabar himself.
"That's two lives you owe me," he said, winking and
finishing off another brave Spanish fool. Calabar's
arms and chest were tattooed with tender nicks and
cuts, and he swore a tooth in the back of his mouth,
right side, was loose. But they had fared well, and the
belly of the large patache seemed swollen with booty.
They were ready to return to St. Eustatia.

But first, they detoured to Trinidad. On Tromp's
orders.

They set anchor far off the northern coast of Trinidad, alongside a Dutch ship called the *Eendracht*.
Calabar asked Moses who they were meeting. Moses
was not certain, which is why he signaled his intent
to come aboard the Dutch ship.

Twenty minutes later, he returned and ordered his
crew to pack a skiff with all the Spanish muskets they
had acquired on their raiding. Then he and Calabar
rowed it to shore alone. There, they met three men,
two of whom were the whitest men Calabar had ever
seen in his life.

One offered his hand. "Aodh O'Rourke," he said,
flashing a wide mouth of mostly straight teeth. "Aide-
de-camp and senior sergeant to the Earl of Tyrconnell,
Hugh Albert O'Donnell." He motioned to his companion with a stiff thumb. "And this sorry son of a bitch
is Malachi O'Mara, my second in command. And this
other fellow is Jacob Jacobszoon, a merchant from St.
Eustatia. Perhaps you know each other?"

Calabar recognized the merchant immediately. He

and his wife had been one of the more difficult couples to get on the ship in Recife. Judging from the look on the man's face as he stared at Calabar now, he remembered that ordeal as well.

Calabar greeted them kindly, but warily. He faced O'Rourke and O'Mara. "Are you two . . . up-timers?"

O'Rourke smiled and huffed. "Not for a moment; we're Irish mercenaries: Wild Geese, or so we're called. *Up-timer* is a label you can rightly affix to our young commander, Eddie Cantrell, and a right good commander he is. You shall meet him by and by, I imagine. Assuming all goes well today."

"And what, may I ask, are we doing today?" Moses said, shaking their hands as well, but clearly sharing Calabar's healthy skepticism. They had been about to tack north toward St. Eustatia when Tromp's courier, a Bermuda-rigged sloop, had found and diverted them. Moses didn't like abrupt changes in course any more than Calabar. "Your crew on the *Eendracht* would not give details."

Aodh O'Rourke looked past them toward the skiff. "Did you bring the Spanish muskets the admiral requested?"

"Yes," Moses said, handing over the one he'd brought ashore, "all of them. Ammunition stocks are low, but there's enough to service a few good ranks. What are they for?"

"Come, I'll tell you." O'Rourke motioned them forward. They followed him and O'Mara up a narrow incline, up into more heavily wooded and mountainous terrain. Calabar enjoyed the walk, was glad to finally be on firm ground again. The smells of the jungle, the sounds of birds and monkeys, all made him think of Brazil and home. It was refreshing and he took it all in as they climbed.

After about a quarter mile, O'Rourke cleared his throat. "The Nepoia tribe here in Trinidad is in desperate need of weapons so that they may wage war on the Arawak. Who seem to be nothing like good neighbors, taking their land as they have. Tromp has agreed to trade them muskets for their permission and protection as our allies busy themselves taking off loads of pitch, and drilling for oil, in this lush paradise. But he also wants us to try to bring back as much food as we can wheedle as well."

"Food I understand," Moses said. "But pitch and oil? Why in the world would Tromp need those?"

"Well, I'm not the man to point out to a captain such as yerself a fleet's need for pitch to tar its hulls. But the oil—well, there we come to matters more rightly addressed to those who've raised them: these 'Americans.'

"As best I understand it, they know—according to maps from their own times—that oil can be easily extracted here on Trinidad. And it is oil that will soon furnish the power for wonders that surpass even those of Commander Cantrell's warships. The United States of Europe, and soon enough the rest of the continent, will be thirsty for it. And having control of its supply shall go a long way toward securing a strong military and economic advantage for our American friends, and for the Dutch and their allies.

"Now, unfortunately, the local Arawaks are a hostile folk. So much so that they've nearly driven the other local natives, the Nepoias, into the sea. Thanks to their friends the Spaniards. However, the chief—or rather, *cacique*—Hyarima of the Nepoias, remains leery of talking to Europeans. Sure an' he's more than enough reason to be cautious—"

Yes, he most certainly does...

"—but we need to make it plain that we are here as his friends. Hopefully, this gift of muskets will show him we mean well, and are willing to help him take back his land from his nasty neighbors and even the Spanish."

"Well," Moses said, "I don't know why the Nepoias would, or should, trust a Jewish pirate in these matters."

"Well now, in point of fact, we've no intent to task yer fine self with taking charge of that conversation," O'Rourke said. "It's more Mister Calabar we've been thinkin' of."

"Me? Why?"

"Well," O'Rourke began, "since ye're native to the area—"

"Trinidad is very distant, both in miles and customs, from Brazil."

O'Rourke nodded. "Well now, that's right enough, and I repent me poor choice of words. But given all the grand glowing palaver we've heard about your background, your heritage, and your relationship with Admiral Tromp and the Dutch, you're still the best choice by a long stretch of road. Ye've a far better chance than any of us at ensuring that this first meeting remains peaceable and productive. As I said, Hyarima has agreed to consider a trade for guns, and more food is a daily want on St. Eustatia. Hyarima himself will not attend this meeting, but shall send a man who will stand on his behalf, and who speaks Spanish. Or so I'm told. O'Mara and I have a reasonable understanding of the tongue, but—"

"I can speak it," Calabar said. "Fluently."

"Excellent! Then you're our man, right enough. If, of course, you agree to help."

Calabar looked into O'Rourke's eyes. He liked them. They were deep and sincere. But what kind of relationship could Calabar really claim with Tromp and the Dutch, specifically? The Nepoia would presume that he had the power to speak for those great powers, that his support of them was complete. But on the other hand, could he even refuse to help them, particularly in a matter that involved getting food for a colony that had spent half a year hovering on the brink of famine?

"I will help you." Calabar said. "St. Eustatia must have food."

O'Rourke nodded slowly, eyes still upon Calabar's own, perhaps wondering at the measured tone in which the other had agreed. "Thank you," he said almost solemnly, and resumed their inland march.

Another quarter mile up the narrow passage brought them before three Nepoia tribesmen, modestly dressed in loincloths and holding spears. They uttered a few words in their language, which Calabar tried to understand but could not, and then gestured that the party should follow them. As he and the rest lined up behind their escorts, Calabar leaned into O'Rourke, and whispered, "Why is he here?" He pointed to Jacobszoon.

"He's going to keep track of the amount of food negotiated per gun barrel," O'Rourke whispered back, "to ensure that it's a fair trade."

"How does he know what a fair trade is in this situation?"

O'Rourke shrugged, offered a hint of a rueful smile. "A fine and just question. Damned if I can answer it, though."

Their Nepoia escorts led them off the path and through dense foliage. Calabar and Moses had little difficulty navigating through it all. Jacobszoon and even O'Rourke and O'Mara had a more difficult time, falling back on occasion, thus forcing their Nepoia escort to pause and wait for them to catch up. Eventually, they broke into a small clearing.

Ten more Nepoia were waiting for them, all males, dressed similarly to the escorts, with spears and axes and even a few bows held at the ready. Many had beads around their necks, some wore feathered head-dresses, others with a narrow strip of bamboo slid through their nostrils. Some had bright red and white clay smeared across their faces and chests in precise lines. They had come in their finest, and Calabar was impressed. They were a beautiful people.

O'Rourke stepped forward, his posture fixed straight, his head raised in a position of authority. He spoke to them, through Calabar. "Greetings. We are honored that you have agreed to speak with us. I hope that this first meeting will not be our last and that the goodwill that we share here today will persist far into the future. May I ask who among you will speak for Cacique Hyarima?"

A man stepped forward. He possessed the most striking headdress, festooned with what Calabar thought were dark cormorant feathers, softened with light blue tanager down. O'Rourke nodded slowly in respect. Calabar and the rest followed the example.

"I am Sukumar," the man said in Spanish, "and I stand in Cacique Hyarima's place."

O'Rourke nodded once. "Very well. We recognize your authority in these negotiations, Sukumar."

Sukumar nodded back, then gestured at the ground. "Please sit, that we may talk."

All the principals sat, including two other Nepoia bearing spears who took places near Sukumar. Calabar sat on O'Rourke's immediate left, and Jacob Jacobszoon slightly further away to his right. The Dutch merchant kept sending disapproving and suspicious glances in Calabar's direction.

"Sukumar," said O'Donnell, "we are prepared to give you fifty Spanish muskets, with ample ammunition so that you may protect yourself from the Arawak and from the Spanish. In exchange we request that you grant us drilling rights at Pitch Lake and potentially elsewhere for the oil which Trinidad has in abundance in the earth beneath us. We have great need for this oil and would welcome any assistance and security that you might provide to us as we extract it."

O'Rourke motioned behind him, and Moses handed over the sample musket that he had brought along. O'Rourke checked to ensure it wasn't loaded, then handed it to Sukumar.

The man inspected it. He cocked the hammer, held it up in a shooting position, and pulled the trigger. He laid it in his lap and nodded agreement. "We have skill with firing muskets. We have taken pieces in the past from the pirates and buccaneers and Spanish that have tried to kill the Nepoia. But we welcome any help that you might give us in the *proper* shooting of this gun."

O'Rourke nodded appreciatively. "We are not planning to stay for very long, Sukumar, lest the Spanish colony here learn of our presence, but perhaps my second, O'Mara, can offer some assistance with that before we depart."

O'Rourke waited for Calabar to finish the translation, then continued cautiously. "We were also hoping to acquire food for the guns."

Sukumar raised his brow. "What kind of food? How much?"

O'Donnell shifted in his seat and looked at Calabar. "I will let Domingos Fernandes Calabar speak to you about that."

Calabar looked at O'Rourke, at the Dutch merchant, who was now staring at him harshly. "Don't tell them about Eustatia," Jacob Jacobszoon hissed in Dutch. "They cannot know. The Spanish here cannot learn of it."

Calabar cleared his throat, nodded humbly to Sukumar. He pointed to Moses who sat at the other end of the delegation. "My friend and I have been raiding against the Spanish for nearly forty days now, attacking their ships, stealing their gold and silver. We have acquired quite a bit of food for... for distribution among the few Dutch colonies and their ships. But it is not enough. We would like to..." he tried finding the right word "...increase our supplies."

Sukumar leaned toward Calabar, squinting. "You are not from across the sea, but still, I do not know you. Where do you come from?"

"Brazil."

Sukumar smiled and began speaking in Tupi, though some of his words were muddled and incorrect. Calabar followed along as best he could and even dared to correct the man when his phrasing was close, but not quite accurate. They had a most pleasant conversation about their respective homelands for a few minutes, but Calabar kept his story general wherever it touched upon what he had done for the Dutch and his changes of fortune in Brazil. He said nothing about St. Eustatia.

The Dutch merchant, clearly not understanding a word of it, scowled at Calabar as if he were the devil. "I'm warning you. Don't speak about Eustatia!"

Calabar shrugged him off.

Finally, the conversation returned to the matter at hand. "How much food do you need, Calabar?" Sukumar had resumed speaking in Spanish.

Jacobszoon tapped Calabar on the shoulder, tore a page from his log book, and handed it over. Calabar looked at the numbers. His eyes grew large, but he read them aloud to Sukumar anyway.

Sukumar's expression was the same. He jumped to his feet. Everyone followed.

"You lie!" he said to O'Rourke. "This is enough food to feed an army. You lie to me. You are here to deceive us. You may even mean to feed an army that will come here and kill us! The Spanish have done no less."

O'Rourke shook his head vigorously, waved his hands. "No, that is not true. Why would we give you guns if we expected you to turn them on us in an attack? I assure you, the food is not for an army."

Sukumar shook his head; the plumage of his headdress shook fitfully. "You are tricking us, offering a few muskets while planning to attack us with hundreds more. I do not believe you. We have been lied to before by white-skinned men who speak kindly and promise friendship, only to rape and kill us." He turned to Calabar. "You. I trust you. You tell me why you need so much food. And speak the truth. I will know if you are lying."

Calabar looked to O'Rourke, O'Mara. They didn't know what to say any more than he did. He saw no other option but to tell the truth. "It's for . . . it's for St.—"

"Stop!" Before Calabar could react, Jacobszoon had a pistol trained at his temple, cocked and ready.

O'Mara moved fast, pushing the merchant's hand away. They fell to the ground. O'Mara tried wrestling the pistol from Jacobszoon's grip, but the gun went off, knocking the Nepoia closest to Sukumar off his feet with a bloody shot to the shoulder. The man hit the ground and screamed in pain.

The Nepoia behind Sukumar raised clubs, spears, and bows and trained them forward. O'Rourke and Moses tried pleading for restraint, though their rudimentary Spanish was difficult to hear over all the shouting and posturing. Calabar tried to retranslate their words correctly to Sukumar.

The Nepoia leader, enraged and ignoring Calabar's pleas for calm, came forward with a knife drawn at the moment that O'Rourke tried to join O'Mara in pinning Jacobszoon to the ground. Sukumar drew the knife back and slashed at O'Rourke's back.

Calabar jumped in between the men, shielding O'Rourke from the knife and taking the cut across his shoulder. He cried out in Spanish, in Dutch, in Portuguese, and in Tupi, for peace, calm, his heart racing with fear. He expected another strike, but Sukumar stayed his hand, stepped back, held up his arms. His men halted, their eyes still wide and bright. At a gesture from their leader, they lowered their weapons.

Several long seconds of awkward silence followed. Jacobszoon groaned under O'Mara's and O'Rourke's combined weight, stopped struggling. Calabar offered a hand to help O'Mara up. Smiling, the Irishman accepted. "You saved my life, O'Mara. I thank you."

"Yeh did no less for me, Calabar," O'Rourke said, coming up beside them.

Calabar nodded, turned quickly toward the Nepoia, held up his hands to mirror the gesture of the other, and said in Spanish, "Honored Sukumar, I wish to give you personal assurances. We are not here to bring war upon your people. The request is exactly as Aodh O'Rourke has said. Guns for oil drilling rights and for food. That is all. And I promise you, on my *honor*, that the food is not for an army. I cannot tell you where the food is going, but I can tell you that it will be given to women and children in a town that can no longer receive their food from across the ocean. They must get their food here, in the Caribbees. No army will be brought against you. And if any of these men ever take up arms against you and your people, I will fight at your side against them. That, I promise, above all."

That drew an inquisitive look from O'Rourke, who seemed to be weighing whether Calabar meant his words. Calabar stared back, but did not allow his feelings to show on his face. *I took a slash in the back for you, but I mean what I say.*

Sukumar sheathed his knife and nodded. "Very well. I will trust you, Calabar. Food for guns. For drilling rights, I cannot agree to that now. That is something that Hyarima will decide. I will explain to him what has happened today, and he will decide if you are worthy of further attention. Much will depend upon you, Calabar. We will give *you* the food, and we will require that *you* help train our men with the muskets. You and you alone. Do you agree to this?"

Calabar looked at O'Rourke and O'Mara. They appeared anxious and genuinely confused; not the reactions of men who had come with a hidden agenda. From the moment he had met them, they had seemed sincere, and had not given him any reason to believe that they were not being utterly truthful about USE and Dutch intentions. Of course, it was still possible that they had been lied to by the representatives of those powers, but Calabar had no better chance of discerning that than they did. He had come this far; there was no strong reason not to play out his role to the end.

"I agree to your terms," Calabar told Sukumar. "We may begin whenever you are ready."

Sukumar nodded. He turned to his man who had been struck by Jacobszoon's foolish action. Luckily, the ball had been small and passed straight through flesh without hitting bone. The man was already sitting up and having his wound dressed. Sukumar patted the fellow's head, gave a small, reassuring smile, then turned back to Calabar. He then bent down and picked up the empty musket. He turned it upside down, stared at the stock, the butt, then said, "Very good. But there is one more thing I ask of you."

He thrust the butt of the musket up under Jacobszoon's chin, and pulled the merchant's head up until their eyes met. Sukumar spit into his face. "Get this *pedazo de mierda* off our island."

Chapter 15

Bom Jesus, Brazil

"*Açúcar mascavado.*"

Pedro Álvares stood before Matias de Albuquerque. "Sir?"

"Do you know what that is?"

Álvares nodded. "Of course I do. It is unrefined, brown sugar. Sugar cake."

"Indeed. But do you know what it *is*?"

Álvares did not know the answer Matias was seeking. He waited.

"It is the lifeblood of Brazil. The product through which all of this is made possible." He motioned around his office, to the silver wine goblets nearby, the paintings on the walls, the beautiful dinner table and chairs, the thick, rich rug on the floor, covering the smooth, polished hardwood. "All of this. I'm here because of it. And you are here because of it. We serve Portugal, but sugar cane is our master. Do you know how it's made?"

Álvares nodded. "I have a basic understanding of

the process, sir, but it has been a while since I've visited a mill."

"Then I will refresh your memory. Juice is removed from the cane stalk through pressers or rollers. It is then channeled into pots and cauldrons, and cooked and cooked, until the major impurities are skimmed away. A thick, brilliant molasses is made from that cooking, which is then put into sugar loaf molds to cool. Sometimes it's brown, sometimes golden yellow, sometimes red. The color depends upon the process itself, but in the end, it's always the same: *Açúcar mascavado*. It is then either further refined or shipped directly to Europe, and all of this—and a great deal of money—is shipped back."

He rose from his chair and walked to Álvares. "There used to be splendid sugar mills on Antonio Vaz. Do you know what happened to them?"

"They were destroyed."

Matias nodded. "By Calabar, that useless filth. When he first deceived us, he burned them. Stole our slaves, set them free, set fire to our ships at port. He took the trust we bestowed upon him, and like the devil himself, turned it against us." He huffed. "It is good that he is dead, no?"

Álvares nodded. "Yes, indeed."

Before he could say anything further, Matias pulled his pistol and struck Álvares in the mouth, sending him reeling across the room and into the table that he had just admired. The silver goblets flew through the air, crashing to the floor, spilling red wine everywhere. Matias followed and struck him again. Álvares fell hard; the fine rug did little to cushion his landing.

As if on cue, two guards came into the room and took positions near the toppled table and Pedro Álvares.

"You lie! We followed you to that ruined mill. We saw who you met there. You have been lying to me all along, and like Calabar, I believed you. He's alive, isn't he? And you have been protecting him and his family, and Luiz, all this time. Where is he, Pedro? Where is Calabar?"

Álvares spit blood, adjusted his jaw, and tried to get up. Matias held him down with a boot to his chest. "You will never find him," he said, chuckling through the pain. "He's long, long gone. Like the Dutch."

"Why did you do it? Why did you betray me?"

To Álvares, there seemed to be genuine hurt in Matias' voice. He looked up, tried to smile through his swelling lips. "There are more important things in this world than you, Matias. The world is changing, and your days are numbered. Enjoy all of these *things*, all of your wealth, my friend. You will not have it much longer."

Matias moved to strike him again. Álvares could see the rage in the man's eyes, but Matias paused. "Take him," he said to the guards, "to San Jorge. Lock him away, and may he rot there."

The guards picked Álvares up and dragged him out as Matias' enraged declarations became increasingly shrill. "I will find him, Pedro. I will find him and kill him. I will find his wife and children. I will execute them all! They will all die for your betrayal!"

Pedro Álvares listened to Matias' ranting as he was being dragged away. He was momentarily pleased to have finally—*finally*—brought so much pain, anger, and doubt to Matias' smug, comfortable life, and he hoped that the gnawing wound he had inflicted upon it would persist for a long while. Then the image of a small, sick boy came to him, and his satisfaction turned to sorrow.

O Calabar. I'm so sorry. So, so sorry.

Outside Puerto Cabello, Venezuela

Calabar held a flintlock pistol half-cocked and at the ready. There was a lot of commotion ahead through the thick foliage, and he wasn't sure who, or what, it was. It might be Aodh O'Rourke with his small group of raiders, ready to attack Spanish warehouses. But if so, they were out of position. Calabar shook his head and sighed. *No need to expose the men so soon, Aodh.* Although this jungle was somewhat different from the ones in Brazil, Calabar still knew how to move, how to scout ahead of an assault force without putting himself in undue jeopardy. These men, no matter how good they were on the battlefields of Europe, had a lot to learn about the bush.

Moses had left Trinidad shortly after the food from the Nepoia had been placed aboard the *Sword of Solomon*. Calabar had been left behind to train the Nepoia as he had promised. The tribesmen fared well with it; Sukumar had been right when he asserted that they knew their way around a musket. They knew which end fired, at least, which was half the battle. It didn't take long for them to develop proper skills. Their reload efficiency was less than desirable, but that would improve over time.

After the training, he had expected to be left on Trinidad until Moses returned to collect him and so, sail back to St. Eustatia together. Instead, only two days after he had finished training the Nepoia, he boarded the *Eendracht* with O'Rourke and O'Mara as it was preparing to set sail west along The Main. The young captain of the jacht, Floriszoon, presented him with a promissary note signed by the Statian merchant from which he had received the brick and coral rag for his home. The substance of the letter was that his debt to the merchant would be forgiven in exchange for further "indispensable services" in support of the *Eendracht*'s mission.

Calabar initially considered refusing. But then he reconsidered: obviously, this was at the behest of Tromp, and there was little to be gained by refusing a request from that benefactor. Especially this one, furnished as it was with a reward that the admiral himself had no doubt pried from the merchant with a considerable amount of both argument and political pressure. Besides, the reward itself would reduce Calabar's debts by half. So he agreed, met the commander of the Irish mercenaries (who also seemed to be a prince of some kind) and asked what service he was being asked to provide.

Calabar looked around at the nighttime jungle, and suppressed his reluctance at once again agreeing to help Europeans conduct their wars upon each other. But a deal was a deal, so he would do his best to help the Irish mercenaries conduct a raid against a sizable Spanish port and the supplies that had been stored there to support an incoming fleet.

Happily, he was not asked to lead the attack, as he had done outside Pontal over a year and a half ago, but rather, merely to serve as a guide, a scout. And maybe this time, he could do it without putting himself in too much danger.

He crept closer to the men that were waiting. Leaves rustled as he passed. A multibarreled pistol emerged from a wall of grass and bushes, and a voice called out, "Advance and be recognized."

Calabar smiled and stepped out. "It's Calabar," he said. "What are you doing this far forward on the path?"

"Being where I'm not supposed to be," O'Rourke answered, waving for the men behind him to rise and prepare to move.

"And why is that?" asked Calabar, who eased the hammer forward again on his pistol.

"Because if any of the Spanish bastards had caught you and indulged their taste for torture, I didn't want to be where you'd have told them we were."

Calabar nodded and whispered, "I'd not have told them anything. Not unto death."

"Which is as may be, friend, but I'll not be trusting the lives of twenty mothers' sons to any man's resolve when his captors start playing mumblety-peg with his fingernails. Or his manhood."

Calabar shrugged. "Very well. The path ahead is overgrown. It is not much used, possibly only by hunters."

"I thought Puerto Cabello was mostly home to fishermen," put in Malachi O'Mara from behind.

Calabar's voice was half-droll, half-annoyed. "As I said, the path is not much used. Aodh, are your men ready?"

O'Rourke nodded. "The oil and charges are ready, and the men are arrayed in their pairs."

"You've reapplied mud?"

"We've done as you instructed."

"And look like a horde of Moors, to boot," mumbled someone from farther back in the column.

"You mind yourself, you blue-eyed Moor," scolded O'Rourke, who kept his focus on Calabar. "Have you seen the warehouses?"

Calabar shrugged again. "Their roofs, only. I did not wish to go closer. But they are where Moses reported them to be."

"And you trust this pirate friend of yours?"

Calabar paused before speaking. Moses had not stayed long on Trinidad, and he had kept mostly to his ship, so O'Rourke had had little contact with him, other than the meeting with the Nepoia. He knew Moses, but he didn't *know* him, at least not well enough to take him at his word.

"He is my friend," Calabar explained, "and I saved his life near Recife. We've saved each other's lives a few times, in fact; so yes, I trust him. He is a pirate, but a selective one. He rarely takes a ship lest she be Portuguese or Spanish. Most importantly, no one knows this coast half as well as he does. His men were in Puerto Cabello only two weeks ago and saw war material being moved into the warehouses, saw the guards standing watch night and day, saw that most of the crews were being kept aboard their ships, not billeted in town."

O'Rourke nodded. "Meaning the Spanish are presuming they could receive orders to weigh anchor any day. Very well; we'll trust your Hebrew pirate friend." He turned to his men. "Blades, not pistols, until we leave the jungle. If we bump into patrols, we take them quietly. Once at the outskirts of the town, it will be guns and fast feet, lads. We'll not have much time."

The path to the warehouses was lightly patrolled, much to Calabar's relief. One unfortunate Spanish guard was relieved from his post by a knife across the throat; another was skewered through the liver by O'Rourke's own blade. Calabar was impressed at the immense respect O'Rourke commanded among the Irish soldiers of fortune who called themselves Wild Geese. Given their easy joviality on the journey to Puerto Cabello, Calabar had worried that, when the time came, they would not show the discipline needed to make this raid work. But as they drew closer to their targets, they became serious, quiet, and quite efficient.

Calabar held up a hand, waving O'Rourke's column down into the ferns at the edge of the jungle. Gesturing for the sergeant to come forward, Calabar pointed toward low, squarish outlines that were located halfway between their position and the sparse lights of Puerto Cabello, only six hundred yards to their northwest. "The warehouses. Simple frame construction. Recent. Almost certainly to house fleet stores."

O'Rourke scanned the bay. Ten large ships pushed their masts toward the stars. Half again as many smaller hulls rode at anchor around them. "That's not the whole fleet from Cartagena, is it?"

Calabar shook his head. "No. According to Moses, they're not all here yet. Those are probably from Maracaibo and Coro. The galleons—any square-rigged ship—have a hard time heading east along Tierra Firma. The current and winds are both against them, and they can't tack well." Calabar considered. "But the Cartagena fleet can't be too far off. A week or two at the most."

Calabar was pleased with himself. Forty days a pirate, and he had learned quite a lot about ships. He had always been a quick study, but life at sea was so much different than life on land. It was the physical equivalent of learning a new and unfamiliar language. But learn it he had and was now proud to speak so competently about maritime matters.

O'Rourke nodded. "Which of the warehouses are our main targets?"

Calabar shrugged. "All are worth destroying. Most only contain food and casks of water and wine, but after all, a fleet without provisions is hardly a fleet. However, if you mean powder and shot..." Calabar pointed at a smaller warehouse located at the center of the larger ones. Patrols moved in a more open pattern between the other buildings, but the guards around the munitions warehouse circled it endlessly, and in tight pairs. And they were armored.

O'Rourke turned to the men behind him. "Listen closely, lads. When we get close to the powder and shot stores, we're going to have to fight genuine Spanish regulars; breastplates and morions all. So don't load lead bullets. Iron's what we need. Double shot for the musketoons and the balls for the pepperboxes." He looked across the ground to the warehouses. "Assume they'll hear us coming at about one hundred yards, see us at about seventy or so, if we're running."

"We could crawl to the warehouses," Calabar offered.

"We could, but it's too easy for us to get spread out that way. When we attack, we have to be close enough so that our numbers sweep them aside and give us a direct line to the munitions. So we crawl the first twenty-five yards, then up and a crouching approach until we're spotted. Then kneel, fire a round, and charge."

Calabar nodded. "Let us do so then. Spread your men along the edge of the jungle. I have been here once before, so I shall lead the way."

Calabar led them down to the warehouses, first crawling, then crouching, then charging. They were spotted by the Spanish not too far from the first warehouse, at which point O'Rourke rose up and yelled, "Fire!" The roar of muskets and pistols was deafening—nothing secret about their attack anymore—but the fire shocked and halted the Spanish in their tracks. Calabar knew, however, that that would not last. O'Rourke was right: these were Spanish regulars, hardened men who knew how to take punishment and recover quickly. One volley would not be enough.

Calabar held his shot on that first volley. One extra ball in that wall of musket fire would be meaningless. He kept his pistol cocked and ready as he charged in with the rest of them. He wasn't required to; his orders were strictly to get O'Rourke's men to the warehouses, and then he could fall back if desired. He had considered it; he certainly didn't want to get wounded—or worse—in Venezuela, not with so much at stake on his fledgling plantation, and with his family still in Brazil. But seeing the flash of musket fire, hearing the roar of the guns, the shouting of men, the desperate fire in fearful eyes, a pulse of wild energy surged not only through his muscles but also into his heart.

Calabar spotted one stalwart Spanish soldier readying his snaplock musket, aimed his pistol, and fired. The shot caught the man in the shoulder; he stumbled and fell. Not a mortal wound, for his armor had absorbed much of the bullet's force, but one of O'Rourke's men finished the job with another shot in the face. That was a ghastly wound, and Calabar turned away, hid behind a pile of barrels, and reloaded his pistol.

He could hear a commotion around O'Rourke, who stood about thirty feet from his position. Sporadic gunfire obscured the details, but the conversation pertained to their explosives. Apparently the fuses on some of their bombs were soaked through. *I hadn't thought about that*, he admitted, finishing his reload. He had dealt with explosives in Brazil, especially in the early days when he had first turned on the Portuguese and was setting their plantations alight. It never occurred to him that these men might not appreciate how hard it was to keep their wicks dry in a rainforest. It was hard enough to get them to cover themselves in mud for night operations. But O'Rourke had another idea, and it sounded like a good one. They were going to hit the food stores first. All they needed to accomplish that was a good fire.

The thought of all that food and wine going up in flames gave Calabar pause. Too bad that their mission was a quick hit and run. With more time and more ships, those stores could have gone a long way to easing the problems of St. Eustatia. But O'Rourke had his orders. And in order to carry them out, he needed Calabar to help keep the Spanish at bay while charges were being set.

Spaniards were moving up from behind the munitions house. Some of O'Rourke's Wild Geese were trying to turn their fire in that direction, but Calabar had the better angle and position, and besides, their services were needed elsewhere. He could hear Spanish being shouted through the darkness, as guards streamed into view and moved toward better firing positions. They did not see Calabar, who waited until the closest dropped to a knee and sighted along his musket's barrel. He aimed his pistol through a small gap in a pile of crates and pulled the trigger.

The man went down with a ball to the throat. Instantly fatal, since he didn't yell out, either when hit or as he fell. The man behind him fell back in surprise, lost his footing, and tripped backward. The rest ran for cover, some of them wildly firing into the darkness.

The Wild Geese closest to Calabar saw this and fired as well, dropping a few of the Spanish, and driving the rest back to more distant defensive positions. Calabar loaded quickly and moved; no reason to give the Spanish a chance to find his position and retaliate.

He fired, moved, fired, moved again, and continued doing so until his ammunition ran low. In the darkness, it was difficult to know where O'Rourke was and how far he and his men had progressed in setting the explosives. But nothing had gone off yet, and so Calabar took a chance and moved closer to the warehouses.

In the faint light he missed a wagon rut and stumbled, falling face first in a pool of mud. He tossed the pistol as he fell, so as not to drown and foul it. But before he could think of rising, he went motionless, his face covered in muck, as three approaching Spaniards trotted toward him. They passed within a few feet, barely giving him notice. Just one more in a growing number of bodies.

Calabar held his breath and pinched his eyes tightly to keep out the muddy water. When the Spaniards disappeared around the corner of a small stable, he rose slowly, his eyes still closed. He rolled free of the mud, rolled until he was in the waist-high weeds growing in the narrow margin between back-to-back warehouses, then wiped his face clean with his shirt. But that was caked with mud as well, so only one eye came out clean. He looked around and tried to stand.

And was struck by what felt like an iron bar across the back of the head.

Thankfully, it was an off-angle blow, but still stunningly painful. Calabar had been in enough close-combat situations that, as soon as he was struck, he leaped sideways so as to prevent a further attack. This bought him a few seconds. Staggering away, he reached instinctively for the point of impact, felt a small cut, a welling lump, and a minor amount of blood. Shaking his head in an attempt to clear it, he wiped more mud from his face and saw his assailant closing.

A big, hulking Spaniard, dressed in fine armor, a morion fastened tightly to his head, and a long saber in his hand, blood flecked on its side rather than edge. He cursed, "*Muera, bastardo mestizo,*" and, with almost exaggerated care, swung his sword again. This time, it was edge-on.

Calabar ducked and reached for the hunting knife at his belt. He tried a counter-swipe, and nicked the exposed part of the man's hand, but did little damage. The Spaniard cursed again and stepped into another swing; although clearly a veteran, he was not a very accomplished swordsman.

Calabar ducked underneath the man's guard and thrust a shoulder into his sternum, which drove him back and down into the spot where the cart track widened into a full mud hole. As he fell, the Spaniard kicked up with his legs and flipped Calabar over.

Calabar gritted his teeth as the small of his back

scraped against rock. He swallowed back a cry of pain and surprise, and came up quickly.

The Spaniard was not so fast. The weight of his armor had driven him deep into the mud. He was fighting to break free. Calabar stepped into the muck and fell on top of the man. He tried driving his knife into the man's eye. The Spaniard caught the blade in mid-thrust, and held it tightly. God be merciful, but he was monstrously strong! Calabar had fought strong men before, but this man was uniquely powerful. Calabar couldn't help but admire the man's drive to live, and for a second, he regretted having to kill him.

Then hell erupted.

Explosions roared behind him: O'Rourke's munitions blowing up the first warehouse. The blast threw Calabar forward, driving him into the Spaniard's face and pushing his morion into the mud. He could feel the heat of the fires building behind him as splintered wood and banded steel from the riven building and shattered casks bounced around him.

Too mired in the mud, and in the veteran's one armed bear-hug, it took Calabar the better part of a minute to roll off his enemy.

The Spaniard had drowned, more on mud than water.

Calabar pulled the man's head out from under the sticky muck, removed his helmet, and looked deeply into the lifeless eyes. "*Perdon, senor. Usted peleó valientemente.*"

Another explosion drove Calabar back to the tree line, where he watched as fire engulfed the warehouses. As he waited for the blasts to subside and until he could get a glimpse of O'Rourke's attack force, he put careful fingers to work feeling, measuring the cuts and bruises on his head, neck, and shoulders. He was just thankful to be alive and that the raid had seemingly succeeded. Squinting against the glare of the multiple warehouses-become-infernos, he wondered how many of O'Rourke's men lay dead in that chaos of fire, mud, and blood. Too many, probably, but hopefully such a successful raid would undercut the power and reach of the Spanish in the Caribbean before they could find the Dutch at St. Eustatia. Before it was too late to save them.

Wait: "too late"? Mierda! I'm *late!*

Calabar, recovering while contemplating both his and the region's future, had forgotten how tightly timed the attack plan was. He jumped up, and taking cover by following the edge of the tree line, he made his way to the harbor, where he and the rest of the Wild Geese—whoever was left—were to gather and swim out to Spanish ships that the prince—O'Donnell?—and his men were securing for their escape.

One of the Wild Geese spotted Calabar as they converged on the rendezvous point. "Come," he said, in his deep Irish accent, "let's be off."

Calabar scanned the beach, glanced toward the burning warehouses. "Where is O'Rourke?"

"I don't know," the man said. "Come on!"

Calabar hit the water and swam like he had in Oranjestad Bay a few months ago. The thought of his prickly pirate friend warmed him, and he swam faster. He was anxious to see Moses again and to get back to St. Eustatia, and to leave this bloody war behind.

Back near the beach, more gunshots were answered by gunshots, screams by screams.

Calabar swam harder and dreamed of the taste of fresh cane juice.

Chapter 16

Igreja da Conceição, near Olinda, Brazil

"Break it down."

Matias' order was clear and unequivocal, though his men seemed reluctant to assault a place of God. "I said, break it down!"

Two men hefted the makeshift battering ram once again and struck the door, once, twice, three times. It cracked despite being a good, healthy piece of hardwood. They struck it twice more, and it burst open. Matias was the first through.

"Look around," he told his men, as he walked slowly up the aisle toward the altar.

It was a beautiful altar, and the walls were richly adorned with gold-inlaid paintings of Our Lady. Matias remembered coming to mass here many times, as a child and as a young man. His duties now did not afford him the time very often. A pang of guilt struck his stomach; not for his absences, but for the door he had left broken in his wake.

But this is necessary. Absolutely necessary.

Father Araujo came through the side entrance that connected the church to the rectory. He was in evening attire, a thin black cassock and a small cross hanging from a chain around his neck. He was an imposing man. Taller than Matias and a little thicker around the waist. His gray hair was thinning. He held a Bible and a lantern.

Matias put his hand on the pistol tucked in his belt. "Where is she?"

"What is going on here?" Father Araujo asked, neglecting both Matias' name and proper title. He swung his lantern forward to get a good look. His eyes fell upon the ruined door. "This is God's house, Matias. Why have you brought ruin to it? Why have you brought a pistol into my holy place?"

"*Your* holy place, Father Araujo?" Matias pulled his pistol and held it forward. *May the Lord forgive me.* "I want her, Father. Give her to me now!"

Father Araujo stood firm, hugging his Bible tightly. "You have no authority here, Matias. The Jesuit order is an autonomous entity, as agreed by—"

"You may file an official complaint with Lisbon, though I doubt your message will be delivered and a response received before I leave here with what I have come for. So I say to you again: bring her to me."

"Who?"

"Calabar's wife and children. You have them. I know it. Do not lie to me, Father, under the eyes of Our Lady." Matias grabbed Araujo's collar, pulled him closer, and placed the barrel of his pistol beneath the priest's chin.

There was a commotion behind the altar, behind the false wall that separated the back of the church from the sanctuary. A woman's voice, anxious, muffled but distinct. Matias backed away and waited.

One of his men came into the room holding the arm of a woman who struggled against him, flailing her arms, trying to pull away. He threw her onto the altar steps. Her gown was white, loose, and revealing. She had dark skin, but she was beautiful. Whatever else she was, she was most certainly that.

Matias knelt beside her. "Celia. It is good to see you again."

She spat at him. Matias closed his eyes and wiped the saliva away from his cheek and chin. He slipped the pistol back into his belt slowly, calmly, smiled, then struck her across the face. She fell backwards with a scream.

"Please, my lord," Father Araujo said, coming forward, one hand held up in an appeal for peace. "I beg you. It is my fault. I am the one to blame. I am a man of God. I help those who cannot help themselves. They were under my care and protection. Blame me and punish me if you must. But please, be merciful to them."

"Where are your children?" Matias asked Celia, ignoring Father Araujo's entreaties.

Celia recovered. She sat up, holding her split lip. She shook her head.

"I will *see* your children, or you will see the back of my hand once more."

"You will never have them."

Matias turned to his men. "Burn the place down. Start with the altar."

"Yes, sir."

One of his men took the lantern they had brought

and moved as if he were going to fling it forward. Celia put up her hands.

"Stop...stop," she said, tears streaming down her swelling face. She sniffled, several times, then called out. "Come, my children. Come to your mama."

Slowly, Martim and Lua emerged from the back of the church. Lua held a doll of loosely stitched rags and dried grass stuffing.

Matias smiled and motioned them forward. He spoke in a higher, friendlier tone. "Come on out. Let us see how you've grown." As they approached, Matias stood very straight and put his hands on his hips. "My, my, my, you *have* grown. Martim, you are becoming quite the strapping young man. And Lua, what a pretty thing you are. Close to marriage age, I would imagine, no? You will make fine babies for a man someday." Matias looked behind them and furrowed his brow. "And where is Carlos?"

No one spoke. No one had to speak.

Matias frowned. "That is too bad. I had high hopes for that one. But, it was not meant to be. What is that passage from the Bible, Father? *Then shall the dust return to the earth as it was: and the spirit shall return unto God who gave it.* So sad, but..." He straightened his belt, adjusted his hat, and said in a defiant tone, "I am glad to see the rest of you so well, but your time here is at an end. Celia, you are an enemy of the state. You have aided and abetted the traitor Domingos Fernandes Calabar, and for that, you shall be sentenced to death."

Martim and Lua began to cry. Father Araujo fell to the floor and wrapped his arms around Matias' legs. "Please, my lord. Do not shed blood here. In the name of God, show mercy. Celia has done no wrong in loving her husband. Her children have done no wrong in loving their father. How can you be a man of God and do such a thing? If you do this, Matias, God will strike you dead. He is watching."

Matias sighed and looked at the walls. Eyes, many eyes, abundant eyes, staring back at him, cold and unmoving. He looked down at Celia. She was lovely, indeed, and still of age to bear children, and to do good work for some man. But she was Tupi, at least partially, just like her traitor husband. Her life didn't mean as much, and God understood that.

"Very well," he said, kicking Father Araujo away. "For you, Father, I will show mercy. No blood will be shed here today." He turned to his men and motioned to the door. "Take them to Bahia and sell them to the slavers. Do not haggle; turn them over requiring but one condition: that all three are to be shipped *out* of Brazil."

"Sir, wouldn't it be easier to take them into Recife?" one asked. "It is much closer, and slave ships arrive all the time, and—"

"I said Bahia, damn you! I do not want any Dutchmen in Recife to see her. Some may be loyal to me, but I cannot be sure that all of them are. I don't want word to get back to *him* on where they were discovered and where they have gone."

"But . . . what price, sir?"

"Any price. No price. My only price is that the slavers get them out of Brazil. Now go!"

Matias dragged Celia up from the floor. He held her arm tightly. He pulled her close, smiled. "It was nice *seeing* you again, Celia. If you weren't a half-breed bitch, I might take you for my own."

She spat at him again. He pushed her away. His men grabbed Martim and Lua and pushed them out of the building.

When they were gone, Matias grabbed a handful of Father Araujo's sleeve and wiped his face clean. "She's a feisty one, isn't she?"

Father Araujo's stare was as sharp and bright as any murderous *bandeirante*. "May God show you mercy, Matias. I will pray for you tonight."

"May he show mercy on us all," Matias said.

He walked down the aisle, out the broken door, and away from all those staring, accusing eyes.

Tobago, Spanish Main

The ship that Hugh Albert O'Donnell had stolen at Puerto Cabello made rendezvous with the *Sword of Solomon* many days later along the Spanish Main, and Calabar climbed aboard. It had one more stop to make: Tobago, where a small Dutch colony had been established only two years before. Admiral Tromp wanted Moses to check on the folk there, and to give them some of the food, supplies, and coin that they had acquired from raiding. The rest would be taken back to Saint Eustatia on another Dutch ship that would be waiting in port. And Calabar was returning with them.

He was ecstatic, though he constantly daydreamed of Celia and the children. He would go back to his plantation to ensure the supplies were delivered and distributed properly. He would secure the needed acreage that connected his land to the bay, and then, as soon as it became possible, he would return to Brazil and see his family again, their bright, hopeful faces just as he remembered. He would bring them to the new plantation, and they would be safe.

Shortly after arriving at Tobago, he stood on the town's small dock, supervising the lading of barrels from Moses' ship to the other, when its Dutch captain walked down the boarding ramp plank and handed Calabar a letter.

"From Admiral Tromp."

The captain said nothing else. He nodded politely, turned, and strode back up to the deck of his ship, giving orders and directing crewmen where to stage the dunnage for proper lading.

Calabar stared at the letter in his hand. It had been opened and folded, and folded, and folded again, until it seemed as if one more fold would cause it to fall apart. The letter had traveled a great distance and had passed through many hands. It had gotten wet and dried. It smelled of sea salt.

He opened it carefully. His heart leapt. It was Luiz's handwriting!

But...the words were not his. These were the words of a classically educated man, one with an air of both propriety and formality, transcribed into an old Brazilian language that he and Luiz used on occasion to pass notes through enemy lines. Calabar did not know what the language was, in fact, and never asked. Luiz had taught him enough of it, however, for it to be useful for their clandestine endeavors. The language that Luiz had picked was too simple phonetically for the words that needed to be included, and Calabar could tell that the boy had struggled with the transcription.

Sentence beginnings were muddled, meanings were slurred, endings were inconclusive. But Calabar got the essence of it, and his heart ached.

He found Moses in his cabin counting Spanish coins. He held the brittle letter up to catch the irregular patch of light that eked through the small stern window. "I must go back to Brazil. Now."

Moses peered up from his counting, a look of confusion on his gray-bearded face. "What?"

"This letter," Calabar said, "is from Luiz. Celia and my children are in danger."

"What has happened?"

Calabar shook his head. "Nothing yet, but from what I can understand of his words, Matias is seeking them, and he may find them soon."

Moses stood up, shook his head. "Wait a moment. How close is Luiz to Matias? How does he know what Matias knows, or what he is doing?"

"The letter is from Pedro Álvares, I'm certain of it. It's Pedro who knows."

Moses' confusing stare grew worse. He shook his head. "Why would Pedro Álvares, a confidante of Matias, tell you that?"

Calabar was about to reveal the ties that bound them, then closed his mouth. He hadn't told anyone about Pedro and their familial connection except Luiz and Celia. What should he say to Moses? He could certainly trust Moses, but what if Tromp found out, or Jol? Would they care, or would they begin to wonder if Calabar's loyalties could be compromised by having a relative so close to Matias?

Calabar felt his closed mouth become taut: he had to remain silent. There was some of his personal business that no one—not even a close friend like Moses—needed to, or could safely, know. "I just know, Moses. I must leave it at that."

Moses shrugged, nodded, and leaned back in his chair. "Well, the transfer of goods and our survey of the colony here will take a few days. Then I'm supposed to put you on that other ship and send you back to Eustatia. Tromp has proposed another venture that will be advantageous to both him and to me. So, for now, this is where our courses must part."

Calabar frowned. Moses' words had become vague, indefinite as he had finished. Very unlike him. Sensing evasion, Calabar stepped closer forward. "Where are you going?"

Moses hesitated, averted his eyes, as if he were embarrassed with the truth. "Just some simple survey work elsewhere."

"Moses . . . tell me!" Calabar stuffed the letter into a pocket as he closed the remaining distance and leaned forward over the counting table. He glared into the Sephardic pirate's eyes.

Moses wiped his chin, pulled whiskers. He sighed loudly, grabbed a mug of rum well to the side of the coins, and took a drink. "Off the Brazilian coast, near my islands."

"And you were going back to Brazil without me?"

"Not Brazil. Off the coast. There is a difference." Moses stood, the mug of rum still in his hand. "Calabar, listen to me. Your agreement with Admiral Tromp and the Company ensures that your property will remain in your name and in your control until year's end. If you don't go back on that ship, there may be no plantation to go back to. So, go back to

Eustatia, take care of whatever it is you need to do, and perhaps within a few months, an opportunity will present itself to go back to Brazil. That is the right course of action here." Moses looked away, put the mug up to his lips to take a sip.

Calabar smacked it away.

The rum and mug flew through the air, spraying Moses, spraying his bed, spraying across the room. Moses fell back in surprise and almost lost his footing, but recovered quickly. "What the hell do you think you're doing? Are you mad? This is my ship, Calabar. I'm the captain. You don't knock a drink out of any captain's hand, and you most certainly don't do it to *me*. You'd best get control of yourself, my friend, or I'll—"

"You'll what?" Calabar asked, moving forward, his hand reaching for the knife at his belt. He chose not to pull it. Yet.

"I have saved your life more than once," Moses said.

"And I you, so do not hold that over me. This is my family we are speaking about. Do you understand? What good is soil back on St. Eustatia? What value sugar? What need, what desire, do I have for a farm if I have no family? I don't wish to hear about the right course of action. Eustatia is but a dream, my *friend*. It serves no purpose to me unless Celia and Martim and Lua and Carlos are there, too, safe under my care. So I ask you in the name of God and as a friend, *please* take me back to Brazil."

Calabar backed away and removed his hand from his knife. Moses eyed him carefully as he wiped rum from his beard. The pirate picked up his mug and set it back onto the table. He moved forward, his eyes never leaving Calabar's face. They stood nose to nose.

"Very well, Calabar. You may come with me. But let me make this very clear to you. You will help me complete my mission first... *first*! And then I'll take you to shore, and you may do whatever it is you wish to do, and may God keep you in his care, for I can do so no longer. I will not risk my men or my mission or Tromp's favor on this impulse of yours, no matter how much I, too, wish to see Celia and your children safely away from danger. And I do, friend. I do. Don't ever doubt that.

"But do not doubt my resolve either. We finish my mission first. Then I shall set you ashore, where you will have only your own wits and God's love to help you. Do you understand me?"

Calabar nodded. "Yes."

"Good." Moses turned away, took his seat, and began counting coins again. "Now, get the hell out of my cabin. And call me up another goddamned mug of rum!"

Part Three

November 1635–February 1636

"Blessed is the man who remains steadfast under trial, for when he has stood the test he will receive the crown of life..."
—James 1:12

Chapter 17

São Salvador da Bahia, Brazil

Matias de Albuquerque's order to his men was still clear in Celia's mind. *Take them to Bahia and get them out of Brazil. I don't want word to get back to* him... But who was "him"? Pedro? Luiz? Or was it Domingos?

The night raid on Olinda by Calabar had been over a year ago, and word had spread fast throughout Pernambuco that the remains of a mameluco had been found in the black ash of the Jewish houses that had burned there. The corpse was so badly damaged that a face could not be discerned, but Celia knew who it was. She knew in her heart. *My husband is dead,* she had said to herself over and over again in the claustrophobic darkness and cloying old-incense reek of the Jesuit church, repeated it so that she might burn the truth of it into her mind. She could not believe it, but she had to, had to accept the fact that she was alone in the world, and from there on, she and Martim and Lua and Carlos were on their own. Her children had no father anymore.

But that one word: *him* . . . Did she dare believe again? Perhaps Matias meant Luiz, but why would the most powerful man in the Pernambuco be concerned if an impoverished young man learned that the Portuguese had discovered Celia's hiding place?

Could Matias have meant Álvarez? Calabar had told her before leaving for the attack on Olinda that Pedro was his half-brother, but why would Matias keep the man as an assistant and confidante if he could not be trusted with such information? Indeed, if Matias suspected Pedro's deepest loyalty lay with Calabar and his family, then Álvarez was unlikely to live long enough to hear that Celia and the children had been found.

No, Celia almost whispered aloud, it had to be Calabar. It had to be. And she allowed her heart to believe it, and *feel* it, once more.

That meant that her husband had survived, and that he had left with the Dutch as he had planned. But if he were alive, why hadn't he returned to Brazil by now? Perhaps he was dead after all, or was still in the Caribbean, fighting Dutch battles, making a glorious name for himself while Carlos . . . Celia forced back the tears. For a moment, she grew angry. *How dare he not return to us. How . . .*

Then the swayback mare she was tethered to almost lost its footing—and she remembered her fate.

She sat on an almost skeletal horse, facing the rear, tied to both the crude saddle and her captor so that she could not fall off at a gallop. Her arms were tied behind her, a sack fixed over her head. It was hot and hard to breathe. Martim and Lua were being transported in a similar fashion, she figured.

She could hear them whimper from time to time, particularly as the pace of their travel grew slower but more painful over rough terrain. They had been riding like this for quite a while, stopping only briefly for a meager sip of water and a sliver of dried fruit.

Celia's legs hurt. Her back hurt. She purposefully tried falling off the horse at one point, but her bindings were tight, and her efforts earned her a sharp smack over her ear from her rider. Her children fell silent. She wavered in and out of fitful sleep.

They arrived in Bahia late in the afternoon. She didn't know what day, nor did it matter really. When they cut her from the horse and removed the sack from her head, she saw that her children were alive. That was all that mattered.

Bahia was a larger port than Recife, and many slaves were brought there from Africa. Celia knew this, for she and Calabar had traveled here in the early days of their marriage to buy supplies that they could not obtain in Recife. She remembered seeing those poor black people hastened off the ships and poked and prodded, then lined up to be haggled over like livestock, naked as the day they were born.

It had been so humiliating that she had turned away from it. But Calabar had stared at the horrid spectacle, his jaw muscles clenching, his eyes growing wet with anger. In those days, slaves were sold in Recife as well, but here in Bahia, the practice seemed more feral, more dangerous, as if it didn't matter if any one slave lived or died. They left that day, and Celia made Calabar promise that they would never return.

Yet here she was, now standing before a slaver herself.

He was a heavy-set, stoop-shouldered man. Doubtless Portuguese, though his attempt at shaving was what one would expect from a man who had grown up far from European customs, and so, had never seen it done properly. Celia could see new cuts and old scars across his cleft chin. His clothing was new, but he had dark sweat stains in his armpits that had turned his tan vest into dark umber. His breath smelled of rum and raw pepper.

He walked behind her, running pudgy fingers across Celia's shoulders. She tried moving away. Her captor pulled her upright and tight.

The slaver cleared his throat. "We don't take many natives anymore. Mostly Africans these days. Better workers. More docile. Easier to train. Natives are lazy and uncooperative. And these don't look like pure-bloods, anyway." He stopped and stared at Martim. "Who are they?"

"That is not your concern," said the man who had guarded Martim closely throughout the journey. "By order of Matias de Albuquerque, you are to take these three and get them out of Brazil."

The slaver huffed. "Does your captain realize that I'm in the business of selling slaves *into* Brazil, not out?"

"I can deliver that message to him if you wish, but I daresay, he may deliver his reply in person, with you on the wrong end of *his* whip."

The slaver stopped his inspection. He seemed genuinely shocked at the boldness of Matias' man. "I'm not beholden to Matias de Albuquerque, sir. I am a merchant in the service of Portugal and, specifically, Brazil. Exactly where does the good captain wish me to send them?"

"Send them to Africa, to Benin, to Luanda. Sell them to the Spanish. Or send them to the bottom of the ocean. He does not care. Just get them *out* of Brazil."

"Please, sir," Celia said, in perfect Portuguese, "do not sell us to the Spanish. I won't be sold to the Spanish."

The slaver turned to her and grabbed the back of her neck tightly. She tried twisting away, but could not escape his grasp for, despite his paunchy, sweaty girth, he was strong. He pressed his face close to hers as if he were inspecting her teeth. She made a good show of it, revealing few problems save for one chipped tooth in the front. He eyed the cut that Matias had put on her mouth. He smiled. "She can take a punch. That's good." His free hand moved down to her right breast. He cupped it and gave a tight squeeze. "And she's still of breeding age." He then put his hand between her legs, letting his fingers slide along the back-running crease of her sweat-slick gown. She closed her eyes, held her breath, fearing what her son might do if he should see. *Please, Martim, no . . .*

But it was too late for entreaties, silent or otherwise. Seeing the violation of his mother's body and dignity, Martim kicked the slaver in the side of the leg. It was a strong kick for a boy; the slaver staggered back, limping and yelping. He nearly lost his balance, but recovered and quickly backhanded Martim. The boy sprawled on the ground of the dusty paddock just behind the slave market.

Celia pulled away from the slaver's grip and fell on her son. "Please, sir. I will do anything. Do not hurt my son. He is just a boy."

"A boy who needs to show respect." The slaver moved to kick Martim in the gut, but it was Matias' man who stopped him, stepping in the slaver's way and holding up a musket to shield the boy from another blow. "We don't have time for this," he said. "Whip him later if you like. Are you going to take them or not?"

The slaver, still enraged, and still smarting from the kick, paused, breathed deeply, and got his anger under control. "They're worthless to me. Just kill them, I say. The children are too young. The woman, she's—"

"We can all read," Celia said, her heart racing. "Even Lua. And Martim knows numbers. So do I. We can clean and cook and work fields. I used to keep the books on a plantation, run a master's kitchen. We can do anything."

She had never been any "master's" slave, but this heathen didn't need to know that, and she didn't think Matias' men knew enough about her to know she was lying. She had done the books for her husband's plantation, and she was a hard and efficient worker. It was essential that this was how they would value her, rather than inspecting her body and face with the intent of making her a breeding whore. Maybe some slaves were willing to be such, in order to secure a bit more safety, garner a few paltry benefits, but not her. Not ever. She would kill herself first.

But she had to live, to take care of Martim and Lua. So if she had to become a slave—and she saw no way to prevent it—then her survival and her children's depended upon her being valued for tasks that would profit a master's household, rather than for compliance she would never show in his bed.

The slaver backed away, rubbed his sweaty chin,

fixed his pant leg, and considered. "I have a ship arriving from Benin in twenty-five, thirty days, depending upon wind and currents. Some of the stock is going up the coast. I suppose I could impose upon the captain to take them. Perhaps they can be given to the Spanish. He may even have need for an accountant, if what the bitch says is true and she can count beyond three. But I'm not sharing any payment for them, you understand. I get full price. Matias gets nothing. And I expect that in writing."

The guard nodded. "I'll sign any contract you write to that effect. He wants nothing. Just move them out."

"Very well."

Martim was pulled back up to his feet, and the guards pushed them forward. Celia hugged Martim close. She rubbed his cheek, rubbed away a tear that mixed with the blood from his nose and mouth. Lua held her mother's hand. She was shaking, and Celia could smell the terrified girl's urine as it trickled down her leg: the strong scent was a reminder of just how insufficient their water rations had been on the journey.

Celia felt she might start quaking uncontrollably: *we are walking to our deaths*. There was no reasonable chance of rescue, no hope of escape or survival. However, her exaggerated show of fearing the Spanish had given the slaver enough malign incentive to promise to send them into the Caribbean. She could only hope that, for reasons of profit, spite, or both, he would keep his word, and that his circumstances hadn't changed by the time the ship from Africa arrived. For they needed to go north; north into the islands.

Because if Calabar was still alive, that's where he would be.

Rocas Atoll, off the coast of Brazil

Moses' spirit quickened as they made their way down the South American coast from Tobago, and Calabar began to believe that his friend had forgotten their little incident with the rum. Calabar wanted to apologize for his angry outburst, but could never quite bring himself to say the words. It was hard to look a pirate in the eye and tell him you were sorry. They seemed to revel in that little show of weakness. Their relationship had evolved beyond such puffery, Calabar knew, but in his heart, Moses was still a pirate. And pirates were proud, frequently arrogant, and many held personal honor above all else. Moses could have easily pulled his pistol and shot Calabar where he stood, and perhaps he might have, had their argument not been in private. But Moses smiled more often than not these days, and Calabar was glad of that.

He found a new spring in his step as well, and by the time they reached the Rocas Atoll, Calabar was relieved that things were returning to normal. Well, perhaps not normal, for he still had to get Celia and the children out of Brazil, but he could certainly focus more readily on the mission at hand. And that mattered to Moses.

By paying a substantial sum in coins they had taken along the Spanish Main, Moses convinced two other pirate crews to meet them at the atoll. He also managed to secure additional men to replace the casualties they had suffered in the process of accruing that wealth. His spirit improved even more after that. They were at full strength again.

Moses' good mood was contagious, spread to his crew—but came crashing down again when the negotiations with the two other captains began.

All were gathered on the *Sword of Solomon*, senior members of Moses' crew flanked by French buccaneers and various British cutthroats and Spanish rebels who smelled even worse than they looked. Even a few runaway slaves who had taken up the rogue's pistol and sword stood in attendance, one of them sporting a wooden leg like Cornelis Jol. Another was missing three fingers from his right hand; a third, an eye which he refused to cover. He smiled madly like a bush dog.

One of the French buccaneers—a short, stocky fellow—kept staring at Calabar as if he knew him, though Calabar had never met a Frenchman in his life. It was annoying, but he let it go. More important issues were being discussed.

"We are not like you, Moses," one of the French pirates, Captain Arnaud Blanchett, said. He seemed to be the only Frenchman in attendance that could speak Dutch. His light brown hair was braided to the waist. He wore a messy goatee, was missing two teeth, and had a red scar across his neck. "We are not allies of Admiral Tromp, or the Dutch. We serve only our own interests. Besides, what you propose requires safe refuge. You have one, here in Rocas Atoll. But it is your playground . . . not ours." He almost sneered. "We are not as fortunate in our friends as you are."

Over the years, Moses had had a number of islands that he considered his base of operation. They changed when his circumstances changed. The Rocas Atoll served as one of those bases, and Calabar had to admit, for sheer beauty, it was a marvelous location.

Not too close to the Brazilian coast to be constantly threatened by the Portuguese navy, yet close enough to enable routine raiding and even interdiction of ports and ships along that same coast. The problem for Moses, at least in these negotiations, was that the Rocas Atoll served as the northernmost point in a long line of islands that stretched as far south as Rio de Janeiro. His pirate friends were not pleased with any plan which put them frequently—or more to the point, predictably—in any single location that was so close to the Caribbean.

"We do not wish to put ourselves in jeopardy for Dutch gains," Blanchett said. "If we operate out of here, that puts us too close to Admiral Tromp and his USE allies in the Caribbean. Have you seen those USE ships, Moses? They belch smoke and fire. Their guns are more powerful than anything ever seen on the ocean, and they shoot further and more accurately as well. You say they would not seek our blood. Perhaps. But things change, my friend. What is to keep your masters from deciding one day that their little pirate operation no longer serves their interests, and then they come for us? I am willing to face any foe on the sea in a fair fight. But that is no fair fight. We would be slaughtered."

Moses sighed deeply and rubbed his eyes. They had been going at it like this for quite a while. "Then as I have said again and again," Moses replied, "you may operate further south."

"That takes us away from ships arriving from Europe," said Jon Cadogen, a Welshman and the captain of his ship, "and puts us right in the middle of those god-damned slave *naus* from Africa. Good money there, yes, but too much trouble."

"You would profit from human flesh?" Everyone turned to stare at Calabar in surprise. He himself was surprised at how quickly the bold words had flown from his lips. These pirates did not know him and perhaps did not expect a man of his...color... to be so outspoken.

"There's good profit in that flesh," Cadogen said, "and I'm not so humble as to ignore that profit. But slave ships are large, heavily defended for the most part, and difficult to board. Larger crews than I have, and if you manage to subdue the crew, then what? You got a pack of Africans to treat with, who don't know a damned thing about sailing. Best thing to do is shoot half and feed them to the sharks."

"And where would you sell the ones you do not shoot?" Calabar asked, moving closer to Cadogen. "Back to the Portuguese? The whole purpose of Moses' proposal is to interdict—to deny—the Portuguese their livelihood."

"Why should we be more concerned about the Portuguese than the Spanish or the USE?" Blanchett said. "I have no love for any of them, you understand, but I don't see any profit in tearing down the Portuguese when they serve as a counterweight to the Spanish. We bring the Portuguese down, and the Spanish and whoever else fills the gap. We're better off staying in the Caribbean, moving between its many refuges, and taking our chances there."

"And you may return there at your leisure," Moses said, reaching the end of his patience, "and take your chances against those mighty ships that belch fire and smoke. And may the sea take you, for that is where you will find your last repose. I have indeed seen those USE ships, Arnaud, and the time is coming when no pirates will be safe in the Caribbean. I am doing you a favor by changing your area of operation and giving you the opportunity to work in partnership with the Dutch and the USE."

"Proposing a sixty-forty split of the spoils is no favor to us," Cadogen said, trying and failing to stare down Calabar. "The starting number is seventy-thirty, and I'm more comfortable with eighty-twenty if I have to deal with slave ships."

"And you will neither kill them nor sell them back to the Portuguese," Calabar said. He could tell that the Welshman was about to say something he'd regret. But Cadogen kept his tongue, gritted his teeth, nodded, and said, "And what do you propose I do with them, then?"

"You will set them free," Calabar said, "or take them as crew. But they won't be bought and sold like chattel."

"And what do *you* say about all this?" Moses asked, interrupting and turning to Arnaud. "Where do you stand now?"

The Frenchman shook his head. "I don't know. I haven't decided yet. We need to venture further south, look at islands near Recife and Bahia. I may be inclined to support your plan if we can find a viable location there."

Moses nodded. "Then that is what we will do. We'll head out in the morning. Get your ships and crews ready."

The meeting ended, and Calabar walked to the prow. He breathed deeply, the first time he had done so since Moses' friends had come aboard. *Some friends!*

An overly cautious Frenchman and a Welsh bigot. *Folly! Utter folly!* Moses would say that it was a good start, but they needed more crews, many more crews if they were to make this plan work. There was too much ocean to cover, too many ways that Portuguese ships could slip through, and too many opportunities for a man like Cadogen to cheat and deceive—and sell or kill the slaves he acquired. Perhaps it was a start, but it was a weak one at best.

"What do you think?" Moses' voice asked from behind.

Calabar started, then turned, tried putting a good face on his reservations. "It *is* a start, I suppose. But I don't trust those men."

"Neither do I," Moses said, "but they are good at what they do. They will be an asset in time, assuming we can persuade them."

"Persuading them is not what concerns me. Can we *control* them?"

Moses huffed. "Good question, and I don't have an answer for you. We'll have to try. Life isn't perfect, my friend. But we dance with the girl that shows up."

Calabar turned to the prow and looked toward the Brazilian coast. It was a full day's sail, when the wind was just right. Not close, but not too far away. "We sail south tomorrow, did you say?"

"Yes."

"Then I ask that you take me to Ilha Itamaracá or Itapessoca. They are just north of Olinda."

"I know where they are," Moses said. "But I'd prefer to take you to Tinharé."

"Why? That's near Bahia. I am going to Recife."

Moses nodded. "Yes, but Recife is too close to

Matias' fleet, too close to eyes cast toward the sea. Tinharé is farther, yes, but safer, and it puts us near other islands that we need to survey. From Tinharé, you can work your way back up the coast to Recife."

The mission is paramount. His friend did not say those words, but Calabar knew that he was thinking them. He nodded. "Yes. That's the best course of action. We will go to Tinharé. If you'll excuse me..."

Moses stepped out of the way, and Calabar moved past him toward midship. The pirate frowned. "Are you well?"

Calabar stopped, turned, and smiled again. "Of course, my friend. Just a little headache from all that bluster and negotiation. Tomorrow will be a busy day, so I should eat and find some rest. I'm fine. We will speak later."

They headed out in the morning, the *Sword of Solomon* in the lead. The wind and currents gave them a great boost, and Moses ordered that they shift their route and head closer, not fifty miles off the Brazilian coast. It was a significant risk since the Portuguese could easily mobilize ships and give pursuit, but being so close also gave the pack a chance to perform a bit of interdiction if the opportunity presented itself. Moses figured that, if they got lucky, they'd come across a Portuguese *nau* or carrack with little or no escort, its belly fat with treasures from Europe, or sugar cake en route there. A three-to-one advantage would spell doom for the poor merchant ship, and Moses intended to let his pirate friends pick over all the bones, to give the sea wolves a taste of blood, and so wear down their reluctance.

No ship, unfortunately, presented itself.

So one night, when Calabar knew that the Recife coast was near, he waited until Moses had fallen asleep to the sweet lullaby of rum, then slipped quietly into the small compartment up near the prow: the one most susceptible to swells, closest to the head, and therefore, the customary billet for the newest and greenest of the crew. He found two such in their bunks; there wasn't room enough to hang a hammock. One was a young man named Richard, who had transferred from Blanchett's ship. The other was a runaway named Casper, who had had his tongue cut out by his former master.

"Wake up!" Calabar whispered.

"What is it, sir?" Richard asked, bleary-eyed and wobbly.

"Come with me," Calabar said. "Both of you."

"Where are we going?"

Calabar did not answer. Instead, he led them first to the weapons locker and secured three muskets with good ammunition. Then they went to the deck, and there, he explained his "mission" to the night crew.

"I'm taking these two with me to shore," he whispered to the men on guard. "Moses has given us a very important task, and it's to be kept quiet. Do you understand?"

They were reluctant at first to agree. But they understood that Calabar was, in effect, second in command to Moses, and that he had the captain's ear and his complete trust. Eventually, they nodded and stepped aside.

Calabar led Richard and Casper to the skiff, lying on the deck alongside the starboard gunwale. It was a light wooden craft with a small sail, but getting it

over the side was not a two-man job; nor was rowing
it all the way to shore. "Let's get this in the water."

"What are we doing?" Richard asked.

"Like I said, it's a secret mission. Captain's orders.
You two know how to sail one of these, yes?"

They both nodded.

"Good, then let's get started."

"The coast is at least fifteen, maybe twenty miles
away," Richard said, "and it won't be easy in the dark,
even with moonlight."

Calabar ignored the statement and continued working. They untied the straps that held the boat to the
deck. Casper manned the tackle they used to help hoist
it up and over the side. Calabar motioned Richard to
board first. The boy did as he was told, accepting all
three rifles and ammunition once he was in the gently
rolling boat. Then Casper and Calabar climbed in.

Casper fixed the sail and turned it to catch the
wind in a broad reach. Richard set the oars. Calabar
checked their muskets.

"Please tell us what we are doing," Richard said.

Calabar looked at the boy. "Righting a wrong that
should have been fixed long ago."

"I don't understand what that means—"

"Shut up and start rowing. We don't have time to
talk."

Richard started to mutter, but went silent at a look
from Calabar. He grabbed the paddles and began to
row.

Slightly less than twenty miles to shore. They had
to make it there by dawn. He hoped they would,
because once Moses awoke and found them gone,
he'd turn his ship in pursuit with guns at the ready.

He would not like having his property stolen and his men commandeered. Calabar understood, even acknowledged the justice of such a response, but he didn't care anymore. He was tired of letting white men determine where he was to go, when it was best to act, and how to carry out a plan.

I'm sorry, Moses, Calabar thought as he watched the lights from the deck of the *Sword of Solomon* fade away, *but your mission means nothing to me anymore.*

Chapter 18

Portuguese slave ship Santa Catarina
do Benin, *the waters off Brazil*

The slavers of Bahia did not care that Celia and her children were native Brazilians. Though their skin was lighter than the Africans remaining on board for auction stops up the Brazilian coast, they were shackled and led toward the ship, Celia and Lua wearing nothing but threadbare white shifts, and Martim in a pair of tan-stained pantaloons. As they shuffled aboard, Celia heard one slaver tell the first mate in Portuguese that "these three" needed to be sold to the Spanish. The first mate tried to dispute the order, but to no avail. Celia heard nothing else on the matter, as a deckhand pushed her down the companionway and into the darkness of the hold.

Martim was housed with the men, who were placed primarily amidships because they were generally taller than the women and required more room. Celia and Lua were placed with the women near the stern, and the only light that they could see was through the cracks in the deck planking. The heat, and the smell of feces and vomit, body odor, and menses, made Celia retch. She threw up more than once, finally dry-heaving with the sway of the ship on the waves. Lua cried constantly. She was not near her mother, but Celia would call out to her, singing Bible quotes, making up the tempo and rhythms to match the sway of the ship. Some of the African women did the same, singing songs in their language, which Celia could not understand, but it helped soothe Lua and some of the less robust girls whose skin was dry and stretched tight due to dehydration.

At some point of every day, everyone coughed, everyone moaned, everyone whimpered. Though they were packed more loosely than during an Atlantic crossing due to the reduced number of slaves being carried, Celia found it difficult to turn onto her sides with bound wrists and ankles. She slept fitfully, and mostly on her back. She hurt everywhere and after a few days, the shackles on her ankles began to cut into her skin. Her arms would fall asleep constantly, forcing her to shift from side to side. That helped keep sensation in her arms, but it made her wrists hurt even more. And then they too began to rub raw and bleed.

She would try to hide her tears, as if doing so convinced her of her own uncertain bravery, gave her strength in the midst of these poor, strange women who had lost hope long ago. Most of them simply lay flat, eyes open or shut, as if fixed in an unshakable melancholy. They all seemed to want to die, and some of them did. The woman to her left died where she lay two days into the voyage, her eyes open, a faint, serene smile on her dry lips. Celia said a prayer for the woman as her spent corpse was pulled free and dragged to the deck.

They were let out each day, under armed guard, to get fresh air and to eat. Buckets were placed on the deck and the women would squat over them to conduct their toilet. The men were lined up on the port side and made to relieve themselves into the ocean. Celia tried to steal a glimpse of Martim as the men were taken below and the women brought up. She thought she saw him once, but it was difficult to know for sure. She had not heard or seen anything to lead her to believe he was in danger, but she nonetheless prayed constantly for his welfare.

The fresh air and the hot sun always brought Lua's energy back quickly. She perked up as Celia doused her with water and cleaned her with a strip from her dress. She did this many times for other women as well, taking it upon herself to clean them, especially their raw ankles and elbows. She wound up removing her dress altogether, an act of solidarity that was also her one clear opportunity to communicate to her hull mates. *If they cannot wear clothing, then neither will I*, Celia said to herself as she ripped her dress apart and helped to bind wounds and blisters. She insisted that Lua should keep her dress, hoping that it would spare her young soul the additional vulnerability of perpetual nakedness.

But when the cleaning was over and the meager food eaten, they were hustled back into the hold, and in the unbearable heat of the equatorial Atlantic, the misery would start all over again.

They landed at the first port, and Celia wondered

if it were Recife. She and Lua were not permitted above deck, so she tried to listen, hoping to overhear conversations that might, if only indirectly, suggest where they were.

About a third of the women were taken above and never seen again. But other cargo, casks and grain, sugar loaves, and building materials, were brought aboard, and so the amount of room allotted to the women remained roughly the same. Their misery was unrelieved, and since they were not allowed on deck while in port, it got even worse than usual.

Celia did not know when they set to sea again. She had passed out from dehydration and awoke only when a swell caused the woman lying nearby to roll on top of her. She awoke and tried pushing the woman off, but she was dead weight, and Celia was too weak.

Then the woman was pushed abruptly away, and a rough hand slapped Celia's face.

"Wake up, mongrel!" The voice was male.

Celia opened her eyes. "Water—I need—"

"Yes, yes, you'll get it. Bring her up."

Her shackles were removed—even the individual ones clasping her wrists and ankles—and she was hauled to the deck. She was dropped harshly onto the planks, and a bucket of ocean water was thrown onto her. The sting from the salt made her entire body ache. She cried out. They tossed another bucketful directly into her face. She lay there and let the pain subside, rubbing her raw wrists and wincing as her fingers worked the tender flesh. Then she was given water to drink, and some pawpaw juice. The juice was wonderful, rejuvenating, and she lay back again and let the sweet flavor cradle her tongue.

"That useless auctioneer in Bahia told me that you are good with numbers."

Celia opened her eyes. It was dusk, and so the light from the sun did not hurt so much. She kept them open, giving them time to focus. She stared up into the waning light, into the silhouetted face of the captain.

Celia nodded. "My name is Celia. I am the wife of..."

"And I am Captain Emilio Ramires. We all have names, even slaves."

Celia ignored his insult, and continued, "I am the wife of Domingos Fernandes Calabar. I and my children have been illegally taken and placed on this ship. I am a free woman, and I demand that—"

"You may make no demands here, half-breed. I do not care why you are on my ship. I have my orders, and they shall be carried out. But, if you are good with numbers, then I have need of you. *Are* you good with numbers or not?"

Celia nodded.

"Speak!"

"Yes, sir, I am."

Captain Ramires nodded, but he did not seem pleased. He looked tired, and annoyed. "Because of you, and my orders to hand you over to the Spanish, we have taken on a fair amount of cargo: hardwood planks, dried meats, casks of nuts and cashew seeds, less perishable produce, some iron ore and a little gold, which I am being allowed to trade in Spanish ports as we sail further north into the islands. In turn, I may get whatever I can in trade for the trip back to Benin, no questions asked." He pulled a piece of paper from his vest and unfolded it. "This chicken scratch is indecipherable to me, and not a goddamned one of my crew is capable of parsing it out, nor do I trust them to be fair even if they could, the *filhos da putas* . . . Half of them deserve to be clapped in irons. No matter; if you can divine the reckonings on this page and give me a full accounting of what I have so that I can determine what would constitute a fair trade to the Spanish, then I'll let you find some little corner belowdecks to call your own, without those shackles. Maybe an additional crust or two at night."

He handed over the paper. Celia looked at it closely, straining to read the scribbled lines in the weak light. It was very difficult to read. The numbers were adequate, but the instructions in between were some of the worst handwriting she had ever seen. But she had seen a lot of poor script when she had worked on Calabar's books. This would be a challenge, but not impossible. And if in doubt, she could simply lie about it, just like his crew could. How would he ever know?

But should she help him at all? Why should she cooperate, trade her skills for advantages when the women and men below were still suffering and dying? How could she justify to their meek, lost eyes that, because she was not African, because her skin was lighter than theirs, because she had the luck of understanding Portuguese and knowing numbers, that she would have access to privileges that they would never have? Or dispel their suspicions that she had traded her body for a few creature comforts and marginally better treatment?

They were in no position to act on whatever resentment or contempt they might feel, and perhaps they wouldn't even care. But Celia would, and she would not be able to face them when they were brought up for food and exercise. And yet, how long could she survive in those chains, lying on those stiff, urine- and blood-soaked planks? If she died down there, then what of her children? She had already lost one. The thought of losing more was too terrible to imagine.

"Yes," she said, finding the resolve, and then the courage, to stand, "I can do it."

"Good, then go to the stores and find some clothes. And get those damned wrists looked at by the physician; I don't want you bleeding all over my books. Then report to the cargo master...the useless whelp. Maybe you can teach him how to read."

Captain Ramires turned to leave. Celia asked, "What about my children? Lua and Martim?"

"What about them?" he asked.

"They are still below, and they are very weak. Can they be let free too?"

Captain Ramires stood looking down at her. He chuckled. "What for? They're not worth anything to me."

Igreja da Conceição, near Olinda, Brazil

Calabar, Richard, and Casper stared out at the Jesuit church through heavy foliage beside a modest stable. The darkness obscured much, but not the thick smells of decaying hay and horse dung. However, Calabar discovered that they were strangely welcome scents; he spent so many weeks away from land that almost any smell—even horse shit—was better than the constant odor of dead fish and sea salt. But he hadn't come here to smell the land, as much as he enjoyed it. He had come for his family, and somewhere inside that church, they were waiting for him.

He looked carefully through the foliage for any sign of guards or Portuguese soldiers. They were unlikely to be stationed at a house of God, he knew, but he was taking no chances. He had come this far; he would not allow himself to get captured by Matias' thugs, or anyone else, so close to his objective.

They waited a long while, staring up at the few specks of light emanating from candles inside the church. One light in an upper window would flicker into existence; another on the ground floor would flicker out. But there was one constant light, in the window of the rectory's small second story. Father Araujo's private residence.

Calabar gave his musket to Richard. "You two wait here. It is better if I go in alone and unarmed. Keep your eyes open. If anyone approaches, fire once into the air."

Richard and Casper looked at each other. Casper blinked and hefted his musket. Calabar nodded his approval, then stepped out into the courtyard, keeping low and close to the shadows.

It was a beautiful church. He had always thought so. He had attended mass in it many times with Celia and the children. Matias had even been in attendance on some occasions, though they had never sat together. Good times. Lost times. Lost, now, forever.

He crouched at the front door. A new door. Fresh wood. Clean iron. Well-crafted hinges. He could still smell the dark wood stain. He tried the latch. Unlocked. Calabar opened the door, slowly, and stepped inside.

He knelt and crossed his chest. He prayed, for the first time in a long time, taking a brief moment to confess his sins to the watchful eyes on the walls. There were many sins, so many that God would likely never forgive. Father Araujo might even absolve him of those sins, but Calabar did not want that priestly intercession. He just wanted to mouth each sin silently and let God decide for himself if Calabar was—could ever be—deserving of forgiveness for so many horrible sins. *I am not worthy. I never will be.*

He stumbled to the altar, fighting back tears. He knelt again. "Celia!" He cried out her name. "Martim... Lua... Carlos! I am here. *Papai* is here!"

Nothing. Not a sound. Not a whisper. Not even a faint breeze to shiver the dim flames of the candles that framed the altar.

He called again, and again, and again. It was Father Araujo who finally answered.

"They are gone, Calabar," the tall priest said, emerging from the door that connected the rectory to the sanctuary, just to the right of the altar. He smiled and held his arms open wide. Calabar stood, walked forward, and fell into his embrace.

"Where are they, Father? Was it Matias?"

"Yes."

"Where has he taken them?"

"To Bahia," he answered, through his own tears. "They were to be given to the slavers there."

"Bastard!"

He did not care if he was in a church. He could not contain his anger, his frustration, any longer. God had to understand and forgive his profanity. "How long?"

"Near two months ago," Father Araujo said. "I am

sorry. There was nothing I could do. I tried. But..."
Father Araujo lowered his head and the tears flowed
down his face.

Calabar nodded, stepped back, turned to leave.

"Wait!" Father Araujo said. "He...he did not take
them all, Calabar. Carlos...he did not go."

Calabar stopped, turned. "Where is he? Where?"

Father Araujo lifted a shaking finger and pointed
through the wall, toward the cemetery outside.

Calabar found his youngest son's grave near the
middle of a cluster of older tombs, a wooden cross at
the head, the mound of dirt worn down from rain,
but still visible through patches of growing weeds.

Calabar fell atop the mound and cried hard. He
reached out to the cross and held it firmly, begged God
to give him back his son, begged to be taken instead.
Carlos was young and innocent of everything. *But not
me. I am innocent of nothing. Take me, for I have lived
enough; I am ready. Please, please, bring him back.*

God, of course, did not answer Calabar's prayer, nor
was it proper to think He would. It was blasphemy,
Father Araujo had always told him, to expect God to
answer such demands. There was a purpose in Carlos'
death, even if we, as sinful mortals, could not see or
comprehend it. That's what Father Araujo would say
if asked. But what kind of God would take such a
young, innocent boy? How could his death have any
meaning, other than to remind Calabar of what a
terrible father he had been? To Carlos. To *all* of them.

"When did he die?" Calabar asked Father Araujo
as the priest approached the grave.

"Several weeks before Matias took them. The medicine that was being delivered stopped. Suddenly,

without warning. We don't know why, and we were reluctant to send inquiries, to find out, lest Matias discover your family's whereabouts. The poor boy just could not go on. But he was brave, very brave, and he died peacefully, Calabar—believe me when I tell you this. He died sleeping, in Lua's arms."

"Was he baptized? Celia wanted him baptized."

Father Araujo nodded. "Yes. Last year."

Calabar closed his eyes and wiped his face. "That is a blessing. What of Luiz? Pedro? What do you know of them?"

"I know nothing. I have not seen or heard from them in a long while. There are rumors that once Matias learned the truth, Pedro was seized and put in prison. But I feared to try to confirm those reports. I did not wish to draw more attention to this church, you understand. But I failed them. I failed them, Calabar. It was too dangerous to keep them so close to Bom Jesus. I should have sent them to—"

"No, Father." Calabar shook his head. "*I* failed them. I failed to protect them. It was not your responsibility. It was mine. I should never have left Brazil. It was foolish of me to think I could find security and comfort with the Dutch. I should have stayed. I should have fled to a *mocambo*, close, where I could look in on them. They could have come with me, perhaps. Maybe Carlos would still have died, but at least he would have seen his father's face before the end, and known that I loved him.

"No amount of prayer will bring him back, I know. But I can do something to honor his memory. My path is clear to me now." Calabar climbed to his feet. "I need a strong horse, Father. Do you have one? One that can get to Bahia by morning?"

"Yes." Father Araujo motioned to the stable. "Take what you will, my son. And may God be with you."

They embraced again. Calabar hugged the priest tightly, not wanting to let go. Finally, he pulled away, bid him farewell, and went to the stable.

There he found a patchy gray Lusitano, tall, perhaps a little underfed, but strong. Calabar was not the best horseman, but he had ridden horses before for the Portuguese.

He prepared the horse for riding, affixed the saddle, fastened the girth and flank straps, and checked the stirrups. He set the bit and fastened the bridle carefully over the mare's head and ears. He clutched the reins tightly and soothed the horse with cooing sounds. He rubbed her neck, and led her out of the stable.

"Richard, Casper," he said. He got no reply.

He called to them again. "You can come out now." They did not appear. He went around the stable to where they had been waiting. They were no longer there; neither was his musket. *Where have they gone?* he wondered. Were they spooked or scared off? He looked around and saw nothing, no signs of any intruders. He called for them again, a little louder. Still nothing. His heart sank. This didn't feel right. There was no reason for them to be gone. But he didn't have time to worry about it. His wife, his children, were being sold into slavery. By comparison, Richard and Casper meant nothing.

He climbed into the saddle, turned the horse toward the road, and urged it into a slow trot.

Calabar worked up to a steady gallop, fast enough so that he felt wind against his face. The horse was strong indeed, and more than capable of maintaining such a pace. He switched it lightly with the reins. It felt good to be going to Bahia, despite what he might find there. It felt good to be in control of his own fate.

He turned a corner, and a long wooden pole came out of the darkness and struck the horse in the flank.

The horse whinnied loudly, reared, shied when the pole poked at her again, tumbled, and threw Calabar into the thick brush. The brush cushioned his fall, and he tried climbing out of it. But as he tried, another pole struck him in the head.

Chapter 19

Portuguese slave ship Santa Catarina
do Benin, *the waters off Brazil*

Celia was so impressive with the accounting that Captain Ramires put her in charge of issuing and tracking the slaves' daily rations, both men and women. She handled these duties in fine fashion as well, until the cook decided that their food had to be more tightly rationed, though Celia did not know why. There was plenty of food to last, given the fact that the captain continually said that they were going to make port soon in Spanish territory, and that everyone would be off-loaded, trades made, and then the trip back to Benin would commence.

But as the days wore on, Celia discovered that the cause of the severe rationing could have been personal rather than practical: one of the female slaves, the prettiest and liveliest of the bunch, had bit the cook's hand when he had squeezed her left breast. The crew who saw it had laughed at the disgusting lout. Embarrassed, he hit the girl in the face, then proceeded to break her ribs with swift, sharp kicks. Captain Ramires saved her in the end, telling the cook, "Go fetch an older one, if you need it that bad. This one's mine." Celia had never seen the Captain take a woman to his quarters, but she would not have been surprised. Many of the men did, and rape was rampant throughout the ship during the evening.

So the food was cut back, and the slaves became restless and hungrier. Soon after, a branding iron was brought out and, once glowing orange, was put to its brutal work. By the time it had seared a small mark into the back of half of the slave's shoulders—proof of legal importation—something dangerous was in the wind.

The women spoke in whispers to themselves during their meals and exercise, and when Celia came around, they would go quiet and speak only about good times in their villages and dreams of freedom. Celia had learned a few of their words, and she knew the differences based on their tone and inflection. She was permitted more frequently on deck now, and so, was occasionally there when the men were brought above. Their tone and behavior had grown decidedly angry, hostile.

One man, a tall, lanky fellow with wiry arms and powerful legs, broke free from the sailors holding him down during his branding, grabbed the branding iron, and pushed it into the face of a crewman. He was chased around the deck for several minutes before a cutlass slash to his leg ended his flight. He was then strung up on a yardarm and the other slaves made to watch as he bled to death. "A warning to you all," Captain Ramires said, though it was doubtful that many knew his words. "I will bleed *all* of you out if this happens again." The man's sunbaked corpse was then cut down and fed to the school of sharks that had been following the ship since Recife.

Things calmed down for a few days after that. Then two belaying pins went missing.

Celia had been asked by Captain Ramires to count them, and count them daily, for fear that they would disappear. She counted them, correctly in her head anyway, but when the count made it officially to paper, she added two. Then a few marlinspikes disappeared. Then a fish gig. They were such small, simple little things, and with a crew like this, one that had been at sea well past what they were accustomed to, such little things could go missing for a number of reasons, she imagined, such as falling innocently over the side, or breaking off in a fish. So, Celia didn't worry about it. Her numbers came out correctly every time. The captain remained content, and so, lax.

After a long day of counting food rations, Celia took time to help a small group of women bathe as the sun began to set. As punishment for the man that had been allowed to bleed out for turning the brand on a crewman, the slaves were forced to stay belowdecks during the hottest part of the day, and then only allowed in small groups to come above near dusk. The group that Celia now helped contained some of the youngest and most vibrant women that remained unsold.

They began to dance, a dance that she had seen before but in more modest expression, earlier in the journey. Now, these women held nothing back. They were vigorous in their movements, as if they were free and dancing in the middle of their own villages. They were naked, of course, and so their breasts bounced side to side as their motions flowed rhythmically, almost wraithlike, back and forth. Their voices were pleasant and dreamy, and some of them even smiled as they articulated a language that, in musical form, Celia could not interpret. Their arms were long and sinuous, their legs spread and muscular, their buttocks arched and exposed.

The crew watching was mesmerized and growing lustful, Celia knew. If this persisted much longer, these agile, joyous young women would be bent over the railing and taken like dogs. *Why are they doing it?* she wondered. Why were they putting themselves on such display, when they must know what might happen, what *would* happen. Why?

Then she saw the first shadow emerge behind a cluster of crewmen whose eyes and attention were drawn to the dancing women. Their skin was pitch black in the waning light of the sun, but Celia could barely see them. Even though her watchfulness was primed, she could scarcely make out the shapes that slipped, one after another, out of the slave hold and into positions behind crates and carelessly piled tackle. Each shadow was careful and smooth, like a jaguar approaching prey through the thick jungle.

She caught the glint of a marlinspike as one of the shadows drew up behind a sailor. A swift motion with the spike through the back, an ink-black hand across the mouth, and the man dropped back, suddenly limp. Not a word spoken; not a sound uttered.

The women never flinched, never broke their strides. They danced on as if only they mattered, as if nothing of any significance was transpiring behind them.

Another and another of the crewmen disappeared as more shadows reached up and snatched one from the rear ranks of the onlookers. Two, three, then four. All silent and dead.

In her mind, Celia rejoiced. It was happening, really happening. Soon, all the captives on this bloody vessel would be free, and the *crew* fed to the sharks. For a moment, she considered jumping into the dance, though she did not know the movements very well. What did it matter? She would strip off her dirty shift and dance, and give the men a show, so long as, at the end, they were all dead.

Lua! Martim! Sudden images of her children's faces, of their vulnerability, first paralyzed, then ended, her eagerness to help seize the ship. Were they safe? Would they remain so? Both of them were still shackled below—or was Martim part of this ambush? Was he somewhere belowdecks, holding a knife, a spike, following other, older men into this desperate struggle?

A new misgiving made her gasp: and what would happen if they succeeded? Not a single speck of land could be seen anywhere around. They were at sea, and what did these poor Africans know of sailing? Celia herself knew next to nothing. Without anyone to navigate, to handle the sails, this revolt was also suicide.

As the fifth crewman fell silently out of sight, Celia closed her eyes, struggled to determine the best course of action, gave up and simply screamed, "MARTIM!"

The women stopped dancing, their song dying in their throats. The crewmen who would have been the sixth victim of the silent attackers turned just in time to thwart his assailant. He pushed the African back, raised and swung the muzzle of his musket toward the man, pulled the trigger, and put a gory hole in his face.

The women screamed, but not in fear. They leaped into the fight like scalded cats, teeth bared, nails extended. They grabbed and clawed and scratched at the eyes of the Portuguese crewmen still alive—six or seven, Celia could not tell in the scuffle—as the African men, now resigned to fighting hand to hand, tried wrestling the crew's weapons away from them. It was an increasingly bloody mass of bodies, the distinction between white and black growing steadily more uncertain in the failing sunlight. Celia thought to jump in as well, to help the women that she had betrayed more by maternal reflex than intent. But no. She had sounded the alarm for a reason—survival—and she needed to hold to it.

She worked around the fight, dodging and ducking as she skirted the mass of legs and wrestling arms. Muskets went off intermittently, with some discharges finding flesh, both black and white, and some sending their balls harmlessly into the sky. But that gunfire brought more to the deck, white and black in equal number, in the struggle to control the ship. As Celia drew near the companionway down to the midship hold where the male slaves were shackled, more gunfire and muffled screaming and howling came through the dank and putrid air from below.

A crewman, one Celia knew by face but could not recall his name, pushed her down, turned his pistol to her head. She squeezed her eyes shut, waiting for the blast. But it did not come. Instead, she heard the meaty *thunk!* of his body as he hit the deck. She opened her eyes. Behind him, an African stood holding one of the missing belaying pins. He shouted something to her in his language. All she could say was, *"Obrigada."* He turned and ran across the deck and forward, toward a small cannon that was mounted so as to be turned on a pedestal. Many men fought over this swivel gun, and it seemed as if the pedestal would break. Celia considered moving in that direction to find a better way belowdecks, then reconsidered as one of the crew fell dead at her feet with a fish gig sticking through his throat.

She turned in the other direction and made her way toward a ladder that disappeared into the dark hold where the women were being held. The companionway she had tried first was now filled with sweat-shiny bodies stabbing, punching, kicking, and biting. Where was the captain? The first mate? The coxswain? She could make out none of these officers, just slaves and crewmen, black and white, fighting to survive.

She reached and worked down the ladder until she found herself in the women's compartment. Surprisingly, she found no guards there. No one was watching the female slaves; she supposed that any guards had been drawn into the desperate fray, now raging both topside and belowdecks, for control of the ship. She could still hear the fight from where she stood, but here there was no movement, no sound.

She entered the hold and found the women sitting upright, but all quiet and still, listening to what was happening around them. She could tell that these women had known what was coming. They were hopeful, but afraid. *And I betrayed them . . . all of them.* She called out to Lua.

"I am here, Mama."

Her voice was faint but clear. Celia went to her, hugged her tightly, and kissed her repeatedly on the forehead. "Pray with me," she said, rubbing tears away from Lua's face.

"Which prayer, Mama?"

"The one Father Araujo taught us."

Lua nodded, and they prayed to Saint Ignatius . . .

> *At the hour of my death, call me*
> *Into your presence, lead me*
> *To praise you with all your saints,*
> *Forever and ever*
> *Amen*

The women around them had heard "Amen" enough to speak it back. They recited the prayer once more, then Celia pulled away. "I must find Martim, sweet bird. Stay here. Do not move. You will be safe."

She didn't believe her own words. No one was safe. She should stay with them, she knew, for anyone caught in the fight could be killed. *Would* be killed.

She left the hold and worked her way through the ship, up and down small flights of stairs, through other companionways, until the sounds of revolt were all she could hear. She moved into the crew quarters, hammocks strung up everywhere, mugs of rum and uneaten strips of meat lying on wooden plates on a three-legged table. In the adjoining compartment, she could see the shapes of men fighting, like a child's shadow play she had seen once in Rio de Janeiro. She moved closer, closer, grabbing a discarded knife as she made it past the table and to the exit. She gripped the knife firmly.

She dared look into the compartment. Three crewmen were there and one African on the floor. He was clearly dead, yet the three crewmen kept stabbing him, again and again, until his stomach and chest were nothing but mush. They were mad with fear, with rage, and they were proving their point by a useless display of savage brutality. For a moment, Celia longed to rush in behind them and plunge her knife into their backs.

As if summoned by her desire, another blur of African men came streaming down an adjoining companionway, shrieking their language, holding belaying pins, knives, and marlinspikes. One even had a musket, though he held it like a club.

They charged the crewmen. Celia ducked back and retreated to the far shadows of her own compartment. She waited there, listening to the sounds of struggle, the disgusting sounds of flesh tearing, skulls cracking, the last whimper of breath from dying mouths. It was madness, and she wanted to float away, to curl up and sleep. She was tired, so tired. She closed her eyes and prayed again.

Then she heard a voice she knew well, cursing in Portuguese. "Martim!" she cried as she darted back to the entrance joining her compartment to the larger one in which the battle was taking place.

Her son had clearly come into the chamber in one of the later ranks, his small frame lost among the larger, darker men. She saw him now, standing in front of a crewman, driving a knife into the man's bloody chest, while two Africans held him up. Celia ran from her hiding place and caught his arm in mid-thrust.

"Martim," she cried. "No!"

He turned on her, as if he were going to drive the knife into her heart. Then he recognized her. His eyes lit up. "Mama," he said, "get out of here. We are taking this ship. Go hide, and—"

"No," she said, tugging him away from the corpse. "You come with me. To Lua. You will stay there. *We* will be safe there."

She tried pulling him away, but he was too strong, too angry, too filled with rage and excitement to listen. He pushed her back. "No! I am going to help these people. We must help them. We are going to take this ship."

"And then what?" she asked. "Do you know how to pilot it? Do you know the way to land? You know nothing of sailing, and neither do these Africans, from what I have seen. It is too dangerous, Martim. All of this is for nothing. Even if you win, we are going to die at sea."

Martim paused as if he were considering her words, then his face grew red and stern. "No! We have to find the weapons locker. We have to."

He pushed her away again and raced out of the room with the other men. She followed, calling his name, but he did not listen, did not respond. He was the same as they were now, she knew, regardless of his lighter skin color. He was an African now, and he would support his brothers in their fight.

Half blind with fear for Martim, she stumbled back toward the women's hold. But everywhere Celia tried to go, wherever she turned, there was fighting. Close in, hand-to-hand action. There were always more Africans than Portuguese, but the Africans were weak from months of poor food, inadequate drinking water, disease, and lethargy.

They fought bravely, they fought hard, but they were

still struggling just to gain the advantage. One, she saw, had wrestled the first mate to the floor and was biting his neck as dogs did, when they were made to fight each other. Blood flowed out from around his teeth as the first mate tried pushing him away. Another was trying to take Captain Ramires' pistol away from him, but the passageway in which they were struggling was narrow, and the man didn't have the proper angle or leverage. Captain Ramires prevailed, turning the barrel so it was pushed against his assailant and pulled the trigger. The man fell atop Celia with a smoking hole in his chest. She lay still, protected and concealed by the larger body, waiting for the captain to move on to the next fight. When he was gone, she pushed the dead man away and kept going.

She caught another glimpse of Martim and followed him into another room, one that she had never been to before. She immediately saw why.

A row of lockers lined the far wall. Chains ran through the handles from locker to locker, and each had a strong cast-iron lock affixed to its handle.

A mass of African men had already pressed into the room, as if they were trying to crush the crewmen, who were lined up in front of the lockers. Desperate, the Portuguese fired pistols into the tightly packed attackers. One shot hit the man just in front of Celia. He convulsed and fell back, his blood splattering on the deck beside her. Then she saw Martim, in the middle of the press, swinging a belaying pin at a crewman.

"Martim!" she screamed, but he didn't hear her.

A little further into the room, the right side of the angry mass lurched forward, and the crewman on that side of the defensive line went down. The Africans rushed through the breach, reached the locker, grabbed its chain, and started pulling. Martim tried moving to help. Celia, hardly thinking, only knew that she had watched as much as she could.

With all her strength, she pushed through the mass until she was behind her son. She grabbed Martim's hair and yanked back so hard he fell to the floor. She did not let go. She pulled and pulled, heedless of his struggle against her. He screamed; she screamed back. She pulled him free, and then grabbed him in a hug, wrapping her body around his. He struggled. He punched, pulled, and pushed. He was strong, and it hurt, but she did not let go.

Until an explosion rocked the locker room. The mass of upright, struggling bodies shielded them from the worst of the concussion: Africans were flung against the bulkheads, some into the air itself. Mangled, shrapnel-torn bodies fell around and against them, knocking Martim out of Celia's arms—

Another explosion, this time from the other side. Newly wounded men shrieked as the blast threw them aside, some flailing and writhing, a few already limp. Celia rocked up, tried to catch a glimpse of what was going on, but slipped on blood just before a tall slave fell atop her, senseless.

She heard more screaming, large blades whispering and then thudding deep into bodies. She wriggled out from under the body on top of her, discovered herself on the edge of a heap of dead or dying men, saw Martim pinned near the bottom. It was hard to breathe, but she wormed into a gap close to her son, pulled his arm and helped tug him free. Together, they crawled in the opposite direction, but were uncertain exactly where they were. There was smoke, thick choking smoke, filling the ship's locker and trying to fill their lungs as well: they could not get a fresh breath.

But they were alive and unwounded, putting them in a very small minority of the people who had, just moments before, so crowded the compartment that it had been almost impossible to move. The moans of the injured became hoarse coughing and desperate, plaintive cries in several African dialects. No one stood, no one called to their comrades to resume the battle; those who could crawled away, most of them leaving gleaming trails of blood as they did.

Celia pulled Martim with her as she found the exit. His rage, his enthusiasm for the fight was gone, and when, breathless, she fell forward, he grabbed her arm and pushed her the rest of the way out of the ship's locker.

Groggy, she turned her head to smile at him—and found herself yanked roughly to her feet and pushed out of the bloody hold. Martim was being dragged behind, coughing raggedly. A few moments later they were propelled out onto the lightless deck. The stars seemed to wheel overhead as Celia gasped for air.

They lay side by side, drawing in great, wracking breaths as the surviving crewmen stacked the dead Africans—men and women alike—in a pile against the starboard gunwale. Then the dead Portuguese were brought up slowly, their bodies laid out in a nice, uniform line, as if they were being prepared for a Christian burial.

The few slaves left alive on the deck stared unblinking at nothing. Their spirit was as broken, as finished, as their revolt. Celia hung her head, and cried.

Captain Ramires knelt close, grabbed her chin, and pulled her face forward. He had a growing bruise on his left cheek and a cut across his forehead. "This is all because of you." His mouth was so close that his rageful spit showered into her face.

Celia shook her head feebly. "No. I . . . I alerted the guards. I . . ."

He flung her face away. "I am aware of that. They told me you screamed your son's name, and that alerted us to the attack. But *none* of this would have happened if *you* and your little whelps hadn't been on board. If we weren't forced to turn you over to the Spanish. All the cargo would be gone by now, we'd be on to Benin, and my men wouldn't have been slaughtered." His eyes roved over her face, as if he expected to see a different face, a face that she kept hidden beneath the one she showed the world. "Who *are* you, bitch?"

"I told you who I was," Celia said, opening her eyes wide and staring him in the face. "I am Celia, wife of Domingos Fernandes Calabar."

"And who the hell is this *Calabar*?"

She sat back on her calves, and, without conscious effort, discovered that she had composed herself. That although she was a slave, she was only conscious of one reaction to him: contempt. The voice that came out of her mouth was unfamiliar: a deep-toned rebuke that was almost a sneer. "You will know soon enough who Calabar is. And so will the rest of your kind."

He slapped her. She fell backwards, against Martim, who got an arm around her before she hit the deck. She held her son tight, and forced away the tears that wanted to start from her eyes, but which she would not give her adversaries the satisfaction of seeing.

"Captain!"

A crewman had emerged from the companionway just forward of the stairs to the quarterdeck. He saluted when the captain turned, said, "The grenades worked, sir. They killed the crew defending the weapons locker, but it remains unbreached. Some of the muskets were damaged by the shock of the blast, but nothing that can't be repaired. No significant losses, sir."

Captain Ramires nodded. "How many did we lose?"

"Don't know the full figures yet, sir. We're still working through the ship, but I'd say around half the crew is dead or wounded."

"Who among the officers and masters?"

"The first mate. Coxswain. Bosun. All dead, sir. I know that for sure."

"Africans?"

The young man shrugged. "Sixty, maybe. Hard to tell at this point, with so many bodies still tangled together in the ship's locker. It's a mess, sir. More men than women for sure. Perhaps she can count them for us." The crewman pointed to Celia.

Captain Ramires shook his head. "No. Her days of counting for us are over. Throw her back into the hold with the rest of them."

"Yes, sir. I shall alert the crew that we're heading back to Recife."

"No. We're not going back. I'm not going to limp back into port with half my crew dead and nothing to show for it. We're going to unload this cargo first, and then—"

"Sir, we don't have enough crew to handle this ship properly. If a storm comes up, we'll likely be wrecked. And we might not even make it back to the coast before it hits." He leaned in and whispered the rest. "And if we have another revolt, they'll roll over us for sure."

Celia watched as Captain Ramires considered the situation. He was angry, uncertain, and trying to conceal the fear she could see in his eyes, hear in his voice. *Good*, she thought. *A man who is afraid is a man who makes mistakes.* Maybe he would buckle under and turn the ship around, take them all back to Recife or Bahia. Anything was possible then.

"No," he said. "We're not going back yet. How close are we to the Spanish shipping routes?"

The young fellow shrugged. "I don't know, sir. Not too far I'd figure. A day, perhaps two. I'll have to check with the sailors to estimate our position."

"Estimate?"

The crewman shrugged. "Sir, the navigator is wounded, and without the first mate and the coxswain..."

The captain nodded angrily. "I see, I see. So get me estimates, then. And get this ship cleaned up. We're continuing onward. Possibly on a new course."

He looked at Celia again. She stared right back. He shook his head and walked away. She lay back and ran a gentle hand back and forth across Martim's bruised, bloody forehead.

"I'm sorry, Mama," he said, close to tears. "I was so angry. I wanted to fight for them. I wanted to help. I—"

"I understand, my sweet boy," she cooed, rubbing his wet hair. "Do not be concerned. I love you still. God loves you still. Always believe that."

They lay back, waiting to be sent down into the belly of the ship. Martim dozed. She held him tightly, singing to him that small prayer that she and Lua had shared, and watching as the surviving crewmen lifted ruined African bodies from the top of the bloody pile and tossed them overboard to the waiting, swarming sharks.

Chapter 20

The Sword of Solomon, *at anchor*
near Ilha Itamaracá

Calabar groaned under the pressure of a blinding headache. He touched the back of his head, felt the tender
bump there. He tried to sit up. The world flipped, and
he fell back down, wanting to vomit, but there was
nothing in his stomach to expel. A bucket of water
was thrown into his face. A familiar laugh followed.

"That's another life you owe me," said Moses,
somewhere in the dim light. "It's becoming a habit.
Maybe a bad one."

Calabar wiped his face with his sleeve and sat up
slowly. He reached out and found a barrel to lean
against. "You are wasting my time, Moses. Go off
and complete your mission for Admiral Tromp. You
no longer have to worry about my safety. I relieve
you of any obligation you feel toward me. I can take
care of myself from now—"

Moses grunted. "Horseshit!" There was real anger—
and, perhaps, fear?—in the pirate's voice. Calabar

hadn't heard that sharp, high timbre in his friend's tone in a long, long time. Maybe never. "Where were you headed on that horse?"

Calabar cleared his throat. "To Bahia. That's where Matias has sent Celia and—" He stopped himself; he couldn't simply say "the children" anymore. Because to refer to the two who survived "the children" made it sound as if that was *all* of Calabar's children, made it sound as if Carlos had never existed. And Calabar would not—could not—do that. Not yet. Maybe never. "Matias handed them over to the slavers."

Moses paused a long moment. Calabar could hear the man's faint sigh despite the incessant cawing of seagulls and the slap of water against the hull. Then Moses said, "And you thought you could just ride into Bahia, at full gallop, and save them? Matias has a lot of soldiers there, Calabar. Soldiers with guns. Far more than you can handle. Your search would end in a matter of minutes—with a hole in your back."

"I thought you said you cared about my family." Calabar did not stand up, but strained his neck to glare at Moses with wide and accusing eyes. "I guess you're just like all other white men. You speak to each other with one side of your mouth; you speak to mameluco dogs with the other."

Moses started forward. "Who the hell do you think you're talking to? I'm not white. I'm a Jew." He removed his hat and ruffled his thinning hair. "You see these horns? No? Well, those 'white men' you refer to believe that they do . . . many of them, anyway. Even Tromp, as honorable a man as he is . . . well, I wonder what he truly thinks of me when he stares me in the face, just like you are doing now. What am I to him? What am

I to any Dutchmen but a Sephardic pirate that God has forsaken? So don't presume to tell me what side of my mouth I speak out of. I speak with one mouth, one voice, and I stand here before you, a man, trying to beat some sense into your foolish head."

Calabar closed his eyes and lay back against the barrel. He wanted to scream, to grab a belaying pin, and beat some sense into Moses; or, at least, drive a greater sense of urgency through his thick skull. But more than anything, he wanted to sleep, and perhaps, when he awoke, all of this would have been a bad dream, a nightmare. He imagined himself lying next to Celia, her arms wrapped around his chest, her soft, subtle breath on his neck, his children giggling in the dark in the next room. A gentle breeze floating off Recife harbor and through his window. What he wouldn't give to hear his neighbor's annoying dog barking just one more time. But now all of it was gone. And here he lay, on the deck of a pirate ship, head ready to burst, being scolded by a privateer.

"Moses," Calabar said, opening his eyes and pulling himself up on wobbly legs. Moses moved to help. Calabar calmly waved him off. "I know you're a good, righteous man, with the best intentions. But I'm at the end of my patience. No; I am well beyond its limits. I can't wait any longer. Not for better winds, nor for a better opportunity, nor for more men. The time to act is *now*. If you were a scout like me, you'd understand that footprints fade, trails grow cold. Minutes, hours, can be the difference between finding what you track and losing it forever. I *must* follow whatever trail remains of my family's movements.

"You know how brutal the slavers are and how

little time they waste. They are likely already gone from Bahia. But I have to find them. I've already lost one child. I won't lose the rest of my family through delay or inaction. I must go to Bahia. The only way you will stop me is if you shackle me belowdecks. Or kill me. Make your choice."

They stared at each other for a long while. It was Moses who spoke first. "You don't realize just how important it is to keep you alive, my friend. How many people are working to keep you alive. Going to Bahia may be the death of us all."

Calabar said nothing. He stared into his friend's eyes and waited.

Moses sighed again, shook his head, turned, cupped his mouth, and yelled, "Hoist anchor!"

Bahia, Brazil

Calabar was quite impressed that the pumpkin-shaped man's ankles didn't break when they tied a slip knot around them and tossed him over the railing. The fat slaver dangled a few inches above the rippling water, screaming.

"He's got good lungs," Moses said, leaning over the railing to watch the man sway back and forth. He leaned back and nodded to Casper and three others holding the rope tightly. "Let's see if he screams as well when he's below the waves."

The man tried to protest, but his mouth was suddenly filled with salty froth. He wriggled and jerked against the rope like an immense worm on a hook. Moses counted to ten. "Let him up."

They pulled the slaver out and slowly, slowly, began to lift him to the railing. Calabar leaned over and grabbed the man's chin and yanked high and hard right so that he could stare into his pudgy face. The slaver's eyes were closed; salt water dribbled out of his gaping mouth. "Your previous answers to my questions were unsatisfactory, sir. Do you care to respond more appropriately this time, or shall we continue with your bath?"

The man shook. "No . . . no. Bring me up, I beg you. I'll tell you what you want to know. I swear it!"

Moses gave the nod. They pulled until the slaver's bound feet were at the railing. Calabar reached over and grabbed the man's pantaloons. Moses grabbed his shirt.

They brought him over the rail and let him fall to the deck. They stepped back and gave the man a moment to collect himself. Then Calabar knelt beside him. "I will ask you again," he said. "Three people. Native Brazilian and Portuguese. Two children. One named Lua. The other Martim. And a woman. Her name is Celia. Where did you send them?"

The man spit more water, coughed, then said. "I . . . I put them on the *Santa Catarina do Benin*. Big ship. A *nau*, though it had light cargo when it set sail."

"By cargo, you mean Africans, don't you?" Calabar slapped the man sharply behind one ear. "Where was it bound?"

The slaver cowered, shook his head. "I don't know for certain. Up the coast. Recife was one of their stops, I know. Fortaleza, maybe. Belém. I was ordered to hand them over to the ship's captain and get them out of Brazil. The man who brought them did not care where, just so long as they were out."

Calabar looked at Moses. "They're probably up to Belém by now. Could Cadogen or Blanchett have run into them?"

Moses shook his head. "It's a big ocean, Calabar. We'll be lucky to find them ourselves."

"The Spanish!" The slaver blurted, trying to pull himself up into a sitting position. Calabar drove his boot into the man's chest, keeping him down. "The Spanish. They were taking them to the Spanish. The bitch—I mean—the mother, she was terrified of the Spanish. That's where they were probably taken."

"That means the Caribbean," Calabar said to Moses, his hope piqued momentarily.

The pirate frowned sadly. "Again, it's a big ocean, my friend. They could be anywhere."

"Still, we have to try to find that ship."

He could tell that Moses was reluctant to go along, to chase a Portuguese slave ship up the coast. It would likely be heavily armed and crewed even if they found it. Could Moses take it? Calabar had no doubt in his friend's abilities as a pirate-turned-part-time-privateer. And all along the Spanish Main, he had seen the fighting prowess of the crew firsthand. But Moses' lack of enthusiasm was a problem in itself, forced Calabar to push less urgently lest he anger the pirate again and lose his cooperation entirely. And right now, the biggest obstacle was not even the lack of information about the destination of the ship, but its capabilities.

Calabar turned back to the slaver. "What did you observe of the ship which took them? How was it rigged, armed, crewed?" Calabar nodded as the answers tumbled out from between the panicked slaver's heavy lips, but kept an eye on Moses. Like the sea wolf he was, his eyes were sharp and unblinking as he learned about his potential target. The more he learned about it, the more he was thinking about how to take it. It was just the scent of blood he needed.

When the slaver was done blubbering out what he knew, Calabar turned to Moses. "Well, what do you say?" he asked calmly.

Moses pulled on his beard. He folded his arms, his gaze moving from Calabar to the slaver, and back again. Finally, he nodded. "Very well. Let's go get them."

Calabar nodded, and allowed himself a smile, refused to show his relief and residual impatience behind it.

"Hey, what about me?" The slaver looked up at them with cold, cautious eyes.

Calabar grabbed his shirt and pulled him up.

"Cut these ropes," the slaver demanded. "I've told you what you wanted to know. Now set me free."

Calabar nodded. He made a move to draw the knife at his belt, as if he were going to cut the man's bindings. Then he grabbed the man violently by the belt and the nape of his neck, and threw him overboard. He waited to speak until the man stopped screaming, until he hit the water and disappeared below the waves.

"There you go, you son of a bitch," Calabar called after him. "There's your freedom."

Chapter 21

Calabar stared at a large ship through Moses' spyglass. At their distance, Calabar could only make out vague shapes on the deck. The details of the ship itself were somewhat clearer.

"Is it the one we're after?" Moses asked. He leaned on the railing beside Calabar.

Calabar shrugged. "It fits the slaver's description. It's Portuguese. It's square-rigged fore and main; lateen-rigged on the mizzen. Of course, that describes most of the larger Spanish and Portuguese ships. For all I know, it may just be an old carrack out of Fortaleza."

"That's doubtful." Moses took the spyglass and had a look himself. He adjusted the focus, walking it up and down the railing, changing his angle. "It's a *nau*, all right, and it's in pretty good shape. So it's worth a closer look. But where's the crew?"

"That's what I was wondering." They had been shadowing the ship for a full day, and Calabar had only seen slight and very intermittent movement on the deck or aloft. Couldn't have been more than a few men active at any given time. "We have an opportunity here."

"They have a full gun deck," Moses said, changing focus again. "And I see a swivel gun on the fo'c'sle, but it looks damaged. There's a chase gun there, a fixed forward-firing falconet. Can't see her stern. So the armament is close to what we were told—but also, pretty common. And pretty dangerous to the likes of us."

"Yes, but if they are under-strength..."

Moses nodded. Calabar could almost see drool at the corner of his friend's mouth. "I wouldn't mind getting my hands on whatever cargo they are hauling. But we can't know for sure about the crew. If we attack and are mistaken about them being shorthanded, we may be in for a deadly fight. And you could find yourself once again meeting the slaver who gave us the information—under the waves."

"This ship can sail circles around that big box of lumber," Calabar said.

"Yes, but one mighty broadside, and we're kindling," Moses grunted. "I wish Blanchett and Cadogen were here. Three against one; we'd make short work of it."

"We're wasting time talking. Let's go get it."

Moses lowered his spyglass and looked at Calabar. He cracked a smile. "Under better circumstances, you'd make a fine pirate captain. But you're angry, Calabar. I've seen angry men such as you throw themselves against wall after wall, and get pounded to dust. Anger got you that nasty wound in your shoulder near Bom Jesus, and anger will get you killed. We'll follow the *nao* for a little while longer, see if we can better

ascertain numbers for their crew. Then we'll rake their
sails from the rear. That'll get the bees buzzing, and
then we'll know her complement for sure. All right?"

Moses was correct. Going in without better intelligence would be foolhardy, but it was difficult for
Calabar to suppress his anger, to be patient under these
circumstances. Just out of reach, his wife and children
might be suffering. Acting as quickly as possible felt
far more crucial than proceeding with due care. But
he nodded, and tried to return Moses' smile. "You're
right, my friend. We'll do as you say, but when the
time comes, I will lead the boarding party."

After a few more hours of shadowing and watching
the Portuguese ship from a good distance, Moses
finally brought *Sword of Solomon* closer and, at one
hundred meters from the *nao*'s port side, he shouted
the command that Calabar had been waiting for. "Fire!"

Round shot roared out of the starboard side muzzles just as the pirate patache crested a swell. Moses
preferred to fire at the top of the roll, as it more
readily guaranteed at least some hits on the initial
volley, though they could range from the rigging to the
hull. Unfortunately, the shot was at an oblique angle,
the Portuguese ship moving as fast as she could to
evade, and thus about two thirds of the balls missed.
The rest of the volley, however, struck the *nau* and
splintered the midships gunwale on the port side. From
this distance, Calabar could not see if any shot found
flesh, but all in all, a decent first volley.

The gunners loaded quickly and, at Moses' command, fired again. Although at an even more oblique
angle, they correctly anticipated the pitch and relative

motion of the ships. Solid shot tore through the *nau*'s aftercastle, from the poop deck on down to the ports for the stern chase guns. Calabar waited to hear any explosions that the shot might have caused further within the hull, but there were none. The Portuguese ship was still mostly intact, still sailing well, and still looking very formidable. A belowdecks explosion would have been good for them tactically, Calabar knew, but he was glad one did not occur. If there were still slaves on that ship...

As Moses had predicted, that volley also got the "bees buzzing" on the *nao*'s deck. Men scrambled about as the Portuguese ship labored to come to starboard and cross ahead of the *Sword of Solomon* in an attempt to bring its entire starboard battery to bear.

"She means to stand and fight," Calabar said, adjusting the focus on the spyglass.

Moses nodded. "Yes, but look: still very few crewmen. I figure they have half their complement, at best. They've realized that between their sparse sail handlers and our superior speed, they can't outrun us. So they'll try to catch us with one good volley and then make a good show if we survive to board." He leaned back, cupped his mouth, and shouted, "Crowd sail, three points port. Quickly now, and ready chain shot!"

By turning sharply to the left, they gave the Portuguese ship the freedom to turn fully to its starboard and open its gunports. Men readied half-ball chain shot below; Calabar could hear their muffled voices through the planks, but kept his eye on the Portuguese ship and watched as, one after another, the gunports were opened along the gun deck and the cannon run out. Far fewer than should have. He shook his head. "That's only half."

"Mhmm," Moses grunted. "Steady now! We've the wind gauge and will be behind her in a moment. Starboard gunners: stand to!"

The Portuguese ship opened fire. Calabar observed the jets of smoke that seemed to carry thunder toward them from each barrel. His instinct was to duck. Moses stood there like a rock, arms folded over his chest, a small smile on his face.

The Portuguese ship, desperate to hammer her antagonist before it could slip out of and behind the spread of her broadside, had fired at the top of the roll. But it would have been better for her captain to have waited another second, maybe two, for the *nao* to go over the crest and her muzzles to dip down. Well over half the broadside of round shot flew harmlessly over *Sword of Solomon* or through the gaps in her rigging: she had too low a profile and was angling too sharply astern to present a frank and easy target.

A lucky ball hit on the crow's nest and shattered it into a flurry of kindling. The lookout's scream ended abruptly, his upper half flying high and far into the portside swells. His lower half had simply disappeared. Another round struck the deck, bounced low and straight across the boards, smashing everything and everyone in its path until it broke through the portside gunwale. Three more crewmen were left dead in its wake, but Moses didn't blink an eye.

"Goddamn!" Calabar said, collecting himself. "She may be weak, but she's got some powerful guns."

"Aye!" Moses said, shifting his stance a little to get a better view of the situation. "We were lucky, but we won't be next time if she gets off another volley at us. We have to bring this to a close. Starboard guns: *fire chain!*"

They fired a full load of chain shot. They hadn't reached the ideal position to rake the *nao*—about fifty meters directly astern—but it didn't matter. The *Sword of Solomon*'s starboard guns spoke and the lateen sail vanished from the mizzenmast of the Portuguese ship. More of the chain shot swept beyond it into the mainmast, ripping deep gashes into the canvas and bringing about half of it down. Calabar saw some of the crew ripped apart by shot that flew head-height across the poop deck.

Everything grew quiet, save for Moses' crew who scrambled to reload another volley of chain shot, and the wounded on the Portuguese ship screaming their last. Calabar waited as the *Sword of Solomon* swept astern of its adversary and immediately heeled to starboard, bringing it along the port side of the Portuguese ship, almost within optimal firing range.

"Will she try another broadside?" he asked.

Moses shrugged. "Due to her limited crew, they'll have to shift men from starboard to port both to reload and train her guns. So they could fire again, if we gave them the time. But we shall not do so." He barked orders. "Starboard guns: fire at will and on the rise. Let's bring down more of her canvas. Pilot, prepare to go alongside. Boarders: stand to!"

"Get the men ready," he muttered to Calabar out of the corner of his mouth.

Calabar nodded and handed over the spyglass.

His men were assembling on the low fo'c'sle, muskets, pistols, boarding axes, and swords at the ready.

Grapplers with hooks, rope, and short boarding ladders waited closest to the starboard railing. Calabar ran a quick headcount, looked into eyes to determine that the boarders were ready. After a ragged thundering of the starboard battery and more canvas, sheets, and rigging came down on the *nao*, he nodded at them and shouted, "Steady courage, men. They have a weakened crew, and the raking has weakened them even further. But a wounded dog will fight to the death, so stay together and fire en masse. Clear the decks but await my signal to go below. They may have human cargo. Do *not* kill any of them. If you do, I will kill *you*. Understand?"

They gave a collective "Aye" and Calabar led them to the side.

Despite their skill, Moses' pilot slammed the *Sword of Solomon*'s prow into the Portuguese ship at a sharp angle. Not direct or swift enough to be considered a ram, but the first bump sent one of Calabar's newest recruits over the bow. No one was quick or close enough to save him, and as the patache put over toward the *nao* again, the cutwater went over him; he disappeared with a yelp, was never seen again.

By the time the *Sword of Solomon* had come to a stop, the starboard side had reloaded. As Calabar prepared to lead his men up and over the side, Moses yelled, "Battery, on my command: *fire!*"

What flew out from the roar and smoke of the starboard guns was a moaning mix of chain and ball, some of the gunners not having heard their captain's order to shift to standard shot. Both hit the Portuguese ship at point-blank range. The *nau* had a higher deck than the patache, and most of the chain was angled upward, although not all of the muzzles were able to clear the enemy's gunwale. But it hardly mattered. Wood splintered. Men inside the Portuguese ship screamed as both shot and chain howled through the gunports and slaughtered cannon crews. The enemy gunwale was shattered from amidships to the aftercastle. The few men who had been defending it with musketoons and pistols either died in place or fell back from the concussive rush of the torrent of lethal iron.

One culverin from the Portuguese ship fired a half load, cutting a swath through Calabar's boarders as they moved to the gunwale and raised the first ladders. Half a dozen fell flailing and crying, three more who neither moved nor made a sound. The rest of the first boarders shied back. For a moment, it seemed as if they might lose their heart, might give the Portuguese enough time to organize a ragged defense, discharge a few of the cannons staring level with the pirates' eyes.

Calabar jumped forward, shouted the order which matched his own action: "Attack!"

The gap between the hulls was small but the angle of the boarders' ascent and the higher deck of the *nao* gave the defenders the advantage. Grapples were tossed, tugged tight, and men began to climb up hand over hand.

Each grapple line had a man assigned for sharp-shooting duty. Any Portuguese sailor brave enough to return to the gunwale to either attempt to cut the grappling lines or lean over to fire at the climbers became a target for the sharpshooters. Although they often did not hit defenders, they almost invariably ruined their aim or thwarted their efforts.

Calabar led the way up his line, pistol and boarding

axe tucked into his belt. Despite the grapple hooks set all along the middle of the *nao*'s port side, the movement of the waves made climbing difficult. His hands, his shoulders, ached at the effort. But he kept pulling his weight up from one knot to the next until he was able to fling himself over the gunwale to land unsteadily upon the enemy's deck.

Where a man rushed at him, blade in motion. Calabar pulled his pistol and fired into the face of a Portuguese crewman whose cut at Calabar's head dropped as he did. The sword skittered to the gunwale not far from the facedown body, from which blood was already running toward a nearby scupper.

Further back from the side, other Portuguese defenders had hastily assembled a ragged firing line among crates and ruined spars. They finally readied and fired their musketoons as Calabar's first boarders rushed them. A few men went down before the ragged volley, but Calabar gathered more new boarders and pressed the attack. Without time to reload his pistol, he tucked it away and drew his axe, hacking and slashing his way through the defenders as if they were a wall of raw meat.

A nearby explosion staggered the attackers and even a few defenders. Calabar half dove, half fell to the deck, balling up and rolling against a crate to keep from being crushed by the press of his own men, some who were running past, others tumbling to the sides, wounded. Through the rushing legs, he saw the source of the explosion: an older Portuguese sailor with a bag from which he was just producing another grenade. He tried to light the fuse with one of the cannon's tapers, but as Calabar's boarders reached him, he had to give ground, struggling to keep the grenade and flame steady.

Calabar sprang up, starting low like a sprinter and launching himself forward to muscle through his own men and emerge close to the sailor-turned-grenadier. He slipped around a cutlass-wielding crewman and slapped the taper out of the fellow's hand before he could steady it to make contact with the grenade's fuse. The sailor spat a curse, stepped back, tried to draw his weapon.

But Calabar was quicker; with his free hand he grabbed for the grenade but, missing it, pulled the bag of others off the lanyard holding it close to the sailor. But with his own weapon hand, he hammered the man's face with the spike of his axe, cutting deep, bloody tracks there, the man abandoning the attempt to draw his own weapon; he was just barely able to successfully fend off what would otherwise have been lethal blows.

Calabar put a break in the rhythmic sequence of attacks: a pause-feint that threw the other man off for just a moment. But in that moment, Calabar sunk the axe's back spike deep into his eye. The sailor screamed, his other hand unclasping; the grenade rolled free and was quickly lost in the mad scuffle of running, leaping, dodging feet and legs.

The Portuguese were putting up a good fight, particularly along the side where the boarders had initially streamed up to the deck. But with pirates and Portuguese now so closely mixed, the covering marksmen were unable to shoot for fear of hitting their own men. Calabar measured the decreased flow of boarders against the steady trickle of new crewmen coming up from the lower decks and, for the first moment, feared that the attack might be repulsed.

And rushing right behind that panic were the faces of Celia, Lua, and Martim, their eyes surrounding him, damning him for not having come sooner, for not having fought harder—

Calabar swung toward the swivel gun just two steps up on the fo'c'sle. Casper was the only surviving boarder still fighting to keep the crew from gaining control of the weapon. Its base was damaged, it teetered on the swivel, but the barrel itself appeared to be in fine order. Was it loaded? The Portuguese were certainly fighting hard to keep it on their side: a sign that it was ready for use.

Calabar fought his way through the intervening melee, taking down one Portuguese sailor with a single flat-sided crack of the boarding axe across his bald pate. Before he could pull his arm back, Calabar took a cut across his right arm. He rolled away from the blow, lessening it, but his knees trembled at the shock and pain and he fell to them.

But he bounced up off them, resolved to keep moving as he staggered forward the last few feet to where Casper clutched the swivel gun with his left hand while fighting off three Portuguese sailors with the sword in his right. But he was badly wounded. Deep lacerations on his torso and limbs, blood seeping out of them like a mounting tide. He was holding his ground, but his strength was waning.

Take a rest, Casper, Calabar said silently as he pushed the former slave aside and took his place.

He killed the closest combatant outright by driving the back spike through his throat. The others hesitated, considered the new opponent, then flanked him more broadly as they edged in to reengage. As they did,

Calabar saw the closest holding a long smoldering match in his hand. He spun the barrel of the swivel gun sharply, knocked the man aside. But the swivel itself cracked at the force of the blow.

Calabar had to catch and hug the barrel to keep it in place, damning himself for having used the weapon as the equivalent of a big club. One more harsh push or yank and the barrel would fully detach from the swivel and be unusable.

The Portuguese came at him again. Calabar ducked, let the barrel take the first saber slash. The blade skidded off with a spark. Another cutlass-wielding sailor struck at him. Calabar dropped into a quick crouch: this sword hit the barrel as well, raising a small spray of even larger sparks. One of which landed near the weapon's readied wick. Had it landed just a little further down the barrel—

Calabar glanced at his first attacker; the fellow was climbing to his feet, the match cord still in his hand, the end glowing red.

If he had that match...

He spun away from the third attacker's clumsily swung belaying pin, shoving his hip against the barrel until it pointed at the largest concentration of Portuguese. It was pure chaos just beyond the foot of the fo'c'sle. Both sides were hopelessly mingled in a seething mass of rising and falling swords, pistol handles, clubs, gigs, axes, and spikes. Teeth flashed white or yellow where some had resorted to biting each other.

Calabar knew it would be disastrous to both sides to fire the gun into the center of that, but if he cheated it away from the side that the pirates had come over...

He shoved the barrel so that it jammed down into the narrower gap where the swivel's arms separated like the two halves of a wishbone, swung wide with his axe—and dove under the weapon.

As the two Portuguese recovered from their surprise at his unexpected movement, Calabar came up and rushed at the fellow who could not seem to decide between holding a weapon, clutching his broken ribs, or grasping the lit match. Startled, he backed away, sword up to block, the opposite elbow steadying his opposite ribcage—and the forgotten match falling to the deck, its end dark but still smoldering.

Even as the sailor stumbled over his own feet, Calabar watched as combatants surged into the open space. The match was free, but he couldn't reach it anymore. Not until he cleared a path to it.

The angle of his crouch put him beneath eye level of the others in the melee, long enough to get in a surprise attack: he thrust his axe spike up into the tender belly of the closest Portuguese sailor. Calabar felt it go deep, gave it a twist, and blood flowed down the man's dirty shirt. The sailor neither screamed nor fell, but stood rigid, his stomach muscles tensing against the imbedded spike. Then he collapsed to his knees and Calabar finished the job by pushing the man away and twisting out the axe as he did. He started to rise—

A boot struck him in the side of the head. Dizzy, Calabar rolled toward the wick, flinching and dodging to avoid another kick, and then another. The blows stopped coming; either Calabar had rolled away from where his assailant could reach or he had been confronted by a more dangerous opponent.

Calabar lunged toward the wick, grabbed it. He pulled it close. He blew a few times on its end, until the embers glowed again.

The blood-slick boarding axe was slippery in his hand as, gripping it tightly, he wormed his way back around to the swivel gun's pedestal—where one of the two men he'd fought earlier was still protecting it. They saw each other at the same moment. The sailor's sword came down first. Calabar raised the axe, blocked the cut with its iron-backed haft, and rolled his wrist so that the blade was deflected away before it could take off his knuckles. As he did, he slipped lower, lashed out with his left leg and got his foot behind the sailor's leading leg. Continuing with one fluid motion, he hooked his pant cuff with the back spike and, rolling back, Calabar kicked his right heel straight up. The blow to the man's groin was so sharp that Calabar felt it in his own hip. The sailor groaned and fell sharply as his doubly hooked leg went out from under him.

Calabar tried to leap to his feet, but instead, had to drag himself up by clutching the top of the tipping pedestal. He reached for the barrel of the swivel gun. He turned it back toward the highest concentration of Portuguese sailors. He placed the faintly glowing coal into the touchhole.

Fire burst from the barrel. The spread of small-gauge grapeshot was broad, but it struck the Portuguese sailors at point-blank range, ripping bloody holes through their bodies and then into those of the men behind, sending them all to the deck. Some of the shot struck Calabar's men; inevitable and unfortunate. But the blast opened a gap in the enemy mass and they exploited that space and the enemy's shock immediately.

Calabar's men charged forward, some making short
work of the sailors wounded by the grapeshot, the
rest swarming around them to crash headlong into
the startled Portuguese survivors. A moment or two of
fierce combat...and then the Portuguese at the rear of
the melee melting away, desperate to find exit points.

The fight was over. Although Calabar could hear
the shrieks of those who had fled beneath the deck
as pursuers caught up with them. That persisted for
almost a full minute.

In that time, Calabar took a moment to catch his
breath and to check on Casper who lay facedown in
a pool of blood and seawater. He rolled the dead
runaway over and cradled him. He said a silent prayer,
held him a moment longer, and laid him back down.
He rose slowly, favoring the side of his head where
the sailor had kicked him.

The remaining Portuguese crew had surrendered
and were herded to the waist, compressed into a
rough cluster around the damaged mainmast, as their
captors bound their hands behind their backs. There
were even fewer than Calabar had estimated. Those
who had died were left lying where they perished.
Moses liked to intimidate prisoners—particularly if
he might need to impress some of them as a prize
crew—by keeping their dead in plain view.

Calabar's men found the captain not merely belowdecks, but cowering in the bilges. They brought him
to the weather deck and made him stand amidst his
dead men. "It is a coward who hides while his men
fight and die," Calabar said loudly, slowly waving his
pistol below the captain's chin.

"I am Captain Emilio Ramires," he announced.

"You have assaulted a Portuguese ship sailing under the banner of King—"

Calabar flipped his wrist hard; the barrel of his pistol struck Ramires across the mouth. Blood and teeth sprayed as the captain fell to his knees. "I don't care about your king," Calabar replied calmly. "But I do care about your human cargo. Where did you take them?"

Ramires grunted, spit blood. He straightened and his jaw moved as if he were about to say something, but then lowered his head when he saw one of Calabar's men—Richard—come up from the hold. The young pirate was frowning as he dropped iron shackles at the captain's knees.

"There is a lot of cargo, Calabar," Richard said, "but no slaves. There are a lot of those." He pointed to the shackles. "Rows upon rows of them. And it stinks like hell down there, Calabar. Vile. Disease-ridden."

Calabar slowly reloaded his pistol as he watched Captain Ramires rub his chin and spit more blood. Something in the captain's eyes gave him pause. "You recognized my name, sir." Calabar kneeled to stare him straight in the eyes. "We have never met, but still you know of me. How? From whose lips?"

Captain Ramires seemed reluctant to answer, but his eyes grew large when Calabar resumed moving his cocked pistol slowly before his bloodied face. "Your wife. She spoke of you. Screamed your name in the night." He forced a chuckle. "She was good at numbers, I'll give her that. Not much good at anything else. But she saved us from a revolt. The Africans hated her after that. I should have kept her for myself, but she and your little whelps got a good price."

Calabar smiled, lowered his pistol. His men quieted. Probably unable to believe that he had not slain the Portuguese on the spot for insulting his wife. "Where did you take them?"

"I took them nowhere," Captain Ramires said, coughing. "A Spanish ship pulled alongside and we made an exchange."

"Where did this Spanish ship take them?"

Captain Ramires shrugged. "Who can say? They mentioned Cartagena a few times, but I asked no questions. I was glad to be rid of them. And of the Africans. And of your wife, especially."

Calabar nodded. "Thank you for your help and honesty, sir." He straightened, raised his pistol so that it pointed at the captain's chest, and pulled the trigger.

"Calabar."

He turned to see Moses standing there, staring at him blankly. Calabar joined him. They walked to the starboard gunwale alone.

"My apologies, Moses," Calabar said, tucking his smoking pistol beneath his belt. "I just couldn't let that son of a bitch breathe any—"

"I don't care about him," Moses said, interrupting. "I'd have killed him myself, but you spared me the trouble. However, I must be clear: I will *not* take my ship into Cartagena."

"I have to go there."

"I will take you as far as Curaçao. From there, you will have to get to Cartagena on your own."

Calabar looked around him. "What about this ship?"

"Depends upon the wind, the weather, and how much spare canvas we find in stores. If she can't keep up, we'll scuttle her after transferring the best of her cargo," Moses said. "We'll probably take on most of the crew as well. Portuguese make good pirates when they put their minds to it, and always having to give in to the will of arrogant Spaniards makes more than a few of them ready to string up their old masters."

He glanced northeast. "The Rocas Atoll isn't far; three days sail, five if we have to tack constantly. We'll stop there and give Blanchett and Cadogen a taste of the cargo to help them make the right decision. And then I'll take you to Curaçao. But that's where we must part ways, Calabar. I've made promises to the Dutch: promises that make it impossible for me to undertake the journeys, and fight the enemies, you have sworn you shall."

Calabar could tell that the frank statement of their separation hurt his friend. It hurt Calabar too. Despite their recent disputes, both at Tobago and after Calabar's flight to the Jesuit church, he respected Moses and valued his counsel, even when it ran contrary to his own impulses. In retrospect, perhaps that was the counsel he had ultimately valued most.

"I understand, Moses," Calabar said, offering his hand. "And thank you. For everything. I hope we meet again someday."

Moses brushed aside Calabar's hand and pulled him in close for a hug. It was an uncomfortable embrace. Perhaps because Moses' crew was nearby, and a good pirate captain could not show such womanly emotion in front of his men. But Moses didn't seem to care, and neither did Calabar. They let the trials of the last several months wash away in a long hug of brothers saying farewell. Perhaps for the last time.

Moses then pulled away. "Now, get your foolish ass to my ship. Get cleaned up, and have my physician check those wounds. And get some food and rest. You've done enough for today. You'll need all the strength you can muster for Cartagena. Because for those such as us, going into that port is like going into the mouth of Hell."

Chapter 22

Cartagena, Viceroyalty of Peru

When Celia's bare foot touched land, she wept. When she saw Martim for the first time in several weeks, after being transferred from the *Santa Catarina do Benin* to the Spanish slave ship, she fell to her knees and cried again. Finally, they were on solid ground and alive. All three.

There were times during their journey that she thought they'd all die. Late at night in the hold, as the waves pounded the creaking, bending planks of the ship, through the terrible chorus of moans and screams of the women who had survived, she could not drive away waking nightmares of watching Martim or Lua being thrown to the sharks like those who had died during the revolt. She prayed to God to give her strength, to drive away those horrible images, but they crept into her thoughts every night, sometimes lurking there, hiding, only rousing when she slept. *I'm a terrible mother*, she'd say to herself in the pitch dark, *for not being strong enough and for not fighting harder to keep them out of this situation.*

And if the situation seemed to have fewer immediately mortal dangers, it also seemed to be one step closer to a life of hopeless misery as a slave. She had heard of this city, this Cartagena, while still in Recife. A large, bustling port. A place of extraordinary wealth. And a veritable citadel of slavery.

Moments after kneeling in thanks, Celia was yanked roughly to her feet and pushed along with the others who had survived the voyage, as if they were just so much cattle. They were stripped of all clothing and put through a rigorous inspection that assessed the health of their bodies and minds. Celia's Spanish was not perfect, but as they worked her over, she heard terms like *"fondeo"* and *"visita de sanidad"* and then, during the final and most rigorous inspection, *"palmeo."* It was in this last part of the process where the physicians asked her the most questions, personal and private ones, as if they were trying to provoke a response, good or bad. They tried to frighten her with intimations and then threats of physical and sexual abuse. After the first few minutes, she realized but did not reveal that she understood what they were doing: provoking her in various ways to assess her demeanor, her level of energy, her reflexes, her tendency toward defiance. She gave them what she presumed they were looking for: demure compliance.

In the end, they classified her as *"pieza de india,"* which near as Celia could figure, meant that she was considered a full "unit of work." Martim and Lua, because of their youth, were not classified as such; in the eyes of the slavers, they were worth much less.

After the inspections, Celia and Lua were placed in a barracoon holding cell not far from Martim's. The only difference between this cell and the hold on the slave ship was slightly better airflow and fresher food. Now that they were to be shown on the block to the final buyers, the quality of the "product" mattered more. No *amo* wanted to buy a physically weak, or intrinsically hostile, slave. But they were still packed in tight, this time with Africans from other ships, all waiting to be sold to the highest bidders from all across the territories of the Caribbean and New Spain.

The African women who had been on the same ship avoided Celia and Lua as if they were traitors. Now Celia understood how Calabar had felt when he had come home from Pontal and told her that de Gama had labeled him with that same word. Celia *had* betrayed those Africans, and they would never understand why she had done it, and she could never explain her actions, mostly because they shared no common language. But even if she was fluent in their language, what could she have said that mattered? She was a mother protecting her children; it did not matter that, in her place, they would have done no less. Fate had given them their roles, and in this tragedy, she was a traitor to them all, and would be guilty of that—both to them and to herself—forever.

The days blurred together. The stagnant heat and the unremitting body odor of too many women packed in close became almost unbearable. Only a cool breeze in the evenings, off the bay, gave Celia and Lua some comfort. When water and modest amounts of food were ladled out in buckets, she would pick up a phrase or two from their keepers.

"Es un grupo lamentable. No tienen bastante carne en sus huesos. Ellos necesitan mas tiempo para recuperarse si quieren criar con estos."

"Pero no hay tiempo. Estan hablando sobre un pelea grande pronto."

She did not know what a scramble, a *pelea*, was and she feared the worst. Three days later, she found out.

The barracoons were opened. Buyers poured in, pushing and prodding their way through the mass of African women while other men stood nearby with pistols and whips and chains, to ensure that none of the stock tried to run away or fight back.

Celia scooped up Lua and huddled in the corner, making herself as meek and as obscure as possible. The buyers who had entered were excited, brusque, and shameless, yelling and pushing through the bodies, picking this woman and that one, making swift inspections of their own, and then hustling their desired purchases to a handler who would line them up and slap chains and rope around their wrists to bring them out of the cell and into buying lines to finalize their purchase. It was chaos. Two buyers even began to fight in the middle of the cell, throwing fists over one particularly young and buxom girl whom Celia did not recognize. She had not been on her ship, but she was quite lovely, an opinion that the buyers obviously shared. They fought and argued over who was going to whelp young off her first. The argument became increasingly disgusting, and was settled only by an auctioneer who took the side of the wealthier one and threw the other out of the *pelea*.

After about thirty minutes, things quieted. Celia and Lua had not been picked, thank God, and so she settled down again and began to fix Lua's hair in a long braided tail. *Perhaps we won't get sold at all. Perhaps—*

"Levantense."

The man's voice startled her. She looked up and saw a Spaniard staring down at her, a small paunch sticking out over his thick leather belt. He wore a broad-brimmed hat. His tunic and pantaloons were dark tan and loose. He had a beard and mustache, black and well groomed. He appeared to have most of his teeth, and he had a scent of perfume about him. He was sweating, but she couldn't smell that through the pungent odor of her cell mates.

Celia took Lua's hand and they stood. She stared the man right in the face.

"I don't normally buy natives," he said. "They are lazy and prone to escape. But the captain of your ship insists that you can keep accounts. And that you can read. Are these claims true?"

Celia hesitated, then nodded. "Yes, I can do both."

"And can you cook?"

"Yes."

"I have sent my foreman here on several occasions to fetch me one such as you, but he has not been successful. So I made the long journey myself, and so I can ill afford the time and expense of returning if what you say about yourself is not true. So be warned: if you fail to meet my needs, I shall be extremely angry."

He watched her eyes as he resumed. "I have a large family and many workers on my plantation. I need a woman who can keep accounts, can read, can cook, and can manage at least three or four other women.

None of these Africans can do that, but maybe you can. You're caboclo, no? All the way from Brazil?" He lifted her arm and inspected the color of her skin. "I will have a caboclo in charge of my kitchen, but not an African. It is a demanding job. Can you do it?"

Celia nodded, enthusiastically. "Oh, yes, sir. I can do all that. Just..."

"Yes?"

"I need my children with me." She patted Lua's head. "My daughter and my son, Martim, must come too."

The man shook his head. "I don't need useless children, eating my food, needing a place to sleep, clothing. Just you."

He turned to a bookkeeper, a young man who stood beside him, holding a manifest. They discussed the list and her price. Celia grabbed the man's shirt-sleeve and tugged. "Sir, I promise you, if you take me away from my children, as soon as I am able, I will kill myself. And you will have wasted a lot of time and money."

Both men stared at her for a long moment; the buyer the longest. Finally, he cracked a smile. "Feisty, eh? I'll beat that out of you in time. You'll learn to hold your tongue and show respect." He moved closer and walked around her slowly. He lifted strands of her hair, smelled them, and put his hand on her waist. Celia tried not to flinch or retch at his touch, but his hands were thick and coarse. He leaned over and whispered in her ear. She could smell a touch of rum on his breath.

"They are very smart children, sir," Celia said, trying to sweeten the idea even further. "They can read and they are learning to write. In time, they could also keep accounts and help you manage your affairs, if you would have further need for that."

The man nodded. "Very well. I can be a fair man. I'll take your children. For now, the boy can work in my fields, and the girl can be a playmate for my youngest. You...well, I want you to remember this favor I am granting you, the kindness I am showing you by keeping your family together. We will be working very closely. Late nights, on occasion. Alone." He stepped closer; there was less than an inch between them. "Do you hear me? Do you understand?"

She nodded, though it was hard for her not to shed tears of rage, fear, and regret. *Do not cry. Do not give this brute the satisfaction. Play for time, Celia, like Calabar always says. In war, you play for time...* "Yes, sir, I hear you."

He nodded. He turned to the bookkeeper. "Get her boy, too. And have all three at my ship within the hour."

He turned to leave. Celia called after him. "Sir, where are we going?"

He stopped, turned, and said. "Far away."

Part Four

March 1636–May 1636

"Stand fast therefore in the liberty
wherewith Christ hath made us free, and be
not entangled again with the yoke of bondage."
—Galatians 5:1

Chapter 23

Cartagena, Viceroyalty of Peru

Calabar was delivered to Curaçao. There, they met with some of Moses' so-called "friends." Spanish pirates. And it was clear to Calabar that they had a love-hate relationship with the Sephardic Jew. Not because of his religion or heritage, but more because he was known to cooperate with the Dutch. But they apparently remained unaware of just how much Moses was now aligned with, and guided by, their interests.

To Calabar's mind, Moses had always been supportive of the Dutch, even when their often similar interests were not evident to others—including the Dutch themselves. But times were changing, and the Spanish raiders knew this. Both parties now expected that, at some point, they'd face each other across broadsides and crossed swords. Neither party wanted to admit this openly, certainly not face to face, but the tension between them hung in the air as thick as cannon smoke.

It was unclear at first whether or not the Spanish pirates would help Calabar reach Cartagena. In the end, they agreed, once Moses shared some of the booty he had acquired from the Portuguese slave ship. So they bid their final farewells, and Calabar climbed aboard the Spanish raider.

But not even these Spanish pirates would sail into Cartagena. Instead, they dropped anchor off the coast and delivered Calabar by skiff near Punta Canoas, a tiny strip of beach about fifteen miles north of the great port. The men who delivered him were evidently quite eager to see him gone, as they forced him off at gunpoint. Calabar wasted no time scrambling up the shore and disappearing into the jungle's edge.

He had a good sword, a knife, a musket, a pistol, and some dried meat and fruit. He had a water skin, a bedroll, and a purse of coins. He had acquired some new clothing from the Portuguese ship. He had even taken the time to clean and shave before departing the Spanish raider. He needed to look as dignified and as presentable as possible. He intended to work and move at night, but even in the low glow of candle- and lamplight, a dirty, disheveled mameluco might raise the suspicion of slavers and bush captains who searched New Spain continually for runaways. His skin color, in combination with being unaccompanied and independent in his interactions, would raise suspicions anyway, but there was no reason to make things worse by looking unkempt and smelling foul. In truth, he had no idea what to expect in Cartagena, but whatever lay waiting, he intended to navigate through it as subtly and skillfully as possible to find his family.

Calabar spent that first night moving south, keeping close to the shoreline but never setting foot on the beach lest he be seen in moonlight. He had more than enough experience moving in darkness, and despite the fact that Colombia was less heavily wooded than Brazil, he managed to move fast and keep hidden.

By first light, he had reached the outskirts of Cartagena, and on that first day, he did nothing but remain in the shadows and observe.

Cartagena reminded him of Recife: a rich port town, always moving, always alive with voices, activity, and the sounds of commerce. A dozen Spanish ships were anchored in port, many of them heavy with guns and crewed with experienced seamen. He could understand why a lone pirate ship, even a Spanish one, would not dare enter Cartagena unless given permission. It certainly seemed to Calabar that this place had to be the jewel in Spain's extensive New World empire, let alone the Viceroyalty of Peru. Admittedly, he had not traveled much in other Spanish territories, but he couldn't imagine a place more active or more extensive than here. He liked the energy of it, despite the fact that it was controlled by the enemy.

He could tell, however, that there was a tension in the air, that everyone was on edge. Perhaps that was due to the pressures the Dutch and their new USE allies had been placing upon the Spanish everywhere in the New World. Perhaps the anxiety shared among the Spanish pirates toward Moses, his crew, and whose interests they might represent, was contagious.

The economic differences between the various social classes were on full display as well. Rich merchantmen, planters, and government officials shared the streets with poorer citizens. And Calabar was happy to see that there were many *mestizos* about, though he did not know if they moved independently or if they were on orders from masters or employers. He assumed the latter. Spain had occupied this part of the Caribbean for a long time, and Calabar knew that there had been a great deal of interbreeding. Most of the slaves were now acquired from Africa, but that didn't mean that the Spanish were above taking natives as slaves. After all, they had obviously done so with Celia and his children. But were they still here? Calabar wondered. They might be, but where?

Seeing the *mestizos* unaccompanied by their masters or other Spaniards gave Calabar some confidence to walk among them, though first he had to find a safe place to store his weapons. It would not do to have a mixed-race man wearing a sword on his hip or a pistol at his belt as he strolled through Cartagena's streets. Despite the many reasons he might suddenly have need of them, he'd have to risk not carrying his weapons, at least for the first few outings.

He found a small, abandoned, and partially crumbled stone building overlooking the port. The area was heavily overgrown, and Calabar deduced that the building had once been a storage house for grain; it still had a few rotten bags tucked into its corners. He cleaned out a small space on the dirt floor for his bedroll, and found a hiding place for his weapons. He tucked them away carefully, but kept the knife in a sheath at the small of his back. He needed to appear completely nonthreatening as he walked the streets, but he wasn't going to be foolish: the knife was easily concealed and even poor workers kept one on hand, both to use as a tool and for defense. Cartagena was a city, after all, and cities bred crime.

Calabar approached the barracoons the first night. He watched and waited from a distance to ensure that he understood the guards' patrol routes, then he moved in quickly and tried to strike up conversations with the African men and women inside. They were not very responsive to his presence, let alone his questions, which was not improved by the fact that neither he nor they could understand each other very well. None of them were fluent in Spanish or Portuguese, and he was unfamiliar with their languages. But he kept at it, pronouncing his family's names clearly, slowly, over and over again: "Do you know a woman named Celia? Do you know a girl named Lua? Or a boy named Martim?"

At one point, a small, timid girl reacted to the name Lua, but before he could ask any further questions, the guards came back around, and he had to seek cover. When he returned, the girl had moved to the center of the cage and refused any further questions. He tried again the next night, but she was gone.

After that, he decided to take to the streets at dusk and try his luck with the *mestizo* population. Most of them were willing to speak to him, if briefly, but none had heard of his family. Some of them seemed to mistake him for a bush captain; those people refused to speak and, instead, flashed parchment or brandings that proved their status, and then politely moved on. In a way, he was pleased to see their unwillingness to speak, to readily give information about possible runaways to just anyone who approached them, no matter their reasons. It gave him hope that there was at least a silent solidarity between the tribes and peoples of this country that had been so brutally assaulted by Europeans, and specifically, the Spanish. It gave him hope for the future. It gave him pause to think.

Two days of searching left him empty-handed, and

Calabar grew anxious. Not even the workers on the dock had any information about his family. There was only one group left for him to speak to, and he had no desire to do it.

He approached the first slaver near the barracoons early the next morning. A fresh shipment of Africans had arrived and were being processed near the auction block. It sickened Calabar to see them being poked and prodded like cattle, their heads inspected for lice, their mouths opened, their genitalia checked for warts and other signs of disease. He hesitated a moment to refocus his mind, then in his most respectful voice, he said to the one apparently in charge, "Sir, if I may approach to ask a question?"

The man turned and looked Calabar from head to toe. He was a small man, shorter than Calabar, standing no taller than five and a half feet. His well-groomed Vandyke moved up and down as his tongue fished around in his mouth for—Calabar figured—the remnants of his morning meal. His clothing seemed newly pressed. His boots were made of clean, black leather. "Yes, what do you want?"

Calabar took a humble step forward and removed his hat. "Sir, my master has asked me to inquire here about a family. A mother and her two children. They were not African. They were lighter-skinned like me. *Mestizos*, if it please you, sir. They—"

"I don't deal with natives or mix bloods," the man blurted, turning his attention back to the line of Africans before him. "You'll have to speak with the auction house."

Calabar grit his teeth, controlled his tongue, politely nodded, and walked away. "Thank you, sir."

He spoke with two other slavers as he made his way toward the auction house. Their reactions were much the same as the first, caring little about his inquiry. They eyed him with almost as much disdain as they did the Africans they were inspecting, and he suspected that if his skin were any darker, they'd have seized him. He moved carefully, slowly, and averted his eyes from their infuriating contempt.

He reached the auction house. It was a small, shed-like structure. One room with one window. Around the entrance stood several Spaniards who looked somewhat bored and disinterested in the morning's activities. Talking amongst themselves, they barely noticed Calabar as he walked right through their midst and into the building.

He was standing in front of the lone desk in the middle of the room before he was noticed by the man sitting behind it. "Who are you?"

The room went silent, and those at the door stopped their conversations and wandered in. Calabar was surrounded by surprised white faces. "Forgive my intrusion, good sirs. My name is . . . Gonzalo Cerrada. I am here on behalf of my master, Carlos Barrosa. Perhaps you know of him?"

The man at the desk looked at one of his assistants who stood nearby. The assistant shook his head. "His name is not familiar," the man at the desk said, turning his attention back to Calabar.

"A fine man, sir," Calabar said, "and a good, honorable master."

"Why are you here?"

Calabar smiled, bowed. "Master Barrosa wishes to know if a woman and her two children were sold here in Cartagena. They were *mestizo*, you see, and they were promised to Master Barrosa exclusively. Her name would have been Celia. Her children, Lua and Martim. Did they pass through here, sir?"

"Why didn't your master Barrosa come and ask these questions himself?"

Calabar nodded humbly again. "Well, you see, sir, Master Barrosa is a very busy man, and I volunteered to come on his behalf because, well"—Calabar looked left, right, then leaned in and whispered—"she was promised to me, sir."

The man at the desk smiled and gave a hearty laugh. The other men laughed as well. Everyone in the room seemed to enjoy the statement, save for Calabar. He hated that he had to say such undignified and degrading things about his wife. He hated that he had to play this game with these vile white men, but what choice did he have? He had walked into the jaguar's lair; he needed to make sure he could get out.

The laughter died down. The man at the desk motioned for his assistant to fetch an accounting book sitting on a shelf to his left. He accepted the book, opened it to the middle, and ran a boney finger down a list of scribbled names. He nodded.

"Indeed," he said. "There is a listing of a Celia. No last name, and no children."

"I see, sir." Hope piqued, Calabar leaned slightly over the desk, trying to surreptitiously steal a glance in the book. "Can you tell me where she was sold?"

The man opened his mouth as if he were about to answer, then paused, eyed Calabar carefully, and closed the book. "Who did you say you belonged to?"

Calabar's heart sank, but he kept calm, and spoke

in a slow, deliberate manner. "His name is Carlos Barossa, sir. He is a plantation owner here, on the outskirts of Cartagena. You may check it yourself if you wish." Calabar fished around in his pocket for a few coins. He laid them on the table. "But first, if it please you sir, I ask again: Where was Celia sold?"

The man stood up abruptly. The others gathered closer to Calabar. "If your master wishes to have that information," the man said, "he can fetch it himself."

Calabar eyed the men who had almost surrounded him, confident that, if they tried to seize him, he'd have just enough time to cut one of them with his hidden knife. But he'd wound or kill only that one; he'd not survive the rest.

"Very good, sir," Calabar said, bowing and taking steps backwards between the men and toward the door. "You have my word that I will tell him directly. And I thank you."

He turned, pausing to allow one of the men barring the exit to finally step aside and allow him to pass.

Once he was clear of the auction house, Calabar put on his hat and walked out of the slave market and into the town proper.

For the rest of the day, he continued interviewing any persons whose activities or station suggested that they might have information about where Celia—and pray to God, his children—had been sold. The fact that there was no listing of Lua and Martim with their mother was not necessarily a concern, since they could have easily been listed on another page, or not listed at all. He knew from experience with slave auctions in Recife and Bahia that children were not considered very valuable in the eyes of sellers and buyers.

Calabar hoped that that was why their names were not listed and that they had simply been picked up to accompany their mother to ensure her stability and tractability in the service of her master. Calabar had never known slave owners to be that generous—most of them could care less about such things—but Celia was a special case. She had to be. She was a mixed blood like him. Surely she would be treated better.

By the end of the day, Calabar noticed that two men from the auction house were following him. For how long, he was not sure, but fortunately he noticed them at a distance and before he headed into the jungle to return to his hideout. Instead, he circled the last few blocks again, trying to lose them in the crowd. But they were persistent and did not let his heightened pace thwart their pursuit. It was growing darker, and he realized that if his next movements did not suggest that he was heading back to his master's property, they might feel justified to apprehend him forcibly. Maybe lethally. He needed to end this chase: end it now, and on his terms.

He wandered down to one of the many staging areas that were just landward of the docks, where empty casks and crates lay in large piles. He had watched this area long enough to know that, when the sun set, it was populated only by men too drunk to know where they were going, whores with clients, and a few vagrants. And tonight, the area was quiet.

When he reached a line of empty barrels that hid him from his pursuers, Calabar crouched quickly in the shadows cast by the moon and drew his knife. He waited, listening for the sound of following boots on the dock.

On the first creak, he sprang and caught the first man around the waist and swung him down to the dried and cracked planking. The man yelped like a wounded dog when they hit; Calabar felt the man's ribs crack under his full weight. He grabbed the man's shirt as he rolled off and, before the other could react or recover, pulled his knife and drove it up through the solar plexus, the tip angled toward the heart. The man gasped and went limp.

Calabar did not take the time to watch the man's final moment, however; he was already turning and rising, hoping that the abruptness of the first attack would momentarily shock the second man into inaction. However, Calabar did not get a chance to strike before his new adversary responded. The second man was unshaken, swift, and precise. He drove his boot into Calabar's face. Calabar lost hold of his knife and scrambled backwards, tasting blood in his mouth. His vision was not impaired, so he could see what the man was going to do next. Unfortunately, he hadn't the balance or position to do anything about it.

The man grabbed up a barrel and slammed it down into Calabar's gut like a hammer. Calabar blocked it with his arms, but the pain of the blow shot through his hands and down into his chest. If felt like every bone from his fingers to his shoulders were on the verge of breaking, and memories of the Spaniard he had fought in the mud in Puerto Cabello came to mind. In some ways, this man was stronger, for he was taller and had better leverage.

As the man raised the barrel for another attack, Calabar tried to kick the man's knee. His heel caught it with a glancing blow, and the man fell back a few paces, lowered the barrel, but did not fall. In the moonlight, Calabar could see the fury in the man's eyes, his rage at the very idea that a nonperson like Calabar would even dare to strike him.

But Calabar barely noticed; he moved to take advantage of his enemy's instant of hesitation. He kicked out again, and this time hit the shin bone. The man roared, dropped the barrel, limped back another step as he drew a pistol.

Calabar reached up to try to pull over an uneven stack of crates behind him, hoping that, in falling, they would not only shield him from the shot, but possibly hit the man. But before he could reach the closest of them, the man cocked the pistol, took aim, and fired.

The shot went wide. Not due to poor aim; an arrow shaft was protruding from the man's right side. Then another hit him, and another. The pistol dragged in the man's hand as, reeling, he tried to turn to see from whence the arrows had flown—and got another shaft in the throat.

He toppled his length, falling dead at Calabar's feet.

By this time, the fray had attracted the attention of a few guardsmen further down the dock. People were coming, and Calabar tried to stand. Out of the darkness, a hand gripped his shoulder and steadied him.

"Come," said a muffled voice. "We must go."

There was no arguing; the guards were closing in, and it would not do to be seen standing over the corpses of two Cartagena slavers. Calabar followed the stranger through the maze of empty crates and barrels, out the back of the staging area, and into the jungle.

They ran until the shouts of the guards and the lights of the dock were gone. Then the stranger slowed as they reached the bank of a small inlet river. He guided Calabar across a meandering set of rocks, and when they reached the opposite bank, they stopped.

Calabar fell to his knees. He was not badly wounded, but his mouth hurt from the kick, and his forearms ached. He checked them. They were not broken, thankfully.

"I thank you, sir," Calabar said, as he leaned against a tree to regain his breath. "Who are you? And why would you bother saving me?"

The stranger knelt. He removed the scarf that covered his face. Calabar looked up into the moonlight and saw a pair of dark eyes. Eyes that he had seen hundreds of times.

"It's me, sir. Luiz."

Calabar grabbed Luiz's arm and pulled him down. He hugged the young man so hard he thought he might break his ribs. He felt like crying. It was like meeting family again after a long, terrible ordeal. Luiz *was* family, as far as Calabar was concerned. A brother, a son. Suddenly, it seemed as if a mighty weight had been lifted from his chest.

"Praise God," Calabar said, close to tears. "You are alive. What are you doing here, my boy?"

"I came here to find Celia and the children."

"Tell me everything."

Calabar let go. Luiz straightened himself and sat upright on a rock nearby. He cleared his throat and began. "When I heard that Matias had sent Celia and the children to Bahia to be sold, I went there, hoping to find them. But I was a little too late. They had already been put on the ship and sent up the coast.

I wasn't sure where they were going, but I spoke to some of the African dock workers there and they told me they thought Recife. Naturally, I went there right away, but I was afraid to enter the port."

"Why?"

"Well—" Luiz told how the doctor had discovered who he was, and how Matias had begun searching for him. "So, I convinced a Portuguese merchant from Antonio Vaz to go there as if he were trying to sell his wares. The slaver's ship was there, he said, but no sign of Celia and the children. I don't think they were allowed off the ship, and of course he didn't risk sneaking aboard."

Calabar nodded. "Go on."

"So when it left port, I went to Olinda and signed on with a French buccaneer that does silver trade with a dealer there. He agreed to take me on, but he was not interested in tracking a Portuguese slave ship, no matter how much I pleaded with him to do so. He threatened to throw me to the sharks if I dared bring it up again. I kept my mouth shut after that and did my duty, though by this time it was clear to me that the slaver must be heading to the Caribbean. It was the only logical path for it to take.

"We sailed to Tortuga, and once there, I learned that one of the largest and most active slave ports on The Main was Cartagena. If Celia and the children were to be sold in the islands, I figured it was likely they would be taken there first. None of the French pirates, unfortunately, had any desire to come here. So I spent many weeks finding working passage on several ships before I could finally make port here. Or, to be more exact, over twenty miles up the coast, at Zamba. So close, but few ships stopped there. So I walked south, which took several days; the coast has many dangers. I've been in Cartagena now for nearly three weeks. Much too late to find Celia and the children, I'm afraid."

Calabar stood slowly and stretched his sore arms. He took a deep breath and said, "Where have you been staying?"

Luiz pointed south through the jungle. "About three miles south, sir, along this river. It winds its way through a sugar mill. The Africans there have been hiding me in their quarters." He tried to smile, but it seemed forced. "My own African heritage makes them trust me, I suppose."

"I suspect they trust you because they know a good and true heart when they find one," Calabar said, placing his hand on the young man's shoulder. "You are a good man, a better man than I've deserved to have at my side, one who has never failed me. Or my family."

Luiz tried to smile again, tried to accept the compliment, but a tear brimmed and ran from his eye. "Thank you, sir. But I did fail you. I failed Celia. I failed Carlos. I failed Pedro. I—"

"I won't hear it, Luiz!" Calabar snapped, more harshly than he wanted. He lowered his voice. "You did your duty. You served my family well, and it would not have done you or me any good if you had disobeyed Pedro's order and tried to retrieve additional medicine. Then I would be grieving over your death as well as my son's. Enough of it now. What matters is the family I still have. Do you *know* where they are?"

Luiz nodded. "Yes, sir. They have been taken to

Hispaniola. There is a fairly new plantation there run by a man named Velasco de las Quintanillas. He bought them only a month ago. I am not certain, but I believe that his property is located somewhere near a place called Boca de Yuma. That is what I have been hearing. It's on the eastern side of the island, but that is all I know."

Calabar pulled back, cocked an eyebrow. "And how do you know so much?"

Luiz lowered his head as if he were looking at his feet, as if embarrassed by what he was going to say next. "I have learned that slavers get loose in the mouth when plied with rum and furnished with prostitutes."

Calabar smiled, shook his head. "Luiz, your resourcefulness never ceases to amaze me. God, I've missed you."

He gave the young man another hug and patted him generously on the back. "Very well, then. We must get to Hispaniola."

Luiz shook his head. "I have tried to find passage there, sir, and indeed, there are ships that go frequently, but we cannot possibly get hired on as crew, nor can we stow away."

"Indeed. And given the fact that we have just killed two slavers, I, at least, cannot possibly walk the streets any longer. The slavers who were following me have friends back at the auction house: friends who were almost certainly informed of their resolve to see where I went. And those friends must now presume that it was I who killed them."

Luiz paused, scratched the top of his head. He probably had lice, Calabar figured, or worse. He had a long beard, and it seemed as if his hair was slick with grease and matted down by humidity and lack of hygiene. He smelled ripe, but then, so did Calabar.

After a few reflective moments, Luiz murmured, "I know of a man who visits one of the city's less favored brothels. He is English, and a pirate, they say. I have only tried to speak to him once, and he did not give me a moment's attention. He is surprisingly young, a bit of a drunk, and an unrepentant foul mouth. But rumor has it that he sometimes buys African slaves and then frees them to serve in his crew . . . if they so wish. If not, he sets them free." Luiz shrugged. "If these rumors are true, then he will have a ship, and maybe we could prevail upon him to take us to Hispaniola."

Calabar nodded, rubbed his chin. Reaching beneath his belt, he showed and bounced the concealed purse of coins that Moses had given him before they parted ways: it made a promising clinking sound as it moved. He smiled. "Let us go find this man. And let's give him an added incentive to agree to our request."

Chapter 24

*Quintanillas sugar plantation, near
Boca de Yuma, Hispaniola*

It did not take long for Celia to become familiar
with the rather unstable behavior of Master Señor
Quintanillas. He was what Father Araujo would often
refer to in his sermons as *"falso"*: those so-called
Christians who claimed to worship God in public
and to follow the precepts of the Church, but then
behind closed doors, committed all forms of sinful
acts, such as drink, gamble, carouse, beat their wives,
their children ... and own slaves. Celia had never seen
Master Quintanillas beat his wife or his four children,
but he was not above beating his slaves or drinking
heavily. He was also not above showing them mercy,
especially the slave women he considered *hermosas*.

As soon as they had arrived in Hispaniola, Celia was
put in charge of the kitchen and of all the cooking on
the plantation, including the food prepared and served
to the slaves, field hands, and house servants alike. It
was a full day's work, and sometimes more, when the

mistress of the house, Señora Violeta Mendoza, would be holding a dinner party for other local plantation families and visiting Spanish dignitaries, such as naval captains, admirals, government officials, and whoever else of import might pay a visit. Master Quintanillas was a well-respected man among the other plantation owners and in the capital of Santo Domingo. It was a busy household, and Celia rarely had time in private with her children.

Lua had been permitted to live with her mother, but her days were filled with hot, difficult work in the smaller side gardens that Master Quintanillas allowed the house slaves to farm for themselves. She and three Africans worked the garden, tending crops such as cauliflower, radishes, peppers, beans, cassava, and a varied assortment of herbs and spices that grew reasonably well in the local climate. She also assisted in tending to a small pen of hogs which fulfilled some of the meat requirements for the entire plantation. And when she had free time, it was often filled with catering to Master Quintanillas' youngest daughter's playtime whims.

Martim, because he did show promise with numbers, was sent to serve the harbormaster in Boca de Yuma. Celia was never permitted to see her son, though she did inquire about his welfare whenever Master Quintanillas sent slaves there to deliver sugar loaves to waiting cargo ships. By their report, he was healthy and growing well, and she thanked God for that. She missed him terribly.

"Celia!" Señora Violeta Mendoza's shout carried over the clamor in the kitchen even as it crushed her brief reverie. "You make sure the pork is cooked

properly this time. I do not want my guests getting
sick. Do you hear me, or must I ask my husband to
beat you next?"

Celia and her modest staff of seven African women
and one mestizo girl they called Consita were preparing for the Señora's next dinner party. The kitchen
was frantic as everyone tried to keep ahead of their
mistress's wrath, which was not as unpredictable as
her husband's but just as terrifying.

"Yes, Señora," Celia replied, accepting a big bowl
of cauliflower soup from the mestizo girl. "It will be
cooked to your satisfaction. I promise."

It would be cooked to her satisfaction, indeed, for
Celia did not want to be beaten like the poor man
strung up on a tree just outside the kitchen window.

That morning, he had been caught heading to
Higuey, a town several miles up the Rio Yuma. Celia
did not know the man; he was one of the many African
field hands. Just days before, his son had been sold
up river without warning or explanation. The man
had simply been trying to see his son, but he'd been
caught, deemed a runaway, and strung up to a tree,
where he had hung all morning in the hot, humid
air. And then, when he was limp on the chains, his
back was opened by the lash until he bled like a
butchered hog.

Celia had forced herself to watch, so that she would
know the man's pain and thus stand with him, at
least in spirit. But after the seventh blow, she could
endure no more, as Master Quintanillas stood near the
whipped man and proclaimed, in his loud, booming
voice for all the gathered slaves to hear: "Let this
be an example to all of you. You do *not* leave the

Quintanillas plantation without my permission. Never!"
It was more important now than ever to stress that
point, for the cane was being harvested and Master
Quintanillas needed every man in the field without
fail. Perhaps the man's punishment would have been
lighter during the slow season—the summer and early
autumn months—but not now, and the man's flayed
back would remind everyone of that fact.

Yet, just this morning, Master Quintanillas had
come to the kitchen seeking a cool drink of water
and had given the sweet mestizo girl a flower from
his garden. He had smiled at her, had accepted a hug,
and had pinched the girl's cheek. The little girl had
beamed with delight and had smiled back with the
same-shaped mouth and same-shaped face as Master
Quintanillas. They had the same eyes too. Celia wondered if Señora Mendoza knew.

Their mistress threw a few more threats at them
for their lack of respect and lack of discipline, and
then left. Celia breathed a sigh of relief. She was also
relieved that the beating had finally stopped, and the
man had been dragged away to the slave quarters. The
world, for a few hours at least, would now be quiet,
and she and her ladies could work in peace.

Her ladies. Celia cursed herself for such an insult.
They were not *her* ladies, and she had to remind herself constantly not to fall into that old trap that she
had seen play out time and again in Brazil. A slave
would be given preferential treatment and authority
for one reason or another, and then overnight, they
would start behaving just like the master. It was a
survival tactic, she knew: a way for those privileged
few slaves to never have to return to the day-to-day

depravities of the most basic and brutal form of bondage. But Celia would not do it, no matter how often Señora Mendoza pushed her to be tougher on the kitchen help.

Of the seven African women under Celia's guidance, five were already on the plantation when she had arrived. The other two had been purchased in Cartagena on the same day as Celia, but she did not recognize them from the ship. Those two were the most temperamental, the most prone to emotional outbursts and crying. She could not understand their language, and they could not understand hers, though she tried her best to keep them in line, not for her own protection and status, but for *their* own welfare. Señora Mendoza had slapped them both, very hard, for being disrespectful, and Master Quintanillas had threatened them with the lash. Celia had done everything she could to keep them safe. Everything, except one unthinkable act that she was almost daily pressured to agree, or at least succumb, to.

"Hard at work, I see."

Master Quintanillas' voice startled her. He stood at the entrance to the kitchen with a big, happy smile on his face, as if the morning's beating had never occurred. His shirt was stained with armpit sweat, and even across the room, Celia could smell rum on his breath. Her heart started as she glanced to either side, made sure everyone was doing their duty.

"Yes, sir," Celia said. "We're working hard for Señora Mendoza. She wants the food ready by six, sir. Señora Mendoza's guests will be arriving at eight."

Keep saying her name . . .

Master Quintanillas stumbled into the kitchen, put his hand out to rest his weight on the closest chair, then tumbled into it. "Get out," he said, waving his arm toward the door. "All of you. Except Celia. We must talk about the party."

Celia nodded quickly to the ladies. They filed out, one after the other. Master Quintanillas gave a little playful wave to the mestizo girl and made a clicking sound like the one used to get a horse moving.

When they had all left, Master Quintanillas spoke. "She's a most lovely girl, wouldn't you say?"

Celia did not turn to acknowledge him, but nodded as she kneaded dough. "Yes, sir, she is very beautiful and sweet. Lua is quite taken with her, but I do not know if Señora Mendoza agrees with you."

"Bah!" His outburst startled Celia, almost as much as his entrance had. "My wife does not appreciate beautiful things. Her head is a-swirl with matters of state and politics. She cares more about impressing administrators than, well, the flowers in her garden."

Celia could tell that the couple's different priorities were a constant tension between them. Apparently, Señora Mendoza had come from a higher station in life. She had married down, as the rumors went among the staff, though not too far down. Master Quintanillas was a prominent man in his own right, and he was quite skilled in the operation of the plantation. But his wife was the face of their business. Together, they ran a successful plantation. Too bad they were such terrible human beings.

Master Quintanillas was on her before she could turn to deflect his hands. "My wife does not appreciate your beauty either, señorita," he said, his wet mouth close enough to put a mist of spittle in her ear. "But I do."

"Please, Señor Quintanillas," she said, trying to wriggle out of his arms. "Señora Mendoza is near."

"She will not disturb us, I promise. And it is time, Celia, for you to pay me back for all the special treatment that I have given you. I allow you to run my kitchen when I could have easily put you in the field, or given you to one of my bucks. Hector is very taken with you."

Hector was a young slave who had shown great affection to Celia, and his tentative advances had not gone unnoticed by her, though he was always respectful in his attempts. He maintained a polite distance, never laying one finger on her, but he was always the one to come in from the field to collect the water jugs for the other workers, and he was always the first in line for food when supper was called.

"Your daughter lives with you, don't forget," Quintanillas continued, as he moved his palms up and down the front of her dress. He pressed himself into her backside. "And Martim could be put straight into the field. We need all the men we can get, right now. I can make things harder for you; I can take it all away. All the extra food, the nice clothing. But I want to be friends. You are a good worker, Celia. Good at accounts. A good mother. I see it every day. You treat these women very gently. You have a soft touch. Share that with me, Celia, and everything will stay as it is."

His rough, drunken hands worked up and down her dress. One stopped, cupping her breast, the other ran lower until he could push two questing fingers between her knees. His movements were growing faster, rougher, his breath on her ear heavier. She could feel him leaning forward to pin her against the table at which she had been working. She grew nauseous, dizzy, thought she might throw up. Wondered if that would drive him off—or damage his ego and trigger the consequences he had threatened.

"Sir, if you do this, your very intelligent wife will surely learn of it, and then she will send me away before I have a child like that mestizo girl you are so fond of. She will send me away, and then your kitchen will fall back to the chaos it was in before I came—or so you have told me. Your important dinners, your important social functions with those people who reduce your taxes and tariffs, who give you money for products that you have not declared: that will all stop—"

His drunken advances suddenly turned to rage. He grabbed her throat. Celia fought to breathe. "Are you threatening me?"

"No, sir," Celia said through the tightness of her windpipe. She tried staying calm, still. She swallowed with difficulty. "I am just stating the truth, sir. If we do this, your wife will know. She will send me away, and you will no longer have peace in your house."

"She would never know."

"But I would be honor bound to tell her."

He emitted a wordless roar and pushed her away. Celia slid along the table, grabbed its end to keep from falling to the floor. Master Quintanillas fell back into his chair and rubbed his sweaty face.

A long, tense silence filled the space between them. Celia dared not speak nor move. It seemed as if Master Quintanillas dozed for a moment. She could hear faint snoring sounds come from beneath the canopy of his messy hair. Then he perked up suddenly, grabbed the table for support, and climbed to his feet. He turned and stumbled to the exit.

When he got there, he said, "Do as Señora Mendoza says. Get the food ready by six. I must prepare for my guests. And Celia"—he turned and cracked a smile—"my patience is gone. One of these days, I will not be so drunk, and you will not be in a position to refuse."

He disappeared. Celia remained motionless for a long moment, looking up and out the window toward the tree where the beaten man had hung. She thought of Lua, of Martim. She thought of Calabar, and she could no longer control herself.

Oh, Calabar. Where are you?

Celia let herself slip the rest of the way to the floor and cried.

Chapter 25

Cartagena, Viceroyalty of Peru

The discovery of the two murdered slavers near the docks had Cartagena on edge. At first the authorities were looking for a mestizo named Gonzalo Cerrada, but in the first twenty-four hours, it was discovered that no one in town knew anyone by that name, nor was there a local planter by the name of Carlos Barrosa. And since the mestizo in question had no particularly distinctive features or marks, physical descriptions were not much more helpful to the investigation and search than the worthless alias with which he had introduced himself. Still, the militia remained watchful and more present in the streets.

But their efforts would ultimately be unsuccessful, Luiz promised Calabar. He had perfected a route into and out of the city at night that ended in a narrow alley behind the brothel which the young English pirate frequented.

As Luiz led them effortlessly yet quietly down that crate-cluttered alley, Calabar wondered if his young friend had perhaps become a bit too familiar with the establishment, had even partaken of its services? Calabar was not about to ask, and it wasn't any of his business anyway. Luiz was young, perhaps too young for such things, and Father Araujo would certainly have given him one of his strident lectures against fornication beyond the marriage bond. But Luiz had grown into a man, at least in Calabar's eyes, and if he wished to engage in such things, why—

Luiz rapped his knuckles on the door in a short but distinctive pattern. A few moments later, it opened. A dark-haired woman in a long, silken robe poked her head out, saw Luiz, and smiled. "Ah, my sweet, dark little boy. You should not be calling tonight. There are too many guards out on the streets. Slavers have been killed, haven't you heard? Boys like you can find themselves dead just by walking the streets."

"We need to see Captain Geare," Luiz said. "Is he here tonight?"

The lady nodded. "*Si*, but he is occupied with Rosalita and Carmen." She chuckled. "And a bottle of rum."

"We'll unoccupy him," Calabar said, moving closer to the door so that the woman could see him.

By now, whatever description of the man being sought in the slavers' murders had spread through the town. The woman stared at Calabar as if she were working it out in her mind. Did this man in the shadows meet that vague description? If so, she did not give anything away in her blank expression, and Calabar helped end her indecision by placing a silver coin in her hand.

She nodded, and smiled ear to ear. "Right this way, *chicos*. I'll take you to *el capitan*."

Calabar tried to ignore the other women they passed as their guide took them through a kitchen and up a small flight of stairs. At the top was a long hallway with rooms on either side. The doors themselves had been removed, and in their place, long, colorful sheets had been tacked up to allow quick access to each room should a problem arise with a client.

As they walked down the hallway, Calabar tried closing his ears to the sounds coming from several of the rooms. It was proving difficult. Luiz seemed to take it all in stride, however, as he had been here before, and was familiar, even comfortable, in the environment.

It had been a long time since Calabar had stepped foot in such a place. Indeed, he had a distinct dislike and distrust of brothels. Not because he had any moral or religious convictions against unsanctified fornication, but because of the potential for violence that was always lurking just beneath the surface in such places. Dangerous men frequented them, many of whom were quite ready and willing to harm the women. More than a few seemed to find a savage delight in it. And Calabar was in no mood to tolerate any violence toward a woman or girl tonight. The thought of Celia and Lua, and what they might be enduring in Hispaniola, undercut whatever small patience he had for such establishments and, in particular, the men who frequented them.

The woman leading them stopped, pushed a sheet aside, and walked in unannounced. Calabar and Luiz followed.

Lying on a rough, unraised mattress was a man and two women, all naked, and all wrapped in each other's sweaty arms. The proprietress's abrupt entrance shook the women from their light doze. They got up quickly and gathered their robes. The man in the middle, a short, stocky creature with an ample beard and long ponytail, and a rum bottle laying at his side, gave a little grunt, whisked away a few flies, and tried to roll over.

"Out, ladies, out," the woman ordered, shooing them away like chickens in a coop. When they were gone, she spoke directly to the sleeping man. "Captain Billy. Wake up, now. You have visitors."

The man stirred, mumbled something under his breath. The woman rolled her eyes and turned toward the door to leave. "Kick him in a minute or two if he doesn't move. He looks like a useless savage, but he's harmless."

Calabar waited a minute, then did as the lady suggested, planting the toe of his boot right into "Captain Billy's" backside.

"Son of a bitch!" The man rolled over twice, then scrambled backwards toward the lone table in the corner. "Who the hell kicked me?"

"I did," Calabar said, moving forward as if he might unleash another kick.

Captain Billy put up his hand. "Okay, okay, give me a minute, goddammit."

Calabar moved back to give him a minute. The man felt around for his pantaloons and shirt and started putting them on. "You interrupted a wonderful dream, sir. I dreamt that I was in an exotic place with two beautiful Spanish ladies—two beautiful *naked* Spanish ladies—at my side."

"You were not dreaming," Luiz said. "That was real."

Captain Billy eyed Luiz and wagged a finger at

him. "I remember you. You had some wild notion to visit Hispaniola."

"It is no wild notion," Calabar said. "We have to get there."

Captain Billy finished dressing, smoothed his greasy hair back, snorted, and spit into a cup on the table. "That is no small undertaking, sir. And given the heightened anxiety among the Spanish due to the activities of the Dutch and their USE friends, Hispaniola is beyond my safe reach, these days. Did you hear about the raid against Puerto Cabello?"

Calabar nodded. "I was there."

Captain Billy perked up. "Were you, now? Hmm! I find that hard to believe, but if so, you should understand my concern. The Spanish have bolstered their land defenses in places like Hispaniola so that similar raids will now be exceedingly difficult. One cannot simply waltz into Hispaniola. At least not for free, anyway."

Calabar drew the bag of silver from his belt and tossed it over. "Perhaps that will improve your willingness."

Captain Billy grabbed it in midair. The jangle of coins inside made the man's eyebrows rise high on his shiny forehead. He thumbed around in the bag, his lips moving silently as he counted. He closed the bag and tucked it away in his shirt. He smiled.

"Where are my manners?" He wiped his hand on his pant leg and offered it to Calabar. "My name is William Geare. My friends, and enemies, call me Captain Billy. And you are . . . ?"

Calabar took Captain Billy's hand reluctantly, not knowing exactly where it had been. "I am Domingos Fernandes Calabar."

"A pleasure to meet you, sir. And may I know why you wish to go to Hispaniola?"

Calabar nodded. "My wife and my children have been sold to a plantation there. I mean to get them back."

"I see." Calabar could see real concern in Captain Billy's eyes as he backed away and found a seat at the table. He sighed. "I'm sorry for your situation, sir. I'm sure it is difficult for you to think about anything else."

Calabar opened his mouth to speak, but thought the better of it. This Englishman seemed genuinely concerned and thoughtful, despite having just awakened from a night of drunken debauchery, but it was best not to say too much. Not yet, anyway. Perhaps later, if they got to know one another better on the way to Hispaniola. Assuming he would take them.

Captain Billy cleared his throat again. "My grand-father was a very pious man. I'm sorry to say that his piety did not manifest itself in any of the subsequent generations of his line. I am my father's son, alas. But we heard my old grandad speak out about the horrors of slavery and chastised those who supported it." He shrugged. "At least I inherited that conviction from him."

"Luiz tells me that your crew is mostly runaways and that you also buy slaves for the sole purpose of making them crewmen."

Captain Billy nodded. "Sometimes, though I have British and Frenchmen and even the occasional Span-iard. I buy slaves here in Cartagena, primarily. That's why I am able to enter port and sample this estab-lishment's lovely offerings. The ladies here know me, you see. Once I've bought the slaves, I give them a choice. Join my crew, or go free."

"You can speak their language?" Calabar asked.

"I've learned a few words over the years," Captain Billy said. "My first mate, though, knows most of them. He was once a slave himself."

"The slavers here in Cartagena do not object to your actions, your intents?" Luiz asked.

Captain Billy chuckled and stretched in the chair. "Well, I don't discuss my actions or intents with them, you understand. Besides, slavers may be wicked men, but they are *business* men first. As long as the price is right, the few that get wind of what I do can be persuaded to look the other way."

"And the slaves that you set free: where do they go?"

Captain Billy shrugged. "I don't know. Some have told me they intend to join runaway communities—*palenques* I think they are called. Those who lack a plan are more likely to be recaptured. Not sure about the rest."

"They should be given passage back to Africa," Calabar said, "if they wish it."

"You've not seen my ship. It's not a vessel equipped for sailing the open ocean. I dare say it's barely equipped for Caribbean travel either, though we get by."

"So will you take us to Hispaniola or not?" Calabar asked.

Captain Billy stood and jiggled the bag of silver that Calabar had given him. "And you just want to be dropped off? Where, exactly?"

"Boca de Yuma," Luiz said.

Captain Billy shook his head. "That's a busy waterway, my friends. How do you intend on getting inland?"

"With respect, sir," Calabar said, growing weary of the banter. "That is not your concern. You may drop us off and then depart."

Captain Billy jiggled the money bag again. "For all these coins, you just want to be dropped off? Do you realize the difficulties that you will face trying to reach the plantation where your family is enslaved? You'll be killed or captured the moment you're spotted."

Calabar eyed the young captain carefully. He nodded and forced a smile. "I can assure you, sir, that Luiz and I have dealt with far worse." He did not elaborate. Instead, Calabar waited.

Captain Billy stalked around the room, seeking something in between all the sheets and pillows. Perhaps his boots, Calabar figured. The man had on a pair of stockings that were almost equal parts hole and cloth. Then Captain Billy's gaze drifted to Luiz, and he stared for a long moment. Then he walked toward him, then around him, taking Luiz's measure as if he were a slave at auction. "Yes . . . yes, you just might do, young man."

"What are you talking about?" Calabar asked. "Why are you eyeing him in such a manner?"

Captain Billy stood back and crossed his arms. "Very well. I agree to take you and Luiz to Hispaniola. But I won't just drop you off. No. I want a bigger stake in this endeavor. Can Luiz here recognize your wife and your children?"

"Of course," Calabar said.

"Good. Then I have an idea. It's risky, by God it is, but if it succeeds, then perhaps we can save your backsides from certain death."

"What is your plan?"

Captain Billy shook his head as he pulled on his boots. "Not here. These goddamn walls are too thin for such topics. Come to my ship and meet my crew. And then let us be off to Providencia, where we will make plans."

Chapter 26

Quintanillas sugar plantation, Hispaniola

The morning was chaotic, confused. Celia was awakened by Lua, who had heard women's voices outside their room, speaking of some new visitor. And not the more pleasant, important kind that Señora Mendoza often invited to her dinner parties. Judging from the worry on the faces of the kitchen help, the person who had arrived on the plantation was not paying a courtesy call.

They threw on simple shifts and made their way through the kitchen and out onto the front yard of the plantation house. Señora Mendoza was there in not much more than a shift herself, though hers was silken and opulent to the point of ostentation. It was more of an elaborate nightgown. She didn't seem confused or worried, just angry for being awakened at such an early hour. The sun had barely risen above the line of trees that faced the distant, narrow bay. It had rained overnight. The grass was wet, and Celia's bare feet were cold.

"What is it, Mama?" Lua asked as they took their place in the line.

"I don't know, child," Celia said, gripping her daughter's hand tightly and praying that this wasn't some form of group punishment that Master Quintanillas had devised as a show of authority. He did that sometimes when he drank heavily.

They stood for almost thirty minutes by Celia's estimate. The day promised to be very hot; even at this hour, it didn't take long for everyone in the line to be wet with sweat. Celia rubbed Lua's head and face to keep her comfortable, praying to God that, whatever this was, it would end quickly so they could begin their day. Master Quintanillas was making a concerted effort to end the harvesting by the end of the month. The field hands were hungry and exhausted. They needed the kitchen help to be at its best, and standing in the hot sun, unmoving for so long, would not help.

Two wagons came up the road from the direction of the port. Riding in the first one were Master Quintanillas, his foreman, and another white man that Celia did not recognize. In the second sat a group of five men, three white and two with dark skin. From this distance, she could not make out who they were, and the sun's glare did not help. The wagons rolled up the long drive, and then came to a stop in front of the slave line.

Master Quintanillas was the first out, and Celia could tell that he was angry. He always rubbed his red, sweaty face when he was about to fly into a rage. The rest of the men jumped down and took up positions in front of the line. Celia could now see all of them clearly.

Her heart leapt into her throat, and she put her hand over Lua's mouth before the girl could raise a stunned finger and point at the darkest man in the group. A man that Celia recognized immediately, though his thick beard covered the baby face that she adored. It was a man she knew well, and one that she loved as a son, a brother.

Luiz!

"Quiet, now, child," Celia whispered to Lua, "and do not speak a word." She did not know if Lua even recognized Luiz in his current state, but she could not take a chance on it, though she herself wanted to leap into his arms and hug him till his breath stopped. Her hand shook. She took slow, deliberate breaths to try to calm herself.

"I want to state again, Señor Geare," Master Quintanillas said to the unrecognizable white man who had gotten out of the wagon with him, "that I resent this intrusion. I assure you that I do not buy runaways. This is a waste of my time, and that of my staff. We're harvesting."

The man replied in English. Luiz translated into Spanish. "I have no intention of wasting your time, Señor Quintanillas. But if my employer's rightful property is among your chattels, then they will be returned to me."

"I buy all my slaves through Cartagena. They are legal, documented transactions."

"That is as may be, sir. But I have been charged with visiting all the plantations in this part of Hispaniola to ensure their recapture and return."

Master Quintanillas grunted. "How is it that a woman and her children can so easily slip away from your employer's plantation? That sounds like incompetence to me."

"You are aware of the raid on Puerto Cabello?" Señor Geare asked.

"I am."

"In that chaos, ten of my employer's slaves went missing. We believe that the Dutch and their lecherous Irish Wild Geese kidnapped them and sold them further to Windward along The Main. Into Cartagena perhaps, and if that is the case, some could have easily fallen into your hands. I have traveled a long distance, sir, and do not wish to waste any more time, as you so eloquently put it. Now, if you will assist me, I shall inspect your staff, and be done with it."

Master Quintanillas stood red-faced, gnashing his teeth. In the end, he stepped aside and Señor Geare got to work.

He started on the far end, inspecting each slave— men and women both—as Celia had seen on the docks in Cartagena. After each inspection, he would look to Luiz who would shake his head gently. One after the other, they moved down the line toward Celia. She could barely breathe. She felt like her bladder might release, she was so scared, so weak in the knees, so afraid that something would happen and alert Master Quintanillas that this was some kind of ruse. She put her left foot back a little to gain better support as she stood there, keeping Lua firmly at her side, hoping the dear girl wouldn't suddenly recognize Luiz and blurt out his name.

Señor Geare reached her, and he inspected her like the others, putting his rough hand on her face, turning her head left then right, inspecting her arms, her back, her shoulders. When he was finished, he looked to Luiz.

He nodded. "It is her, sir," he said in Spanish. "Her name is Celia. Her daughter is Lua."

"Nonsense!" Master Quintanillas shouted. "She and the girl are caboclo, from Brazil. They are not from Puerto Cabello. I have papers proving it."

Señor Geare looked at Luiz again and got confirmation. "He tells me otherwise, and he has very good eyes. She and the girl will come with us now, and we shall pay you handsomely for them both."

It looked as if Master Quintanillas was about to drive his fist into Señor Geare's face. He evidently thought the better of it, as he considered the rest of the Englishman's entourage. They were well armed, with pistols, swords, and knives. Master Quintanillas had his sword, and his foreman had a wheellock pistol, a whip, and a sword at his belt. If matters came to blows, then Master Quintanillas and his security would give as good as they got. But he stepped back, fought to clear the anger from his face, and asked, "How much?"

No two words had ever sounded sweeter to Celia, not in all her life. *Is this happening?* she wondered and prayed again to the Almighty. *We're going home!*

Señor Geare produced a bag of coins, opened it to show the money therein, and said, "Three hundred fifty pesos for the woman. Two hundred thirty for the girl, and those are above market price, as you well know."

Master Quintanillas rubbed his chin, stepped forward, and looked Celia straight in the face. He stared for a long while, and Celia was afraid to make eye contact, afraid that she might give it all away with a quiver of her lip, or a blink of her eye. "Celia," he said, very cool, very calmly. "Does this man speak the truth? Are you his employer's property?"

She looked up, tried not to let her fear make her voice tremble. She swallowed, and said very quietly, "Yes, sir."

"Then they lied to me in Cartagena. *You* lied to me."

She said nothing further. She looked at her feet, kept perfectly still. Master Quintanillas cleared his throat, and she could hear his rough hands rub across his coarse chin. "No," he finally said, turning back toward Señor Geare. "No sale. You have no proof that she is yours, and I will not listen to the testimony of a bitch who told me one story before and another now. They are mine, legally sold and duly recorded."

"Luiz," Señor Geare said, holding out his hand. "Give me the writ."

Luiz pulled a heavily stained and wrinkled document from his vest pocket. Señor Geare opened it and read it aloud. "It says here that, by authorization of the governor of Puerto Cabello, any and all slave owners within New Spain are to cooperate with me to secure the reacquisition of all lost and stolen slaves once owned by Señor Sebastian Caballero. Names of all said slaves are listed at the bottom, Señor Quintanillas, for your review."

He handed it over. Master Quintanillas read the names at the bottom. His index finger stopped in three places. Then he folded up the paper and handed it back. "My answer remains unchanged, Señor Geare. Celia and her children will not leave with you today. If your employer wishes to reacquire his slaves—if they truly *are* his slaves—then he may come here himself."

Señor Geare sighed. "I can take this matter up with the governor in Santo Domingo, Señor Quintanillas, if you force me to."

"You may do whatever you deem necessary, sir. But I say again: you will not leave here with my property."

"Oh, for heaven's sake, Velasco," Señora Mendoza said, coming forward, her face a mix of exasperation and anger. "Just let the *puta* go! You will not get a better price for her anywhere, and there are always more to find."

"Quiet, woman," Master Quintanillas barked back. "She is the best kitchen manager we have ever had. You wish to host all your fancy, self-important gatherings without such assistance? You wish to fall flat on your face and be mocked and ridiculed? Now be still, or back to the house with you. I will handle this."

Señora Mendoza huffed and stormed back to the house, leaving a trail of obscenities behind her. Celia blinked at the words, was sure she had never heard such foul words from such a well-born lady in her entire life.

"Very well," Señor Geare said, handing the writ back to Luiz. "There is no need to push the matter any further right now. We are both fair men, and I'm sure that an arrangement can be made. I will convey the sum of our discussion to my employer. I promise you that he—and I—will be back in good time." Señor Geare tipped his hat. "Thank you for your time and patience, Señor Quintanillas. We will see ourselves back to port."

Celia shot a glance at Luiz. She almost cried when he gave her a subtle wink, then turned and followed Señor Geare back to the second wagon. They piled into it, and the driver led the team back into the road.

Master Quintanillas and his foreman waited and watched the wagon disappear, then he turned to his slaves. "Back to the house. All of you! It's a busy day."

As Celia turned to leave, she felt Master Quintanillas' hands on her hair. He yanked her back forcefully. She yelped, but kept her voice down, so as not to frighten Lua, who stood nearby, clinging to her mother's shift.

"I don't know who he was," Master Quintanillas said, his sour breath at her ear. "And I don't know which story is true ... yours or his. But I don't care. You are mine, Celia, whoever you are. You are mine. And you will always be mine. Do you understand?"

He pushed her forward, and she fell to the ground. Celia kept her head bowed, but watched his boots as he and the foreman walked toward the cane fields. She held back her tears, but this time, they were not caused by sorrow or fear. This time, she felt anger, and as he walked away, she recited to herself again and again a line from the Bible.

Watch ye therefore: for ye know not when the master of the house cometh, at even, or at midnight, or at the cock crowing, or in the morning.

"They're coming, Master Quintanillas," Celia said quietly as she hugged her daughter. "They're coming."

Chapter 27

Off Boca de Yuma, Hispaniola

Calabar held his breath as Captain Billy's skiff closed with the pirate's seaworn caravel, the *Wee Skipper*. He leaned over the side before Luiz was halfway up the Jacob's ladder that reached down to the swells.

"What did you find?" Calabar asked, out of breath. "Were they there? Did you get them?"

Luiz's expression was somber, sad. He lowered his eyes. "They are there, sir. But...we could not free them."

"Dammit!" Calabar leaned on the mast, his shoulders low, his brightest hopes draining out of his body like sweat. So close, yet so far. He closed his eyes, breathed deeply, allowing his nerves to settle. "You saw them all? Were they well?"

"Only Celia and Lua," Luiz said. "We did not see Martim, but by Señor Quintanillas' own words, it's clear that he's there. We just didn't see him."

Calabar looked toward the sun. "This time of year?

They're harvesting. He's in the field, most likely." He shook his head. "My poor son."

"Quintanillas lined up the house staff," Captain Billy shouted up the ladder as he followed Luiz's ascent, "and let us go from one to the other. Your wife and little girl both appear healthy, though it's hard sometimes to know for sure. With the *master* breathing down their necks, they ain't going to say much. Señor Quintanillas is a right arrogant son of a bitch, and I'd have run his liver through if the situation were convenient. But that would have been the end of Luiz and meself, to say nothing of a good lot of my men and, dare I say, your wife. The situation was too uncertain, too tense, to try anything more, er, lively."

Calabar nodded. "You made the right choice. It served no purpose for you to go there and get killed. Your mission was a success; you confirmed that they are there. Now we have to get them out."

Captain Billy nodded and waved Calabar and Luiz to follow. "Come with me. My men and I have a plan."

They followed the pirate captain belowdecks where the crew was waiting in a hold that had been repurposed for crew quarters. In the center of the compartment was a long table. Various maps lay unfolded upon it.

Captain Billy's crew was the most diverse Calabar had ever seen. About twenty men in total, it was comprised mainly of runaways and slaves the captain had purchased and then freed. It also included other Englishmen, as well as French, Tainos, and even two Spaniards. It was a rough band, cutthroats indeed, and Calabar figured that plenty of them could care less about his family or his desire to rescue them. What they cared about was gold, silver, and anything else they could get their hands on. Their interest piqued when Captain Billy began his discussion.

"We will help you, Calabar," the English pirate said, "as long as you agree that we have sole claim to whatever we may pluck from the plantation. Any goods, weapons, monies that we find are ours."

Calabar shrugged. "I care only about my wife and my children. Nothing more. You can burn it to the ground if you like, just so long as I get my family out safely."

A pleasant rumble spread through the crew. Calabar could tell by their expressions that they liked what he was saying. Perhaps he had said too much.

"But," he continued, "I ask you to go easy on the innocent. Do not harm the slaves. They can be helpful to us as we make our push. And women and children. If Quintanillas has a family, don't—"

"He has a family," Captain Billy confirmed, "a wife and children. In that chaos, I cannot regulate the behavior of all of my men, nor will I try. But they understand my position on excessive brutality. And besides: look at them, Calabar. Most of them were slaves themselves at one point or another in their lives. They understand what it means to be an innocent in chains. And if they forget, Deebal will remind them by ripping their guts out."

Deebal was Captain Billy's first mate. They called him "The Giant." He was the largest African that Calabar had ever seen. He stood a good six and a half feet tall, towering over everyone in the hold, and having to stoop lest he scrape his head on the beams. He wore two cutlasses at his belt, a wheellock pistol, a light tan vest and breeches, and a simple blue kerchief around his head. He had multiple scars, some of them nearly a foot long, running across his back and chest. He spoke Spanish and English poorly, preferring to mix the languages. Calabar suspected that he was a Muslim, for he had glimpsed the man praying several times each day on his knees facing generally eastward. Islam was not a religion widely practiced in the Caribbean, but no one was going to tell Deebal to stop his "heretical" practice. He was big, brooding, and had little patience for strategic or social subtleties. Calabar liked him immediately.

And judging by the crew's expression as Deebal glared around at them with an evil eye, they understood the limitations on their actions as defined by Captain Billy.

"What is your plan?" Calabar asked.

Luiz produced a map and unfolded it across the table. It was a hastily sketched outline of the Hispaniola coast, with more detail penciled in around Boca de Yuma.

"I could not bring the *Wee Skipper* in close enough to get a better view from the crow's nest," Captain Billy said, pointing to various areas behind buildings, woods, or ridges. "While rowing the skiff into port, my men used our spyglasses and sketched this as they awaited our return."

Captain Billy pointed to several markings. "There's one main dock. It serves several plantations, Quintanillas' being one of the largest. It's long enough that two Spanish merchants can be docked on either side at any given time. There are a few other docks as well, but they serve fishing boats and other, smaller cargo ships. When we arrived, there was one merchant at the main dock, with lots of activity around it. Several wagons of sugar loaves were in process of final lading. Quintanillas is a new owner, it seems, but appears to be thriving. He and his neighbors all seem to make a good profit."

"What of the port's defenses?" Calabar asked.

"There's one coastal battery here," Captain Billy continued, "but I don't plan on bringing this old girl in that close. There may be ships at the dock when we arrive, and they will have their own crews and guns. Merchant ships of course, but still formidable, especially if their backs are against the wall. There was also one old carrack anchored in the middle of the port directly across from the main dock. I believe it serves two purposes. One, the gunports on its starboard side can open up and hammer any unwelcome ships that approach the inlet without permission. And second, it supports the small garrison of Spanish troops stationed there at the mouth of the river."

"How many troops?"

Captain Billy shrugged. "I don't know. Quick count... maybe twenty, thirty men? Maybe more. It's a pretty sparsely habited area, as far as I could tell. There are other buildings, as you can see. The harbormaster's office is here. A few small warehouses here. Some civilian residences back here. Some shops scattered about. Including the troops, two hundred to three hundred souls in total?

"The Quintanillas plantation is one of the largest in the area. There is another town up the river about twenty miles, Higuey, but I don't think it is of much concern to us. If we strike, it'll take a long time for any troops up that way to organize and come down. We'll be long gone." He smiled wolfishly. "Or dead."

Calabar leaned over the map. He ran his finger up the Yuma River to a clump of buildings hugging the west side of the bank. "This is the plantation?"

"Aye," Captain Billy said. "The property straddles the river. He uses the water to power his cane mashers. It's a good operation. The plantation house and slave quarters are here. His sugar mills are here, and his fields are mostly here, on the east side of the river. Slaves move from their quarters to the fields by crossing a bridge here."

"How large is the bridge?" Calabar asked.

"Not very, but it's of good, sturdy stone. It needs to be strong enough to support wagons that carry the cut cane to the mills."

"The slave quarters and the plantation house are both on the same side of the river," Luiz said. "That's to our advantage."

Calabar nodded. "Agreed. We can concentrate our efforts on the west side."

Captain Billy cleared his throat, snorted, and spit into a spittoon nearby. "I have an alternative proposal, if I may."

Calabar stood straight. He eyed the pirate carefully. "Yes?"

"The coastline along the southern approach is pretty steep and rocky," Captain Billy said. "Not a problem for men like us who are experienced with this sort of action. But for a woman, and children, having to climb down into a boat off those rocks might prove hazardous and cause delays that you cannot afford."

He leaned back over the map and pointed to an "X"

that had been scratched on the paper. "But here, we have a far more pleasant beach. Still a little rocky in places, but it's mixed with sand, and some very smooth spots as well. It's further away from the plantation, but if you follow this route through this wood here, you'll find his fields, which will have been harvested by the time we get there. Pretty much a clean, open pathway straight to the bridge. Then it's across and up to the house."

Calabar considered the idea, studied the map, and the route that Captain Billy was proposing. He shook his head. "From that distance, there is no way that all of us can get in there without alerting someone. I've owned a sugar plantation, Captain. There is more activity at night than you may realize. The foreman or some of his assistants may be out in the fields for any of a dozen unforeseeable reasons. A field hand may happen to be out there relieving himself and see us coming. He might not like his master, but if he thinks his home is being attacked, he'll alert someone. By God, if it wasn't for the lack of a moon and the overcast, they might have been working all night in shifts. But since they can't work in the total dark, your idea has merit—but to be sure we won't be discovered, we'll need to stage a diversion."

"A diversion?" Captain Billy said. "And how do you propose to do that?"

"We have to hit the main dock. We have to pull the garrison away from its barracks. We have to try to pull Quintanillas' guards away from the plantation itself. So, we torch the main dock with pitch or oil; whatever we have in the greatest quantities. That will force everyone in Boca de Yuma to focus on putting out the fire, to forming into a bucket brigade. While that's going on, we slip through the fields and take the plantation house."

Captain Billy stroked his stubbled chin; the rasping sound was like a file on coarse wood. He walked around the table, studying the map, rubbing the back of his neck. He snorted and spit once more. He put his hands on his hips. "It's goddamn risky, Calabar. Dividing the crew like that. If it doesn't work, we're buggered."

Calabar nodded. "It is, but it's the best chance we have with so few men. We have to reduce their fighting effectiveness by dividing *their* forces. It can be done. I've made it work in Brazil. The key will be a good first strike against the dock. Who do you have that you can trust to do it?"

"I'll do it," Luiz said, stepping forward.

Calabar smiled and nodded, but hesitantly. "Are you sure?"

"Yes. I'll keep them busy, sir. You just get into Quintanillas' hacienda and get your family out. They've suffered enough."

"And I'll go with you, Luiz," Captain Billy said, grinning ear to ear. "It's been an age since I've set a good fire." He rubbed his hands together as if he were washing them beneath a spigot. "Let's go wreak a bit of havoc."

"I'll need eight men for the plantation house," Calabar said. He turned toward Deebal. The first mate stared down at him as if he were something good to eat or beat. Calabar resisted the urge to step back a pace, hoped his brisk nod covered his nervous swallow, and said, "And your first mate; I'll need a man who can break down doors."

Chapter 28

Boca de Yuma, Hispaniola

Instead of immediately launching their assault, they resolved to sail around the northern coast and approach Tortuga, waiting for the dark of the moon and the darkening horizon's promise of thick clouds to roll in and make it that much easier to approach their objectives undetected.

At the northernmost reach of their cruise, Captain Billy offered Calabar the opportunity to solicit the aid of the notorious French pirates who worked out of that island—"The Turtle"—but he refused. It would be wonderful to have more men, but who could know the motivations of French pirates, let alone the individual motivations of Captain Billy's crew, when bullets began to fly and swords began to clash? It was difficult to gauge the true motivations of any pirates, for that matter, so why exacerbate the problem by adding more? No, Calabar decided, they would go in with what they had, and may God protect those who were landing, or the devil have them all.

They returned under gray skies, the dusk-hour cloud cover absolute as they landed just above Boca de Yuma. It did much to keep them from being detected as they moved inland. The absence of the moon not only meant they were wholly unlit, but they also cast no shadows; as long as they were careful not to silhouette themselves against the lights of a house, the locals would have no reasonable chance of seeing them.

Captain Billy wanted to distribute a few torches among the raiders, just in case. Calabar accepted a couple, but had no intention of using them, at least not on the approach. True, he was not familiar with the terrain of Hispaniola, and in such dark conditions, it would be easy to get lost. But Calabar had traversed more densely wooded and darker areas in Brazil of which he had even less advance knowledge. Besides, Billy and Luiz had been careful to make note of landmarks that would be obvious, even on the blackest night. And if they happened to wander a little off course, lights from the slave quarters or from the plantation house itself would steer them back. Calabar was quite certain his team would be fine, just so long as the men remained quiet and focused. Hopefully, Deebal could ensure that they did so.

The *Wee Skipper*'s weapons locker was opened and swords and knives were distributed to everyone; even a few boarding axes were handed out. Full muskets and musketoons were assigned to those most proficient among the crew. Calabar and Luiz had their own weapons, so luckily the landing party was well equipped, save for ammunition. Bags of bullets, powder horns, and bandoleers of prepared charges were given

out, but it only equaled about twenty shots per man.
Calabar knew that that would not be enough, especially
if the team assigned to managing responses from the
town itself encountered a resolute garrison that fired
back steadily. Luiz and his men would not survive if
they couldn't return fire to keep the defenders' heads
down while they got in and out. So Calabar reduced
his team's ammunition load to about fifteen rounds
per man and gave the rest to Luiz.

The crew of the *Wee Skipper* readied all three of
its skiffs, although one of them was nothing more
than a simple ten-foot fishing boat. Calabar and his
men would take one of the true skiffs and the fishing
boat; he needed both if he was going to have enough
room for his family and for at least a few slaves that
wanted to risk escape. He wished he had twenty boats
to get them all off, but he resolved not to spend any
time regretting the sharp limitations of this mission.

Luiz and Captain Billy would take the third skiff
and try to cause as much trouble as they could in and
around Boca de Yuma. They were tightly packed on
their boat, as it was loaded with small barrels of pitch
and a few casks of lantern oil. Calabar was concerned
that the tiny boat would not take the weight of the
men plus all the pitch, but Captain Billy just smiled
and shook his head. "I know my boats, Calabar. It'll
float, and we'll toss whatever we don't use to make
room for what we steal."

So everything was ready. The clouds thickened, and
a cooler northwesterly breeze set in as the dim orb that
was the sun finally settled below the western horizon.

It was time to attack.

❖   ❖   ❖

Luiz Goncalves was tired of arguing with Captain Billy. He was refusing to listen to reason.

"We don't have time to attack that ship, Captain." Luiz tried once more to get through the Englishman's thick—or at least greed-blinded—skull. "Our mission is to fire the dock. That's what Calabar wants us to do."

"I know our goddamned mission," Captain Billy hissed, "but that ship's not anchored there for show, Luiz. If it stays untouched and unbothered, its crew will man the gunports on its port side, slip in chain shot or grape, and cut us to pieces on the dock. Or they'll take to skiffs and add more men to the garrison. And they probably won't give a damn if their fire hits civilians or even their own soldiers. Don't tell me my business, lad. I know naval tactics. We've got to hit that ship as well."

"Fine," Luiz grumbled. "Then let's get it done quickly."

Their skiff floated slowly forward in the dark, just one hundred yards from the Spanish ship anchored in the center of the inlet. Five additional crewmen were poised behind them as two rowed, dipping and raising the oars slowly, quietly.

Lights were visible on the deck of the ship, and Luiz could make out a few men patrolling the deck. But it didn't look like many more were on hand, and those that were did not seem alert. To them, Luiz figured, it was just another overcast night in Boca de Yuma.

No one on the skiff spoke, though one of the crew gave a tiny cough. Captain Billy tore off his hat and struck the man across the head. No one else coughed again after that. Instead, they prepared the pitch for the hull of the ship. Luiz assisted by ensuring that it was applied evenly and thickly on woolen cloth wrapped around an ax handle. Three other men readied oil, and Luiz could hardly breathe as the breath-stealing combination of both fluids made his nostrils sting.

"Won't they smell this?" he whispered.

Captain Billy shrugged. "Maybe, but once we've spread it, there's not a damn thing they can do about it. Now be quiet. It's time."

Crewmen steadied the skiff along the hull of the Spanish ship, and then got to work, smearing a long stripe of oil and pitch up along the gunports on the starboard side, slowly advancing their boat by towing it along the hull with their palms. It was difficult, slow work, and Luiz had to put his hands on the legs of the men working to give them support. Regardless, one of the men tumbled. Luiz caught him just before he struck the bottom of the boat. They paused, waiting to see if the noise caused anyone on board the Spanish ship to take notice. A few terrifying moments passed, but no trouble. So they continued until the entire starboard side was prepared.

At the stern, they smeared on a good coat, and then applied ten feet of the smelly muck to the port side.

"That's all," Captain Billy said, motioning for everyone to sit back down and tuck away their tools.

They turned the skiff toward the docks. Luiz breathed a sigh of relief. He wanted to cough to clear his lungs of the fumes, but suppressed it. They had succeeded thus far; he wasn't about to ruin it all now.

As they drew near the dock, he wondered how Calabar was faring. Surely he had already landed and was moving inland. But he would not strike until the dock was burning, and now they had lost precious time dealing with the Spanish ship. But maybe Captain Billy had been right. Maybe it was necessary to prepare to cripple it beforehand, lest it prevent them from causing the necessary havoc on the dock. A lesson learned, perhaps.

Luiz dipped his hand into the salty water and cleaned his face. The long, dark shape of the dock grew. Luiz breathed deeply, prepared more pitch, and thought, *now the hard part begins.*

Calabar was impressed with the pirates' noise discipline. They had obviously done this before: row ashore under cover of darkness and move inland carefully on a raid. Such missions were always difficult under the best of circumstances, especially if one had to keep ordering the team to shut up and be quiet. The presence of Deebal helped. The large man didn't speak much himself, but he understood Spanish enough to be given simple orders. The rest of the men took Deebal's lead.

They landed the two boats almost two miles up from Boca de Yuma on a quiet little patch of sand, exactly where Captain Billy had indicated. Ten men total including himself and Deebal. A handful had gone with Luiz and Captain Billy, and according to the plan, they should have already begun to apply oil and pitch to the dock. As he climbed out of his skiff, Calabar paused a moment, listening carefully. Not even the faint reports of musket fire from the general direction of the docks. That didn't necessarily mean anything had gone awry, of course. The night was still young. There was still time for the plan to unfold properly.

"Muskets in hand. Follow me," he whispered, reaching into the bottom of the skiff and pulling out his own weapon. He had a pistol too, and a knife and a sword. The rest had muskets and at least a knife, though some had swords as well. They were not going in with as much ammunition as Calabar would have liked, but it would do. And Deebal had a large pack on his back loaded with a small cask of oil, five torches, and old sail canvas torn into twenty bandages. Calabar had asked for those specifically; he had been on enough raids to know that the difference between success and disaster could depend upon a clean bandage to tie around a bleeding head or arm or leg. He couldn't count the number of men he had seen die in battle due to that simple oversight. Not tonight, however. They were going into a dangerous situation with dangerously few men. He couldn't afford to lose a single one.

The raiders followed Calabar and Deebal into the trees, keeping to the line of approach that Captain Billy had crudely sketched out. Calabar had no illusions about this route. He knew that there would be obstacles and hazards that could not be anticipated. But they needed to be at the cane fields by the time the dock was set aflame. Timing was crucial.

A few weak beams of moonlight tried flitting through the heavy clouds. Beneath the canopy of trees, it hardly mattered, but Calabar took advantage of the small slivers of light that came through and readjusted their course twice, always moving left at an angle consistent with where he estimated the harvested fields to be. At one spot, they had to wade through a tributary off the Rio Yuma at waist height—a feature that had not appeared on Captain Billy's sketch—and Deebal had to hold the pack above his head lest all of the bandages become soaked and soiled. That cost them precious time, but Calabar bit back his impatience and helped each of the men out of the water as quickly as possible.

They reached the edge of the first field around thirty minutes later. It stretched out before them, flat and barren except for the base of the stalks which had been close-cut and left behind like sharp spikes hammered into the ground. Calabar closed his eyes and breathed deeply. The discarded cane was already beginning to ferment, and he could smell its souring sweetness.

"What now, Calabar?" Deebal asked.

"Now," he said, "we wait."

Calabar crouched, and Deebal and the others followed suit.

There were no ships moored at the dock. That, at least, was a blessing, though Captain Billy seemed disappointed. He and his crew hadn't come just to cause havoc. They wanted loot, and having a ship at dock meant just that. As they drew closer, Luiz could see the outline of casks and crates stacked or laying on their sides upon the dock, and along the edge of the shoreline near small warehouses around the harbormaster's office. There was plenty to choose from, though the skiff itself could not hold a lot. That was probably why the captain was testy: he had come to a pirate's paradise, stacked with a wide variety of potentially high-value booty, and his men could take only what they could carry. *Oh, well,* Luiz thought as they made their way slowly and quietly along the pilings of the dock, *life is never perfect.*

They came close to the shore, where the planks of the dock could be touched. The posts here were slick with slime: impossible to grab for leverage to hoist themselves up. Each man had to be assisted out of the boat. Luiz was second to last, just before Captain Billy himself. One man remained in the boat with orders to wait for their return, and if something went wrong, to abandon the skiff and meet them at the rendezvous site further down the shore. He handed up two casks of oil and one barrel of pitch.

"Okay, boys," Captain Billy whispered. "Take what you can and meet us back here. And do it quickly, quietly. Someone will happen across us before too long."

They nodded and headed down the dock and then onto the shore where the warehouses lay. They moved more quickly and more cautiously than Luiz had expected. Of course, they had done this sort of thing before and almost all of them were dark-skinned, which made them even harder to make out in the darkness. But once the fire was set . . .

"Let's get to work."

They did not paint the oil and pitch on as they had with the ship. Instead, they punched holes in the casks and simply let the fluids trickle out as they moved up and down the dock, splashing everything in their path. Luiz could almost hear Captain Billy whining as he applied the pitch to the crates of sugar loaf molds. Luiz could smell the sweet sugar and remembered better times as a boy, when he had worked alongside Calabar in his fields. Would life ever be so simple again? he wondered. Probably not. Too much had changed since those easy days, and not just for him, but for the whole world, it seemed. And those changes had, ultimately, put him on this dock on Hispaniola, carrying out a nighttime raid on a Spanish port in what had once been the unthinkably distant Caribbean. *Tonight I might die.* But the thought did not trouble him as much as he had expected; he was prepared for it. *If Calabar can save Celia and the children, it will be worth it.*

They tossed aside their casks and headed back to the skiff. Fifteen minutes later, the men who had gone off to scrounge for loot began returning, staggering under the weight of sacks bulging with woolen clothing, dried fruits and nuts, sugar loaf molds, casks of wine, bags of grain. They handed down their spoils, then climbed in themselves.

"Push off," Captain Billy said.

"But your last man hasn't returned," Luiz said.

"Forget him! He's late. If he's alive, he knows the rendezvous point. Push off, goddammit."

One of the two oarsmen pushed off and they began rowing away from the dock. They rowed hard and fast, no longer taking care to keep their actions slow or quiet. There was no need now, for once they got far enough away, their own actions would make their presence known.

"Okay, Nestor," Captain Billy said. "Do what you do best."

The man reached down, pushed aside some of the sacks, and took up a bow. From a small quiver, he pulled an arrow whose tip had been wrapped with cotton soaked in oil. Captain Billy lit the tip. With their eyes adjusted to the long, unrelieved darkness, the flaming arrow seemed like a full torch. Luiz held up his hand against the brightness of it, then lowered his head to give the man ample room to shoot. Without a moment's delay, Nestor loosed the shaft.

The arrow arced up, and then down into a pile of

crates on the dock. It immediately burst into flames. He notched a second, and a third, and by the fourth, the dock was burning fiercely. Then he turned his attention to the Spanish ship. It was much farther away, so he raised the bow up higher for a longer, arcing shot to the stern. He missed with the first shaft, and the second. The third, however, sunk into the wood just below the great window of the stern. The pitch that had been slathered there ignited. A hungry, leaping line of flame raced around the hull, giving the ship an ethereal, ghostly appearance as light glowed up and through the rigging and sails. Luiz wanted to shout for joy. The plan had worked. All of it.

The roar of a musket came from the ship. An instant later, the ball hit Nestor in the chest and knocked him off the boat.

Luiz ducked, expecting more shots. But none came as the men on the ship turned their attention to their burning hull.

"Row! Row, goddammit!" Captain Billy screamed as he drew his pistol and raised it in the general direction of the dock. He did not fire, but he held it in readiness, in case someone on the shore noticed their little craft as it drifted away.

The port was waking up. Luiz could hear shouting all along the waterfront. Lights rose everywhere as people rushed out of buildings toward the fire sweeping along their dock, destroying everything on it. He could hear them screaming for buckets and water. A line was beginning to form. A line that would have been quite easy to hit with muskets, picking them off one after the other until they broke and ran back to the cover of their buildings. But many of them were civilians, and

Captain Billy had made it clear that they weren't to be harmed if at all possible. The best thing was to quietly row away, and that's what they intended to do.

There it is, Calabar, sir. Your diversion.

Just beyond the flames, Luiz spotted a boy near the dock. It was difficult to see any details in the inconstant play of light and shadow cast by the burning planks, but his skin was lighter, his hair straighter and longer than any African boy. He was in a simple night shirt that hung to his knees and taking orders from a thick man directing him and others where to concentrate their efforts. Luiz blinked, wiped his eyes to be sure. He looked again; there was no mistake.

"Martim!"

"What?" Captain Billy asked. "What did you say?"

Luiz pointed. "That's Martim. Calabar's son. He's at the dock. Right there. We have to save him."

"Are you daft?" Captain Billy said. "This is one of the best raids I've ever carried off. I lost only one man, maybe two. We created the diversion and got what we came for. There is no way we're turning back into that."

Captain Billy tried reaching out to grab Luiz's shoulder. Luiz shrugged him off and stood, despite the threat of another shot from the ship. "I didn't come here for loot, sir. I'm here to save my friends . . . my family."

"Damn you, don't you jump into that water. It's suicide."

Captain Billy grabbed Luiz's leg. Luiz punched the captain, sending him backward with a grunt. He did not wait to see if he had hurt the man.

Luiz turned and jumped into the water.

Chapter 29

Quintanillas plantation, Hispaniola

A broad grin spread across Calabar's face, though his companions could not see it. But like him, surely they could hear the sound of distant gunfire in the direction of Boca de Yuma and could see a dark patch of smoke illuminated by flames at its base, rising into the night sky. *You've done it, Luiz,* Calabar said to himself as he stood and adjusted his weapons. *You've done it.*

They waited a little longer, just enough to see if the events in the town caused any disturbance around—or aggressive response from—the plantation which lay three hundred yards to their front, just over the Rio Yuma. Calabar could make out small specks of lamplight. The plantation was stirring, but to what extent he could not tell.

"Let's go," he said, staying low and moving slowly at first, and then picking up the pace as they drew closer to the bridge. The ground was wet, but not sloppy, and here, a bed of old, discarded cane stalks

363

both protected their feet and dampened the sound of their approach.

They reached a small section of the field where the cane had yet to be cut, and Calabar used its cover to help hide their approach to the bridge, which he was finally able to see clearly. "Damn," he hissed.

"What is it?" Deebal asked.

"Guards. Three of them."

"We kill them?"

The simplicity of the question made Calabar pause. The answer was yes, of course, but he had hoped that they'd at least get across the bridge before swords were drawn and guns were fired. He nodded. "Yes. I will lead, but no one fires a shot or says a word until I do. Do you understand?"

He waited until everyone gave some form of acknowledgment. Then he stood, pulled his pistol, and walked toward the bridge.

His men followed closely behind, Deebal the closest. They maintained their silence, thank God, all the way across the field and right up to the crossing itself. Three guards stood talking, their muskets lazily held at their sides. They seemed oblivious to the commotion in the town and the increasing activity at the plantation, or perhaps they did not care. Calabar shook his head. *Useless men...*

The bridge was stone, and Calabar's boots gave him away the moment his feet came into contact with it in his steady but unrushed approach to the guards. But in the dark, he was near point-blank range before they bothered to turn and see who was coming up behind them at a leisurely pace.

Calabar raised his pistol, pulled the trigger. The

guard closest to him took the shot right in the chest. He tumbled backwards, hit the stone lip of the bridge, fell over the side and into the river.

Deebal was on the second, swinging his cutlasses until the man's uniform was nothing but bloody tatters. The guard tried holding up his musket to defend against the attack, but that just exposed his arms to the assault. Deebal finished him with a slice across his face, then dumped the man into the river. The third guard was far enough away to try fleeing; he turned and sprinted toward the far end of the bridge. One of the other pirates shot him in the back.

Calabar paused to reload his pistol. A noisier assault than he had wanted, but there was no turning back now. The dock was burning, and the plantation house was not far away, its windows aglow with the light of many lanterns. Celia and Lua were in there somewhere.

"Where we go now?" Deebal grunted.

Calabar suppressed the urge to point to the plantation house. That's where his heart would have taken him. His mind, however, was following a subtler plan. A better one.

"To the slave quarters," he said.

Something was happening, but Celia could not tell what. There was confusion on the plantation and at the docks. Master Quintanillas, the foreman, and his men were scrambling to and fro, trying to learn more and prepare to defend against—well, whatever it might be. Celia and the rest of the house slaves were not permitted to leave their rooms, nor did Señora Mendoza provide any answers when asked what was happening. She probably didn't know herself, as she and her children locked themselves in their rooms soon after.

But Celia was able to peek out the small barred window of her room and saw the running or trotting legs of the plantation guards and Master Quintanillas himself. All of them had weapons. She tried making out their terse conversations, but it was difficult. Something was definitely happening at the docks; that much she could fathom. The plantation? Their comments were too general to know for sure. Maybe they didn't yet know, either.

Moments after coming to that conclusion, she heard a gunshot. It was difficult to say which direction it had come from. Not from inside the house, at least. Then she heard another, and the men that were gathering outside near Master Quintanillas scattered.

"What is happening, Mama?" Lua asked.

Celia only partially heard her daughter. Was it Calabar? She dared not hope for such a thing: Master Quintanillas had steadily increased the forces and preparations with which he could defend his plantation. Being so close to Boca de Yuma and so close to the river itself, coastal raiders might come to believe that an attack would be easy, poorly resisted. Nothing could be further from the truth. So while on the one hand Celia desperately wanted the commotion outside to be the work of Calabar, she wanted him safely away from the dangers of the plantation. The thought of him being killed at this moment, so close to her and Lua . . .

More sporadic shots echoed across the plantation grounds. Celia's heart leapt. Perhaps it was a revolt, just like on the slave ship. It could be; Master Quintanillas had been pushing them hard for weeks in a rush to finish the harvest. A lot of bad treatment, a lot of whippings. A couple had even died while working.

She felt faint, stepped away from the window. She turned to the locked door. Locked from the outside. Just like every slave door on the plantation. Celia pressed against it, then pushed herself into it hard. She threw her shoulder against it. Nothing. Not the slightest budge.

"Will this help, Mama?"

Lua held up a small blade, as small as a nail file. Celia grabbed it. "Where did you get this?"

Lua lowered her head. She clearly didn't want to say. Finally she said, "Señora Mendoza gave it to me."

"Why?"

"The señora gave it to me to protect myself, if Master Quintanillas ever came to . . . ever came closer than he should."

Celia cupped her daughter's face. She felt like crying. She hugged the little girl tightly, kissed her forehead, then took the knife from her.

She pressed against the door again, placed the knife into the thin gap between the door and the frame, and began to saw.

Luiz cursed himself as he swam to the shore. *Damn me, that I have no gun.* He had left his musket in the bottom of the skiff. His only weapon was a sword, connected to his belt by a lanyard. It made swimming awkward, and Luiz was not a great swimmer to begin with. But he paddled hard, arm over arm, until his churning legs finally felt the muddy silt of the shallows.

He staggered up on to the shore, not caring if

Captain Billy lost his temper and tried to shoot him in the back. It had been a very successful mission, and the captain could not be blamed for wanting to get away unharmed. Luiz's impulsive leap into the water and return to the waterfront was certainly risky, even foolhardy—especially without sufficient weaponry. But he didn't care. He was resolved to find Martim in the firelit chaos, grab him, and take him home.

Holding the lanyard steady with one hand, he pulled his sword from its scabbard with the other. It was a good blade, newly sharpened. Luiz hoped he wouldn't have to use it, but he had no illusions about the strong likelihood that he would need to. After serving for several years as Calabar's assistant, he simply accepted that in war, someone always got killed. Killing did not follow Christian teaching, but if the cause was just, it could sometimes be excused, and he could think of no better cause than freeing Martim from the brutal and dehumanizing yoke of slavery. Luiz clenched his teeth: he had nearly been pushed into that abyss himself. Mistaken for a runaway and put in irons, it was Calabar who had saved him on that day, and now Luiz intended to repay that debt. Or die trying.

He ran up the shoreline, ignoring the sharp rocks jabbing at the soles of his thin leather boots. He climbed up a pile of boulders and found a footpath that wound its way around a stack of wood planks and up to the walkway that followed the coast, just behind the docks. They were filled with Spanish soldiers and civilians alike, passing each other buckets of water in a long line that stretched from a cistern on the edge of the town out to the farther, burning extents of the larger dock. Luiz crouched behind the planks and scanned the crowd. No Martim.

Calabar was often fond of saying, "In war, if in doubt of a strategy, charge in and lead from the front." Of course, Calabar's unwavering focus upon victory meant that his actual strategy was always informed by judicious planning. But perhaps just such a rash move was needed at this moment. Not a frontal attack, per se, but why not go right through the enemy's figurative front door?

Luiz stood straight, fixed his shirt, rubbed his beard and slicked his wet hair back, and walked right up to the bucket brigade.

Those gathered were working so feverishly that most did not even notice him; the rest apparently saw nothing particularly unusual about his appearance. One frantic woman even handed him a filled bucket. Luiz accepted it coolly with his free hand and moved it to the next person. He accepted three more, then quickly passed out of the line and toward a small cluster of buildings. The largest was the harbormaster's office and living quarters. Luiz had been in it for a brief moment when he and Captain Billy had arrived pretending to be bush captains, though at that time, Martim had not been present. He paused and looked once more through the crowd, shielding his eyes from the strong glare and heat of the fire.

No, Martim was not there.

He ducked past two Spanish soldiers who seemed to be acting as guardsmen near the smallest of the three buildings. Perhaps they were protecting whatever was in that warehouse from looters. Perhaps they were just being lazy or taking a break. They had muskets, however, and although he did not risk attracting attention by glancing more carefully at the weapons, Luiz decided to presume they were loaded and ready for use.

He kept his head down and moved past the two Spaniards, walking as if he belonged there. They glanced his way, but did not try to stop him, despite his dark skin and the sword in his hand. Perhaps they did not notice it against his leg. Luiz coughed a bit—hardly an act given the irritation of the fumes he'd been working with much of the night—and used the hacking to keep his head low and bent forward. He kept walking.

He continued until he had reached the far side of the buildings and stood near the window of the harbormaster's office. It was covered with a rough, unbleached piece of canvas. A light from inside made it glow a dull orange. He heard voices.

One was Martim's. "Sir, we should be out there helping with the buckets."

The other was the harbormaster. Luiz had only heard the man speak once, but his was a distinctively high-pitched voice. "No. I told you, boy: we're going to defend this building, you hear? Got too many valuables, too many important books. We can't lose an inch of it to fire, to looters. Now do as I say."

Luiz lifted the canvas an inch to peek inside.

Martim was standing in front of the harbormaster. The man handed the boy a club which resembled a belaying pin that had been carved to better fit a hand. Worked into its head was a rough constellation of wicked, rusty nails. Primitive but potent, and judging from Martim's expression, Luiz guessed he wanted to drive the crooked iron points into the man's skull.

The harbormaster held a wheellock pistol. He motioned toward the door. "Now," he said, "you go over there and keep an eye out for anyone coming near. If you see someone you don't know, you shout. You understand me?"

Martim nodded. The harbormaster gave him a light tap on the face, then stepped away to a row of books in the far corner. Martim took his place beside the door.

Luiz paused and took a deep breath. He closed his eyes and prayed, asking God for strength, for courage. His heart was beating wildly. He was both excited and scared, but there was only one thing to do with time so short.

He stood, walked back around to the door, and revealed himself to its young defender.

Martim was about to shout, then he paused, the words sticking in his throat.

Luiz put a finger to his mouth. "Shh! You remember me?" Luiz whispered, holding his sword down, rubbing back his beard so Martim could see his face better in the faint light.

Martim shook. His knees bent, his eyes grew wet. He nodded. He stepped aside, and Luiz walked into the harbormaster's office as if he had business there.

The harbormaster had his back to the door. He had placed his pistol on the counter that separated him from his clients, and his face was buried in a large book he had pulled from a shelf. The room was quiet, save for the echo of voices and activity from the burning dock. The harbormaster finally turned to see who had entered.

"Who are you?" he asked, slamming the book shut.

He looked at Martim. "Boy, I told you to shout if someone you do not know came near."

"But I do know him, sir," Martim said, a small grin on his face. "I know him well. This is Luiz Goncalves."

"Luiz Gon—"

Then the harbormaster recognized his face. And then he saw the long sword in Luiz's hand, which was now raised and pointed forward.

The man dropped the book and reached for his pistol.

Chapter 30

Quintanillas plantation, Hispaniola

Quietly, Calabar and his men moved toward the slave quarters: two rows of small, connected huts just back from the river bank, lined up neatly like barracks in a fort. The gunshots at the bridge had awakened some of the occupants, and they had come out with torches to see what was happening. When they saw Calabar and his men, they were afraid. Some ran back into their hovels. Others shouted, trying to alert the guards at the plantation house. But when Calabar thrust a knife into one of their hands, and then spoke to them in Spanish, they understood enough to know what was happening: they were being freed, or at least, they could choose whether to join Calabar's men or not.

Weapons were handed out to those who chose to join. Six men, one woman, and a child who had to be turned away three times: all contrary efforts notwithstanding, tonight's raid was almost sure to claim enough innocents as it was. Many of the rest chose to simply flee; men and women grabbed each other's hands, or those of their children and disappeared into the darkness. Some were far too afraid to leave their homes.

Calabar called Deebal over. "I want you to lead these people to the mills. See them over there? Just where Captain Billy's map showed. I want those mills burned to the ground, you understand? Burn it all, burn everything. Burn everything leading right up to the house, and you meet me there directly."

Deebal nodded, re-secured his pack. "I will, Calabar. I promise. Now come with me," he shouted to the freed slaves. "We go and burn!"

"The rest of you men are with me," Calabar said to his remaining pirates.

They left the slave quarters untouched, along with those inside who chose not to join. Instead, they began to approach the house—and the man beside Calabar fell dead with a musket shot through his chest.

Calabar returned fire, though he could not see who had fired upon them. His men fired back, and for a few long moments, they exchanged gunfire with an unseen enemy. Calabar dropped to the ground, reloaded his pistol while pinned behind a tree stump. Another of his men fell with an agonized scream. Calabar rose quickly and shot again.

As he did, a thick yellow-orange flame leapt up into the sky from the nearest sugar mill. Calabar rejoiced. Deebal had done his job. And now shouting rose up from that direction as well: slaves, happy to see that symbol of their servitude erupt in fire. There were gunshots and when more of the mills torched, the unseen foe in front of Calabar shifted his fire to the slaves silhouetted by the flames, faint sounds of movement suggesting that he meant to get closer to that mob of attackers. A few scattered shots continued to zip and raise wood chips near Calabar's position, but they were not well aimed. Clearly, even some of the house's defenders had shifted their efforts to repel the attack upon the source of the plantation's—and therefore, their own—livelihood: the sugar mills.

Calabar reloaded again, then said, "Let's take them."

He and his men stood. "Fire!"

They sent a disciplined volley ripping through the bushes and thin walls that a number of the defenders had used for cover. Whether they hit any, drove them back, or the positions were already empty was unknown, but there was no return fire.

Calabar regretted not reloading, but seizing the initiative was more important. "Move!" he yelled to his men.

They ran up the long narrow road that led to the plantation house. Calabar could see the building's full outline now. It was well built, quite large, and clearly designed to be impressive. The many windows suggested many rooms, which would in turn mean losing more crucial minutes searching each of them. All made more difficult by the likelihood that the master had locked all the doors and had instructed his slaves to hide.

And what kind of resistance would they encounter inside the house? And was the master inside, or had he gone to fight the flames of his burning sugar mills? And worst of all, when they got to the front door, Calabar would confront the tactical conundrum he'd faced from the start: he might need a door breaker to get in. But Deebal had been the only one whose imposing size and daunting personality was likely to organize the slaves long enough to set fire to the mills. So if the entry to the main house was particularly sturdy, well . . . Calabar sighed. Well, then he'd just have to improvise.

For the first time, and only for that instant, Hispaniola felt a little bit like Brazil.

The gunfire outside had increased over the last several minutes, and then a fire erupted by the mills. Celia stopped sawing at the wood around the lock long enough to glance outside again.

The fire was high and still growing. She could not see it all, but life on their old plantation in Recife had taught her that mills could catch fire and burn with sickening speed. She could already smell the characteristic scorched-caramel scent of the smoke. There was also sporadic gunfire down near the slave quarters. She could hear it, but could not see anything. Perhaps it was a slave revolt after all.

And perhaps we should not leave the room. She had struggled with Lua's tiny knife to cut out the lock from the door frame. She had made progress, but it was a strong lock in thick wood.

She went back to it. No, this wasn't just a slave revolt. She couldn't be sure and was taking a great risk in freeing herself and her children if it proved to be a revolt that was eventually quashed. What would Master Quintanillas do to her when he found she had damaged the door trying to escape? His retribution against any slaves who had revolted would be swift and savage. No one would avoid his wrath. She and her children might not fare much better.

But no, this did not sound, or even *feel*, like a slave revolt. An uprising would not have involved a fire on Boca de Yuma's waterfront; even if it could have been arranged, it would not have helped any slaves escape. On the contrary: it roused the countryside to greater alertness. For the first time since the glow of the fires had sprung up at the port, she thought of Martim. Where was he? What was happening to him? Was he alive?

Celia could not think of her son dead. No God in heaven would permit her son to be killed under such circumstances, without first letting her see him once more.

She repeated that over and over as she resumed cutting away at the wood around the lock.

The harbormaster was quick for a thick man, quicker than Luiz expected, but not quick enough. As the Spaniard grabbed his already-cocked pistol and raised its muzzle, Luiz rushed forward and slashed at the man's wrist just before the gun went off. The ball went wide and the man screamed and dropped the smoking gun, clutching his bleeding forearm. Luiz leapt forward, pinning the man against the table. He pushed his sword's handguard into the man's throat.

"I should kill you," Luiz said, spitting the words, "for *owning* Martim. You are a disgrace under heaven, and in the eyes of God."

"I do not own him," the harbormaster gasped, choking the words out as Luiz pressed harder. The Spaniard's face was beet red, his eyes watering under the pressure at his throat. "He is on loan to me. I—I have never harmed him."

"He is telling the truth, Luiz," Martim said, stepping

forward and putting his hands on Luiz's sword arm. "He is a nice man. Don't kill him."

Luiz looked at Martim, then back to the harbor-master. "Hmm," he grunted. He stared at the cowering man. "Martim, as young as he is, is a far better human being than you will ever be. You are lucky today."

Luiz raised his sword and brought its hilt back down hard against the bridge of the man's nose. He heard—and felt—it crack under the blow, and blood ran down the harbormaster's face as he fell to the floor like a bag of rocks. The blood running out of his nose bubbled regularly, though: he was still alive.

"Come," Luiz said, grabbing Martim by the arm and pulling him toward the door. "We have to go."

Martim resisted. "Where?"

"Away from here. There's a ship waiting."

Martim resisted again. "No. We must get Mama and Lua. They are at the plantation."

Luiz nodded. "I know. Your father is getting them."

Martim's jaw fell open. "Papi? He is alive?"

"*Si*. Now come, we must get away."

They turned to the door—and discovered the two Spanish guards that Luiz had passed earlier staring at them. They held their muskets forward, cocked and ready to fire.

"Do not move, mestizo bastard," one said, curling his finger around the trigger. "One move, and I'll kill you. Drop your sword. Quickly now."

Luiz did not move. He did not drop his sword.

"I said drop it n—"

A report from just beyond the doorway cut the man off in mid-word: his chest burst open in a gout of blood and ripped clothing. He fell dead.

His partner tried to turn and confront the threat, but he took a pistol across the mouth so hard that Luiz could hear his jaw snap. Blood and teeth flew through the air.

Captain Billy stepped through the door and over the bodies, a spent pistol in his hand. "Do I have to save your hide every time, Luiz? Come on, let's be off. We don't have all night."

Luiz breathed a sigh of relief. "Thank you, Captain. I owe you my life."

Captain Billy nodded. "Seems so. We'll settle up later. Now let's *go*." Luiz picked up one of the muskets, Martim the other as the pirate captain peeked out the doorway. "I already sent the others ahead to the rendezvous point. We'll have to move through the woods this way to skirt the dock and the bucket brigade. And right now: all this gunfire will most assuredly draw more men."

Luiz followed Captain Billy in the direction he indicated, but Martim took off in the other direction.

"Martim!" Luiz stopped. "No. This way."

Martim turned and shook his head. "I am going to get Mama and Lua."

"No. Your father will get them."

Through the wood in the direction of the plantation, Luiz could hear faint, intermittent echoes of gunfire. "You hear that? He and his men have reached the plantation. It's a bloody fight, there: far too dangerous. So come with me . . . now!"

Luiz tried to infuse his tone of voice with the gravelly impatience of a father who brooked no debate and presumed he would be obeyed. He hoped Martim responded to that tone instinctively, so quickly that he'd be obeying the command before stopping to reflect that Luiz was not his father, did not have that measure of authority over him.

He could understand the boy's fear and agitation. Martim was trying to be a man, trying to go and fight for his mother, his sister, to ensure their safety and avenge every terrible thing that had happened to all of them while in bondage. But given the current situation, it was rash and foolhardy, and it could not be allowed.

Luiz lowered his musket, smiled, and walked calmly to Martim. He nodded. "I understand. So did your father. He foresaw that we might find you separated from your mother and sister. And he gave me orders to pass on to you."

"Let me guess: 'follow Luiz.'"

"Actually, it was 'obey Luiz,' but since I'm telling you to follow, that's the same thing at this moment. Now let's get moving."

Martim frowned. "Stay here. Wait for my signal."

"Because you're going to give us the slip?" Captain Billy hissed.

"No, because I can tell you when it's safe to come out. People from Boca de Yuma won't be startled to see me come out of this building. Both of you—well, you look like pirates."

Billy cracked a reluctant grin. "Well, then—get on with yerself and yer scouting."

Martim nodded quickly and left. The two men leaned close to the thin margin between the still-open door and the rude jamb, watching for the boy's signal.

Captain Billy glanced sharply at Luiz. "And just when did Calabar give you these orders for his son?"

"Never," Luiz answered with a sad smile.

"You're a liar!" Billy exclaimed.

"Today, yes," Luiz answered. "And as soon as we reach a safe harbor with a church, I shall be a penitent in a confessional, being absolved of this very necessary sin."

"Assuming we live that long," growled Billy, beginning to move in response to Martim's hasty, waist-high wave.

Gunfire from guardsmen defending the plantation house met them as they advanced. But in the poor light, none of the rounds found targets, and it did not slow Calabar's advance toward the long stone staircase that led up to the double doors. He and his men fired back as they pushed forward, pinning the soldiers behind the cover of the veranda that fronted the house at the same level as the top of the stairs. Some of the pirates wanted to pause, reload, and fire back. Calabar stopped them.

"Forward!" he shouted. "Don't give them time to reload."

They reached the stairs before the guards could fire again. By that time, most of the guards' firing angles were either blocked or awkward, forcing them to leave the cover and lean over the balustrade of the veranda. The pirates were ready, and they traded shots, staying low, denying the defenders easy targets. Musketballs spalled chunks and dust out of the stone near both groups. A guard went down with a shoulder wound. One of the pirates tumbled down the steps, shot through the throat. Calabar crouched lower to avoid the fire, drew his sword, and raced up the stairs.

He reached the first guard as the man was trying to raise his musket. One swift slash across the face and the man went down, dropping his musket and clutching his bleeding mouth and neck. Calabar pushed the man out of the way and attacked another. This one, however, was ready for the blow. He brought up his musket and blocked Calabar's sword slash, then drove the butt of his musket toward Calabar's throat.

Calabar reared back as the strike came in; it became a glancing instead of direct blow. Painful, but not critical. Calabar staggered a step to the rear, clutched his Adam's apple for a second: nothing broken, nothing bleeding. Feigning fear and distress, he backed away a few more paces and the guard foolishly followed—only to be taken in the flank by the pirates charging up the stairs.

With bloodthirsty howls, the pirates split into two groups, each one charging along one wing of the veranda. They set upon the rest of the guards with wild fury, swinging swords, fists, and biting as they went. The fight became a confused brawl, and Calabar simply fell back out of the way and allowed the sea dogs to do their work while he studied the door.

It had a sturdy lock, perhaps was even blocked by a crossbar on the inside. He pushed his shoulder into it. It gave slightly, but not enough to suggest that it might be knocked down by force, at least not by anyone smaller than Deebal. So Calabar improvised. He loaded his pistol, aimed it at the latch, and fired.

Splinters of wood and bits of iron exploded out of the door. He loaded again, quicker this time, fearing that the brutal melee that had now moved to the far ends of each wing of the veranda might roll back in his direction. He aimed and fired.

This time, the shot blew a small hole in the door, revealing the mechanism—and a simple and now badly mangled latch. He tucked away his pistol, drew his sword, stepped back a pace, and then kicked up and straight at where the latch looked weakest.

The door swung back into complete darkness, save for a small lantern on a table in the foyer. But it cast enough light for him to see farther into the house. He held his sword forward and stepped in slowly.

He wanted to shout, to scream Celia's name, but he swallowed down the urge. Surely whoever was further in the house—more guards perhaps—knew that somebody was inside; the fierce, desperate melee on both wings of the veranda had surely alerted everyone inside that the house was being assaulted. But he crept quietly forward, refusing to make any sound that might help defenders pinpoint his position.

The foyer led into a long hallway with two junctions. At each of the intersections, he paused, looked both ways as his eyes adjusted to the darkness that was even more absolute than the moonless, overcast night. As soon as he could make out the basic shapes around him, he kept against the right-hand wall and moved straight ahead.

The main hallway ended at a set of three downward steps into a broad space. Calabar paused and crouched on the first riser. He lowered his head to look into the room, his sword still pointed forward.

It was the kitchen. Calabar could not resist any longer.

"Celia," he hissed. Then louder. "Celia!"

Nothing. He moved quietly down the steps and into the kitchen.

"Celia!"

From a small hallway to the left, he heard a door shake. He heard a woman's muffled voice.

He moved toward the voice. "Celia?"

The first door on the right rattled again.

"Calabar?" The voice was clear and so very achingly familiar.

"Celia!"

He was beside himself with joy, relief. Suddenly his legs were weak, he could not breathe. He stumbled to the door and pressed into it. He tried forcing the latch.

"It is locked, my love," Celia said, shaking the door again. Her voice was like honey; so sweet, so wonderful to hear again. "Can you open it from your side? I have been trying to cut around the lock but cannot manage it from here, not with this small knife."

Calabar studied the lock. It was a strong iron lock, but it was slightly loose; probably a result of Celia's determined sawing at the wood around it. He gathered his strength, breathed deep, and stepped back. "Move away," he said. He focused on the lock, willing his heel to hit it squarely, then lifted his boot and kicked as if he meant his foot to go through the door.

The shock jolted his joints—ankle, knee, hip—painfully. But the door had given slightly. If he had to break his leg getting Celia out, then he would. He stepped back again, raised his leg, and drove his heel sharply against the lock. And again. And again.

On the fourth try, his kick was answered by a shriek of rent metal and the door burst open.

The room was lit by lantern light, revealing the most beautiful thing he had ever seen: Celia in a dirty white gown. And Lua beside her, bigger now than he remembered. Almost a young lady. Together, they were as perfect as a picture in a church. Or a dream.

Calabar tucked away his sword, held out his arms to enfold them, and moved forward.

Before they hugged, something struck him in the head.

Chapter 31

Boca de Yuma, Hispaniola

"You three! Stop!"

Luiz heard the command but paid it no mind. Neither did Captain Billy, who shouted "Come! Come!" from ahead as they worked their way through the wood along the inlet's southern shore toward the rendezvous point. The Spanish soldier's imperious bellow began a chorus of other soldiers' warnings, followed shortly by a smattering of gunfire.

Luiz kept his hand on the small of Martim's back, ostensibly steering him, but also shielding the boy's smaller body. Luckily, the darkness was so absolute that the Spanish soldiers were almost firing blind, relying upon sound as well as sight. They would fire and then reload as they pursued, and then fire again. The shots were sporadic and inaccurate, but they did not stop, showed no signs that they ever would.

"How much farther?" Luiz shouted ahead.

"Don't know," Captain Billy replied. "Can't tell in the dark. I'll know when we get closer. Keep running."

Luiz held a loaded rifle in his free hand, and he wanted to fire it, but he couldn't afford to pause to do so. But Captain Billy had a pistol, and fell back to work as the rearguard, periodically firing at their pursuers as he braced himself against a tree. After one bright discharge, they heard a groan from one of their pursuers. Luiz hadn't realized just how good a shot the pirate was until that moment. Too bad he didn't have two pistols.

The Spaniards paused, possibly to care for their fallen comrade. But evidently, they also took the time to wait for the faintest sign of movement in the dark wood, and then volleyed. A searing needle cut into Luiz's calf, felt like the sting of a bird-sized bee. He shouted, as much from surprise as pain, and fell. Martim tumbled forward into brambles.

"I'm hit!" Luiz hissed.

Captain Billy was at his side immediately. "Where?"

"Left leg," Luiz said, gritting his teeth against the spread of the throbbing heat. "The calf."

Captain Billy grabbed up Luiz's leg and felt the spot where the bullet had grazed the skin. "A flesh wound, boy. Just a flesh wound. Nothing to worry about. You ever been shot before?"

Luiz shook his head.

"Well, don't worry. It gets easier every time." Captain Billy chuckled and helped Luiz to his feet. "Can you walk?"

"Yes, I think so."

"Good. Then herd that boy the last furlong to the boat. Just follow the treeline and keep bearing to your left. I'll hold them off."

Captain Billy grabbed up Luiz's musket and turned toward the advancing Spanish soldiers.

Luiz tried to object, but Captain Billy had already moved off into the shadows. As Luiz got Martim in front of him again and started limping forward, he saw the pirate captain lift the musket to his shoulder, aim carefully into the darkness, and fire. Now facing toward the rendezvous point, Luiz heard rather than saw him toss the shoulder arm away and cock his reloaded pistol.

Every stride was painful, but Luiz grit his teeth, and with one hand locked on Martim's shirttails, kept moving, bearing constantly to the left.

Another one hundred yards and the bluff-cresting tree line sloped down and gave way to beach. The skiff was marked by a tiny spot of light in the distance. Behind, Captain Billy sent obscenities and pistol shots at the oncoming Spanish. Luiz shook his head, said a small prayer for the foulmouthed pirate, and moved to Martim's side, boosting the increasingly tired boy on their run through the sand.

As he drew near the skiff, he waved and called out to keep the other pirates from firing at him. Two jumped out of the boat, grabbed Martim and threw him over the side into the bottom.

"Where's the captain?" one asked.

Luiz shook his head as the Englishman's pistol was answered by a Spanish musket. "Back there, holding them off."

The pirates looked at each other. One muttered darkly. The senior of them frowned, spat. "No: we wait."

Before Luiz could even think better of the question, he wondered, *Well, should we*? Captain Billy had not given those instructions . . . but Luiz stopped in mid-thought. He was lying to himself; of course

Captain Billy would want them to wait. It was Luiz's single-minded determination to save Martim, to repay his debt, that had him debating against the right and expected course of action for one second of moral weakness. No: without Captain Billy, he and Martim would have been dead by now. Several times over, probably. He nodded at the senior pirate in the skiff. "Yes: we'll wait."

With stern warnings that Martim was to keep himself down and out of the way, the pirates readied the muskets they'd kept in the bottom of the boat and crouched low, using the oarlocks and the rim of the gunwale as they trained their barrels down the beach.

Almost a minute passed. It was quiet, very quiet. No gunfire, no voices, not even the distant sounds of Boca de Yuma's populace, still striving to save their dock. At this distance, Luiz could not even smell smoke. It was eerily peaceful and quiet. He took a moment to touch the gory seam the musket ball had striped into the flesh of his leg. It was warm to the touch and the slowly seeping blood was black in the lightless night. Some sand had gotten into the wound, as well as some dirt from their dash through the coast woods. But it was, after all, just what Captain Billy had said: a simple flesh wound.

The silence was shattered by Captain Billy's voice, shouting down the beach, drowned out by a few musket shots. Was it possible that the pirate was singing a shanty? Now? The words were unfamiliar, obscured by a thick accent that Luiz had heard from the mouths of a few men from the British Isles—and then the strangely jolly reaver broke from the trees, his dim silhouette waving madly as he came.

One of the crew put his musket to his shoulder. Luiz clapped a hand on the cocked hammer. "No, you might hit him!"

But Billy didn't seem to be worried about that. "Fire, goddamn you! Fire!" he shrieked at the skiff.

The crewman pushed Luiz away. "See? He wants us to shoot. Now do as he says, or get away."

Luiz shouldered his own weapon, and as one, he and the pirates fired the moment Captain Billy dropped into the sand. A few dozen yards behind him, the few Spanish soldiers that were still in pursuit fell as the clouds parted long enough for Luiz to see the balls send up bits of uniforms and faint, dark sprays of blood from their chests, arms, and faces. As the sound of the gunfire echoed and rolled away, Captain Billy cackled madly, and Luiz couldn't help but share in that gladness. No further fire from behind the pirate; maybe the Spaniards were all dead, or had given up their costly chase.

Still chortling, Captain Billy got up and seemed to wipe sand from his shirt. He strolled casually to the skiff, as if he were striding along the deck of his own ship. "Well, that was a right jolly run they gave me. Almost had me a few times, I must say—"

A single musket flashed, roared, from the scrub that fell away from the tree line as it skirted the rear of the strand. Captain Billy fell.

The crewmen who had reloaded returned fire as Luiz scrambled forward. He grabbed Captain Billy by the shirt and pulled him to the skiff. He lifted the pirate, tumbled him into the boat as all but one of the crewmen took hold of the boat and began shoving it toward the surf five yards away.

The bow cut into the low risers and with one last push, the others threw themselves into the boat and grabbed for the spare oars. As they rowed away, Luiz picked up his musket again and fired into the tree line. He kept loading and firing until they were far off the shore. Then he stopped, laid down the musket, and checked Martim. The boy was panting from exhaustion and from fear, but his face was rigid against any possibility of tears.

Captain Billy still lay in the bottom of the boat.

"How is he?" Luiz asked, knowing the answer.

Almost as a matter of ritual, the senior pirate placed two fingers on Captain Billy's throat. He held them there for half a minute as the boat cleared the rolling surf and reached smoother water.

He removed his fingers and shook his head. "He's gone."

Celia screamed when the club struck Calabar in the side of the head. Her husband fell into the room and smashed the small table near the center where she and Lua had their evening meals. Celia pulled her rigid, soundless daughter aside; Calabar's limp body just missed striking her before toppling to the floor.

Now looming in the doorway, Master Quintanillas followed after, the club still in his hand. He did not seem drunk this time. Instead, although steadier on his feet there was an almost feral madness in his eyes, a wild rage that she had not seen before. He stunk of smoke; he was drenched in sweat. His face was red, his breath labored. His body almost steamed. Surely he had rushed from some other part of the hacienda; from the burning sugar mills, perhaps. Strange that he had come alone . . . but then she knew why. He would die before he let anyone take her and Lua away from him.

As the man who presumed to own her strode in, club raised over Calabar, Celia screamed again and jumped on his back. Master Quintanillas stumbled to the left, flailing behind his own back with the club, then losing his footing in the wreckage of the table and tumbling into a chest of drawers against the far wall.

He glared as he fell, and she could read his thoughts in his eyes: *How dare some caboclo slut attack me?* But she hardly stopped to notice; she followed him down, pulling his hair, scraping at his face with work-toughened fingernails, with Lua now screaming and crying behind her, confused and terrified.

Despite losing his balance, Master Quintanillas recovered and grabbed Celia's long hair. He pulled her off his back and slung her down hard upon the floor at his feet. Celia struggled with his thick hand, trying to pry his fingers open, but he hauled on her hair so savagely that it began ripping out of her head. She had to let go.

"Perra!" he spat at her and kicked her once in the ribs. "No one is going to save you. You are mine, you understand? *Mine!"*

Celia clutched her stomach and gasped for air. Master Quintanillas raised his boot again for another strike. Celia closed her eyes and waited.

It did not come. Instead, she heard him scream the same instant his fingers released her hair, followed by a loud crash. She opened her eyes.

Calabar had recovered and had rammed himself into Master Quintanillas, pile-driving him into the chest of drawers. The man went sprawling, but Calabar, although unsteady, did not relent. He kept following his adversary, punched and kicked and punched and kicked again, until Quintanillas' face was a bloody pulp.

But somehow the slave master's instincts ensured that he kept the club firmly in his hand. In between two wide-swung blows from Calabar, Master Quintanillas found strength and a moment in which to act: he jammed the club up into Calabar's groin.

Celia's husband tumbled backwards, hitting the floor once again. He lay clutching his crotch, groaning, his action spasmodic.

Lua ran to her father.

"No," Celia shouted at her. "Stay back!"

The girl's cheeks were rivers of tears. Celia understood Lua's reflex to help her father, but Master Quintanillas was climbing to his knees. The club was still in his hand.

"I'm going to kill you, you son of a bitch," he said as he staggered, crouched toward Calabar, his words slurred with blood and spit. "Destroy my plantation? Kill my men? Free my slaves? Who do you think you are?"

Do something! Celia screamed those words to herself. She rose to rush at Quintanillas again, but the pain drove the breath out of her.

Her "master" had reached Calabar, just as he was beginning to rise. Quintanillas was still too fast, too alert: he crouched lower, raised the club high above his head—

And like the memory of a waking dream, she heard Lua's voice explaining: *The señora gave it to me to protect myself, if Master Quintanillas ever came closer than he should.*

Before she could be stopped by the imagined frown

of Father Araujo, before she could even think, Celia plunged her hand into the pocket of her nightgown and pulled out the little blade that her daughter had given her, the one provided by Señora Mendoza.

Celia rose to her feet as the world seemed to slow down. She brought the knife up above her head just as Master Quintanillas held the club above his own.

She screamed, leaped forward, and drove the blade into his neck.

Through rolling vision that made his head throb, Calabar heard Celia shriek, saw a white blur dive toward the slave master, and a down-flashing knife drive deep into his throat. The man went down hard, the club falling out of his hand. The white blur became Celia, who straddled the back of the motionless body, stabbing in rhythm with her screams.

"No one owns me! You will never own me! You will never have me. You will never have my Lua! You are nothing! You are nothing!"

Calabar stood, stumbled into a wall, put out a hand to steady himself, used the other to hold his head. The haziness of his vision lessened, the world coming slowly back into focus. As soon as he felt steady enough, he closed the distance to Celia in one long stride and caught her blood-spattered arm at the top of an arc. "Enough, Celia! Enough!" He used a softer voice as he felt the impetus of her next blow diminish. "Calm, now, calm. He's dead."

She dropped the knife and fell into his arms. Her knife hand was soaked in blood; she pushed it into his shirt, twisting it in an attempt to wipe off the gore. But he didn't care. She was bloody, sweaty, and dirty—and she looked and smelled wonderful. Because she looked and smelled like Celia, his Celia. In her arms, everything was right with the world once again.

Lua came to them and hugged their shoulders, her head on a level with theirs. Calabar began to shake, but he resisted the urge to cry with them. He wanted to. He deserved to. He was tired, exhausted. So tired that he did not have the strength to cry; he just wanted to hold on and never let them go again.

Hard footsteps and voices echoed along the hallway from the foyer, found their way down into the kitchen. He heard his name, and raised his head to reply. "We are in here, Deebal," Calabar answered. "In here."

The giant entered the room. He, too, was bloody and smelled of smoke. He had gashes on his arms, wrapped with the white bandages that Calabar had insisted on bringing along. His shirt was tattered and dark with soot and ash. He seemed to have lost a cutlass, but he was grinning from ear to ear. "We have it, Calabar. The place is ours."

"Did you burn the mills?"

"Aye. To the ground, and the warehouse, and some of the slave quarters. All the wagons. Killed the fore-man, but could not find the master. He must have gotten away."

Calabar pointed to the body on the floor. "No, he didn't."

"Good," Deebal said, his eyes big and bright "Every-thing is burning... but this house. Do we torch it?"

"Most of the house staff are locked in their rooms," Celia said, stepping back and wiping her face clean. "Many slaves. And Señora Mendoza is upstairs with her children. I'm sure of it."

Calabar nodded and turned to Deebal. "Find everyone. Get them out. Show mercy. Take what you want. Then burn this building to the ground."

The pirates behind Deebal gave a riotous cry and quickly spread through the house. Deebal left the room and began breaking down doors.

By the time Calabar and his family reached the front yard, Señora Mendoza and her children were being escorted out.

"Don't hurt them," Celia said as she grabbed Calabar's arm and squeezed it. "The Señora is not innocent, but her children are. They need their mother."

"I would not dare do that," Calabar said. He walked up to Señora Mendoza. "You forced my family to submit to the lash. I offer you a simple truth which you may reject or accept as you wish. The world is changing, Señora. There is no place in it for people like your husband anymore."

Señora Mendoza stared at him. "Is my husband dead?"

Calabar nodded, and for a moment, he felt guilty as he stared into the faces of her terrified children. Celia was right: they were innocent in all this. They did not deserve to have their father killed, no matter how terrible a man he was. But neither did he, Calabar, deserve to have his wife and children brutalized, sold, and treated like property.

"Here," Señora Mendoza said, grabbing a little mestizo girl that stood behind her. She pushed her forward. "Take her. She is not mine, and I will not claim her. But she does not deserve to be here. Take her, and may God make good use of her soul."

Calabar shook his head. "No. I will not take a child—"

Celia came forward and put her hand on Calabar's shoulder to silence him. "We will take her, Señora Mendoza. Gladly. And thank you for...for—" Celia reached into her pocket and drew out the bloody knife with which she had killed Master Quintanillas.

Señora Mendoza seemed to understand. She nodded, turned to her children, and, holding their hands, led them off into the night, toward the low glimmers that marked Boca de Yuma.

The house was now fully engulfed in fire. Calabar and his family watched it burn while the pirates gathered in the yard, their arms full of booty from the house. They were all smiling and joking, obviously ready for festivities. Calabar could not share their elation.

"Where is Martim?" he asked.

"At the harbor," Celia said. "He was working for the harbormaster. We have to find him."

Calabar fought back his tears. "We can't. Not right now. We have to go. Without delay. Luiz attacked the harbor. Pray that he found Martim. If not, I'll return. I promise."

Celia looked as if she were about to protest, but she bit her lip, wiped her eyes, and nodded.

I will return. She had heard him utter those words before, Calabar knew, and she probably believed them—and him—when he sailed away from Recife. And she had waited. And he had not come back. *Does she believe me now?* he wondered. Would she ever really believe any promise that he would make in the future?

Calabar turned to Deebal. "Let's go." Then he shouted to all the slaves who were gathered in the yard. "If any of you wish to come with us, now is the time. Those who do, walk from this place as free men and women who shall never know manacles or whips again."

He turned to Celia. He smiled. He laid his hands on her shoulders. Her skin was soft, welcoming. He didn't want to let her go. "Are you ready?"

She nodded. "Let's go home, Calabar."

He took her hand, then Lua's, and led them away from the burning house and toward the stone bridge.

Chapter 32

Off Boca de Yuma, Hispaniola

Calabar felt two emotions when they reached the *Wee Skipper* with the first boatload of freed slaves: elation and sorrow. Martim was there, wrapped in a gray woolen blanket but otherwise healthy and overjoyed to see his father. As soon as he left his son's tight hug, Calabar was told of Captain Billy's death, and the dread seriousness of the situation wiped away any joy he felt about his family safe and back together again. There was no one among the crew competent enough to assume the role of captain. Many crewmembers had died in the raid, and there were none among the survivors that Deebal or the other senior pirates would accept as their leader. The first mate himself refused the position out of hand. Not only was Calabar unwilling to argue with the big man, but it was a sound decision: Deebal had no interest in the subtle strategies and wariness that were the prerequisite of a successful pirate captain. That left the crew's eyes turning toward the only remaining, and eminently

399

logical, candidate—who had no stomach for it at the moment. But what other option was there? A ship of sea wolves sailing without a leader would soon argue with, and then fall upon, one another.

Calabar's first decision as captain made his stomach sink and his head hurt. "We have to hoist anchor and leave. Now."

"There are still slaves waiting on the beach for us to return and get them," Deebal said, pointing through the darkness toward the invisible shore.

"I know, but Luiz says that the Spanish ship protecting Boca de Yuma did not suffer as much damage as Captain Billy hoped. If it comes at us—and the pilot tells me that the tide is about to begin running out—we will not survive, not without a proper captain and a full crew. We have to go now, while the sun still sleeps."

So they slipped away, aided by a few brief glimpses of the coast when a providential gap in the clouds admitted a brief wash of ghostly moonlight. Once the sun rose, they corrected course, bending southeast toward the Leeward Islands. To St. Eustatia, to Calabar's plantation, and to freedom. Calabar explained to the Africans who they had been able to bring aboard that they were welcome to live on his property and to share in the profits made from his crops. No chains. No whips. Hard work, yes, but no beatings, and no deprivations. Many of them agreed. Almost as many refused and instead asked to stay on board the *Wee Skipper* as crewmembers.

In point of fact, there was no way of knowing what would become of the *Wee Skipper* once it moored off St. Eustatia, assuming that it was even allowed to do so. It was even possible that the Dutch would seize and repurpose it for their own ends. Would they keep the current crew, ex-slaves and all, or restaff it with their own? Calabar did not know the answer to that, but both the new and old pirates chose to believe that they would not dare do so, no matter how much he warned them of the likelihood that the Dutch would not recognize the ship as their property, since they had no official allegiance nor law to support their claim upon it. Eventually, Calabar accepted that the crew was immovable in this resolve and that further appeals to logic were pointless. Besides, one of the central tenets of genuine freedom was the right to make one's own choices—no matter how wildly misguided they might be.

But as fate had it, they did not make port at St. Eustatia. Instead, after two weeks of tacking against the contrary winds south of Puerto Rico, they were intercepted by a Dutch ship and another flying a flag common among the Brethren of the Coast. Within minutes, her lines identified her as none other than the *Sword of Solomon*.

Calabar was glad to see his old friend Moses again, and remarked upon the fortuitiousness of their meeting by chance in so large an expanse of sea. Moses shook his head; no such luck, he explained. Just a few days earlier, a Dutch jacht—a ship as swift as *Wee Skipper* was slow—had brought news that the docks at Boca de Yuma had been almost completely destroyed and at least one plantation's slaves had been taken off Hispaniola or had fled into the almost impenetrable jungles of the island's central mountains. When it became clear that no one in the allied fleet or its sanctioned privateers had conducted the attack, Moses had begun wondering if the perpetrator might in fact be a foolhardy mameluco "traitor" seeking to liberate his family with some pirate help.

Moses made his suspicions known to Admiral Tromp, who had given Moses a Dutch fluyt and a formal contract to patrol the most common routes that might be taken by a renegade fleeing Spanish pursuit from Hispaniola for at least a month. Happily, the hunch had paid off within their first week out from Statia.

"The course you took here: risky, Calabar. You're getting predictable in your old age," Moses said after he had heard all the details of Calabar's raid on Boca de Yuma.

Calabar huffed. "I told you before, Moses. I'm not a seaman, I'm a soldier."

Moses laughed and slapped his old friend on the shoulder. "And a damn fine one. One of the finest I've seen. Now come. We have business to attend to."

"Where?"

"Just a day south, on St. Croix. There's a gathering, and you are invited."

Calabar started to refuse, then stopped quickly. There was no reason to resist Moses anymore on when it came to helping the Dutch, not on this simple request at least. St. Croix was not too far from St. Eustatia, and a tiny delay getting back home no longer mattered. Celia and Lua and Martim were with him again, and safe. Besides, showing ready cooperation with the Dutch meant that they would first encounter the *Wee Skipper* away from Statia. The thought of commandeering the ship would not occur to them, and they'd be in no position to do so without having a very impolitic fight on their hands. The crew would therefore be free to chart their own course—literally and figuratively—and possibly even get a letter of marque from Tromp or one of the other allies.

Calabar nodded. "Very well, my friend. I'll follow in your wake."

St. Croix, Lesser Antilles

The Dutch and their allies were gathering at St. Croix for two reasons. First, they had decided to establish a lookout post there—which the young up-time commander Edward Cantrell had labeled an "early warning initiative"—to protect St. Eustatia. Both he and Admiral Tromp were on hand to oversee what had been accomplished so far, and what next steps were wanted. Second, the Dutch wanted to survey the island for eventual colonization. As Moses had explained to Calabar after their ships had joined the others at the south-facing anchorage, the Spanish had swept through the Leewards in 1628 and had cleared the Dutch off St. Croix. Now was as good a time as any to reestablish a foothold, before the Spanish or anyone else had their interest in it rekindled.

The original plan had been to meet at the ruined town site further along the south shore. However, this was changed to a gathering on board a Dutch ship that Calabar had never heard of before, the *Vergoeding*: a name which translated roughly as "compensation."

As Calabar's skiff approached the vessel, he understood the origins of its name a bit better. According to the chief at the tiller, it was, in fact, a prize hull taken from the Spanish at the Battle of Grenada late last year. Now repaired, she symbolized not only the victories that Dutch and allied forces had been winning in the Antilles, but the growth of their power and so, the security of St. Eustatia and those colonies and communities that were her friends.

Although still by no means a ship commander, and without any real interest in becoming one, Calabar had nonetheless been around enough of them that he could discern the work that had been done on *Vergoeding* and the changes they brought to her probable performance. Formerly the forty-eight-gun galleon *San Francisco*, her spars were new and her rigging closer to the Dutch pattern. And while her guns were still the large—not to say cumbersome—pieces that were a Spaniard's standard armament, they were all the same type: thirty-six-pounders, except for two lighter chase guns that the rebuilders in St. Eustatia mounted on her bow.

The second ship was similar but more squat, built for cargo, and from the look of her, she, too, had received quite a bit of attention from the ship's carpenters. "And what is her story?" Calabar asked the skiff's pilot, jutting his chin at the hull. It almost looked piebald, given all the bright new wood mixed in among the age-darkened original timbers.

The pilot shrugged. "Don't know much about her. Came into port just two months ago, dragged in by the Jewish pirate, Cohen. Listing, taking on water almost as fast as the prize crew could pump and bail. But they saved her."

Calabar studied the pattern of new wood more closely, the new spars, the atypically uniform cannon. He frowned. "What was her name when she was in Spanish hands?"

"She was Portuguese, actually. And she was called the, the . . . yes—the *Santa Catarina do Benin*. I think. Yes, that's it."

Calabar managed not to smile as he saw the ship anew, recognized its lines. "And now?"

The pilot scratched a furry ear. "Oh, they hung a strange new name on her, they did. And in a strange way, too."

"What do you mean?"

"I mean that all the other prizes which come into our hands have been given Dutch names. And if they're merchantmen, they're christened by the West India Company. Only seems right, *ja*?"

Calabar nodded.

"Well, not this one. When she was finally seaworthy, word came down from Tromp himself regarding the ship's name. And the story I heard is that when the Company representative went out to his flagship *Amelia* to request a change, the admiral chased him out of his great cabin and off the ship without so much as hearing the end of his appeal." The pilot shook his head. "Not at all like Tromp, that."

Calabar waited, sighed, realized he was going to have to remind the pilot what the original question had been. "And the new name?"

"Oh. Right. *Spartacus*. Something of a mystery, that."

Calabar smiled. "Yes, something of a mystery." *But not to me.*

And . . . thank you, Maarten.

Only Calabar and Luiz attended from the crew of the *Wee Skipper*, having been asked to make a report on operations and conditions with which they were particularly familiar. It was no surprise that the rest were desperately relieved not to have to leave their creaky old hull. As renegades, they generally only felt fully safe at sea or ashore in one of the Caribbean's sparse—and notorious—pirate havens. Celia, who had never cared for politics, elected not to accompany Calabar. She was content to stay aboard the *Wee Skipper* with Lua and Martim.

The moment Calabar's eyes drew level with the *Vergoeding*'s deck, he could tell that this was a higher-level gathering than the one he had attended on Tromp's *Amelia* back in Recife. Not as many common merchants and farmers; in their place, a great many more officials from the WIC, including some from the old Recife government: Matthijs van Ceulen and Johann Gijsselingh, Councilmen Jehan de Bruyne, Philip Serooskereken, and Servatius Carpentier. Collectively, these men represented the political and mercantile interests of St. Eustatia and other Dutch colonies in the Caribbean. There were at least as many attendees that Calabar did not know, making it impossible to discern where their interests and motivations lay. But Calabar had no question about his own; he just wasn't sure how many of those gathered would share them.

They spoke first about defense and security matters, though Admiral Tromp and Commander Cantrell left after their brief introductory remarks. Their representatives, Admiral Joost Banckert and Jan van Walbeeck, laid out the details, occasionally assisted by young officers whose names and faces were new to Calabar. After Walbeeck detailed what they knew of the chilling events on Curaçao, he invited Calabar to brief them about the recent "action" on Hispaniola. Calabar also gave them as much pertinent information as he could remember about Cartagena. Where his knowledge was wanting, Luiz filled in the gaps.

Many in attendance believed that Cartagena needed to be attacked, or at least blockaded. *That would be foolhardy*, Calabar thought to himself, but he did not voice his opinion, as the conversation went quickly to discussing the new ships arriving from Europe, USE-built ships, powered by steam and guns far superior to anything the Spanish could muster. Calabar did not know the truth of such talk, for he had never been on one of these marvelous new ships, though he had seen Commander Cantrell's flagship, the *Intrepid*, from the *Wee Skipper*'s quarterdeck when they had rounded the headland that sheltered the anchorage on the west. It was an impressive hull with an impressive smoke stack. But numbers sometimes outweighed better technology, as Calabar had seen time and again in Brazil. A horde of determined men can sweep superior guns from the field. Did the Dutch have the willpower to accept such losses with an attack on Cartagena? Could they even take such losses and still survive in the Caribbean? The world was changing, yes. The presence of Commander Cantrell and his flagship proved that. But did the Dutch have the time to wait until such changes altered the balance of power?

Then the discussion turned to mercantile matters. Calabar listened intently. When the matter of slavery came up, he jumped in.

"Sirs," he said, standing and moving forward so that all eyes could see him, all ears could hear. "Many of you know me personally. I have served with some of you in the past. I am what the Portuguese call a mameluco, a man of mixed Portuguese and native Brazilian blood. It is a term of disrespect, a term that separates me and others like me from being seen as equals in the eyes of lighter-skinned men. Like all of you, for example."

Some tried to raise their objection to the implicit parallel upon which he had concluded, but Calabar silenced them by continuing without pause. "I am not here to lay blame upon any of you, nor am I here to enjoin any of you to fully reject slavery. But I am here to impress upon you the simple truth that slavery is not a viable economic or political tool to wield in the struggle against your enemies.

"As Captain Moses Cohen has explained to me, the USE has banned slavery in its constitution. How long will they continue to maintain an alliance with the Dutch if you continue to keep slaves? I do know—from experience—that the Spanish and the Portuguese are far more brutal to their slaves than the Dutch, but that doesn't make the institution politically wise or acceptable in the eyes of God. You may treat your slaves comparatively well, but if they serve your properties and economic interests against their will, then you are sustaining the institution which the Spanish and Portuguese exploit to brutalize whole races of men and women.

"So I implore you: the gradual reduction, and then elimination, of slavery is not sufficient. You must ban slavery now, immediately, just as your USE allies have done. It will hurt economically in the short-term, yes. But in the long-term, you will gain the support of all native and African men and women who have been taken in chains and made to serve lesser men than they. And here, in this New World, such allies are not just important. They could prove decisive.

"That is all I have to say."

For the first time since the meeting began, no one uttered a word. They stood silent, waiting to see if he had anything to add, despite his last definitive comment. Some averted their eyes; some looked at each other, seeking a response that, Calabar knew, none of them had.

Finally, one of Admiral Tromp's most trusted advisors, Servatius Carpentier, stood forth and responded. "Don Calabar, Admiral Tromp and I have heard your words on this matter and not only take them seriously; we agree and second them. We believe that it is both bad policy and immoral to maintain such a brutal practice, all the more since our chief ally in Europe and here in the Caribbean is the USE. As you say, they do not keep slaves and soon, their superior technology will take hold in this world and render the practice obsolete.

"So we propose that a ban be agreed upon now, to take effect one year hence, so as to give merchants and farmers time to adjust to the economic disruption and even hardships that the complete eradication of slavery will surely cause. At such time as the ban takes effect, all slaves will be free to depart or enter into sharecropping or indentured servitude relationships with the employers of their choice. What say all of you?"

Everyone had much to say, and for a moment, Calabar's heart soared. These men, these pale-skinned Europeans who often placed trade and commerce above their own lives, seemed genuinely in agreement. Slavery was an obsolete institution and something had to be done.

But as the conversation progressed, economic fears and second-guessing of the ban began to take hold. Calabar could see the conversation shift from an outright ban in a single year to a more staged approach. Conditions were attached to the choices that the freed slaves could make among employers. For those who wished to depart, the price of transport had to be offset by a period of unpaid servitude, further increased by the cost of their food and shelter until that labor-price was met. Caveats and provisos accumulated swiftly.

In the end, no ban was declared. Those gathered agreed to it in principle, and promised on the record that they would work toward slavery's final eradication and the implementation of the sharecropping system that Carpentier had urged, but no firm timeline was set to achieving either objective.

Calabar left the meeting as soon as it became obvious that the spark of life had guttered out for his vision of emancipation, that it was, instead, a stillborn hope, strangled by a many-stranded legal umbilicus of ifs, buts, and maybes. In many ways he felt far worse listening to those bureaucrats rationalize away a swift end to slavery than he did suffering bullet wounds or sword slashes. At least there was no obfuscation, no dodging and double-talk, with a gun or a blade.

"It is a start," Luiz said as they left the meeting. "Perhaps that was the best we could have hoped for from these men."

Calabar shrugged. "Perhaps, but with no deadlines agreed upon, they will simply go home and fall back into their easy, complacent lives. No, Luiz. There will be no end to slavery in Dutch territories anytime soon."

They stood overlooking the bay. Calabar's ship lay

anchored on one side of the fleet, Admiral Tromp's and Commander Cantrell's flagships on the opposite side. The USE ship was a mighty hull indeed, as it sat there on the waves, belching smoke like some mythological dragon. It was a wonder to behold, and perhaps it and the other modern ships that had arrived from Europe could change the balance of power in the Dutch and allied colonies, enable a loosening of slavery's yoke. But what about the slaves in Spanish territories? What about the slaves in Portuguese territories?

What about Brazil?

Calabar straightened his spine and looked beyond the ships toward the southeast, toward where St. Eustatia was hidden beneath the blue-on-blue horizon of sea and sky. He thought about his plantation there. For more than a year, he'd badgered Moses to go back, so that Calabar could take up the machete once again and cut cane. As he was born to do, he thought. But every time, something got in the way. Something always prevented him from going back to his plantation and living that life. And now he understood why, what purpose he was destined to fulfill in some fashion. The purpose for which the agonies of his families and friends and fellow dark-skinned peoples had prepared him.

"Luiz," he said, turning, "get to the ship. Gather Deebal and the others who have chosen to remain as crew. Get them together that I may speak to them. All of them."

Luiz nodded. "Of course, sir. But why?"

Calabar cracked a smile. "We have a job to do."

Chapter 33

St. Croix, Lesser Antilles

It was a beautiful, sunny day, the kind of day that Calabar used to enjoy working his fields on St. Eustatia, and indeed, on his first plantation in Brazil, before the Dutch had arrived on the Pernambuco coast and changed his life forever. He paused for a moment to take a deep breath, his nervous hands on the edge of the skiff being loaded with food and blankets and new clothing, all ultimately bound for his almost-completed house. Then the skiff would row out to the *Spartacus*, which, once its new passengers were aboard, would sail to St. Eustatia, where the plantation awaited, just as Tromp had promised it would so long ago.

Calabar stared up into the sun. There was a time when he had wanted nothing more than to work under that bright-burning orb, laboring among the thick rows of sugar cane, feeling it with anxious hands, cutting the stalks with a sharp machete, its green smell growing in his nose as thoughts of mounting profits grew in his imagination. And right along with those images came visions of how they would buy his family a safer, more comfortable life. Indeed, there was a time where that was all he thought about, not so long ago.

Once the skiff was lashed to the side of the *Spartacus*, he helped Lua and Martim on to the floating platform that supported the base of the convenience stairs. And lastly, he boosted up the little mestizo girl—Consita—who Celia had resolved to take with them. Finally, he handed Celia up.

But once her footing was secure and she made to withdraw her hand, he held it. Tightly, firmly, but also gently. She turned, surprised but beaming widely—until she saw his eyes.

Calabar smiled as best he could and said, "Celia, my love, I will not be going with you and the children."

The last remains of the rosy smile that she had worn all day disappeared. "What do you mean?"

"I will not be returning to St. Eustatia with you. I am going back to Brazil. It is clear to me now," he continued before she could respond, "what I must do. Yesterday, the West India Company refused my plea to ban slavery. They are against the practice in principle, so they say, but they cannot bring themselves to rise above their own economic interests to do what is right. But this isn't their war. It is ours. Mine, yours, Lua's, Martim's, even Consita's. It is every mameluco's, mestizo's, caboclos's, and African's war. We are the ones that suffer under the oppression of slavery and of racism. And if there is a change to come, it will be us who will see it through. And that begins in Brazil."

"Who is going with you?"

"Luiz, of course. Deebal. All of the crew that are

left from when I first went aboard outside Cartagena, and some of the Hispaniola Africans. The rest will go with you and help work the plantation, as sharecroppers." Calabar tried to keep his smile from fading, knew he was failing. "You are a far better manager than I am, Celia. You can run that plantation better than me." Calabar swallowed and braced for her anger. He knew it was coming.

He waited, but Celia said nothing. Instead, a single tear crept down her long left cheek. Her silence was even worse than her wrath.

"I *must* go back, Celia. I must," he pleaded. "Don't you understand? Too many of our people suffer under Matias, under the Portuguese. If I wait for the Dutch to decide when it's finally in their best interest to—"

"I know."

Her words stopped him. He wasn't sure he had heard her correctly. He blinked.

She smiled. "That was not the response you were expecting?"

Calabar shook his head.

Celia moved close, put her hands on his shoulders as her body rocked with the swells that moved both the skiff and the float. "I know you must go back, and as painful as it is to see you leave, I understand. For a year, I've been struggling with my feelings on these same matters, on the terrible choices a woman, a parent, must make when she is determined to be both a good mother and to fight the horrors and fiends of slavery. I have no clear answers for that, not yet. Maybe I never will. But now that I have lived as a slave, have experienced it myself, have seen our children suffer under it, I know that it must end quickly.

Now." A memory made her smile melancholy. "Do you remember that I called you a child of Brazil?"

Calabar nodded.

"I'll be honest: I didn't really know what I meant by that at the time. I thought I did. But now I do know. I do not want you to go, Calabar. But a child becomes a man; a man, a father. Your own children need their father, but Brazil needs you more. So, go and be the kind of father that Brazil needs. Go . . . and make every slaver bleed."

She said nothing more. She stood back as he said goodbye to Martim and Lua, and gave a little wave to Consita. There were tears and confusion on Lua's face. Martim said nothing, nor did his expression give away what he was thinking. Perhaps he understood, like his mother, exactly why his father was returning to Brazil. Perhaps he even agreed with it. They did not shake hands. They did not hug. They simply nodded to one another.

The skiff pulled away from the *Spartacus*. He watched the three of them as the stepsail caught a reaching breeze and swept toward the stern. Just before they slipped behind it, he lifted his hand in farewell.

And then they were gone.

Calabar had to stop himself three times from jumping into the water and swimming toward the dwindling shape of the *Spartacus*. Watching it sail slowly away, he cycled again and again through the reasons he was heading to Brazil rather than St. Eustatia. And each time, he came to the same, simple conclusion: trust Celia. She was always right about matters of family and duty. Yes, he was leaving his family once again, but Brazil was his family, too, and still in the thrall of cruel and evil men from foreign shores. They needed him now just as Celia and the children had when Matias had sold them into slavery.

"Your wife is wise. She will come to understand and respect your decision," Moses said as they stood beside each other on the shore, watching Celia's boat shrink toward the horizon. "It may take a while, but she will understand."

"She does already," Calabar said. "She's an amazing woman, my friend. Frankly, I don't deserve her."

Moses nodded. "On that, we can agree."

They laughed together, then Moses said, "So, when will you be off in the *Wee Skipper*?"

"She's called the *Freedom* now. I'm going back within the hour." He paused, regretting the question he had to ask—or rather, the answer he feared he would get. "You will not be accompanying us, I take it?"

Moses shook his head. "Not right away, no. There's more work—and loot—for me up here in the Caribbean. But when those tasks are done, we'll turn our bowsprit south and return to the Rocas Atoll. And then, we'll finish the job we started."

Calabar turned to Moses. He looked the man deep in his eyes. They were dark, soulful eyes. Good eyes. "We've been through a lot together, haven't we, my friend?"

"Indeed. And who could have imagined but a few short years ago that a mameluco dog and a Sephardic pirate could change the world?"

Calabar laughed. "We haven't changed it yet."

"Then go, my good friend, and get to work on it. I'll be along presently."

Moses pulled Calabar in for a strong embrace. "Godspeed," Moses said, then let go quickly and walked away, calling for the pilot of the skiff to return and ferry his friend back to his own ship.

Calabar watched him go. Then he turned back and watched Celia's boat become a black speck on a darkling horizon. He blew a kiss after her, then swung his leg over the gunwale to begin his journey toward *Freedom*.

Epilogue

On board Intrepid, *St. Croix*

"I should have stayed for the meeting," Maarten Tromp muttered hollowly, as he and Eddie watched *Freedom* angle off toward open water.

Eddie shook his head. "You were right to leave when you did. Whatever they decided about slavery, it had to be their decision. You and Jan van Walbeeck have already become suspect by driving policy, even forcing it on the administrators, the governor. It was enough you had Carpentier there."

Tromp shook his head, hung it slightly in the direction of the departing ship. "No, it was not enough. Domingos—Calabar—left before they finished. And you saw his posture as well as I did. Dejected, maybe disgusted. Maybe both. We do not have to wait for the report to be sure of the outcome. They did not take decisive action on slavery."

Eddie sighed. "Not as decisive as Calabar would have liked, anyhow. But like Houtebeen says, Calabar's passion can sometimes cloud his judgment."

Tromp looked up sharply. "Is it clouded judgment to insist upon an end to slavery, immediately?"

Eddie shook his head. "No. But it is unreasonable to expect that people whose opinions—and interests—are diametrically opposed to yours will just roll over in a single afternoon. From their perspective, they've already accepted a huge amount of change. Costly change. A five-year phaseout of all slavery, to be replaced by indentured servitude or sharecropping, depending upon government—rather than Company—adjudication. Official monitoring of conditions until then. A special office for investigating mistreatment or neglect of all slaves and bondsmen until they are freed." Eddie swept a hand toward *Vergoeding* and toward distant St. Eustatia beyond her part of the horizon. "Not only did the owners and Company reps not want it, they only agreed because of implied threats, not democratic debate."

Eddie shrugged. "If it wasn't for the special circumstance of the colony—operating under military oversight until it's deemed sufficiently safe from Spanish elimination—you wouldn't have been able to do *any* of it. You had to nip two revolts in the bud, as it was."

Tromp nodded reluctantly. "Yes. But that doesn't make what Calabar wants—and that he wants it *now*—any less right."

Eddie blew out his cheeks. "No argument there. We lived this same truth up-time, you know."

"And what truth is that?"

"That no matter how fast you want change, the price of having anything vaguely like a democracy is that you never get that change as quickly as you want it." He locked both hands tightly on the top of *Intrepid*'s stern railing. "In our history, it was cotton and tobacco and antebellum slavery. Every bit as horrendous, as monstrous as Spanish slavery now. Arguably worse, in a number of particulars. You probably read that we fought a Civil War over it. Well, over other things, too, but if the issue of slavery hadn't been a point of contention, I doubt it would have come to blows, let alone become the most costly conflict in my nation's history. Hell; it was almost as costly in terms of American lives as all our other wars added together."

Tromp frowned. "And are you saying this is because the change—the elimination of slavery—occurred too quickly?"

Eddie held out his hands in a reflex that was part correction and part revulsion. "God, no. I'd like to say it could have been avoided, but damned if I can see how. My point is that, even after fighting that war, even after the Emancipation Act which freed all the slaves, there still wasn't anything vaguely like equality in the United States a hundred years later. One man—another Martin, in fact—pointed out that the descendants of those freed slaves still did not have the same freedoms, the same safety, as other Americans: that achieving that equality was still, in fact, a dream."

"And did that dream ever come true?"

Eddie sighed. "I'll never know. It sure hadn't when we got flung backward in time. Yeah, things had continued to get better—but how long should anyone be expected to wait, really? And America wasn't alone in experiencing that kind of delay. Former slaves or colonial 'subjects' in other countries were no better off; some had it a lot worse. And it was all as wrong as wrong could be."

"But?"

Eddie closed his eyes. "But the gears grind slowly in anything like a democracy, Maarten. Changes that seem like they should be easy to make seem to take forever. And for decades—centuries—after a change is declared, there are still people working against it. And as long as they don't break the law doing so, by what authority do you tell them that they can't?"

"Is it as the English statesman—Church-Hill?—said: 'Democracy is the worst form of government . . . except for all those other forms that have been tried from time to time.'"

Eddie nodded. "Yeah, but it doesn't sound quite so witty when you're still on the wrong end of a whip." He discovered he was watching the dispersing crowd of Dutch landowners, administrators, and officers on the deck of the *Vergoeding*—and that his hands had become bleached-white claws from his death grip on the stern rail.

Tromp glanced down at them. "I do not seem to be alone in my dismay—and displeasure—at today's outcome."

"Oh, you most certainly are not. I mean, here we are, up-timers equipped with full knowledge of the atrocities and wars spawned by slavery, and we *still* can't get rid of it. Not quickly enough. Because it's *never* quickly enough."

"So you *do* agree: I *should* have forced a different outcome—"

Eddie closed his eyes. "And start a rebellion? Another civil war over slavery? Here, in the only colony in this part of the New World that is even vaguely based on a democratic system? And with what outcome? Destroying the only effective opposition to the *real* monsters, which would leave them free to continue their horrors unopposed?" Eyes still closed, Eddie shook his head. "There are times when revolution is the only answer, I guess. But it is always a roll of the dice and an uncertain leap—not of faith, but desperation. One that often ends in an abyss." He opened his eyes. "I grew up wondering how anyone even came up with the idea of slavery, hating that it had been part of my nation's history, wondering why it had taken so long to get rid of it, blaming everyone who hadn't been John Brown: who hadn't picked up a gun to eradicate it immediately. And here I am, counseling against doing exactly that." Eddie let out a shuddering breath. "If that doesn't make me a hypocrite, I don't know what does."

Tromp frowned, nodded. "That may be the curse and the cost of being a political realist, Eddie—something that I suspect your Michael Stearns understands. Very well. He has fought against these same forces of oppression, but not through rebellion. He has the long view common among compassionate pragmatists, and no doubt shares your regret, even guilt."

Eddie skoffed. "Mike? He's a crusader fighting the good fight. Has been since we arrived here. Well, even before, back up-time. He's got nothing to feel guilty about."

Tromp smiled sadly. "Does he not? No matter our personal dedication to goodness and justice, we are all, in greater or lesser measure, complicit in the injustices of the society which we tolerate. Even if we tolerate it for the best of reasons, it is a constant struggle not to be consumed by the self-contempt that such accommodation threatens to breed in any person of conscience."

Eddie looked up as a new ship steamed into the wide bay: the destroyer *Harrier*, her distinctive armored bridge perched on the forward edge of her quarterdeck like a homely black box. "Which is to say that a guilty conscience is the only consolation we've got?" he muttered, shaking his head.

Tromp frowned. "My countrymen—the slaveholders, I mean—would be easier to deal with if they were not living in fear. And yes, I know that they have more to fear from keeping slaves than from freeing them, but that is rational—and rationality diminishes in proportion to the growth of fear. It is logical, but I know these colonists; when they feel less threatened, they will become more reasonable. More compassionate."

Eddie sighed. "So it sounds like the fastest way to reassure your slaveholders is to accelerate our campaign to control the region. Which means staying focused on getting more allies, more forces, more weapons with which to hammer down the Spanish Viceroys and their slave-economies."

Tromp stood back from the rail. "Which reminds me: I must sail within the hour. There is much business to which I must attend back in Statia."

"More prize ships to bring to readiness, Admiral?"

"Yes. Hopefully, with the arrival of your new ships, we will be able to mount a decisive offensive against the Spanish."

Eddie felt his stomach sink. "Yeah, about that."

Tromp looked over, frowning. Then understanding swept away that expression; when hearing unpromising news, the Dutch admiral was always careful to adopt a neutral expression. "So, it is confirmed?"

Eddie nodded. "Just relayed from Statia before

you came aboard. I got the decrypted message when I went below just before the meeting on *Vergoeding* broke up."

Tromp shook his head. "It seems that problems always accumulate faster than solutions. So: the Turks. How long have they been on the march?"

Eddie shrugged. "Message doesn't say. From what I can tell, Simpson may not know yet. But they are confirmed as attacking along Austria's southernmost borders."

Tromp nodded. "And with your Admiral Simpson's new fleet only partially built, he may need more ships. Particularly the best ones." The admiral glanced around *Intrepid* meaningfully.

"He may, but he hasn't said so. Hasn't even hinted at that. Just that the new second-generation cruisers and destroyers may get their shakedown cruises at the same time they are commencing campaign operations. Never a good situation, and particularly not on ships as complex as those."

"Well, at least he has had the benefit of a year's worth of reports and assessments from your experiences with the first models here in the New World."

Eddie nodded. "Of course, an Ottoman invasion could be a catalyst for even more strategic complications."

"Of course," Tromp agreed, frowning. "Philip is certainly not enamored of the other two branches of the Hapsburg family. He may see an Ottoman attack on Austria as desirable, a means of reducing the influence of his cousin Emperor Ferdinand."

"Yeah, and ever since Philip's little brother Fernando married Ferdie's sister and declared himself 'King in the Lowlands,' Spain's been itching to take them all down a few notches. Maybe more."

Tromp glanced at him. "You think Philip would attack his own brother?"

Eddie cocked his head, considering. "Attack? Maybe. But smother and strangle economically, sure. Besides, Philip doesn't have to attack the Spanish Lowlands to make his brother's—and the USE's—life miserable. He could go after Bernhard in Burgundy, raid commerce going in or out of Amsterdam, or strengthen his own position in Milan or Naples or Switzerland. All of which would have serious consequences for the USE, and about which we could do squat—all if we were locked in a death match with the Ottomans."

Tromp nodded. "So we had best presume that, from here on, we may be on our own." He looked wistfully at *Intrepid*'s smokestack. "I suppose we must even anticipate a reduction in our current forces."

One of the few things that Eddie's mother and father ever agreed upon was that spitting was a filthy habit. But now, he spat over the rail. "From the start, it has been totally screwed up that our alliance has no joint command. And now we might really feel the cost of that. Sure, everybody was more comfortable maintaining full control over their own assets. But now, if any of the allies—including the USE—decide that their forces are needed back home . . ." He shook his head in disgust.

Tromp smiled. "My young friend, you speak as if there is any other kind of alliance. Nations commit to each other only so far as it is immediately expedient to do so."

"Yeah, well . . . that won't always be completely true. Well, it wouldn't have always been true. I mean, if history had stayed the same ... well, if the *future* was going to stay the same—" Eddie rolled his eyes in frustration at finding words to articulate the temporal disjuncture. "I'll start again. World War Two. You've read about it?"

"Briefly. There is much to read about the nations of your world that will never be. Interesting, but not as pressing as becoming acquainted with the new technologies and knowledge that will impact this one."

"Point taken. Here's the bottom line: a lot of the Allies in World War Two operated under a unified command. Their generals were integrated into a single hierarchy. And the operations of their forces were closely coordinated."

"And that worked?"

"Not always. Sometimes not at all. But over the course of the war, it helped *those* Allies keep a common agenda: a shared set of objectives to be achieved in a given sequence as part of a greater plan. We could use that here, right about now."

Tromp looked after the *Freedom*. "Actually, Eddie, we may have a faint, and strange, version of that emerging."

"What do you mean?"

"If I remember what little I read of that history, the great strategic imperative of those Allies was to open new fronts. To confound the powers of their foes, the countries of the ... the Axle?"

"The Axis," Eddie supplied, suppressing a grin.

"Yes. Thank you. The Allies confounded the Axis by forcing them to fight in more regions and so, undercut the concentrations of force their enemies required to achieve decisive victories on any of their fronts."

Eddie nodded and smiled. "For a guy who hasn't read a lot about the Second World War, that's a pretty good strategic synopsis."

Tromp nodded his appreciation, then jutted his chin at the dwindling stern of *Freedom*. "There is the start of our 'second front.'"

Eddie was just able to keep himself from smacking his forehead with his palm. "Damn—er, darn it. Of course. If Calabar can make enough trouble in Brazil—maybe in the entirety of South America—that will make it impossible for the Spanish to mass all their forces against us here."

Tromp nodded after the disappearing ship, his voice sad. "We can only hope that Domingos will live, will enjoy good luck as Brazil's Spartacus." The admiral started when he saw Eddie's reaction: a sly, humorless smile. "What? Americans do not believe in luck? Not that I do, really, but still—"

"No, Maarten. It's not that we don't believe in luck. It's that we believe in making our own."

"What do you mean? That you actually believe you can make your own luck?"

"Tell me, Maarten," Eddie said around a growing smile, "while you were reading about World War Two, did you ever come across the term 'Lend Lease'?"

Cast of Characters

Álvares, Pedro	Assistant to Matias de Albuquerque
Arciszewski, Krzysztof	Dutch officer; Polish nobleman and engineer
Bagnuoli	Portuguese officer
Banckert, Adriaen	Dutch naval officer and Joost Bankert's son
Banckert, Joost	Dutch admiral
Blanchett, Arnaud	French pirate captain
Bosch	Dutch officer
Cadogen, Jon	British pirate captain
Calabar, Domingos Fernandes	Mameluco; sugar plantation owner; scout; Dutch supporter
Cardoso, Alvaro	Portuguese merchant in Olinda
Carlos	Calabar's youngest son

Carmen	Spanish prostitute
Carpentier, Servatius	Dutch councilman, Recife
Casper	Runaway African slave; pirate
Celia	Calabar's wife
Consita	Mestizo girl
Deebal "The Giant"	Runaway African slave; first mate; pirate
De Albuquerque, Duarte	Matias de Albuquerque's brother and former Governor-General, Pernambuco
De Albuquerque, Matias	Portuguese officer; current Governor-General, Pernambuco
De Bruyne, Jehan	Dutch councilman, Recife
De Gama, Pedro Correia	Portuguese officer
De Oliveira, Diogo Luis	Former Governor-General, Pernambuco
De Las Quintanillas, Velasco	Spanish plantation owner, slaver
Diederik	Dutch boy, St. Eustatia
Dircksens, Willem	Dutch sugar plantation foreman
Do Abreu, Antonio	Portuguese settler
Eanes, Moses Cohen Henriques	Sephardic pirate

Erckens, Bram	Dutch physician, Recife
Father Araujo	Jesuit priest
Filipe	African boy; servant
Geare, William "Captain Billy"	British pirate captain
Gijsselingh, Johann	Dutch administrator, Recife
Goncalves, Luiz	Assistant to Calabar
Hector	African slave
Hyarima	Cacique of the Nepoia tribe, Trinidad
Jacobszoon, Jacob	Dutch merchant
Jansen	Dutch soldier
Jol, Cornelis "Peg Leg"	Privateer and admiral of the Dutch fleet
Lichthart, Jan Cornelisz	Dutch naval officer
Lua	Calabar's daughter
Martim	Calabar's oldest son
Mendoza, Violeta	Velasco de las Quintanillas' wife
Nestor	Member of William Geare's (Captain Billy's) crew
O'Donnell, Hugh Albert	Earl of Tyrconnell, Colonel of the Wild Geese

O'Mara, Malachi	Assistant to Aodh O'Rourke, Wild Geese
O'Rourke, Aodh	Aide-de-camp to Hugh O'Donnell and Senior Sergeant of the Wild Geese
Ramires, Emilio	Portuguese slave ship captain
Richard	French pirate
Rosalita	Spanish prostitute
Schutte	Dutch officer
Serooskereken, Philip	Dutch councilman, Recife
Stein-Callenfels	Dutch officer
Sukumar	Assistant to Hyarima, Nepoia tribe, Trinidad
Tromp, Maarten	Admiral of the Dutch fleet
Van Ceulen, Matthijs	Dutch administrator, Recife
Van Walbeeck, Jan	Governor of St. Eustatia
Von Schoppe, Sigismond	German-born officer serving the Dutch

RING OF FIRE SERIES
(with Eric Flint)

1635: The Papal Stakes PB: 978-1-4516-3920-9 • $7.99
Up to their necks in papal assassins, power politics, murder, and mayhem, the uptimers need help and they need it quickly.

1636: Commander Cantrell in the West Indies
PB: 978-1-4767-8060-3 • $8.99
Oil. The Americas have it. The United States of Europe needs it. Enter Lieutenant-Commander Eddie Cantrell.

1636: The Vatican Sanction HC: 978-1-4814-8277-6 • $25.00
PB: 978-1-4814-8386-5 • $7.99
Pope Urban has fled the Vatican and the traitor Borja. But assassins have followed him to France—and not only assassins! The Pope and his allies have fled right into the clutches of the vile Pedro Dolor.

STARFIRE SERIES
(with Steve White)

Extremis PB: 978-1-4516-3814-1 • $7.99
They have traveled for centuries, slower than light, and now they have arrived at the planet they intend to make their new home: Earth. The fact that humanity is already living there is only a minor inconvenience.

Imperative PB: 978-1-4814-8243-1 • $7.99
A resurrected star navy hero attempts to keep a fragile interstellar alliance together while battling and implacable alien adversary.

Oblivion PB: 978-1-4814-8325-4 • $16.00
It's time to take a stand! For Earth! For Humanity! For the Pan-Sentient Union!